T0086049

Good
on
Paper

Valerie Tejeda is an author, journalist, and astrology writer with a BA in psychology and certificate in astrology and music therapy. Valerie is the author and narrator of the best-selling Audible Originals *Self Care by the Signs* and *Self Care by the Moon*.

Her bylines have appeared in publications such as *Self Magazine*, *Vanity Fair*, *MTV*, *Teen Vogue*, *Marie Claire*, *Cosmopolitan*, *Huffington Post*, *Latina*, and more. She is the creator of the pop astrology digital brand Big Cosmic Energy.

Valerie is a Californian who loves iced coffee and asking people, "When's your birthday?" when she first meets them.

Valerie Tejeda

First published in 2022
by HEADLINE ETERNAL
An imprint of HEADLINE PUBLISHING GROUP

2

Cataloguing in Publication Data is available from the British Library

ISBN 978 1 4722 9420 3

Typeset in 11/14 pt Minion Pro by Jouve (UK), Milton Keynes

Printed and bound in Great Britain by Clays Ltd, Elcograf S.p.A.

Headline's policy is to use papers that are natural, renewable and recyclable
products and made from wood grown in well-managed forests and other
controlled sources. The logging and manufacturing processes are expected to
conform to the environmental regulations of the country of origin.

HEADLINE PUBLISHING GROUP
An Hachette UK Company
Carmelite House
50 Victoria Embankment
London EC4Y 0DZ

www.headlineeternal.com
www.headline.co.uk
www.hachette.co.uk

To everyone who needs the reminder:
Life's too short to be unhappy.

Good on Paper

Why Marrying Your Best Friend is a Recipe for Disaster

By Jazmine Prado

Happy couples love giving one piece of marriage advice above all others: Marry your best friend. It's the de facto pearl of wisdom meted out by lifestyle magazines, family and friends (maybe even your own parents at one point or another), cheesy social media captions, and pretty much anyone in a successful, loving relationship. Except here's the thing—marrying your best friend, in most cases, is actually a recipe for disaster.

Divorce rates are through the roof, but that's nothing new. While it's a bit tricky to pin down the exact number, around 50 percent of marriages end in divorce. And one recent study of more than 1,000 divorcees found that nearly 83 percent claimed they had, in fact, married their best friend. So it begs the question: have we been going about finding our perfect long-term partner the wrong way all this time?

Before you write me off as some bitter marriage-hating single, stay with me for a second. There's nothing *wrong* with marrying your best friend. Sure, the familiarity and comfort that go hand-in-hand with knowing someone inside and out is nice—you can probably be completely yourself around them—but can your best friend really check off the laundry list of qualifications needed in a lifelong partner? In most cases, the answer is a resounding "no."

Maybe when it comes to marriage we should be looking for partners who are a match for us on paper, who line up with our life plan, and just learn more about them along the way?

Think about a job interview and the kind of questions asked. They might inquire about your goals and long-term plans, about your qualifications and past experience. They'll almost certainly ask for your biggest strengths and weaknesses, why you want to work there, what you feel you can offer; the list goes on. The interviewer (or company really) is looking for a compatible partnership, one that is mutually beneficial and fulfills the needs of both parties. Maybe you've become friends, or even best friends, with your co-workers or even your boss (I know I've made lasting friendships throughout my professional tenure), but that wasn't the reason you got hired there.

Dating sites and apps use similar data-driven approaches for finding a suitable match. While filling out the questionnaire, it might feel like you're back in the hot seat, interviewing for your next job. There's an endless array of metrics and data points that will be collected to help pair two singles together in the hopes of a lasting relationship, but do you know the one question they won't ask?—"Are you best friends?"

All I'm saying is, best friends are best friends for a reason. Yes, friendships can deepen to an incredible point of trust, blossoming into something truly beautiful. And romantic relationships evolving into deep friendships is a completely different situation. But trying to shift a best friend into the role of long-term romantic partner is like trying to force a round peg into a square hole. It's just not a good fit, and more often than not it will lead to another divorce statistic, not a lifetime of happiness and bliss.

Chapter One

Past: 21 years old

"God, I have no idea what to get," I said as I fanned through the drink menu at an upscale cocktail bar called Taberna in West Los Angeles. The walls inside were dark gray and splashed with paintings from local artists, and a lone neon sign that read, *Sinners and Saints Welcome.*

The whole placed smelt like lavender and strawberries mingled with the bite of hard liquor and bad decisions.

I was there with Leonardo Couture, my childhood best friend whom I promised years ago I'd have my first official bar experience with.

"I have no idea what to get either," Leo replied. "But I know I want something with lots of tequila in it."

I laughed, my eyebrows rising. "Starting out strong, huh?"

"Well, I'm beyond bored of the beer in the dorms. Speaking of which, how are things at that ridiculous school of yours?"

"You mean the school that's way better than yours? It's amazing, thanks for asking," I replied with a hint of sass. Leo chuckled. I was at USC on an academic scholarship and Leo was at UCLA on a soccer scholarship. Of course we would end up at rival colleges; we were always competing.

I sucked in a breath of dry air. "But what about you? How's the photography stuff going?" Leo was studying to be a nature photographer and documentarian, something right up his alley.

"Good. Nothing too exciting going on at the moment." His eyes moved from the menu to meet mine. "By the way, that eyeshadow looks really nice on you. It brings out the gold and copper flecks in your eyes."

Leo always noticed colors. Light. Details. Everything.

"Thanks," I said, turning my face back to the menu to conceal my blush.

"Anything new and exciting going on with you?" he asked. Leo and I had never gone a day without speaking, even if it was just a quick text message. But truthfully, there's only so much you can update each other on via text. We were due for a good catch-up.

"Maybe. Maybe not," I teased, shrugging my shoulders.

"What's with the mysterious-ness, Jazmine Prado?" Leo often said my first and last name together. It was endearing.

"Gotta keep you guessing, don't I?" *Dammit. Was I flirting with him?* I knew I shouldn't be flirting with Leo. That would only complicate things.

My gaze moved away again, but as I slyly looked over, I noticed he was sneaking in glances, scanning me over from head to toe as I sat on the barstool beside him.

I was wearing a little black dress that hugged my body in all the right places, shiny black pumps, hoop earrings, and my Indalo charm bracelet from Spain that I never left home without. I'd styled my long, dark hair with loose, flowing curls, pale pink on my lips, eyeliner framing my brown eyes, and highlighter to complement my bone structure. I went all out.

Blood rushed to my face as I watched Leo take me in. And suddenly, I was captivated by how beautifully his brown, wavy hair fell right around his ears, framing his high cheekbones, and how his golden-brown skin glistened against it. He had on a fitted black shirt and black jeans that perfectly outlined his toned frame and a five o'clock shadow on his face. Twenty-one looked good on him.

I attributed my sudden appreciation for Leo's exterior to the bar's well-placed lighting. It had to be that.

Seconds later, the bartender stepped up across from us and set a Martini in front of me. "Oh, I didn't order that—"

"Complements of the gentleman." He thumbed at a table behind us. I looked over my shoulder and noticed a man in a tailored gray suit sitting alone at a table. He had dirty-blond hair and a nicely groomed beard. When he noticed me look over, he raised his own matching Martini in a kind of salute. I waved back with a hesitant smile.

"Whoa, this is *not* how it's supposed to go. Pretty sure I'm the only one who's buying you drinks tonight." Leo nudged me. He was grinning, but I couldn't tell if he was joking or a little bit jealous. For some reason, I hoped it was the latter.

"You're buying *me* drinks? I don't remember that being part of the plan. I would have picked an even *more* expensive spot," I teased, and he laughed. I reached for the stem of the Martini glass. "What am I supposed to do, reject this dude's drink? Have them pour it down the sink? That would be wasteful!"

Leo rolled his eyes. "I suppose you shouldn't waste it, no . . ."

"Also, if you're planning to buy my drinks, I need to buy yours," I insisted.

"No way! I wanted to take you out as a late birthday thing."

"It was just your birthday too!" We were born only a few days apart. Leo's birthday was November 15th and mine was November 21st.

"And I thought this was more of a thing we were supposed

to experience together. Not *my* birthday celebration." My nose wrinkled a little.

"Can't it be both?"

"I guess . . ." I tilted the glass toward him, then carefully set the Martini back down. When I looked up at him, an unfamiliar warmth swirled in my chest.

"So you wanted to take me out for my birthday, huh? Does that mean this counts as a date? I've never been on an official date with Leo Couture." My grin turned sly.

Then, Leo did something that surprised me. He ran his finger over my hand where it rested on the bar top. Softly. Gently. Tracing the back of my palm in a way that sent shivers down my spine. Heat radiated from his fingertips, and the searing look in his eyes made my stomach flip.

"First time for everything," he replied, his voice softer now. Coy.

I casually drew my hand away, ignoring a pang of regret in the pit of my stomach, and put it around the Martini glass in front of me. I was ready for that drink. Something, anything, to distract myself from those butterflies. But as I raised the glass once more, Leo stopped me.

"Not yet. We have to have our first bar experience together—"

"Well then, order something for fuck's sake." I laughed.

Leo waved for the attention of the bartender and ordered some version of a margarita. Once his drink was ready we held them up for a toast. "To our many years as best friends. And hopefully many more."

"Best friends who apparently go on dates," I said, before grinning and taking a sip of my Martini. *Damn.* It was strong. The vodka made my nose water. I tasted fruits too, cranberries, orange peel, a hint of lime. The sweet cut down on the burn. It was not a drink I would have thought to order, but it wasn't bad. I snuck another sip before I sat it back down. "Wow, that's good vodka," I said before I lightly coughed. "How's yours?"

"Amazing. Want to try it?" He tilted the cup toward me. My gaze drifted to the salt on the glass, to the spot where his lips had worn away the rim. The urge to put my lips where his had been suddenly felt dangerous.

I cleared my throat. "Nah, I'll finish this one first." And after taking a couple of big gulps, I said in a rush, "So, are you still with Elizabeth?" He nearly choked on his margarita.

Leo had been on and off with Elizabeth Milton since we were teens. Elizabeth was blonde, blue-eyed, and deceptively perfect. She was someone who I longed to be like during my awkward junior-high years when I hadn't yet made peace with my brown hair, sharp nose, and bushy eyebrows.

Leo and Elizabeth were always up and down and all over the place. And during the times he was "off" with Elizabeth, he was often casually dating someone else. I couldn't remember the last time Leo was truly single.

"Damn. Cutting right to the chase." He ran his fingers through his hair.

"Well, you said we were on a 'date' so I figured I would ask. You know, I'm not about being the other woman," I joked. Though, there was truth behind it. "Your Facebook said 'it's complicated' so I wasn't sure."

He scratched his head. "But you don't have Facebook."

Fuck. Heat rushed to my cheeks. "Oh, um, a friend of mine told me . . . someone who knows someone who you know at UCLA . . . or something like that." I took another longer sip of my Martini, completely aware of the fact that I gave myself away.

Truth was, I'd had one of my dorm-mates look up Leo's profile a few days before, just out of curiosity.

Leo smiled. I always loved his smile. He had the best smile. It was a beaming ear-to-ear smile filled with so much joy. He was always so present, so in the moment. It made you want to be there with him, too.

"So you were stalking my profile?"

"No," I quickly shot back. "Just getting the most up-to-date information. I'm a journalist major, and a Scorpio, it's practically my job to snoop. Plus, *you* haven't told me anything in weeks, and apparently your Facebook status or whatever it's called changes as quick as I can blink."

Leo flushed, looking appropriately chastised. "We hadn't had a good talk in a while," he protested, before he swallowed a long gulp of his own drink.

I picked up my glass and imitated him. In doing so, I downed the last of my drink. *That went quick*. "So . . . how complicated is it?" I asked, almost afraid of the answer.

Leo tilted up his head and stared at the ceiling for a second before answering. "Not that much, really. We're not together at the moment, but we're still friends."

"Still on and off, it's fair to say?" I side-eyed him.

"I guess so."

My stomach dropped. Strangely, that was not the answer I wanted to hear. I hoped he would say he was done with Elizabeth forever, that this time they'd finally decided they were better off not trying to make this odd thing between them work. But I reminded myself, firmly, that it shouldn't matter to me. I was his friend.

"Enough about Elizabeth," Leo said, his voice rougher than I expected. "What about you? Have you been seeing anyone at SC? I heard the guys are awful there." He said the last as a joke, but I noticed a tension in his shoulders, as if he were bracing himself for a blow.

I rolled my eyes. "Oh please, there's lots of great guys there . . ." I squinted. "But I'm not dating anyone."

"So you haven't found anyone better than me yet?" Leo smirked. His question threw me off.

I started nervously playing with the salt on the bar table. "Oh, I . . ."

"You know, because of the little deal we made when we were eighteen after you turned me down?"

Leo and I made a marriage pact our senior year of high school. He told me he had feelings for me and thought we should give the boyfriend–girlfriend thing a real try. I said we were too young, the timing wasn't right, and that I needed to have my journalism career in place before I got serious with anyone. I was a really fun eighteen year old. But I had my reasons.

My mom not having the opportunity to achieve her dreams made me even more determined to achieve my own. And her and my grandma wanted that for me as well. So much so, that throughout my teen years my mom would take me to her psychic friend who would tell me that if I wanted to be successful, I'd have to stay focused and not get caught up in relationships. I'm about 99 percent sure my mom paid him to say such things. But for someone like me who thrived on being ambitious, and was also superstitious, it was enough to keep me on track.

So to appease Leo, and so our years of friendship wouldn't sink down the drain, I suggested that we make a pact to marry each other at twenty-eight if both of us were still single. Twenty-eight made sense to me. I would have my career in place by then and it was ten years from eighteen, and ten was my lucky number.

We said we'd get married in Cancún, Mexico, where his

father, a French chef, met his mother, a Mexican romance novelist. And for our honeymoon we'd go to Marbella, Spain, where my Spanish-Moroccan parents were from. Leo and I were both mixed race and children of immigrants. Something else we had in common.

Leo thought the pact was just a way for me to string him along until I found someone "better." It wasn't. He'd been my best friend since first grade, lived right across the street from me, and I didn't want to lose him. And I also thought there could maybe be a time for us one day—just not then. But considering a couple weeks later he got back with Elizabeth, I figured he forgot about the whole ridiculous thing. Apparently, he didn't.

I met Leo's gaze. The background noise in the bar faded away as I stared. Soon, the rest of the room seemed to vanish, until it was just the two of us there. Just him. "You remember that?"

"Of course. It wasn't that long ago." He grinned and crossed his arms, his biceps brimming through his tight shirt. Everything he did felt sexy. Every move he made. Every word he said. He didn't feel like my childhood friend who I'd learned how to ride a bike with, and snuck into my first R-rated movie with, and trick-or-treated with every Halloween. He felt like something else, like someone more.

Suddenly, I felt weirdly nervous. My heart rabbited against my ribs. I forced myself to take a deep breath, and tore my gaze from his so as not to distract myself. "So, do we still have a deal then?" I tried for lighthearted, and almost made it work.

Leo tipped back the last of his drink. "Now *that* is up to you."

"Up to me?!" I waved a dismissive hand at him. "You're the one who's always off-and-on with Elizabeth or has some girl on your arm."

Leo leaned in closer and brought his hand to rest gently on top of mine. I froze, aware of every muscle, every inch where his palm rested on my body. I could feel his breath tickle my face. He stared like no one had ever stared at me before. There were flecks of green in his hazel eyes as they caught the dim bar lights.

"Jazmine. Us being together has always been up to you."

About an hour later, a few more appetizers and another drink in, I wasn't wasted but I was certainly tipsy. And based on the empty glass in front of Leo, I wagered he was in the same boat.

Booze-drinking aside, we were high on nostalgia and drunk on memories that night. We reminisced about the time we drove to Santa Monica after Leo got his license and how we ended up eating saltwater taffy on the beach till after midnight. We felt so cool and free and on top of the world and I didn't even care that I got grounded for missing curfew.

We remembered that time in seventh grade when we both got sent to the principal's office for leaving campus during lunch to walk to Taco Bell. Leo told the principal it was his fault, that he convinced me to do it, and got assigned a few days of detention. I felt bad and offered to make it up to him by doing his English homework—an offer that he refused.

We also talked about our first little kiss in first grade. It was a peck on the lips that we briefly shared behind a birch tree. Leo had helped me with my limonada stand that day and I was in an extra good mood because I made a whopping twenty bucks. My glee over earning some money would've probably led to me kissing practically anyone, but I was glad that it was Leo.

"Okay, be honest," Leo said, his fingers grazing my hand again. Maybe by accident, I couldn't be sure. We were both resting our arms on the bar for balance by now. Still, the chills returned. "I know you like to keep things close to the chest, but how many people have you kissed, not including me?" He held up a finger. "Before you say anything, I know we were only kids, but you should know that our first kiss in your parents' backyard rocked my little six-year-old world."

"Oh, come on, no it didn't."

"It did. I thought about it for days. Even started writing 'Leo + Jazmine' with hearts all over my notebooks."

I smiled, unaware that six-year-old Leo was so sentimental.

"Then, spring break senior year, the night of the marriage pact . . ." he made a drum roll sound on the bar table, "Jazmine and Leo kissed again!" Leo changed the tone of his voice to sound like an on-air reporter. I burst into laughter.

His eyes caught mine. Sparked. "And you know what, you're a good kisser. A really good kisser. Hot. Made the fact that you turned me down even more soul-crushing." He winked.

A smile overtook my face and I turned away in embarrassment—though I couldn't deny I enjoyed hearing it.

"Soul-crushing?" I countered. "Based on your constant lack of single-ness, you've seemed to have managed just fine."

"What can I say?" He shrugged. "I'm a survivor."

I laughed and took another sip of my drink. "So?" Leo nudged at my shoulder. "How many people have been lucky enough to make out with Jazmine Prado?" Leo folded his hands innocently, but his smile was all devilry. "Just please tell me you didn't do too much with Brian Doyle." Brian was a brief boyfriend I had during our junior year of high school. Leo didn't approve of him.

"I wasn't aware my dating history was going to be a topic of discussion tonight," I joked. The reality was, I didn't have much of a dating history. Leo was aware of this.

I theorized he was trying to gage if I was still the same picky bitch whose heart had to be earned. Now that we were away at college, we didn't have eyes on each other like we used to.

"Oh, come on. It's fun."

"For you, maybe." I paused and tapped my fingers on the Mojito glass. "Fine. Maybe . . . Four?"

Leo raised his brows. "Four. Wow. Sounds, um . . . wild." He nudged me, teasing.

I playfully slapped his shoulder. "Hey. I've been busy keeping my grades up and working on my craft . . . I'm committed to making this writing dream of mine happen, remember?"

"I've been busy too. Keeping my grades up, playing soccer, working towards my dreams. But I still find time for . . . other things. It's important to experience the full breadth of life."

I rolled my eyes. I got it: he was having fun and I was the boring one who was twenty-one and hadn't even had sex yet.

"What's *your* number then?" I asked, secretly hoping it wasn't in the millions.

"More than four," he admitted slowly, avoiding my gaze. "But not a ton. I've been with Elizabeth more often than not, and you know I'm not a cheater."

And then, for some reason, I blurted this out: "Have you had sex yet?"

Leo looked like a deer in the headlights. Like he was smack dab in the middle of the road and couldn't get away fast enough from oncoming traffic. "Um. Yeah," he answered, while playing with the basket of tortilla chips in front of him. "Elizabeth and I first had sex after spring fling, senior year. But don't worry, we used a condom."

I suddenly couldn't breathe. A lump formed in my throat. It felt so massive, I couldn't swallow. For a brief second, I thought I was having an allergic reaction, but no. I was reacting to the fact that he fucked Elizabeth for the first time just a couple weeks after I was experiencing my first real kiss . . . with him.

Though we never discussed it, I assumed Leo wasn't a virgin. He's twenty-one, extremely attractive, and super-charming. But the fact that he did the deed so close to our "make-out marriage pact" night, threw me for an unfortunate loop. I was disappointed in myself for being so naive.

With difficulty, I kept my eyes focused on the far corner of the bar. Anywhere but at him. I gently twisted the tarnished white-gold talisman that dangled from my wrist—an Indalo stick figure that carried a rainbow in its outreached hands. A gift from my grandma many moons ago, this symbol was believed to be good luck, to protect from bad energy. And my fingers always seemed to find it when I was feeling uneasy. Like right then. I stopped as soon as I noticed.

But he's Leo. He knew how to read me better than anyone. He knew my tells. He reached over and took my hand, not just a light graze this time, but fully interlacing his fingers through mine. "Before you write me off as some player, I know I said my number was 'more than four' but the thing is—"

"I don't really want to talk about this anymore," I mumbled through my tight throat. I shoved to my feet. "I've got to go to the bathroom."

Before I could move, Leo gently grabbed my arm. "I don't understand what I did wrong here." His face went tight with confusion. "You knew Elizabeth and I had dated for years. I thought you would've guessed . . ."

Leo was right. I couldn't fault him for losing his virginity to his girlfriend. If I hadn't turned him down back then, it probably would have been us experiencing that "first" together. "It's okay," I lied through my racing heart. "I really do just have to go to the bathroom. When I get back let's just . . . move on."

The cab ride back to our houses was a lot quieter than I would have expected it to be after our first bar experience together. I hoped the booze and good food would make my upset, confusing feelings dissipate. It did not. My chest felt tight as the cab pulled up to my parents' driveway, and I steadied myself before stepping outside of the car. Leo paid the driver and he drove away.

"Do you want to come over?" Leo asked before I could turn toward my own front door. "My parents are in Europe for my Dad's chef event. They'll be back tomorrow night. My sisters went with them, so it's just me."

I let out a long breath. Leo. His parents' house. Both of us, alone in it. Some part of me wanted to test that out. See what would happen. But . . . "I don't know. It's late, and I have to . . ."

"Do nothing?" He raised an eyebrow. "You're on Thanksgiving break." He inched closer. "Come on. I know I did something to upset you, and I want to make it up to you."

He reached over and took my hand, clutching it softly. "Just come over. I promise, you'll have a good time."

My shoulders sagged, and I gave in. "Fine," I sighed.

I let him lead me across the street, and tried my best not to smile when he made a comment about the deep shades in the midnight sky overhead. Always noticing colors.

We walked into his backyard, which still had the same Mexican rainforest vibe it always had, and sat in reclining chairs under the moonlit sky. The branches from the palm trees swayed lightly in the cool night breeze.

We fell silent for a few minutes. A shooting star passed overhead, and we both exclaimed at the same time, pointing. Then we laughed at how we both reacted the same way, and lapsed into companionable silence again. Leo was always one of the few people in the world I could just be quiet with. No pressure to fill the silence.

Then, I broke the silence by asking him something that surprised me. Something that threw us both for a loop.

"Leo, since you're apparently mister 'More Than Four' why haven't you ever tried to have sex with me?" I kept my gaze fixed firmly on the stars.

I fell silent. It wasn't like me to act this desperate and entitled. But I wanted to know if he simply never wanted to, or if it was something else entirely. I saw Leo turning towards me out of the corner of my eye, and held my breath.

He ran a hand through his hair, sitting up to study me. His posture was tight and I could see his arms flexed under his long-sleeved shirt.

"I guess . . . I didn't know it was an option," he replied, his tone quiet and solemn. "That night after we kissed, when you said the timing wasn't right for us . . . I just figured that meant I should try to move on. And I would never think just randomly hooking up would be something you'd want to do. Friends with benefits never seemed like your thing."

I forced a weak smile. "That makes sense . . . I'm sorry. I'm acting like a bitch."

Leo shifted towards the end of his chair, moving closer to me in the process. "If I'm being honest, I wish that night after spring fling was with you."

The jolt in my body returned. This time, with more intensity. He inched a little closer. "But you know, first times are overrated, anyway. You're still figuring things out. It's probably better it didn't happen then—"

"What about now?" I interrupted.

"Wait. What?" He blinked, eyes going wide.

"Let's do it. Let's have sex. Tonight. Do you have any protection?"

His eyes locked on to mine. His chest rose and fell,

definitely a little faster than it had been before. "Yeah, I have some condoms upstairs." But when he spoke again, it was hesitant. "Not that I don't want to, because *believe* me I do. I mean, I've thought about it so many times—"

"You have?" I asked, startled.

He laughed. "Is that a real question? It's just . . . We've both been drinking—"

"So? I'm not tipsy anymore . . . Are you?"

"No. But still . . . I've always wanted it to be right, 'cause it's you, and I would never want you to think I was taking advantage of you or something—"

Before he could finish his sentence, I leapt from my seat and moved over to his. I leaned in, so close that our noses touched. "Leo. I want to do this if you want to," I whispered.

He hesitated for a second before pressing his lips softly against mine, telling the sweetest story. A story of lifelong friendship. A story that's always been leading to more. A story of repressed desire and love. A story that should have started a long time ago.

His hands ran up and down my back. He cradled my body with the perfect amount of strength—enough for me to know that he was there, but not so much that he was overpowering me. I still felt in control.

Our tongues slid in and out of each other's mouths to the beat of a perfect rhythm. Like we had been doing this dance for years. He put his hand under my thigh and flipped me onto my back on the reclining chair. We stopped for a moment to gaze into each other's eyes. Our chests rose and fell in time together. My body filled with tingles as his lips found my neck, and he traced a slow path under my jawline. I softly moaned.

His mouth found my mouth again and as he lay on top of me, I could feel the hardness of his body against mine.

This is it, I thought. *Leo and I are going to have sex and it's going to be amazing.*

But then, suddenly, Leo stopped, turning his head away.

"What's wrong?" I clutched his face in my hands and gently tilted it back toward me.

His eyes searched mine, desperate, wanting. "I'm just worried about what this means for us. Who are we? Are we Leo and Jazmine, best friends who are also fuck buddies? Or are we Leo and Jazmine, best friends who are finally going to give dating a real shot?"

I raised my eyebrow. "Are you really going to ask me this while you're on top of me? Shouldn't you be ripping my clothes off and taking me upstairs instead of wanting to talk?" I joked.

"I'm just thinking, before this gets any more complicated, maybe we should talk about if we actually want to do the relationship thing. You know that's what I've wanted for years."

I sighed, more loudly than I realized. "I know. And I want that too . . . Eventually."

"*Eventually.*" Leo backed away from me. My body went cold all over again from the absence of him. My arms ached to be around him again. "Is this about the 'timing has to be right' again?"

My hand came to rest on his arm and I squeezed gently. "Leo, we're seniors in college. We don't know where our lives are going to take us after graduation. We both have our own ambitions and dreams . . . All I know is that my parents only married because my mom got pregnant with me. And she gave up all of her dreams because of that."

"I would never want you to give up on your dreams, Jazmine. You know that, right? Your ambition and passion is one of my favorite things about you!"

"Well, what if after college we got jobs in other states?"

His gaze remained firm. "We could make it work if we wanted."

"I'm sure we could. But it makes more sense to wait. Otherwise we're risking our shot way too soon—"

He pivoted away from me. My arm dropped to my side. "So you want to just, what? Wait until we're twenty-eight? I think making this marriage pact with you was a huge mistake. I know the whole thing was partly a joke anyway, but it feels like you just want to string me along until this bullshit deadline."

"That's not it!" I shouted, louder than I intended.

"Then what is it?" His voice rose too. Leo almost never raised his voice. He noticed it at the same time I did, and softened. "I love you, Jazmine," he murmured, quieter now. "I've always loved you. I don't want to wait until I'm twenty-eight to be with you. That's *seven* damn years from now. Tomorrow isn't promised. Anything could happen by then!"

I swallowed hard, trying to hold back the tears forming in my eyes. I was suddenly paralyzed with fear of what loving him could mean. The fear overtook my body, and I couldn't find the words to speak. To tell him how I felt. Or what I wanted.

I wanted him, but I also wanted my dream job. I couldn't fall into the trap my mother did, of falling in love too young and losing out on my ambitions. My family was counting on me to make something of myself and I couldn't risk letting them down.

We both jumped at the sound of Leo's phone ringing. At that moment, I was extremely grateful for the distraction. "Shit. I have to get this. I'll be right back."

"Okay." I sat back on the recliner and tried not to look too relieved.

As Leo walked inside the house, I wondered who could be so important for Leo to step away from *this* conversation. The one we'd been overdue to have for years. But his parents were traveling. Maybe something went wrong with their trip?

When Leo stepped back out onto the patio he looked like he'd fought off an evil spirit. His face was long, his eyes tired.

"What's wrong? Who was that?" I sat upright again, worried.

Leo's shoulders tensed. "Elizabeth."

I flinched. "Why did she call you?"

"She's at a party in Beverly Hills and apparently her friends accidentally left without her. She can't get a hold of her parents. She asked me to come pick her up."

"Is the party unsafe or something? Is she in a bad situation?"

"Oh no." Leo shook his head. "Nothing like that. She just doesn't want to wait around for her parents all evening. Apparently they're at a play or something."

Fire coursed through my veins. I forced myself to breathe. He'd just told me he'd always loved me, and now he wanted to go pick up Elizabeth?

I hopped to my feet, unable to fight the anger anymore. "That's ridiculous. So you're supposed to stop what you're doing and go pick her up because she doesn't want to wait around at a party in Beverly Hills? Tell her to call a fucking cab. That's what I would do if I was in her situation!"

"She doesn't like taking cabs in the U.S." He rolled his eyes. "She thinks they're gross. She says she'll only take them in Paris."

"Well, Princess Elizabeth can find another way home. I can't believe you're even considering leaving me here to go get her." I crossed my arms.

Leo looked bewildered. "What? I wasn't going to leave you! I was going to ask you to come with me."

"Oh, sure, because she'd love that. You showing up with me! You know she's always been weird about our friendship." I shook my head. "And fuck, maybe now she has a reason to be. Plus, you can't just rush to her every beck and call. She's just taking advantage of you, can't you see that?"

Leo stepped closer. Tension radiated from his every step. "Elizabeth and I are still friends, Jazmine. I'm not going to not help out a friend."

"Which is exactly why she called *you* and not any of her millions of girlfriends. She knows you're a nice guy, and she knows you'll come get her no matter what hour of night or day if she asks you. It's probably just a ploy to get back together with you. This is what she *always* does. She's been doing this since high school. It's unhealthy and you fall for it every damn time!" By the end of my sentence I was jabbing my finger into his face.

He backed away. "What is your deal?"

"My deal is I'm sick of playing second fucking fiddle to perfect Elizabeth."

"Second fiddle?" He laughed, looking incredulous. "You've always been first fiddle. I'm the one who's been trying to get with you for years. I just told you I loved you. You're the one who keeps saying the timing isn't right and pushing me away. Seems like I'm the one who's second fiddle to whatever your perfect life plan is."

My body felt tight, my fingers numb. I took a long, slow breath, trying to steady my heart rate. It pulsed so hard my eardrums felt like they were about to burst.

"Leo," I replied in a more composed tone. "If you go pick her up right now, you guys are going to end up back together. It's just what you do." I would know. I'd seen it happen enough times.

"Well, the girl that I want to be with doesn't want anything to do with me for another seven fucking years. So I'm kind of in a dilemma here." Leo fished for his car keys in his pocket.

"Don't go to her."

"Look." He let out a long breath. "If you don't want to come, I'll try to be back as fast as I can. If you want to stay here until I get back, you're more than welcome to."

My very bones ached with rage. Leo moved towards the patio's back gate. Watching him walk away made the anger and fear more palpable.

And then, I said something regretful: "If you leave to go to pick her up, right now, after everything we were just talking about . . . then we're done. We can't be friends anymore. Dating is off the table. *This*," I pointed back and forth to us, "is done."

My bottom lip started to quiver. I immediately wished to retract my words. But it was too late. I couldn't take them back.

Leo stopped in his tracks. He turned around, shock stretched across his beautiful face. "Are you seriously giving me an ultimatum? We've been friends since first fucking grade. *Best friends.* Friends who've stood by each other through *everything.* You would give that all up because of your stupid jealousy of Elizabeth?"

"I'm not jealous of her, Leo," I spat back. "It's not about that. It's about the fact that you can't say no to her. It's about that we weren't done talking, we were in the middle of a serious conversation, and we were even about to maybe have sex, for fuck's safe! And still, you're leaping up to do her bidding. Frankly, it's bullshit."

He shook his head. "Look, I've got to go."

"I'm serious, Leo. You do this, it's over."

Leo let out a long sigh and gave me one last, lingering glance. Then he walked out the gate to his car.

I considered going after him, but I didn't.

A week after our fight I was sitting in my car at a nearby shopping center and nervously fiddling with my keys. It was breezy and drizzly—the type of weather that'd usually put me in a good mood. But that day, it didn't.

I couldn't quite recall why I went to that center in the first place. I was parked near The Coffee House. A place Leo and I would often go to read, listen to music, or muse about life. Maybe I was there for coffee. Or to grab a late lunch. Or maybe I just went there instinctively. My mind was in a fog and had been for that entire week.

Usually when I felt this way, I'd hang out with my best friend. But we weren't talking.

By the time I realized I was wrong for giving Leo an ultimatum, apologizing felt impossible; humiliating. I was too proud to say, "You were right. I was just jealous and acting immature and my ego got the best of me." Instead, I was silent. Avoidant. Pushing him away like I never had before.

I wanted to make things right—I just wasn't sure where to start.

The gaping hole in my chest was substantial. I couldn't imagine not having Leo in my life. It was foolish of me to even suggest it. The phrase, "think before you speak," cut a lot deeper after that day.

But we had to address the elephant in the room: Were we going to try being more than just friends? Another conversation I was dreading.

As my mind continued to race, I looked over and noticed what appeared to be an envelope poking out from under the passenger seat. I reached over to grab it, thinking it was possibly a bill I missed or maybe a copy of next semester's schedule.

But my breath hitched when I saw the handwriting. It was Leo's.

This wasn't the first time he'd slipped a note in my car. I had the bad habit of leaving my windows just slightly cracked, something he'd constantly hounded me about, claiming it was "unsafe." At that moment though, I was grateful for my bad habit.

I took a couple deep breaths before tearing open the letter.

Jazmine,

I tried calling, but kept getting your voicemail. I just needed you to know that I'm so sorry. I shouldn't have left you to pick up Elizabeth.

That night, our first bar experience together, was supposed to be a time for us. I fucked it up. I'd blame it on my age or the fact that I sometimes have a savior complex (at least, that's what my psych major roommate tells me), but really there's no excuse.

You joked that we were on a date, and if I were on a date, I would've never left my date like that. I wouldn't have even answered my phone.

I'm really sorry. I am. I hope you can forgive me. I know it's only been a couple days but I really miss you already.

I'm going to be at The Coffee House on Tuesday editing some photos. If you're around, come by and I'll get your coffee. I owe you one anyway.

I love you,
Leo

A tear trickled down the side of my face. Seeing his letter, knowing how he felt, I knew right then I had to call him. I could muster up the courage to apologize for how I acted. To own my part in this, too.

But then, my eyes focused on the day. *Tuesday.* Today was a Friday, and the following Tuesday we'd both be back at college.

Based on that, and the "I know it's only been a couple days," I suspected Leo slipped this through my car window the Sunday after our fight, but I missed it. I hadn't left the house all week.

Suddenly, reaching out to Leo felt pressing. Urgent. I didn't want him to think I was ignoring his apology.

Just when I'd summoned the courage to pick up my phone, the hairs on the back of my neck stood up. I felt something familiar nearby. I knew exactly who it was.

I wiped my eyes and looked up through the rain-spattered glass, only to see Leo standing in front of The Coffee House. My heart dropped. It was no surprise that he was there. This was our favorite spot.

Through the lens of the water, he looked like a painting. Something from a storybook, all watercolor streaks. *You sound like him*, I told myself.

As I gazed at Leo, my heart raced in my chest. I put my phone down and unbuckled my seat belt. I didn't need to call him now, I could apologize face to face. It seemed the universe had given me the perfect opportunity to make this right. To put this silly fight behind us.

And just as I was about to open the door, I froze.

Standing behind Leo was Elizabeth. She looked even better than she did the last time I saw her. Her bright blue eyes and blond hair glistened, even in the gloomy light. I suddenly felt like I was dog-paddling in the sea of my insecurities, trying my best not to sink below the surface. My skin itched as if hives were forming on my chest.

Leo glanced over at my car. *Shit!* I ducked, hoping he didn't spot me. Outside it began to rain harder, obscuring the windshield. Making it a little harder to see outside.

As I carefully peeked over the steering wheel, I saw Leo move closer to Elizabeth. A lump formed in my throat. He tucked a strand of hair behind her ear before delicately caressing her face. Then, he leaned in. Slowly. Brushing his lips against hers, soft at first, gentle. Elizabeth sank into him. His lips consumed hers, his strong hands running up and down her back.

It was a real kiss. A sexy kiss. A kiss that made the hole in my chest grow even wider.

When they came up for air, Leo grabbed her hand, and they walked off in the opposite direction, leaving the front of the coffee shop.

Bile rose in my throat as I watched them move away. The sound of the water hitting the windshield matched the pattern of the tears that were now running down my cheeks. My heart sank into my chest so deep, I feared a part of it would never emerge again.

I wondered if he saw me. If he knew I was in my car. And if so, did he kiss her on purpose? Or was it simply that spotting my car brought back the heartache from our fight and me never responding to his apology?

Regardless, this was a slap in the face. No. It was more than that. My sadness morphed into anger. It was visceral anger. Soul-eating.

I almost burst into more tears, but I swallowed my emotions instead.

He was hurt and dealt with it his way—by seeking comfort in the familiar. And I was hurt and would deal with it my way—by never talking to him again.

Don't Be Fooled by the Highlight Reel

By Jazmine Prado

Long before the days of social media apps there was a different way to humble brag to your friends: A high school reunion.

Generally speaking, high school reunions took place every ten years after graduation, giving attendees ample time to prep their outfits, craft witty stories and other anecdotes to create the perfect highlight reel of their life. It was one day, a decade after high school, to shine as brightly as the glory days. It was something to look forward to.

During high school reunions you could stretch the truth about how successful you were in your jobs, show photos of your kids, your pets, your home, and paint a rosy picture of how happy and perfect your life was. And then, several hours later, it was all over. You would return to your normal routine and tuck away your highlight reel until the next one.

Enter social media: a place where users post a never-ending string of curated photos of their alleged "life," each with their own perfectly crafted captions. And just like a high school reunion, very little of what we see online reflects reality. Even posts that claim to be "real" or "raw" oftentimes serve a purpose to enhance one's "brand," just like everything else.

There's no doubt that this disconnect between fact and fiction can have a lasting impact on our brains, and our self-esteem. Yet even so, many cannot look away.

But just to be clear, there's nothing wrong with enjoying social media! There are positives to it as well, one big one being its ability to connect people from all around the world.

This article isn't here to shame social media lovers or influencers. It's here to argue that it might serve us better to accept social media for what it truly is: Fiction. Fantasy. A never-ending highlight reel of our best, most shining moments. A mere fraction of our truths.

So next time you're scrolling through your feed and feeling like a piece of shit after coming across a post of someone's vacation, promotion, or engagement, or perfectly positioned photo, just remember you're only getting a small peek behind the curtain. The real story is, more often than not, a lot less glamorous.

Chapter Two

Present day: 28th Birthday

"May I ask when the hotel will be open?" I said on the phone to the man I was interviewing for *Style&Travel.* His name was Alan Yorkshire and he was announcing his plans to open a state-of-the-art hotel in Iceland with money he'd inherited from his father. Not that I didn't *love* interviewing rich, Beverly Hills-born socialites about their upcoming business ventures, but truth be told, I found this story to be a bit . . . dull. Probably because it was a piece that was assigned to me—not one I came up with and pitched myself.

On the other end of the line, Alan took a deep breath. He sounded as if he didn't expect me to ask such a standard question. "Well." He loudly cleared his throat. "I would say as soon as humanly possible."

I rolled my eyes. I never liked it when interviewees gave vague answers. "Do you have a general time frame I could maybe give our readers?" I asked, hoping my tone didn't give away my annoyance. "It's November now. Is summer a realistic timeline, or maybe next fall—"

"How about we just say ASAP," he replied, a bit sternly.

"You bet." I tightened my jaw. I was thankful at that moment the interview wasn't a video call.

"But could you please stress that our hotel will be five-star and that we'll have a luxurious, top-of-the-line spa and salon," Alan added. "I know your readers love that stuff."

What Mr. Yorkshire failed to realize was that the demographic for *Style&Travel* were readers who weren't only looking to stay at five-star resorts with over-priced amenities. They were looking for an experience, to make a long-lasting memory.

I knew this first-hand because I once wrote an essay about the topic, titled, *Traveling Has Become More About The Experience And Less About The Flex.*

Alan would have known this if he did his market research. But that's how it went when one lived in a bubble.

"Well, I think I've got this all down. Thank you so much for taking the time to speak with me, and for choosing *Style&Travel* to announce this exciting new hotel of yours," I said politely. *Always stay classy on the job.*

"No problem. And thank you for being willing to talk with me at this hour, I know it's evening where you are. I've been traveling all over Europe, it's hard to keep track of the time." I let out a quiet chuckle at his humble brag. "Can't wait to read the story!" he added.

I hung up the phone and squinted at the desk calendar in my apartment. Deadline was in two days. Not bad. Totally doable. Problem was, I was dreading writing it.

Gone were the golden days of journalism. The days when magazines were filled with short stories, celebrity tell-alls, thought-provoking opinion pieces, and in-depth destination features that transported a reader to another time and place. Written stories in print and online publications were dying. Well, more like they were dead.

In its place were videos to try to keep up with our ever-declining attention spans, as well as social media posts with photos and inspirational quotes. I often lost sleep about how over 62 percent of people got their news from social media. It was definitely not how I predicted things would go when I graduated summa cum laude with a B.A. in Journalism six years ago.

I missed writing stories that made my heart sing.

Essays like, "Why the Phrase 'Bikini Body' is Bullshit." And, "How Not Being a Mother Doesn't Make You Any Less of a Woman." And one of my all-time favorites, a story about being the daughter of immigrants, titled, "Caught Between Two Worlds."

Stories that started conversations. Made people think. Some that even went viral, won me a couple awards, and earned me a Wikipedia page.

I let out a long sigh as I tapped on my desk, running my fingers against the worn wood on the edges. The fact that I'd gone from "think-pieces" to interviewing spoiled entrepreneurs like Alan Yorkshire about his latest cash-grab for a paid advertisement article, made my stomach sour a bit.

But I reminded myself I was grateful to have work. Thanks to pivot-to-video initiatives, many of my journalist friends were unemployed. I was one of the lucky ones. I'd rather be writing something I hated than not writing at all.

I turned at the sound of my phone buzzing. It was a text from my boyfriend, Hudson.

Can't wait to celebrate your birthday tomorrow! 28 is gonna be great! I love you!

A smile tugged at my lips.

Hudson planned to come into town from Toronto for

meetings but was arriving a couple days early to spend my birthday with me, and to be my date to my birthday dinner.

I'd never been big on birthday parties, but after constant nagging from my cousin Gal, I'd agreed to a small dinner—just my family, even though that felt like more than I'd bargained for.

Having Hudson in town would make it a little more challenging to get my article done. But I was a pro and used to pulling all-nighters to write stories if I had to. *I got this.*

I texted, "*Love you*" back before reaching for a half-eaten croissant and a glass of CBD-infused soda that I poured and forgot about before the interview started.

After taking a long sip, I geared up to send some weekly pitches to my editor, Kelly Jameson. We had a system: The writers sent their pitches Wednesday night and she'd always get back by noon on Thursday. Like clockwork.

I leaned back in my chair as I brainstormed some story ideas. My mind went blank. What I really wanted to pitch was a story about inspiring women who were left out of history books. Or maybe something about astrology and tarot and how they're being used in therapy. Or even something health related, like the rise of telemedicine and how it's pushing us into the future.

Something. Anything that made me feel like I had a pulse.

But stories like that weren't really on brand for *Style&Travel* and I was determined to get one of my original ideas picked up this week. Mainly, so I wouldn't be stuck interviewing more people like Alan Yorkshire.

After staring at the wall for a few more minutes I finally came up with some concepts: Tips for traveling during the holidays, where to find the best fall scarves, and how to do a pumpkin spice latte tour. All stories I thought my editor would eat up.

"She has to take one of these," I muttered to myself. The

unfortunate reality was, it had been about three weeks since *Style&Travel* commissioned an article that was originally mine. And I had noticed a pattern: Whenever a magazine was about to do a lay-off, they took less and less original material from their writers.

I had experienced two editorial staff lay-offs in the last three years. I didn't think I could weather another.

I pressed send on the email and then scarfed the last of my croissant and leaned back in my seat, drink in hand.

I closed my eyes and took a few deep breaths. It had been a long day staring at screens and my eyes were feeling the weight of it.

When I cracked them open my heart fluttered as I watched the clock on my computer tick over to 1:12 a.m on November 21st. Officially my twenty-eighth birthday. Allegedly, I was supposed to be born a minute earlier, at 1:11 a.m., which would've blessed me with a life full of peace. But my stubborn soul decided on a minute later—just to keep things interesting. At least I was born on a full moon. That had to count for something.

My hands felt damp as I gazed at the date and time on my home screen. I put the glass back on my desk, worried the added moisture would make it slip through my fingers.

Turning twenty-eight isn't usually a stress-inducing birthday for most people, but it was for me, for a reason both absurd and ridiculous: It was the date I'd set for the marriage pact I made with my former childhood best friend, Leonardo Couture.

I didn't allow myself to think about Leo. It was a self-preservation thing. One thought from our past would lead to countless others, spreading deep into my psyche like a lethal virus with no cure in sight.

It may have gone against my personal rules, but this was one of the rare times I wanted to think about him.

Though I happily voided the pact we made years ago after our crushing fight, I was curious to know if he was single, nonetheless. If there was ever a day to do some digging on him, this was it.

I opened my phone and went straight to Instagram. In the search bar, I entered his name: Leo Couture. He was the first result, because we had lots of followers in common.

Just not each other.

Ignoring the little pang, I went to click on his profile. As my hand hovered over my phone, it started to shake. My heart raced in my chest and I felt like I was breathing through a very thin, constricted straw. It may have been seven years since our falling-out, but my body still reacted like it happened yesterday. My fingers traced over my Indalo bracelet as I took a long, deep breath.

Despite what some say, time doesn't heal all wounds.

After a few more minutes of internal emotional battle, I finally clicked over to his account.

My stomach churned as I stared at his profile picture. It was like looking at a ghost. A ghost that still haunted me, usually at my lowest moments. It seemed that all the black tourmaline I collected couldn't quite keep this spirit away.

While gazing at his photo, the tiniest of smiles tugged at my lips. He looked like the same Leo, just more mature. A few more lines on his face, a little more dark hair on his chin, but the same wavy hair, golden-brown skin, and bright hazel eyes I last gazed into what felt like a lifetime ago.

A shred of sentiment threatened its way to the surface and I quickly stuffed it away like I always did. I was there for facts, nothing more.

I moved my gaze towards his Bio section, which simply stated, "I take pictures and make documentaries about nature," and then scrolled down to his grid. It was full of beautiful posts about the outdoors, except for his most recent one. The moment I saw the photo, I felt the bile rise up my throat.

It was a picture of him and a blonde woman holding hands but my eyes latched on to who was tagged in the post . . ."Elizabeth Milton," and then to a word in the caption: *engaged*.

I took another sip of the CBD soda from the glass on my desk and stared at my screen. "Fuck," I murmured to myself. Considering our history, and how everything went down the last time we . . .

This one just stung a little.

Now I remembered why I hated the guy.

I wondered how long he'd been engaged to Elizabeth, of all people, but I couldn't bring myself to gather any more info. I knew myself well enough to know that going down the Leo Couture rabbit hole was a bad idea.

The screen went blurry. Unable to focus, I put down my phone. A ball formed in my throat. I was disappointed in myself for giving a shit. Not wanting to give this anymore attention, I settled into bed and started to watch *Friends* reruns.

Soon enough, Leo was far from my mind and instead I was second-guessing the story pitches I sent Kelly.

My eyes felt heavy and after yawning a few times I reached over to turn off the light, pausing when I noticed I had an unread text on my phone. It was from a former colleague, Amanda Gill. We both worked as writers at the posh lifestyle publication *The Mod,* about two years ago.

The text was from earlier that day. Somehow, I missed it.

Jaz, my magazine laid off the entire editorial staff today, myself included. Can you FUCKING believe it?! Pivoting to video again, just like Mod. I can't believe this keeps happening to us and I've been hearing through the grapevine more magazines will be following suit. You're so lucky to have a good gig at Style&Travel! If you know anyone who's looking for writers, please let me know.

More magazines following suit? I hoped with all of my soul it wouldn't be *Style&Travel.*

Suddenly, my heavy eyelids were nowhere to be found and instead of getting a good night's sleep, I was wide awake, counting down the hours until I'd hear back from Kelly about the pitches.

Chapter Three

As I pulled into the crowded pick-up lane at Bob Hope Airport in Burbank, my palms started to sweat. The traffic was bumper to bumper and I hated the feeling of being stuck between two cars. You would think I'd be used to traffic, being born and raised in L.A., but sometimes, it still made me clammy.

It was 12:03 p.m., and since I was at a halt in the pick-up lane and not going anywhere anytime soon, I grabbed at my phone to check my emails and brace myself for Kelly's reply.

I scratched my head as I stared at the screen. *Huh. That's odd.* To my surprise, Kelly hadn't gotten back to me yet.

I furrowed by brows and refreshed again. Nothing.

My hands started to tremble. Kelly always got back by noon on Thursday. Never a second later. Not since I'd been working at *Style&Travel*, at least.

I gulped as the thought of Amanda's text came rushing into my brain. More magazine lay-offs. More pivot-to-video initiatives. I thought *Style&Travel* was safe, but were they?

My mind started to spin. *What if she hated all the pitches? What if she doesn't have anything to assign me this week? What if they're cutting their editorial staff to run more videos and podcasts like every other fucking publication?*

Maybe it wasn't just the traffic making me clammy. I wiped

my palms on my sweater and pulled at my collar as my neck filled with heat. I knew I was probably just being paranoid. But I couldn't help but worry.

After refreshing my email for what felt like the millionth time, I forced myself to put my phone down. Snafus with my career were always panic-inducing. Some struggle with the fear of flying. Others, the fear of heights, or even spiders. For me, it was the fear of not being successful. And it could send me into a tailspin.

With my phone out of reach, I looked up and caught a glimpse of myself in the rearview mirror and flinched at the bags under my eyes. The concealer I applied that morning didn't seem to be doing much. My hair was pulled back in a not-artfully-messy bun, and my lips were in desperate need of some color. Me looking like death warmed over wasn't necessarily the distraction I was looking for, but it *was* a distraction nonetheless.

I peeked at the cars. Still no movement. I reached into my bag and grabbed my peach-colored lipgloss. *That's a little better*, I thought, pursing my lips at my reflection in my rearview mirror.

The cars began to move again. I inched forward, scanning the crowd for my boyfriend. Several car lengths along, I spotted dirty-blond hair pulled into a familiar low bun.

"Hudson! Over here!" I shouted as I rolled down the window to my Honda Accord. On the sidewalk, a tall, thirty-year-old man turned in my direction. His deep-blue eyes lit up the moment they met mine. I forced a smile, working overtime to suppress the anxiety I was still feeling over my editor. I didn't see the need to pull Hudson into my doom.

Hudson and I had been together for just over a year and a half. He was exactly what I never knew I needed. Easy-going.

Up for anything. Obsessed with his career as much as I was obsessed with mine. And beautiful to boot.

He checked off everything on my list for what I was looking for in a partner. He was perfect for me on paper. And we were drama-free.

He was Canadian and we met at a charity benefit that I was covering in Malibu. Hudson lived in Toronto, but he visited L.A. once a month for work. We talked on the phone or video-chatted every day. Honestly, the distance was totally doable. I liked being involved with someone who didn't live close by. Been there done that.

Hudson finished collecting his bags—really just one impressively small bag, the guy was a pro traveler—and jogged up to my window. Before opening the door, he held up his phone in selfie position. "Hey guys, it's Hudson. I'm here in the lovely state of California again. The weather is beautiful this time of year, probably about seventy degrees at the moment. Anyway, I've got some awesome things I'm gonna be sharing this week, so stay tuned!" He waved at the camera with enthusiasm.

I leaned forward so no one could see me in the background. For the most part, Hudson knew how to angle his camera, but sometimes he'd accidentally slip up, catch me in the frame.

He worked in social media. He was a legit social media star, actually. He had over two million die-hard subscribers who tuned in to watch his videos, which chronicled his travel adventures and daredevil antics: jumping out of airplanes, scaling mountains, and flying to Hawaii just to surf a big wave. That was all just business as usual for Hudson. He made good money from sponsorships and partnerships with clothing or sporting goods brands, too.

It all went a bit over my head, but I had come to respect his job. He worked constantly, whether on planning his next

YouTube video, chronicling his everyday life in digestible clips for TikTok, or editing pictures for Instagram. He was always on, and he had no problem letting his followers into his life.

I was the opposite.

I had Instagram, Facebook, and Twitter accounts, but I rarely used them. I didn't have many followers and I didn't care to try to attract more. Besides, other than posting about my articles, I didn't like to share my life online. Plus, I was bitter at social medial for how it's changed the landscape of the journalism world.

Being with Hudson definitely took some getting used to. But he was great about keeping me off his accounts and never seemed offended that I didn't want to be on there.

He finally slid into the passenger seat of my car with a wide smile. As always, his big blue eyes reminded me of the Malibu sea, the same thought I had the day we met. When Hudson looked at me with those eyes, my stomach dropped as if I'd just barreled over the highest point of a roller coaster. His eyes had that much power.

Well. His muscular build and handsome, sculpted face certainly didn't hurt either.

But my favorite thing about him was the fact that he didn't take himself too seriously. He was always goofing around or doing something silly, he was very likable.

"Hey." He leaned in real slow. Then paused, his lips inches from mine. Teasing. "Happy birthday, love." Only then did he finally kiss me.

Kissing Hudson was an *experience*. Soft, but not too soft. Wild, but not too wild. Every kiss filled me with a newfound sense of adventure. He pulled away, just far enough so we could both catch our breaths, and stared at me again. I blushed and quickly looked the other direction.

Sometimes his gaze could be intense. In a good way, but . . . my whole body felt flushed right then, and I was conscious of the other cars around us. *People might see.* I'd never been good at affection in public.

"How was your flight?" I asked, clearing my throat of the lump it always seemed to grow around him.

"Comfortable. I slept or read most of the way."

"Damn. First class sounds great."

"The company I'm doing a sponsorship with offered to pay for it. I didn't protest." He grinned. "You look beautiful, by the way."

I laughed, catching a glimpse of the bags still bulging from my eyes. "Thank you," I replied, because Hudson always threatened to compliment with more compliments unless I accepted said compliments. "Are you sure you want to stay at my apartment? I'm sure they offered to put you up in some fancy hotel. My place is such shit."

"Jaz, we go through this every time. I love staying at your place. Hotels are boring." He leaned his seat back, eyes still on me.

I maneuvered back into traffic as we spoke. "That's not true. Hotels are awesome. Soft sheets, room service, no cleaning . . . Not boring, in my book."

"I'd rather stay with you." He paused. "Unless you don't want me to stay there?"

"What? No, of course not! I love when you stay with me. I just feel bad because it's so small."

"I'm Canadian. The country full of happy people, remember? I don't give a shit about ridiculous things like apartment size. I just want to be with you."

I squinted at Hudson from the corner of my eyes. "Okay. But just know I won't be offended if you change your mind."

"My mind is happily made up." He grinned. "By the way, I'm looking forward to dinner tonight."

"Well, that makes one of us."

He reached across the gear shift to nudge my arm. "Come on, you should love your birthday. It's Jaz Day. The best day. The day you were born."

I let out a quiet chuckle. "Was your cabin pressurized? You seem even more chipper than usual. And you're *always* chipper." Hudson was usually super upbeat. He was an Aries—lively, optimistic, fearless. His positivity helped to balance out my brooding Scorpio soul.

"I'm just happy to see you, that's all." He finally glanced away from me, toward the window, and I relaxed a little at no longer being the object of his loving gaze. Or his birthday conversation. "Do you mind if we stop by that famous street before we go to your apartment? Ro-de-oh Drive or something like that."

I burst out laughing. "It's pronounced Ro-day-oh, not Ro-de-oh like a cowboy." I grinned. "But sure, of course."

"Great. Just wanted to do a little shopping."

I raised an eyebrow. "Wow. Fancy." I couldn't remember the last time I went to Rodeo Drive for anything. Most of my days were spent at home writing and trying to keep up with the hustle of the journalism world. Shopping for fun hadn't been on my agenda—or in my budget, to be honest—in forever. But I was always happy to go along.

We circled for about ten minutes before I could find an open parking spot. The second I stepped out of the car, Hudson picked me up and swung me around in his arms, before laying another kiss on my lips. I wrapped my arms around his neck, sank against him.

I loved the way he could just pick me up so effortlessly. And the way his stubble scratched my cheek gently, as he lowered me back to the ground. "Is that new cologne?" I asked as he perched me back on my feet.

I was five four and Hudson was six three, so he towered over me. The top button on his cream-colored long-sleeved shirt was unbuttoned as usual, and also as usual, it made me blush. He was a fitness buff (a passion we did not share) and his toned pecs peeked through his shirt.

"The cologne? Just a product I'm trialing," he said. "They asked me for a sponsorship, but I wanted to try it first . . . You like?"

He smelled like woodsmoke and oak. "I don't usually like things that woodsy, but this one's nice!" I added.

I tilted my head back so he could give me another kiss. "I'm really happy you're here," I murmured.

Between my nervousness over not hearing back from Kelly that afternoon, and my moment of weakness when I looked up Leo's profile the night before, I was more than happy to be in the presence of Hudson's good vibrations.

He was like an energy cleanse. A human equivalent to the crystal, selenite.

"Me too." He grinned and pulled out his phone. "One sec." He winked, before stepping away from my side. "Hey guys, I'm here at the infamous Rodeo Drive—" He still pronounced it Ro-De-Oh. It took all my effort not to laugh and ruin his take. "—in Beverly Hills. About to do some shopping before a big night I have ahead of me. Hope you all are having a wonderful afternoon." He flung up a peace sign before he disconnected.

"A big night ahead?" I lifted an eyebrow.

"Well, um, yeah. Your birthday dinner, of course." As he spoke, he fumbled with his cell phone, made a grab for it, and dropped it again. It landed face down on the pavement, and I winced. Hudson quickly leaned down and scooped it up.

"Are you okay? I can't believe you just dropped your phone!" I stared. He wasn't usually clumsy.

"I'm fine. And look, no scratches!" He spun the uncracked screen toward me to demonstrate. "You're my good luck charm." He draped an arm around my shoulders and tugged me against his side.

We were walking hand-in-hand up Rodeo Drive when Hudson suddenly stopped. Right in front of Chanel. "I have to pop in here. That okay?"

"You have to pick something up in Chanel?" My eyebrows rose. "Is that the brand you're working with this trip?" If so, it was a step above the others. Not that they weren't brands I recognized, but, well . . . Chanel was Chanel.

"Not exactly."

I squinted, trying to get more out of him. But Hudson's face could be totally blank when he wanted it to be. The man did once make it to the finals of a professional poker tournament, after all.

When we stepped inside the store, Hudson waved to a woman in the back. She motioned to another guy to bring forward a couple boxes. It all happened so fast, I couldn't even process what was going on until the woman stood in front of us.

But she wasn't looking at Hudson. She held out a hand to me.

"You must be Jazmine. I'm Melody." Melody had long, strawberry-blond hair that went perfectly with her gorgeous shade of burnt-orange lipstick. Her gray dress didn't have a crinkle in sight and her snakeskin pointed shoes were so shiny they were almost appetizing.

"I hope you like what I picked for you," she said. "But if you don't, we can always find you something else."

"For me?" I turned toward Hudson, confused. "I thought we came here for you."

He just smiled, wide and innocent. "It's your birthday present, Jaz. Well . . ." He shrugged. "One of them, anyway."

My jaw actually dropped. I wasn't used to shit like this. "*Seriously?* You didn't have to get me anything! You being here is my present."

"Think of it as a bonus gift, then."

"Wait. You just said this was just *one* of them?" I groaned. "Please tell me the others aren't this fancy."

Hudson just laughed. "I make no such promises."

Hesitantly, I walked over and opened the first box the woman laid on the counter. I gasped. Inside lay a black dress with black lace around the collar and waist.

As I stared, Melody reached over to lift it from the box. It was perfect. Something I would have picked for myself—if I'd ever thought to shop somewhere this fancy.

I was still staring when Melody nudged another box in my direction. This one was smaller than the other. I glanced at Hudson, torn between happiness and embarrassment. I felt like the main character in a cheesy, holiday movie because, "hot boyfriend comes to town and surprises girlfriend with Chanel," seemed more like something I'd write than something I'd experience first-hand.

"Go ahead." He grinned.

I opened the box to find a black Chanel clutch with the iconic gold Cs on the front. It couldn't have matched the dress any more perfectly. Unable to resist, I lifted it to my nose, inhaled the brand-new smell.

"Do you like it?" Hudson asked, and for a second he almost looked worried.

"Are you kidding? These are *amazing*." Not to mention

exactly my style. "Thank you so much." I reached out to hug him, but he raised a palm, stopping me.

"There's one more box."

"Okay, you got me *way* too much," I protested.

He motioned to a man in the back, who carried up a garment bag.

"Hudson, seriously."

"Just open it."

Inside the garment bag hung a beautiful black pea coat, complete with signature Chanel buttons. I reached over to touch it. The fabric felt soft and warm against my skin.

"So you don't get cold tonight," Hudson explained. "That is, since I assumed you'd want to wear all of this tonight—"

"Um, of course I do." I grinned. Then I shook my head. "But really, you went above and beyond. This is all too much."

"But do you like it?"

"Well, yeah, how could I not? Everything is beautiful. Thank you." I reached up, and this time he leaned down, let me fold my arms around his neck. "You really didn't have to do this."

"I know," he murmured, his face inches from mine. So close I caught the minty scent of his breath. "But I wanted to."

"Would you like to try it all on?" Melody asked. "We want to make sure everything fits. We have plenty of options if they don't." She turned around and grabbed a bottle from behind the counter. "But first, champagne?"

"Um, sure," I answered giddily, accepting a flute as I followed her into the dressing room.

On the drive home from Chanel, I couldn't stop thinking about how much Hudson had just spent on me. I didn't think I'd ever had someone spend that kind of money on me before.

I knew Hudson made good money, but he had never been

one to flaunt it. He dressed pretty casual on most days, in jeans and a T-shirt. He was just as happy eating at a fast-food joint as a Michelin-starred restaurant. And he was *way* less of a coffee snob than I was. This was the first time I'd seen him flex his income.

As much as I loved it, I didn't want to get used to this. Or expect it. Or depend on it. Plus, with my writer's budget, I'd never be able to spoil him back.

When we arrived at my one-bedroom apartment, my stomach went queasy with nerves. I paused at my doorway. "Last chance to book a hotel instead," I warned him. My apartment only accentuated the differences in our lifestyles.

"I told you: hotels are boring. I'd rather stay at the Jaz Pad."

I snorted. "Oh Jesus. Let's never ever say that again."

He laughed, and I turned the key, my nerves skittering. The apartment looked just like it had when I left. Spotless, because I'd cleaned for his arrival. The air smelled fresh with hints of rosemary from the incense I burned a few hours ago.

I plopped onto the couch, the one I bought secondhand from some friends who were moving, and Hudson set the bags beside the door and joined me. We barely fit side by side. Normally, I'd be glad to feel the warmth of his body pressed close to mine. But right then, it just reminded me that the couch I really wanted wasn't in the budget. Or a larger living space, for that matter.

I pulled my phone out of my pocket and refreshed my email one more time. Still nothing from Kelly. And it being the end of the workday, it was safe to say I wasn't going to hear from her anytime soon.

Suddenly, I didn't care about not having the budget for the perfect couch. If *Style&Travel* were doing an editorial lay-off, I wouldn't have any budget at all.

I swallowed hard, trying to distract myself from the anxious feelings. “Thank you again for my presents.” I smiled at him, then flipped over to drape a leg over his, until I straddled his lap, facing him. Trying to push my stresses far from my mind.

His eyes widened, his mouth curling into a grin as his hands slid down my waist to settle on my hips. “Do you mean me or the Chanel?” he asked, a teasing note in his voice.

“Both.” I ran my fingers through his hair. Leaned closer. “Though, right now . . . Definitely you.”

“You sure you don’t wish you were playing with that pea coat instead?” He smirked as his hands slid lower. Around the arch of my hip bones, then down, until his fingers found my ass. He squeezed lightly, just hard enough to make me slide closer to him, my heartbeat picking up speed.

“Hmm . . . I mean, that pea coat *is* pretty damn nice,” I teased, before letting one hand glide down his back, the other buried in his hair.

He chuckled softly, and I could feel the vibration of his laughter in every spot where my body was pressed against his. My belly tightened, my nerves firing overtime everywhere we touched.

That feeling only heightened when he slid one hand back up along my curves, tracing his fingertips up my body until he wrapped his hand around the back of my neck. Used it to pull me closer, our lips a mere breath apart. “I know I already gave you some of your birthday presents, but I *think* we should keep the celebration going.” His lips brushed mine. Light. Teasing. “We have time, right?”

My breath hitched. I wanted more. But my eyes flickered toward the clock on the side wall. “Well, we have to leave for dinner in one hour.” My eyes twinkled.

"Hmm . . ." His eyes narrowed. "You sure we can't be a little late?" This time, he kissed me for real. Hard, his lips parting mine. I sank into the kiss, let him take control, his tongue twining around mine for a second, until he drew back, nipping my lower lip gently in the process.

I gasped, slid closer to him. I could feel the hard press of him through his jeans, excited already just from my proximity.

I knew the feeling.

"Mm . . . maybe a *little* late," I admitted.

"Good." With that, he grasped the hem of my sweatshirt and yanked it up and over my head.

I grinned and reached down to undo the buttons on his. But he made that difficult. He dipped his head to start kissing his way down my neck, that faint stubble on his cheeks tickling my sensitive skin, making me inhale sharply, every time his mouth found a new spot to kiss.

He traced his lips over my collarbone, his tongue dipping into my clavicle for a moment, until I shivered. A full-body shiver, all the way from my scalp down to my toes.

This man always knew exactly how and where to touch me.

His lips shifted down the slope of my chest, as his hands slid around my back, one questing for the clasp of my bra. But then he paused. Tilted his head back, so his chin rested on my chest, with me gazing down at him for once.

"Is this okay?" he asked softly, his breath hot everywhere he just kissed me.

"Oh, yes. Very, very okay," I murmured.

He undid the clasp. Let my bra fall between us. My head fell back. He gently cupped my breasts in his hands, his mouth dipping to kiss one after the other, before sucking a nipple into his mouth and lightly tugging it with his teeth. A faint moan escaped my lips, as his tongue traced the delicate skin.

Then I remembered his shirt, and forced my head back into the game. *Buttons. Undo the buttons.*

Hudson was an expert at distracting me.

I lost track of how long we spent undressing each other. In fact, I forgot about the clock entirely, as he finally flipped me over on the couch, so I was pinned beneath him, both of us completely naked.

I loved the way our bodies felt, pressed together like this. We fit each other like puzzle pieces: my petite curves to his sculpted muscles. I reached down between us, stroking his hardness while he touched me. His eyes rolled back in his head as if he were putty in my hands. He grabbed under my hips, pulling my body even closer to his. When he pushed inside me, my head fell back, my body arching up against his, as sweat slicked between us, his hands tight on my hips as he drove into me again and again.

"Fuck, Hudson . . ." I forgot how to form words, as he brought me closer and closer to that peak.

And suddenly, for the first time that day, I wasn't obsessing about my email.

Caught Between Two Worlds

By Jazmine Prado

We all want to belong to a community, a special place filled with people who accept and understand us. These feelings are universal. But what if you're someone who belongs to multiple communities, while at the same time being rejected by them all for being too ethnic, not ethnic enough, or simply for being foreign and different. Some say you're not enough like them, others will say you're too much like the "others." You're somewhere in the middle, caught between two worlds.

When you're a person of mixed race, or a first-generation immigrant, it's easy to feel caught between worlds—not American enough, not Latino enough, not Black enough, not Asian enough, et cetera. But being somewhere in between is its own, beautiful world altogether. It's not as simple as checking one box or another—it's accepting that you are a category of your own. And finding solace in the things that make you uniquely you.

It's growing up to know and love traditions, food, and holidays your peers probably have never experienced, or maybe even heard of. It's having a diverse perspective and seeing the many layers of the world that are invisible to most. It's having a real, living piece of your family's heritage right in your living room. It's about finding the strength to be your true, perfect self, even if it means others might not accept you. This unique experience isn't explored much, yet there are *millions* living in the U.S. who fall under this category.

I am mixed race. Spanish and Moroccan. Born in the U.S., daughter of immigrants. Both my parents are from the Andalusian region of Spain. Marbella to be exact. We have Spanish and North African (Maghreb) heritage from Casablanca, Morocco, which isn't uncommon for people from Andalusia. The mix of cultures is evident in everything my family does, from their cuisine, to their choice in music, to their shades of brown skin and prominent features, to the fact that we often ate dinner around 10 p.m.

But though I've experienced all this culture, I still can't speak Spanish, my family's native tongue, yet I can understand it. In other words, I sometimes feel like I'm in a cultural limbo. But I wouldn't have it any other way. I am American. I am Spanish-Moroccan. I am somewhere in between.

Chapter Four

Hudson and I arrived at the restaurant about twenty minutes late, though I couldn't bring myself to feel bad about it. After our sex on the couch, we both got ready as fast as we could—and all things considered, we cleaned up quite nicely.

Hudson was wearing black jeans, a white collared shirt, and a black blazer that perfectly accentuated his broad shoulders. His dirty-blond hair, that fell just under his chin, was pulled back per usual, his hands studded with rings he collected on his many travels.

As for me, I wore my birthday presents. Dressed in Chanel, I felt like a million bucks. It was the most I had dressed up in a long time and the fanciest outfit I've worn in . . . well, ever.

We stepped inside the posh bistro hand-in-hand, and right away, I caught a whiff of garlic bread. My stomach growled. I had worked up quite an appetite.

"Hi. I'm Jazmine Prado . . . The reservation is under Gal Berdugo," I said to the hostess at the front. "I apologize for being late."

"Oh, no worries. And perfect. Right this way." The hostess escorted us to a private room in the back. The sound of clinking dishes as we weaved in and out of tables was music to my ears; I've always been a fan of white noise.

"It's the birthday girl!" Gal shouted the minute we walked into the room.

As the hostess turned to leave, I noticed she snuck in a side glance at Hudson. I couldn't tell if she knew him from online or if she was just admiring his natural beauty.

Seated already at the table were my cousin Gal and her boyfriend, Anik. At first glances, you could probably tell Gal and I were related. Our Spanish-Moroccan roots showed in our dark hair, high cheekbones, and thick brows. But Gal's Ashkenazi Jewish half meant her skin was a shade lighter than mine, and while we were both petite, she was a bit leaner, and I had a few more curves. As she put it, I got the good ass and breasts from the family. Seemed fair, since she got all the legs.

Our mothers were sisters and I often thanked my lucky stars that they both decided to immigrate to L.A. around the same time, because I don't know what I would do without Gal in my life. She was my rock.

Gal worked in PR and met Anik Singh, an Indian-American doctor, while doing some marketing for a hospital. They lived together and had been dating for about three years. It was one of those relationships where they "weren't sure if they believed in marriage" but they were dedicated to each other as much as any married couple I'd ever met.

I glanced over and saw my mom, dad, and my brother Oliver, along with his new-ish husband, Gabe Sato. Oliver and Gabe were both E.R. nurses. They had just returned from a trip to Osaka, Japan, where Gabe's family was originally from. To judge by the pictures Oli sent me, it looked like he had the time of his life.

"Look! It's my daughter and her beautiful man." My mom jumped to her feet and walked over to us with open arms. Her red dress swished around her knees and matched her crimson pumps perfectly. Her dark hair was pulled back in a low bun. She looked like she had just left a flamenco club. It was a very dramatic ensemble and very fitting for Lucia Prado. "Feliz cumpleaños, Jazzy."

She gave Hudson a hug—before me—and squeezed his bicep in the process. "Dios. That's *very* nice."

"Okay, Mom." I laughed and gave her a hug to rescue Hudson.

My dad came up behind her and shook Hudson's hand, before he embraced me. "Happy birthday, Jaz. You look beautiful."

"Thanks, Dad," I said, smiling as I looked at his shirt. All the buttons were in the wrong spots. Something about the sight of it warmed my heart. He often missed those sorts of details. Which was ironic, considering he was an eye doctor.

"Omar, come back to your seat," Mom interrupted. Dad shrugged his shoulders at me and moved in her direction. She was always bossing him around.

Seated near my dad were my grandparents, Mamá and Papá Prado. They'd planned to come into town from Spain for the upcoming holiday season, and had arrived early for my twenty-eighth birthday. But my jaw practically dropped when I saw who was seated across from them. My other grandparents, Lito and Lita Durán. They also lived in Spain, and from what I'd heard, they had not planned on coming to California anytime soon. They hadn't traveled much over the last few years—we were more likely to visit them—so I was shocked to see them there.

"What are *you guys* doing here?" I asked. "I hope you didn't come all this way for my birthday!"

"No, no." My mom waved a hand. "They decided to take a random trip and it just happened to be at the same time as Mamá and Papá Prado." A devilish grin found my mom's face.

I wouldn't have been surprised if she convinced her parents to come all this way for my birthday dinner since she knew my dad's parents were going to be here. Regardless, I was so happy to see both sets of grandparents at once. I couldn't remember the last time they were all in California at the same time.

"It's so great to see you guys! I'm so happy everyone is here." I turned towards Hudson. "Hudson, you remember my Mamá and Papá Prado?"

"Of course I remember." Hudson was way ahead of me, already shaking their hands. "So good to see you both again."

"And these are my mother's parents, Lito and Lit—"

My lita jumped from her seat before I'd even finished speaking. She reached up and grabbed Hudson's face, planting a huge kiss on each cheek. *What a trooper.*

"I've heard so much about you," Lita exclaimed. Both sets of grandparents could speak English but had thick Spanish accents. "Lucia sent me lots of pictures. She said you're famous online. Like a movie star."

"Oh, I don't know about that . . ."

"He is. He has over two million subscribers," I added proudly, putting my hand on his chest.

She reached up and adjusted her glasses as she stared at Hudson's face. "Joder, Jazmine, no wonder! Que guapo." Lita Durán batted her eyelashes and hovered a little too close for comfort.

She then planted a kiss on my cheek, still not taking her eyes off of Hudson. "He has a good energy, I can feel it."

In addition to pulling tarot cards, practicing tasseography, and reading palms and birth charts, my grandma also claimed to be able to sense good or bad energy in people. She had never been wrong.

"Jazmine, honey, I looked at your birth chart today and did your horoscope, and this is going to be a big year for you," Lita said, reaching into her purse and grabbing a small rose quartz crystal and placing it in the palm of my hand. "Love is the theme."

Love? Usually my birthday readings were very career centric. *Why the sudden shift this year?* I wondered. My chest filled with heat.

"Thank you, Lita." I hugged my grandma and slid the rose quartz in my bag.

"And I can see why love is a theme," she said, winking at Hudson. "Look at him!"

"Amelia, would you let them go to their seats," Lito Durán interrupted, placing a hand on his wife's shoulder. His accent was thicker than everyone else's in the family.

"Oh quiet, Yosef. I am just being friendly." She swatted her husband's arm, but with affection. "Mierda!" she grumbled reluctantly and moved towards the table.

"They do this all the time," I whispered to Hudson. "They like to lovingly bicker."

"They seem great to me." Hudson squeezed my hand, and I relaxed. He appeared to be enjoying himself, in spite of my fawning relatives.

I took a seat right next to Gal and Hudson sat on my other side. "This is going to be *interesting*," I murmured to Gal, who laughed knowingly.

"Lita makes everything interesting. That's why she's so awesome!" The Duráns were Gal's grandparents too. "And holy shit can we talk about how amazing your outfit is? Did Hudson get this for you? I know you didn't buy that for yourself, you're such a fucking penny-pincher."

I glanced over, but Hudson was already deep in conversation with Papá Prado. Another thing on my list that I loved about Hudson—he could blend in to any social situation and enjoy himself.

I tore my gaze away from Hudson's sculpted face, my own heating up as I remembered the way he pulled me onto his lap earlier, determined to make me late for dinner. I cleared my throat and smiled for Gal. "He said it was *one of* my birthday presents." I lifted an eyebrow as if to ask *how much more could there be?*

Gal only chuckled. "About time someone spoiled you." She reached back to touch the coat I'd draped over my chair in appreciation as she spoke. "He's a winner. Hold on tight to that one."

We ordered appetizers and multiple main courses and Papá Prado spent about ten minutes questioning the server about the wines they had available on-site.

Wine was *very* important to the Prados and the Duráns. It practically coursed through their blood.

By the time the vino started flowing, I was already feeling more relaxed than I ever had at one of my birthday dinners. Maybe because for once, there were so many relatives in the room, nobody was too focused on talking about me getting older.

I grinned, watching my parents and grandparents, already a couple glasses in, compete to talk over one another as they all tried to share stories about their lives at once.

Halfway through Mamá Prado's story about one of her neighbors she thinks is stealing oranges from her tree back home, Hudson's phone buzzed on the table. "Oh shoot. I have to take this." He leaned in to touch my shoulder. "Okay if I excuse myself for a minute?"

"Of course. Take your time."

"I'll be right back." He kissed my forehead and strode outside. Once he moved away, I spotted Oliver, seated across from me, smirking. My brother is two years younger than me. He and I shared similar features: dark hair, bushy brows, sharp cheekbones, medium-brown skin. Sometimes, it felt like looking in a mirror.

"What are you smiling about?" I kicked his foot gently under the table.

"Nothing." His smile turned coy. "You look really nice tonight."

"Thank you, but I know you well enough to know that's not what you're smirking about. Come on, what?" I leaned around to peer at the big mirror on the far wall of the restaurant. "Do I have lipstick on my teeth or something?"

Oliver rolled his eyes and leaned in closer. "Okay, fine. I watched a couple of your man's videos the other day. My God! He's nice to watch. Plus my guess is he's *big-ish*?" He raised a brow. "How's the sex—amazing?"

My face—hell, my whole *body*—flushed bright red. "Oliver!" I groaned. "I am not discussing my boyfriend's penis size with my baby brother. Plus, *hello*?" I pointed to Gabe, seated on Oliver's other side and leaning in to hear what we were talking about.

"Please, my husband knows I love him."

"I do." Gabe shot Oli the fondest of smiles. "Besides, we talk about stuff like this all the time. Hudson Taylor is on both of our 'celebrity men we'd love to fuck' list. Normally it's only movie stars allowed, but Hudson's videos were too great to ignore."

"We've never had a social media star make the list before," Oliver pointed out with pure delight. "You should be proud."

I couldn't help but laugh. Well, in between groaning. "This is ridiculous."

On my left, Gal swirled her glass of red wine. "Hudson is on my list too, actually," she admitted before taking a huge gulp.

"Oh, come on, you still have a *list*?" I leaned around her to eyeball her live-in boyfriend. "Anik, help me out here?"

"Gal is allowed to have her list and I am allowed to have mine." He shrugged, hands spread wide, as if to indicate his own helplessness.

"For God's sake, you're no help at all." I picked up my own wine glass, suddenly aware that all eyes at the table were focused on me. I studied my family, one after the other. "So . . . *everyone* just wants to fuck my boyfriend?"

"Yes," almost everyone there replied, practically in unison. Even my mom, Lita, and Mamá Prado.

I groaned and laid my head down on the table, only to feel Gal nudge my knee underneath it.

"Heads up," she murmured. I looked up and noticed Hudson moving back toward the table.

I cast another glare at the group. "Can you all just keep it in your damn pants for now? He's coming back."

Shoulder shrugs and head nods followed. When Hudson sat back down beside me, awkward silence filled the room, all the more noticeable for how boisterous we'd been when he left. I took a sip of wine, lips pursed, trying my best not to laugh into the glass.

"Jazzy, I'm so proud of how well you're doing," my mom broke the silence before taking a bite of a bruschetta. "You've been able to take care of yourself since college, and make a name for yourself too as a journalist. I hope you know how impressive that is."

My mother always dreamed of becoming an actress in Spain. But she got pregnant with me (it wasn't planned) and married my dad, opting instead to raise us kids and support him with his optometry ambitions. She didn't follow her dreams, so I always felt like I had to keep following mine for the both of us. She was living vicariously through me. She told me so all the time.

"I tell my friends to Google your name so they can see how successful my daughter is!" She leaned over the table and gave me a kiss on the cheek. "Feliz cumpleaños, my baby girl. I am so proud of you."

My heart sank. Would she still be proud if she knew that I'd gotten laid off from two publications in the last three years? Or that my editor still hadn't gotten back yet about my pitches?

She raised her glass, and everyone at the table followed suit. Over her shoulder, Oliver grinned at me.

"To my big sister, twenty-eight and fucking flourishing and only just beginning," he smirked, knowing he was embarrassing me. I glared before rolling my eyes.

"To Jazmine," they toasted.

My stomach dropped. I didn't have the heart to tell any of them the truth: that my career of choice felt increasingly grim in the now video-dominated media. And that I was scared shitless that my achievements and experience might not be enough to solidify my future.

Then, just when I thought things couldn't get more awkward, Lita Durán decided to follow up the uncomfortable toast with something even more uncomfortable. "And Jazmine, honey, I am so happy to see you happy. You finally moved on after being so sad about Leo Couture for all those years! I told you the tea leaves said you'd see better days."

My face went bright red all over again. *Shit.* I never impressed on Lita my "we don't speak about Leo" rule. None of my family knew what happened between me and Leo, except Gal. Whenever they'd bring him up in conversation, I'd change it. And as the years went on, they got bored of prying. Oliver had his ideas, but I never confirmed them.

Lita loved to talk, so it wasn't out of character for her to bring up the past. But still, I was sweating.

Beside me, Hudson was looking back and forth from Lita to me. "Leonardo Couture? The *NatGeo* photographer? The one who just filmed that climate change documentary about the melting ice in the Arctic?"

The fact that Leo's career was thriving and mine currently wasn't, was like salt in a wound. "Yep. That's him," I replied through tightly gritted teeth, hoping Hudson couldn't tell how on edge I was.

"I follow him online, I love his work," Hudson added.

At the far end of the table, Lita sighed dramatically. "Such a nice boy. And guapo too. Though, not as handsome as you." She flashed another sly smile at Hudson.

But Hudson's gaze was fixed on me instead. "You dated Leonardo Couture?" I couldn't read his tone. Was he upset? Worried? Or just curious?

Damn Hudson and his hard-to-read face. I cleared my throat and took another swig of wine. "Not really. It's . . . complicated." I nervously tapped my fingernails on the table. "Does anyone see the waiter? I think I'd like to order something a little stronger."

Dead silence.

"*Boy*, was it complicated," my mom chimed in.

"Mom, please—"

But she'd entered storytelling mode. And once Lucia Prado entered storytelling mode, there was no stopping her. She leaned toward Hudson with a confidential air. "They were amigos since elementary school. Leo lived across the street, but they also had this unspoken romantic thing going on their whole childhood."

"That's not true!" I said, louder than I intended. I still couldn't decipher Hudson's expression. He just watched my mother, smiling, perfectly calm. At least he looked amused. Still, this was just about the last thing I wanted my family to be talking about in front of my boyfriend at my birthday dinner.

Remember that time you got your heart broken by your best friend, and you'd never even officially dated?

"She doesn't want to admit it, but it was true." Mom swirled her wine glass for emphasis. "Then, after years of dancing around one another, they had a serious falling-out. They haven't spoken in years. And I don't even know what they fought about. Nobody does! Jazmine's so damn secretive!"

I wanted to die at this point. I wondered if I could flag down a waiter and ask him for an escape hatch. A secret back entrance I could slip out of. Or maybe I could just melt through the floorboards from sheer embarrassment. It was a sobering reminder of why I disliked birthday dinners so much.

"That's so sad they don't talk anymore." Mamá Prado sighed. "He was always so polite. And his madre, Elena Chavez Couture, writes the best romance novels. Everyone in Spain loves them." Mamá Prado elbowed her husband. "Even your papá reads them in secret."

"I do not." Papá Prado's face turned pink. At least I wasn't the only one blushing now. "Was that the young man who played golf with me a couple times?" he asked. Papá Prado didn't have the greatest memory.

My father nodded. "Didn't you tell me you thought he had a thing for Jazmine?"

"I thought everyone knew," Papá replied, looking bewildered.

"It was pretty obvious," Mom interrupted, never one to let her father-in-law steal her thunder. "Well, to everyone except Jazmine. But then Leo started dating that beautiful blonde chica . . . What's her name? Elizabeth?"

"Wow, guys, thanks for this." I put my head in my hands.

Beside me, Hudson was actually laughing. *Bastard.* I thought he was supposed to be on my side.

"The point is," Gal jumped in, trying to fix things as always. "Jazmine is now happier than ever and has found her perfect match."

Again, I wanted to die. *Thanks for the most awkward birthday dinner ever, everyone.*

"I'm glad you think so, because I have to agree." Hudson's voice sounded quiet, solemn. Not his usual upbeat form.

But then his chair screeched, and I realized he was standing up.

Fuck, is he about to give a speech? I hated birthday speeches. It's right up there with my family bringing up my first heartbreak.

But it was too late now. Hudson was already speaking. "When I went to Malibu for work, I didn't expect to meet anyone, let alone a lovely lady who captured my heart so completely, that I was willing to try and make an international long-distance relationship work."

A few people around the table chuckled.

My face burned, for an entirely new reason now. *What is he doing?*

"But meeting Jazmine has changed my life for the better." Hudson locked eyes with me, smiling. "I can't imagine my life without you in it." Slowly, still holding my gaze, he began to lower himself down.

Onto one knee.

Oh my God. I pressed one hand over my mouth, my eyes going wide.

"And I hope I won't ever have to," he said quietly, as he withdrew a little black box from his coat pocket. Then he winked. "Told you there was another present coming."

I couldn't make my brain work, or catch up to what was happening.

Hudson popped the lid off the box. The diamond within . . . *Holy shit.* Emerald cut. That had to be at least a few carats. On a thin white gold band, because he knew I wasn't big on regular gold—silver and white gold were my preference.

Holy shit.

It was spectacular. *He* was spectacular. My gaze darted back to his face, dead serious now.

But his eyes shone when they met mine. All I could see there was love, pure and simple.

"Jazmine Prado, I love you," he murmured. "I want to spend the rest of my life with you. Will you marry me?"

The room started to blur. I could hear the echoes of my family's claps and cheers—I could've sworn that Lita, who appeared to be right about my horoscope love theme, was about to faint.

Out of the corner of my eye I saw Oliver and Gabe go in for a kiss. Saw Mamá and Papá Prado raise their wine glasses. Saw my dad put his arm around my mom, who had burst into tears. Gal rested her head on Anik's shoulder.

As for Lita, she'd recovered from her swoon and tried to drag a resisting Lito into some sort of flamenco-esque dance with her.

But then everyone else faded into the background and I focused on the man kneeling before me.

We'd been together for a year and a half and the majority of that time had been long distance. Maybe that wouldn't feel quick to others but it felt a bit quick for me. Was I ready for marriage? Were *we*? Hudson did check every box on my list but we'd never even lived in the same city together, let alone the same apartment. Would it work if we could learn more about each other on the way? What if we didn't get along once we got to spend more time together than a week a month?

What if . . .?

But then I thought about all the mistakes I'd made in the past. Waiting for the right timing. Second-guessing myself in doubt. I didn't want to do that again.

I loved Hudson. So there was only one thing to say.

"Yes," I whispered, the loudest I could make myself with my throat so tight.

The room erupted with even louder cheering. Hudson picked me up and swung me in a circle before planting his lips on top of mine. I sank into that kiss, into the feeling of his strong arms around me.

Our lips were still locked when he took my left hand and slid the ring home. Immediately, my hand felt heavier. Weighed down.

I held it up for display, to the sound of more cheering, as my relatives began to grab us and kiss our cheeks, one after the next.

"Do you like it?" Hudson murmured in my ear, between bouts of us being accosted by family members. I grinned, rested my hands on his chest.

"It's perfect. Thank you." With that, I wrapped one hand around the back of his neck and pulled him down into another slow kiss.

But in the midst of that perfect, beautiful moment my mind started to wander, and I realized that it had been almost an entire day since I sent my pitches to Kelly and I still hadn't heard back from her.

And as my stomach started to flip I couldn't tell if it was turning because I had just gotten engaged, or because I had this feeling that the career I've worked so hard for might truly be in trouble.

Chapter Five

I tossed and turned all night next to Hudson, who slept beside me like a log. The clock at my bedside flashed the whole while: 2:15, 3:35, 4:01; 4:32; 4:55. When I finally dozed off, my dreams became fitful. Restless.

By the time the light woke me again at 10:04—way too early, in my opinion—I rolled over to find a note where Hudson had been lying.

> *Had to get up early for some meetings, didn't want to wake you. Will be back tonight and can't wait to see you. I love you, my fiancée.*

My fiancée.

I looked down at the shiny diamond on my finger and a smile tugged at my lips. I was engaged. It was surreal. But I knew I had some time to get used to being a fiancée as I wasn't planning to walk down the aisle anytime soon. I admired the ring for a few more seconds before rolling over in bed and reaching for my phone.

As of the night before, Kelly still hadn't responded to the pitches I sent. But I figured by that point, she would've had to have gotten back. I was eagerly anticipating her reply.

I opened my phone to refresh, and my eyes widened when I saw her email come through. *Finally.* But the subject line of her reply made me freeze right away.

Chat today?

The email itself read: "Hey, Jaz. You free to meet for coffee this afternoon? Got your pitches and wanted to chat about a couple things. Let me know. Xo."

Kelly had never asked me to coffee just over a couple of pitches. Nausea crept up my throat. They had to be doing an editorial lay-off. I was officially screwed.

I took some breaths to settle my racing heart and then reached for the tarot card deck sitting on my side table, hoping to find some encouragement, some insight, some anything. I shuffled the cards a few times before pulling one out of the middle.

The reversed Tower card. It represents loss. Obstacles. Upheaval. *Well, that's not good.* I grabbed my phone to text Gal.

JAZMINE: Can I come by your office for lunch today?

She replied a few minutes later.

GAL: Of course! Everything okay?

JAZMINE: Ya. Totally fine. See you then!

Figured I'd save the panic-inducing rundown for after I got there.

I walked into the elevator of Gal's West Los Angeles building and pressed the button for the third floor. It was just me inside and I nervously tapped my foot, shifting the bag of sandwiches and salads from Gal's favorite lunch spot from hand to hand.

My stomach rumbled, though whether that was hunger or nausea again, I couldn't be sure. Maybe both. Eating seemed a dangerous gamble. Then again, I needed fuel before my meeting with my editor. It didn't seem wise to tackle that with only coffee in my system.

I stepped off the elevator, and the smiling receptionist waved me straight through, not even pausing her phone conversation. I assumed Gal warned her I was coming.

Gal's office, the headquarters of Berdugo PR, had floor-to-ceiling windows and a sweeping view over the city. She'd worked her ass off to get there—head of her own firm, calling all the shots. I was so proud of her. She was killing it.

At the doorway, I tapped on the frame, even though it was open.

"Come in!" she called. I stepped through and swung the door shut behind me.

Gal was wearing her typical professional pant-suit attire, accented by a beautiful beaded necklace with a black rose. Her hair was parted down the middle and slicked into a low ponytail, making her sharp nose and enviable eyebrows take center stage.

"Wow, you're looking rather Spanish-Moroccan today. I like." I dropped into the chair across her desk.

"Really? Is it the necklace?"

"The necklace. The pony. The brows. I don't know . . ." I set the bag of lunches on the desktop between us while she cleared a space among her papers. "But you look gorgeous, as always."

"Well, thank you." Just as she reached for the bag, a knock sounded.

"Excuse me, Miss Berdugo?" Gal's new assistant cracked the door cautiously. He looked to be in his mid-twenties, lean with long legs, black hair and a thin moustache, a matching tight beard. "Sony Pictures asked if they could move the meeting to 3:15? And—" He paused and glanced at me. "Wait, is this Jazmine? Your infamous cousin." His eyes lit up.

"The one and only," Gal replied, grinning.

"Oh my God, I've heard so much about you!" He stepped

fully into the office and extended a hand. "I'm Lorenzo, I just started here."

"Nice to meet you."

"I've read a bunch of your articles." He blushed. "Well, actually, all of them. You're so great at opinion pieces and also setting the scene and nailing an interviewee in just a few words . . . My dream is to be a writer one day. Like you."

"Wow. Thank you so much." I could feel my cheeks burning red by now, too. I looked over at Gal, who was grinning from ear to ear. She knew I was uncomfortable with compliments and she loved making me uncomfortable in that regard.

I loved hearing people sing my praises when it came to my work. But my body had other plans. It'd been conditioned to react with embarrassment every time.

"If you ever have any questions about writing or anything, just let me know," I offered. Now my smile turned forced. *If Lorenzo only knew I might be getting fired today.*

"Really? Because that would be amazing! I'd love to pick your brain sometime about—"

"Lorenzo," Gal interrupted. "You can tell Sony that meeting time works. As for Jazmine, I'll send an email, introducing you both so you can talk more about writing. Does that sound good?"

Lorenzo bobbed his head. "Of course, Miss Berdugo. Thank you. I'll go let Sony know. It was so nice to meet you, Jazmine. Have a good lunch!" He smiled and waved, before backing out the door.

"He seems nice," I told Gal, my eyes dancing with amusement.

"The best. I heart him." Gal leaned back in her desk chair.

"I brought your favorite sandwich," I said, nudging the lunch bag toward her.

She ignored it and grabbed my hand to turn it over, admiring the ring again. "Fuck, I'm still not over it. It looks even bigger today, I swear."

"It is gorgeous." I examined the rock on my finger. "But do you think it's a little . . . *too* big?"

Gal lifted a single perfectly manicured brow. "Okay, stop. I refuse to let you gripe about the size of your *massive* engagement ring, brooding writer or no." With that, she grabbed the bag, rooted around for her sandwich. She unwrapped it and took a big bite, still shaking her head at me.

"Fair enough." I fished for my own sandwich before I settled back in my seat. "I'll try to temper my brooding for you."

"Thank you." She finished chewing her first bite, plopped her sandwich down and spread it open to pour a more than generous heap of honey mustard into the middle. "Can we talk about the fact that you're *engaged*? To a social media star, no less." She snorted. "And considering how much you've always loved that medium . . ."

"I know, ironic, right?" I tugged at the button on my blazer and exhaled a little louder than I realized.

"So, not that I don't love you randomly stopping by, but why are you *really* here?" Gal eyed me, my sandwich, then me again. "You aren't even eating. What's wrong?"

Jesus, it's like she's reading my fucking soul. Gal had always been able to get a good read on people. I always assumed she got that from Lita Durán.

I put down the sandwich and crossed my arms. "Well. I'm just . . . nervous about *some* things." My eyes drifted to Gal's massive office windows. It was a beautiful smog-free day for once, Los Angeles sparkling against a blue sky. Rare, those days.

"Jazmine," Gal murmured, dragging me back to reality. "What are you nervous about, the engagement?"

"What?" I blinked, startled. "No. Not at all. I just got a weird email from my editor. She asked me to meet her in person this afternoon. She never does that. I'm worried . . ." I paused, shutting my eyes. "I'm worried I'm getting let go again."

Gal was the only person in my family who knew about the two lay-offs in the last three years. Truthfully, the only reason she was in the loop was because she didn't buy it when I told her I was leaving a publication for a "change of pace." She knew I liked consistency when it came to my work. That I was a creature of habit in that regard.

Gal scoffed. "Come on, Jaz—"

"I'm serious! They've been downsizing like crazy for months. And they haven't been taking any of my pitches. It's become all about videos, and podcasts, and photos, and more things that don't require as many writers like everywhere else. Years of experience and awards don't matter when there's not much to write. It might be my time."

Gal tilted her chair back on two legs. "I'm not trying to be a bitch, but . . . we've had a few conversations about your changing industry. What have I said time and time again?"

"Adapt or die, get more active online, blah blah blah."

"Blah blah blah?" She furrowed her brows. "Jaz, you haven't listened at all. You have a cool job and a strong skill. You could have your own blog or build your own platform. And then you could leverage that platform for more work wherever you wanted. That's the day and age we live in!"

Gal was right. I knew she was. But every time she'd try to convince me to start a blog or build an online platform it always felt way over my head. Instead, I held on to the traditional and hoped it wouldn't bite me in the ass. I guess I was wrong.

"Look. You can ride my ass for being stubborn later," I interrupted. "I'm really freaking out here."

Gal's eyes softened. She tilted her chair back to the floor and crossed her hands on the desk instead. I recognized her posture: Gal's infamous fix-it mode. "Okay, worst-case scenario, you lose your job. I don't think that's gonna happen, but let's just consider it. It wouldn't be the end of the world. You've always wanted to write a book, right? A biography of inspiring women, or a book of poetry, you've published poetry in magazines before! Or, fuck, didn't you once pitch me a young adult novel about a vampire?"

My face flushed. "That's not exactly a viable career alternative. There's no guarantee a publisher would buy my books—"

"Well, Hudson has a solid income. You're engaged now, you'll probably be moving in together soon . . ."

My eyes shot wide.

Gal blinked at me, like she was surprised by my shock. "What? Won't you?"

"Moving in together? We *just* got engaged." My heart hammered. "I can't let him support me. I have to have a career. My own paycheck."

I couldn't be like Mom, losing track of my dreams the minute a man entered the picture. I'd never forgive myself.

Mom would never forgive me, either.

"Okay," Gal said slowly. "If you don't want to do that, do you have enough savings to get you through a few months while you cranked out a book?"

I chuckled. "Gal. I'm a writer. Success as a writer doesn't always equal a big income, you know that. My savings account is leaner than you."

She rolled her eyes and tapped her fingers on the desk. "Any other publications you could write for?"

"I definitely plan to apply. Problem is, most publications are in the same boat, making the same changes." It was a sad time for journalism, and all lovers of the written word, really.

Then she perked up. "I could help find you some work. Companies are always looking for branded content. It would bore the fuck out of you, but it would be a steady paycheck."

I sighed again, and my heart rate eased, just a little. "I definitely would be open to that. Thank you for the offer either way, I really appreciate it." I dabbed the napkin at my temple again. "I just . . ." My chest tightened. "I feel like I'm drowning."

"Jaz. You're my cousin. My friend. My family." Gal reached across the desk to catch my hand, and squeezed. "Though you are a true pain in my ass sometimes, I would never let you drown."

I flashed her a weak smile. Not very convincing.

But it was enough for her to release my fingertips and lean back in her chair again. "Maybe your editor wants to talk to you about something else entirely. You never know."

God bless Gal and her Sagittarius optimism. "I really hope you're right."

I arrived at the coffee shop in Santa Monica early, hoping to steady my thoughts before my editor got there.

Despite my nerves over the current situation, I really loved working with Kelly. She was smart, efficient, and she'd made history as the first Black woman to be named editor-in-chief at *Style&Travel*.

She and I were friendly in an editor-and-journalist sort of way, but we weren't the type to hang out outside of work. Not because I didn't want to, we just kept things strictly business.

As a child, Papá Prado always gave me speeches about how one should never get too close to people at work. Problems with co-workers tend to multiply, he always said.

Lito Durán was more superstitious about it, always telling me not to befriend my neighbors because it's important not to "shit where you eat" as it could bring bad luck. To this day, I keep my distance from people both at work and living nearby.

Leo Couture had been the one glaring exception. Lito was on to something.

Inside the coffee shop, I ordered an Americano with a pump of vanilla and heavy cream, and then sat at a table in the back with a view of the door. My legs bounced nervously. Soon, the shiver traveled all the way up my arms. I hugged myself to stop it.

You are not about to get fired, I silently chanted as my fingers grazed my Indalo bracelet. *You're an award-winning journalist, they can't let you go. Everything is fine.*

Then Kelly strode in. The moment I saw her, my nerves lit up again. She eyed me immediately and waved. She was smiling, but her eyes remained grim, filled with worry. On normally bubbly Kelly, that expression worried me even more.

But despite the impending doom, she looked lovely as always. Her black curly hair fell just at her shoulders, and she wore a beautiful shade of burgundy lipstick that perfectly complemented her dark-brown skin. Her olive-green pantsuit fit her perfectly, and her tall black heels would have knocked me on my ass, but she rocked them.

As she reached me, I stood to give her a hug. But before I could, she spotted the ring.

The thing drew attention.

"Is that an engagement ring?!" Kelly grabbed my hand, ignoring my hug. "Oh my God! When did this happen?"

"Oh, um . . . Last night, actually." I flushed as she turned my hand to admire it from all angles.

At least her gloomy expression had faded a bit. "Are you kidding me? Congratulations! I didn't even know you were seeing someone. Who's the lucky person?"

"A guy named Hudson. We met at a charity event I was

covering in Malibu. It was before I started at *Style&Travel*." She finally released my hand, and I took a seat once more, while she perched across from me, hands on the table, gaze still on my ring.

At my words, she smirked. "You met at a charity event?! That's so sweet. Is he a journalist too?"

"No." I played with the buttons on my blazer. "He's a social media creator. He's pretty big actually."

Her forehead scrunched. "Really? Wait . . . What's his name?"

"Hudson Taylor."

Kelly's jaw actually dropped. "No fucking way." She grabbed her phone out of her purse and opened Instagram, pulling up Hudson's profile. She followed him. Of course she did. "You're engaged to *this* Hudson Taylor? The hot adventurer Canadian?" She waved her phone under my nose.

I cleared my throat to keep from laughing. Or groaning. I never knew how to feel about millions of people following my boyfriend's—*fiancé's*—every move. "That's the one."

"You've been dating Hudson fucking Taylor all this time and you didn't say anything?" Kelly laughed and shook her head, but she was grinning too. "You're sneaky, girl. This is huge! Tell me the whole story. How did he propose?"

The whole story. You would think being a writer, I would enjoy gushing about the details. Instead, my ability to articulate words dried straight up. I just sort of . . . froze.

"Well." I cleared my throat. "He came into town for my birthday yesterday . . ."

"Hold it." Kelly held up her hand. "Yesterday was your birthday? You didn't fill that out on the employee form, so I never knew when it was . . . You've got to stop hiding shit." She pursed her lips. "But happy belated! If I knew, I would've had you come into the office and gotten you a cake."

And that's exactly why I didn't tell you. I appreciated the thoughtfulness, but going into the office so my fellow employees could sing "Happy Birthday" while I cut a cake sounded torturous. Thanks, but no thanks.

"I'm just not that big on birthdays." I shifted in my seat, uncomfortable.

"Fine, I'll let that one slide." I couldn't tell if she was joking or not. Kelly leaned in. "Now, tell me more about the proposal."

There was something about her facial expression. Did she want the story because Hudson was internet famous, or to make a story out of it? Or was she just being nice?

Unfortunately for her, my proposal wasn't really magazine-essay worthy. Of course, that's exactly why I loved it.

I took another sip of coffee and folded my hands in my lap. "Well. We went out to dinner with my family for my birthday. And after we ate, he got down on one knee in front of everyone and proposed. It was really sweet."

Awkward silence followed. "Sounds . . . really sweet!" Kelly smiled again and pushed curls out of her face. "I'm so happy that you're happy."

"Thank you." *Here it comes.*

Sure enough, a moment later, Kelly sat up straighter, and her smile dripped away. *Shit.*

"To be honest, I'm really glad things are going so well in your personal life. Happiness outside of career is very important. So is prioritizing self-care."

She was dancing around her words. Never a good sign. Still, I managed to maintain my composure in the face of one of my worst fears.

"As I'm sure you know, things have been changing a lot at *Style&Travel.* I'm really sorry to bring this up the day after your birthday and your engagement . . . but I don't think the conversation can be postponed any longer." She paused and took a deep breath, looking away for a moment. I wondered how many times in recent months she'd had to give this same speech. How many other hopes and dreams she was forced to shatter against her will. I could tell it was stressful for her. "Unfortunately, the changes here are going to affect all the writers, Jazmine, including you."

Fuck.

"You know this is not the direction *I* want to go in. Frankly, this is not my ideal direction at all. But as the editor-in-chief, I still answer to the higher-ups of our parent company, Mercer Media. They want to cut print editions and stories in general. What we will be doing in print will mostly be photos with very low word counts. And we will be shifting our focus to video and visual media online. Social media channels, podcasts . . ."

My right leg started to spasm. Even my toes felt numb.

A magazine with fewer stories felt like a peanut butter and jelly sandwich without the peanut butter and jelly. Two slices of plain white bread, without any real substance.

"Fewer stories?" I repeated. "I feel like we're already running fewer stories."

"You're right. The thing is, we still have cuts to make. Everything we've commissioned already—so for around the next six issues—will run on the web only. But we aren't taking new story pitches now."

My heartbeat pulsed in my ears. My skin felt like it was on fire. "What are you saying?"

"You're an amazing writer, Jazmine. Literally my favorite. You are over-qualified to be working for us, to be honest. It kills me that I have to say this." Kelly reached over and squeezed my hand. "But unless you have some sort of video or photo skills you can offer . . . your time with *Style&Travel* will be coming to an end. I'm so, *so* sorry."

I felt like someone had just stabbed me in the heart. I suspected this was coming, but suspecting and knowing are two very different sensations.

Kelly's face suddenly went blurry. The coffee shop felt like a sauna, and yet I was shivering as if freezing. I wanted to run outside and gasp for fresh air. Maybe then I'd remember how to breathe again.

But I couldn't leave. Not now. I had to face this harsh reality head-on.

"It's not just you," Kelly was saying. "I've had this conversation with all of our writers this week. You are the last." Kelly frowned as she examined my face. "But hey, have you ever been on camera before? We could explore the possibility of filming some of your pitches as video content?"

Just the thought of being on video made me anxious. I didn't speak well on camera. Always fumbled my words. And afterward, I always picked apart how I looked. One of my favorite things about being a writer was it never required me to speak aloud or be on video.

Until now, apparently.

"No. Videos are Hudson's area of expertise, not mine." I nervously chuckled and wiped my sweaty palms on my pants.

But then the air around us changed. You would have thought a fairy godmother arrived and sprinkled fairy dust all over the coffee shop. That's how much Kelly's face lit up with glee. As if some magical light bulb just clicked on in her mind.

It was such a complete one-eighty from just a few seconds ago that I stared at her, confused.

"Holy shit, Jazmine." She waved both hands in the air like a kid. "I just had *the best* idea!" Then she paused to grimace. "But you're probably not going to like it."

She shifted her chair around the table so she was sitting beside me instead of across. "Okay, hear me out . . . What if you and Hudson filmed your wedding live on camera?"

I squinted. "Like on his social media channels?"

"Not exactly. What Mercer really wants is an original web series. They believe that's the next gold mine for web traffic. It would put Mercer Media at the forefront for lifestyle and travel media." She cleared her throat. "So . . . what if we turned your wedding into a mini reality web series for *Style&Travel*? It could be the first one for our magazine. Hudson is a huge social media star, so he would rake in viewers. The higher-ups at Mercer would flip, Jazmine!"

My head was spinning. My ears buzzed, making it hard for me to concentrate on her words.

But she was on a roll. "We could do a destination wedding, perfect for our travel crowd. We'd only need a couple of days to film it. I know the best videographer, too. They owe me a favor so I know I could get them on board."

My heart raced. Film our wedding? For a web series? "I don't know, Kelly. We literally just got engaged *yesterday*—"

"We don't need to film it tomorrow or anything. We need a little time to prepare, but not lots. We do want to strike quickly before another publication does something similar first. I'm thinking February, maybe around Valentine's Day?"

Valentine's Day? That was three months away. Three months to plan my entire wedding. One I'd barely even begun to think about.

"That gives you some time to make a guest list and get everything in order and we will take care of the rest," Kelly said. "It will be fast but totally doable since we've already been in talks with a handful of brands about the possibility of doing a show and I know Mercer would throw a lot of money behind this. Especially with Hudson involved. They've been dying to collaborate with stars like him. I could negotiate for you both to be paid a salary on top of Mercer covering the costs for the wedding. Room and board, flights for you and your guests . . . Think of all the money you would save! You wouldn't have to pay a cent for your own wedding."

Kelly was very convincing, I'd give her that. Still, my heart wouldn't stop skipping.

Just at lunch, it had seemed outlandish when Gal suggested I move in with Hudson soon. Now we could be getting married in three months?

Kelly continued, "We'd make so much money from views and endorsements . . . And once you marry Hudson on camera, you'll become a star too, which in turn gives you more power. I'm sure you'll be getting offers left and right. It's honestly a brilliant career move, Jazmine."

Getting offers left and right? I liked the sound of that.

But filming my wedding for the whole world to see? I wasn't so sure. Besides my profile pictures, I didn't even have any photos of myself on my social media. Everything else was screenshots of my work.

I thought of all Hudson's fans who would watch our wedding. All the pressure I'd feel—all my hatred of being on video. It would be preserved for ever. Viewed by millions. Not just everyone I'm friends with or work with—the whole world would see me. Strangers, judging my every move, instead of just critiquing my writing.

There had to be another way. "I really appreciate the idea. I appreciate it so much! It's just . . ." I tapped on my coffee cup, searching for the right way to put this. "I'm pretty private . . .

What if I wrote an essay about our wedding day, and chronicled the entire process in a written format instead? Hudson could take photos for us both; I'm sure he'd be up for that. Would that work?"

Please take the bait. Please take the bait.

But Kelly's expression had already fallen. "I'm sorry. But I just don't think that would be enough for Mercer." She gave me a weak smile and leaned back. "Look. I'm not trying to pressure you. I don't want you to do anything you're uncomfortable with." She paused. "Just think about it. Talk to Hudson. Truthfully, I'm just trying to find a way to keep you at *Style&Travel* and I think Mercer would really go for this."

My shoulders sagged.

Kelly winced. "I really am sorry, Jazmine. The industry is changing every day. Sometimes all we can do is change along with it."

A gnawing pain ate away at my stomach. I was drowning, just like I thought. But Kelly was offering me a lifeline. It wasn't the lifeline I wanted, but it was a lifeline nonetheless.

The question was: should I take it? Or should I try to swim upstream on my own without a paddle—hell, without even a canoe?

I couldn't do it.

Social media wasn't my thing. Being on camera was *definitely* not my thing. I was a writer, end of story. Doing this web series was the second-to-last thing I wanted to do.

But the *absolute* last thing I wanted to do was lose another job. I'd worked too hard to get to where I am. I'd built a whole life around this career. I *needed* it, for more than just the money. It gave me purpose, made me feel seen, appreciated, talented.

When it came down to it, this really wasn't a question at all. I knew what I needed to do.

"What the hell, I'm in." I forced a smile. It wavered around the edges, then finally stuck. "Tell the higher-ups Hudson and I are game for this." My hands started to tremble.

Kelly tilted her head, a confused grin tugging at her lips. "Are you sure? Shouldn't you at least ask Hudson before I bring this to them?"

"Please." I waved a hand, dismissive. "He's a social media star, he'll be fine with it. And he's also a sweetheart. If I want this, he will too."

It was true. Hudson was so supportive like that. Another thing he checked on my list.

Kelly chuckled. "Well, I'm sure you know your man better than anyone." She winked. "But I don't, so I'm in a bit of an ethical dilemma. I can't speak on his behalf without his approval."

My cheeks burned. Hearing Kelly use the phrase "ethical dilemma" made me embarrassed for speaking on Hudson's behalf.

But I couldn't worry about that. I was running on survival. Pure survival. And I refused to leave that coffee shop until I felt like my job remained intact. "One sec. I'll ask him right now," I said, opening my phone to text him.

I can explain more later, but my editor wants us to film our wedding as a web series for Style&Travel. Thoughts?

Literally two seconds later he replied.

I'm on board if you are. Whatever you need.

I'm on board if you are. I stared at those words and tried not to suffocate all over again. One of the most intimate moments of my life was going to be a reality web series for the whole world to see.

I would be on camera for the whole world to see.

My head felt fuzzy from the adrenaline. Giddiness over saving my job mingled with terror in my chest. *What the fuck did I just sign us up for?*

But I ignored all that, and held out my phone for Kelly to see Hudson's response. "We're in," I said.

On the bright side, I no longer felt like I was drowning. I did, however, feel like I'd completely forgotten how to swim.

FOR IMMEDIATE RELEASE

MERCER MEDIA'S FIRST WEB SERIES TO DEBUT ON THEIR REVOLUTIONARY NEW APP

Los Angeles, CA: Publishing powerhouse Mercer Media will be debuting its first reality web series *Our Big Day: A Wedding with Hudson Taylor* on their new *Style&Travel* app this Valentine's Day, available to members worldwide.

The app is the first of its kind, a one-stop-shop for entertainment featuring celebrity interviews, podcasts, travel videos, exclusive photos and guides, and will also host a streaming service for their upcoming original shows.

In addition, members will have the opportunity to create their own profiles and interact with the stars of the web shows. The app will be available to download on mobile devices, tablets, and television for a monthly fee of only $3.99.

Mercer Media's first series, *Our Big Day*, will be a reality web show chronicling the wedding of social media star Hudson Taylor and award-winning journalist Jazmine Prado. The show will feature five episodes, including a live-streaming ceremony of their wedding at the La Belladonna luxury resort in Cancún, Mexico.

Jack Paulson, Mercer Media's executive producer of the show, said, "We couldn't be more thrilled about *Our Big Day* and cannot wait to share *Style&Travel*'s app with the world!"

Chapter Six

Three months later

I sat in the departure lounge at LAX mindlessly scrolling through the news on my phone before our flight was scheduled to take off. Reading the news had always been a guilty pleasure of mine, a way to calm my racing mind and still my racing heart, a way to distract myself from the worries of my own life.

But at that point, I found it to be more depressing than pleasant—and not just because I wasn't writing at the moment. There was less fact-checking. Fewer thought pieces. Fewer seasoned journalists.

Just a bunch of clickbait articles competing for numbers.

Of course, there were still outlets producing fantastic work from great writers, reporting facts and truth. But sadly those were becoming few and far between.

I took a long breath and sighed as I closed the tab on an article with at least ten typos and the incorrect name of an actor they were referencing. It was an ugly reminder of where the writing world was at. Where *I* was at. And why I was sitting in that airport in the first place.

"Here's your coffee, love," Hudson said, sliding into the seat beside me. I perked up at the sight of him, forcing my blues back behind the wall I'd built for them years ago. Hudson wore his dark-blond hair in its usual low bun, his body covered in a black sweatshirt and jeans.

I wore the exact same thing, down to the bun, yet somehow his outfit seemed a lot more polished. We hadn't planned to match.

"Just so you know, they might have put two pumps of vanilla instead of one in your Americano. The lady at the counter seemed a bit distracted. Do you want me to go back and get you another?"

"Well, you *are* distracting." I grinned, accepting the cup. "And it's fine, I could use a little extra sugar today anyway. Sugar is supposed to help calm the nerves, right? Or was that just an excuse my mom made up to eat more churros con chocolate."

Hudson laughed. "Do you have a fear of flying I don't know about?"

A smile tugged at my lips. Hudson's Canadian accent always shone through when he said the word *about*. He pronounced it like "a-boot." I loved it.

"No," I answered slowly. "No fear of flying. But I *do* have a fear of my wedding being filmed for the world to see. It's being added to the phobia list as we speak." I tried for a joke, a smile, but it felt painful on my face.

Hudson wrapped one arm around my shoulders. Even through the sweatshirt I could feel his chiseled bicep. "I think you mean *our wedding*," he teased.

I nudged him. "You know what I mean."

"Letting them film the whole thing *was* your idea," he reminded me gently. Before I could glare too fiercely, he added, "It won't be so bad, I promise. I'll be with you the whole time. If anything makes you feel uncomfortable just let me know and I'll talk to the producers about it."

It *did* reassure me that Hudson knew his way around a set. How to talk the talk. He'd been the one to go over our contracts since he knew all the clauses to look out for. He nudged me again. "Besides, you'll be great on camera. You come across more natural than you think."

I doubt that. Being on camera felt like the most unnatural thing to me in the world. But there wasn't much I could do about it at that point. In a little over two days, my every move would be on camera.

I nestled into Hudson's shoulder in an attempt to distract myself. "Remind me of the schedule again."

We'd already gone over this a couple dozen times, but Hudson knew me well enough to know that repetition helped. Having a plan helped. "Let's see." He made a show of checking his watch. "It's Friday now. We have the weekend to prep, then filming begins first thing Monday."

Monday through Thursday we'd be filming a day in advance: so the Monday content would be quickly edited but wouldn't air until Tuesday, and so on. Next Friday, a week from today, was a prep day, and then Saturday . . .

"It's more the live part I'm worried about," I admitted quietly.

Saturday would be the live-streaming of our wedding. No cuts, no re-shoots, no safety net of any kind. If I tripped and fell on my ass—or more likely if I tripped and fell and then shouted "fuck," I was literally fucked because the millions tuning in would see it in real-time.

I let out a long breath. The thought of filming was nerve-racking enough, but being live made me want to vomit.

Hudson kissed my temple, and the sensation made my eyes flutter closed. "You'll do great. I'll be right there beside you for Our Big Day."

I squinted, not sure if he was teasing again or not.

Mercer Media decided to call the web series *Our Big Day: A Wedding with Hudson Taylor.* That title made everything even more vomit-inducing. Not because of the fact that they didn't include my name (fine by me!), which Kelly, by the way, said she fought for. But the part that made my eyes roll was the phrase "Big Day." Really? Completely unoriginal, not the slightest bit creative, and also a bit insulting. Maybe Mercer Media should consider hiring some of their writers back.

Just saying.

"Hey. I have a little something for you." Hudson reached in his carry-on backpack and pulled out a telltale blue-ish-green box with a white bow.

I gasped when I saw it. The box on its own was impressive enough. "Tiffany's? You really shouldn't have!"

"Just think of it as an early Valentine's Day present. Since Valentine's falls the day after our wedding, and we'll be too busy honeymooning to think about it." He winked.

I opened the box to find a delicate necklace inside: a white gold ampersand pendant encrusted with diamonds. Perfection. Absolutely beautiful.

"Because you're a writer," Hudson said. "I thought it would remind you that doing this show doesn't change that." He squeezed my hand. "Also, I looked it up and it represents union and good things to come."

My eyes started to burn. I took a deep breath to fight back the tears that threatened. I had never felt like crying after receiving a gift before. Hudson getting me something to remind me I am still a writer despite all of this, that was just beyond.

Thank God he didn't give me the necklace when we were back at my apartment, because without a crowd of strangers nearby, I would have been swimming in a river of my own tears.

I reached over to rest my hand on Hudson's cheek. "Thank you," I said, before leaning towards him and putting my lips on his. His mouth still held a hint of the sugar-free mocha he just devoured, and it made my breath catch, my hand feeling hot against his cheekbone.

If we weren't sitting in an airport, I would have undressed him right there. His thoughtfulness was such a turn-on. *Now I wish he* had *given me the gift in my apartment.*

"I actually have a little something for you too," I murmured, once we finally parted, both grinning at each other. As I reached into my bag, however, I hesitated, a touch of insecurity striking. "Fair warning, it's not as fancy as Tiffany's, because obviously I don't make the money you make—not yet, anyway," I added quickly, before Hudson could say it for me. He grinned and winked in response.

You've got to put good vibes out into the universe and manifest your desires, he was always telling me.

I took a deep breath and handed him the little brown box. "But here." I kept holding that breath while he worked through the wrapping paper.

But the instant it peeled apart, his eyes warmed, and I relaxed the tiniest bit.

Inside sat a chunky silver ring with an engraving I designed on top. It was handmade, through a company Gal found. "It's the coordinates of where we met in Malibu," I said, pointing to the top of the ring. "I wanted to get you something unique." I bit my lip, hoping that he liked it. He was a big fan of jewelry and particularly loved rings from places he'd traveled.

"Oh my gosh, Jaz, I love it!" He pulled the ring out of the box and slipped it onto his free middle finger. "It fits perfectly, thank you." He grabbed my chin and pulled me in for another kiss.

For a moment, everything faded into the background except for Hudson's soft lips. I forgot that we were in an airport, about to fly to Cancún on the most terrifying trip of my life. I forgot about the pre-wedding jitters, about the film crew, all of it. It was just me and him, here, reminding one another why we were doing this. Why we belonged together.

It was perfect.

Then Hudson jerked back from me mid-liplock, and glanced toward the flight attendant calling our names. I hadn't even heard the announcement.

"That's our cue." He picked up both my carry-on bag and his.

I frowned at the woman, who hurried over to accept our bags. Nobody else in the line had even gotten up to board yet. "What's going on?" I murmured.

Hudson's grin widened. "I talked production into first-class seats. After all, we're the stars of this show. We deserve the best treatment."

I stifled a nervous laugh as I trailed Hudson and the flight attendant, now joined by another man who scanned tickets I hadn't even noticed Hudson hand over. "Wow. Thanks, Mercer Media." I had never flown first class before. I was excited to see what the fuss was all about.

As we were escorted down the airline's gangway, Hudson held up his phone, in what I'd come to recognize as his favorite selfie angle.

Although filming for the series itself didn't officially begin until Monday, we'd gotten enough pointed hints leading up to this trip about how Hudson needed to build buzz on his channels—and on the new *Style&Travel* app where episodes would be airing—to take the hint. They wanted some behind-the-scenes footage, to get people talking before the show began.

And talking they were. My social media following had climbed to the tens of thousands practically overnight and all I'd done was repost a photo of Hudson's where he announced that I was the woman he was about to marry. It was the first time I let him post a photo of me and tag me in it.

As for Hudson, his video post on the *Style&Travel* app last week about the wedding had over six million views—helped in large part by a drive from his own two-million-plus followers.

The app was scarily involved. Viewers would be able to watch episodes, leave comments, and even interact with me and Hudson on our separate profiles.

I'd barely checked mine so far, aside from posting links to all my old articles in the vain hope all this attention might win my writing some love.

Hudson already had half a dozen posts, with thousands of comments on each.

The app would become a hub for all of *Style&Travel*'s videos, podcasts, editorial photos, a few select essays, and future web series to come. Someday, I'd be doing most of my written work for them on there, all going well with the show.

But being that *Our Big Day* was Mercer's first web series, they were putting it front and center.

Hudson was clearly no stranger to constantly updating profiles, but I had no idea what the hell I was doing. I guessed it was time to rip off the Band-Aid, though. I geared up for it to sting.

"Hey, guys, I'm here with my beautiful fiancée, Jazmine Prado," Hudson was saying into his camera. "We're boarding our flight to the resort in Cancún where they'll be hosting *Our Big Day*."

Pro name-drop of the show. I suppressed a smile. Unfortunately, that caught his eye.

"Say hi, Jazmine." He aimed the phone my way. My stomach soured.

"Hi." I waved at his phone, feeling the heat rush to my body. This wasn't even a real camera. *How, was I going to face this next week?*

"Isn't she so beautiful?" Hudson cooed. And then I promptly hid my face in both palms and groaned. He just laughed. Merciless, this man. "Make sure you guys check out Jazmine's profile on the app—she's got some great content posted there, stories that made me fall in love with her from day one."

My heart swelled. This pro knew how to hype even the most inept of social media users, like me.

"And make sure you have those notifications turned on, because you won't want to miss a single thing that's coming. Cheers!" Hudson waved goodbye to the camera before sliding his phone back into his pocket. "See, that wasn't so bad, was it?" He gave me a soft pat on the back.

I finally managed to raise my head from its new home in my palms. "I mean, I feel like a fucking idiot. But other than that, no, not so bad."

"Once we get to our seats, you should post too." He draped his arm around my shoulder easily. "Make sure it goes to your Moments stream."

I reached up to hold his hand. "Okay. What does that mean again exactly?"

Hudson laughed, and I felt the vibration travel through his chest into mine. "Don't worry, I'll show you."

The second we stepped onto the plane, a flight attendant—not the one who'd taken our bags, either, because I saw her across the first-class lounge putting them into the overhead bins—offered us a steaming piece of cloth with a pair of tongs.

"Hot towel?" Her red lipstick practically blinded me. She looked like she'd just stepped out of a different era, with her blond hair pulled back in a sleek up-do and a white button-up shirt tucked into a navy pencil skirt. Effortlessly glamorous. This first-class lifestyle was enticing. Alluring. Easy to be seduced by.

"No, thank you," I replied, unsure what I'd do with the towel. Then I immediately regretted rejecting it, because Hudson accepted his with gusto and pressed it over his face with a groan of pleasure.

Luckily, my disappointment didn't last long. Another attendant arrived with a tray of champagne flutes.

He gleamed at Hudson as we accepted our drinks. "Huge fan, Mr. Taylor."

"You can call me Hudson. And thanks, man." Hudson offered a fist bump of approval, and we leaned back in our huge seats.

There was so much legroom that even when I stretched my legs all the way out, they didn't touch the seatback in front of me. "What's all this room for? I could fit my whole family right here," I joked.

But then Hudson tapped the console between us, with little cartoon drawings of a chair upright, a chair reclined, and a person curled up in bed.

Only then did I notice the padding along the legs of the seat too, and realized the whole thing could transform into a full-on bed with the touch of a button. "Wow."

Hudson laughed at the expression that must have been

plastered all over my face. He leaned in to kiss my forehead. "Hang on, I have to get this incredulousness on camera."

I groaned. "Everyone is going to think I'm some broke girl who doesn't know what first class is like."

"No, they'll think you're a lauded journalist working in a tragic industry," he retorted as he started filming again.

I forced a broad, fake smile and waved my champagne at the camera, trying my best to look excited, until Hudson gave up and pocketed the phone again.

"Your turn," he reminded me.

Damn. I'd been hoping he'd forget.

Hudson took my phone and opened the app, explaining the process of taking a picture or a video, how to edit it (like I'd remember all that), and how to post it to my profile's Moments.

He said the post on the Moments would disappear after twenty-four hours (which I liked), but that any posts on the feed would stay indefinitely. Feed posts were also where people could comment and interact—though they had no ability to like or favorite. He reminded me I'd need to build up both the Moments and the feed itself.

After I got a handle on it, I took a selfie with Hudson kissing my cheek and wrote, *Headed to Cancún with this amazing guy.* "Does that work?" I said, showing him the post.

"You know, for someone who's all about words, you don't say much about yourself," Hudson commented, while I decorated the post with heart stickers and posted it on my Moments.

A picture was all I could muster. I'd work my way up to a video.

"I'm an essayist and a reporter," I told him. "I write thought pieces about interesting topics and I report about other people and places. *Interesting* people and places. Not me."

"You're interesting, Jaz. Believe me." He leaned in to kiss my cheek again, and my eyes fluttered shut. Then he drew back. "Let's get another shot of us for mine. Why don't you put your hand on my chest, so we can get your ring in this one?"

"My ring?" I furrowed my brows. "Why?"

"Well." He cleared his throat. "When I was ring-shopping, I ended up going with a newer, family-owned company called Clides & Gillians. They were very nice and gave me a bit of a deal . . . I think hoping I would post about it. After we signed on for the show, I talked to Kelly about having them design your wedding band too. They jumped at the chance and are making it in exchange for some low-key advertising. Like this." He took my hand and placed it on his chest.

I stared at the diamond glinting between us.

"So they're designing my wedding band completely for free?" My eyebrow shot up. I was intrigued someone would give up a paycheck of that size for just a shout-out.

Hudson shrugged his shoulders. "With the number of people projected to tune in, getting eyes on their product is more valuable than money."

I smiled, and tried to ignore the itching sensation at the back of my mind. The thought that some things maybe shouldn't be so public, or used as advertisements.

The flight to Cancún went smoothly. We landed at exactly 4:44 p.m, which I took to be a good sign. I grabbed a cup of coffee before heading to the private car waiting for us outside.

As we drove away from the airport, I leaned out the window to let the salt breeze dust my cheeks. Hudson leaned over, too, his warm frame resting against my shoulder.

"It smells amazing," I murmured. The scent of the sea always brought a smile to my face, even during my most anxious of times.

"Check out this view." Hudson filmed through the window, catching the palm trees and the azure sky and the temperate seventy-five-degree breeze that drifted past outside. In the distance, we could see rock formations dotted along the coast of the ocean, an even deeper blue than the sky above.

When we arrived at La Belladonna—the resort where the wedding would take place—my jaw dropped to the floor. First class was one thing. The private car, another.

But La Belladonna was next level. It was one of the resorts I wrote about for a *Style&Travel* feature in last April's issue. I interviewed the owners over a video call. It had floored me just seeing it through my computer.

"Oh my God," I whispered as I stepped out of the car onto verdant green lawns that led up to a series of villas, each with adobe walls and red-tiled rooftops. Each villa had its own interior courtyard and pool, to cool down the house in the heat, and the whole resort was a sprawling complex of those villas, trailing down to the beachfront where that warm blue water lapped at pristine white sand.

Despite my job stress, and my disdain for the week to come, I felt deep gratitude to just be there. For the opportunity to see the resort in person.

"This is seriously stunning. Did it get prettier since we saw the photos?" I asked.

Hudson laughed. "Photos can't do some things justice," he said, yet he wasn't looking at the resort when he said it. His gaze burned into mine, and for the first time that day, it seemed that capturing us on his camera wasn't on his mind.

His hand slid down my arm, and his fingers folded between mine. I squeezed his palm, while a cheerful check-in person took our bags from the driver and beckoned us after her.

Even the pathways between the lawns had been decorated—stones lined with colorful sea creatures and faux fossils that reminded me of the Gaudí-style tiles you'd see in Barcelona.

"How are you holding up?" Hudson murmured while we trailed after our guide, who chattered away about all the amenities. Room service, turn-down service, private dinner with a private chef if we wanted . . . My head swam.

"I know all of this happened really fast and I know how you feel about being on camera and being online . . ." Hudson bit into his lower lip.

I smiled. "It *is* a lot. But I'm okay. Just happy to be here with you." It was the truth. Despite what some may think, you can be happy and grateful and also feel anxious and stressed at the same time. Things aren't always so black and white.

Hudson smiled before leaning in and giving me a light peck on my forehead.

Then we reached our villa, and they showed us to our rooms.

I say "rooms" because Hudson and I each had our own separate suite, in a private villa with at least a dozen other rooms, the purposes of which I couldn't fathom. Maybe the film crew would live in those? Or some of our wedding guests? But some looked like sitting rooms, dining rooms . . . It was a veritable mansion.

They put us in suites across the hall from one another because they didn't want us in the same place once the filming started. But until we were told otherwise, we'd be sleeping in the same bed.

The check-in attendant dropped off my bags near the enormous walk-in closet, and then flung open the balcony windows—yep, it had a full-on balcony, overlooking a gently sloping hill down to the beachfront. It was so close I could hear the waves crashing on the shore, and taste the salt in the breeze against my cheeks.

It took me a full minute to drag myself away from the gorgeous view out over the sea, and the glistening white-sand beaches Cancún was known for.

When I managed to turn away, I found the desk near the bed stocked with cashews, Skittles, Takis—some of my favorite snacks. There was also a small bag of palo santo and a mini bottle of lavender oil for relaxation. The mini-fridge had full-size bottles of the brand of water I preferred, too.

Hudson must have called ahead and told them. My heart swelled a little.

I crossed the hall to Hudson's room and tapped lightly on the doorframe, since he'd left the door propped open.

The room looked identical to mine aside from my random snacks. His only had the water bottles.

"This place is incredible," I commented, my gaze drifting past my equally incredible fiancé toward the windows behind him. Then my gaze snagged on the clock beside his bed. "Oh shit. We're supposed to meet Kelly in thirty minutes for dinner."

"Perfect." Hudson took a couple steps toward me, and then his hands folded around my waist. "I guess we'll just have to share a shower then, you know, to save time." He grinned, and I couldn't help but return it, shifting a little closer to him.

His arms tightened around my waist, and the next thing I knew, I was being swept up against his chest while he kicked the door to his rooms shut behind us.

He walked backward toward the shower with me in his arms, and I wrapped my arms around his neck, my legs around his waist. I wanted to savor every second we had alone together before the circus that was *Our Big Day* started.

This was the lead-up to our wedding. We should be celebrating it like this, together, in private.

And for just this stolen little while, as Hudson turned on the rain shower and pulled me into it over my squeals of protest, clothing and all . . . we were able to.

Due to the time constraints, I styled my hair simply, dabbed on some light make-up, and put on a casual little black dress and matching black heels.

In the mirror, I was surprised at how decent I looked after the flight. Maybe thanks to those lie-back seats. Or maybe because I was finally able to sneak some alone-time with Hudson. We'd had precious little of that in the weeks leading up to this day. We'd both been overwhelmed with prep work. But soon, it would all pay off. I was counting on it.

After getting ready, I lit up one of the palo santo sticks and let the fragrant smoke waft through the suite, hoping to bring in some fresh, new energy that I could carry with me over the next few days. Just as I finished, Hudson emerged from the bathroom in a white collared shirt and tan dress pants. I blushed the moment I saw him.

He was still buttoning up the shirt, revealing his chiseled chest and abs. It was all too much for my easily flustered senses and I wished we didn't have to go to dinner at all.

"Ready?" He reached for my hand, and I let him draw me upright.

"To sneak away somewhere together and elope?" I suggested, only half joking. But he just laughed and kissed my temple, before leading me from the room by the hand.

As we made our way down to Gratalina, one of the resort's many on-site restaurants, my stomach knotted.

Kelly had sent us an email explaining that in addition to her, we would be joined for dinner by a Mercer Media executive producer, the La Belladonna event planner, and the videographer. She said it would just be a casual business dinner, more a meet-and-greet than anything. But nonetheless, I was nervous.

This Mercer exec could make or break my career. Hell, this whole project could. It was time to put my game face on and squash my anxiousness and apprehension.

The moment we stepped into Gratalina, an upscale locally inspired fine-dining restaurant with a native Cancún chef, I spotted Kelly's trademark pantsuit (this one was beige) and black curls right away.

We picked our way across the dimly lit restaurant, decorated in a modern open-plan style but with repurposed wooden tables, and Aztec artwork and historical artifacts displayed on the walls.

Sitting with Kelly were two women and a man I had never seen before. The rest of our guests for dinner, I figured.

"Jazmine! Hudson! You've arrived." Kelly jumped to her feet when she saw us and walked over to crush me in a bear hug before she shook Hudson's hand. "I'm so happy there weren't any hiccups with the travel."

We took our seats while Kelly made the introductions. The woman extended a hand first. She was petite, with fair skin smattered in freckles, and golden, wavy hair. "Jennifer Horowitz," the woman offered.

"She's a producer and director at NBC," Kelly added, which made the woman's smile widen.

I shook Jennifer's hand. "Wow, NBC. That's really impressive." I loved me a lady producer in showbiz. Not an easy business to crack into. "Are you our videographer?" I asked.

Kelly had said our videographer was the best in the biz. I wasn't surprised she worked for NBC.

Kelly chuckled. "Actually, Jennifer is my beautiful date for this fabulous week." She draped her arm around Jennifer's shoulders.

My cheeks suddenly went warm. "Oh, I'm so sorry," I replied, embarrassed by my mistake. I glanced around the table again and noticed an extra seat. Someone hadn't arrived yet. Clearly the videographer. *I can't believe I missed that.*

Luckily, Jennifer was still smiling. "I'm just along for the ride this time," Jennifer said with a hint of a New York accent. "Here for play, not work."

"Those are the best trips." Hudson offered his hand too. "Nice to meet you."

"And this is Rosa Gonzalez," Kelly continued the introductions. "She's the event planner here at La Belladonna. She's the one who made everything happen so quickly. Seriously, a god-send."

Rosa nodded her head and I couldn't take my eyes away from the beautiful red rose pinned behind her ear. I also loved how her black hair was loosely styled in a braid. She complemented it with a flowing cream dress and bell sleeves. All very Cancún.

"So nice to meet you," I said.

"Likewise," Hudson added. "Thank you so much for hosting *Our Big Day.*"

I wasn't sure if he used the title of the show intentionally there or not.

"Last but certainly not least, this is Jack Paulson, an executive producer from Mercer Media."

Jack looked exactly how I would have imagined an executive producer from Mercer to look. He wore black pants and a black blazer with a gray dress shirt underneath. He had salt-and-pepper hair and green eyes and a well-groomed mustache and beard. His gaze focused on me immediately, intense. Very "I mean business."

Just making eye contact alone felt incredibly rattling.

He reached out for my hand. "You look the same as you do

in your pictures, which is a good thing. Wasn't sure how much we'd have to photoshop you."

Inside I flinched, but I kept a straight face. I looked over at Kelly who squinted in Jack's direction. Seemed she was taken aback by his comment, too. Jack's handshake was obnoxiously firm, in my opinion. "We're expecting big things from you two," he continued, gazing from me to Hudson, "and we couldn't be more optimistic about the show."

My stomach turned. Knowing that over four million people had already downloaded the app was enough pressure. Hearing his high expectations just made it worse.

Luckily Hudson was harder to fluster. "Happy to hear you're expecting big things, because that's what you're going to get." He offered his charming on-camera grin. "Couldn't be more thrilled to be here."

He wasn't lying. Hudson thrived on pressure. Having high expectations to meet just fueled his Aries fire.

"Why don't we order some appetizers," Kelly suggested. "Our videographer will be here any minute. You're going to love him! He has a fantastic eye for detail. We worked together years ago when I was at The Discovery Channel. Leonardo is seriously talented."

Leonardo. The whole world around me seemed to screech to a halt.

A videographer named Leonardo. With a good eye for detail.

My head started to spin. The uneasiness I'd stuffed in the back of my mind came bursting through the wall I built for it with a vengeance, shattering pieces all over my psyche that I knew would be difficult to clean up.

My legs started twitching in my seat. Hudson noticed, and brought a hand down to rest on my knee, even though he couldn't know where my sudden nerves were exploding from.

I cleared my throat through the thunder of my own pulse in my ears. I almost failed to make my tongue work, but I got there in the end. "Wait. Did you say the videographer's name is Leonardo?"

But Kelly was already glancing away from me, her face brightening with a wider smile. "Oh, there he is." She held up a hand. "Leonardo, over here!"

The ringing in my ears worsened, and it took every effort to stay upright, rigid in my seat. I felt like I was trapped underwater with no oxygen. I fought just to inhale one breath. *It can't be. It fucking can't be.*

But it could. It was.

Striding across the restaurant toward our table was the person I despised more than anyone—Leo Couture.

Chapter Seven

I rubbed my eyes as the ghost from my past strode across the Gratalina lobby, intent on haunting me once more. I tugged at my Indalo charm, hoping that its protective energy combined with the palo santo I burned earlier would make this ghost go away.

It did not.

My hands went cold and numb as if I had just submerged them in ice. I sat there in my seat, equally frozen, unable to budge. Unable to process this as reality.

A smile stretched across Leo's face as he waved at Kelly. *He had to know, right?* When he agreed to do this, he must have known it was my wedding. Why the fuck would he agree to that?

From a distance, Leo looked like no time had passed at all, even though it had been seven years since I'd seen him last. He still wore a long-sleeved fitted black T-shirt that hugged his body. Still complemented it with dark jeans molded to his hips. His brown hair, golden-brown skin and sharp cheekbones hadn't changed much either.

I blinked a couple times. *I'm dreaming. I know it.* There was no way Leo Couture would agree to be the videographer for my wedding. No one could be *that* unlucky.

With each step that Leo took towards our table, however, I became more and more aware that this was certainly not a dream. Not a hallucination.

But a moment later, his eyes found mine. He staggered mid-step. His face grew pale like he had just seen a zombie rising from the grave. But I'd rank the reuniting of two people who didn't want to be reunited much worse than the zombie apocalypse—it felt more like the end of the world.

Based on Leo's deer-in-the-headlights expression, I guessed I was wrong: he also had no idea we would be working together. Did he even know who I was marrying? Or that I'd gotten engaged in the first place?

My mind started racing for possible explanations. Adding to the irony was that Cancún was the place Leo and I said we were going to get married when we made our marriage pact. But this city meant a lot more to Leo than our voided deal.

It was where his father met his mother. Cancún marked the beginning of his parents' romance, and because of such, it was where his family visited every year. It was a city steeped in Couture memories. *Maybe he took the gig because it was in Cancún?*

As he approached the table everyone rose except for me. I couldn't have stood if I'd tried. My legs were like Jell-O. The room was spinning. My stomach queasy.

We stared at each other, eyes wide, for what felt like hours. Surely everyone around us must have noticed. Surely Hudson had noticed. But only a few seconds later, Hudson offered Leo a hand.

"Leonardo Couture. You're the one filming our wedding? I am such a fan of your work, man. Hudson Taylor, great to meet you." It took Leo a minute to register the offered hand, and accept it. At least it got Leo's gaze off of me. "I just watched the mini-doc you did about the Aztec ruins. The photos were just breathtaking!"

"Thank you. I really appreciate that." Leo crossed his arms and stared at Hudson, inspecting him as if he were his understudy. It was a familiar look—the same one I'd often give Elizabeth while trying to discern why she was cast as the role of the leading lady in the fucked-up production that was Jazmine and Leo.

"And I didn't know I'd be working with you either," he added loudly, directing his voice towards where I was still seated at the table. He laughed. It sounded nervous. Was it weird that I could still tell when he felt nervous?

"I owed Kelly a favor. When she called to ask for my help with a project down in Cancún, I agreed, no questions asked. Anything for Kelly. And to visit one of my family's favorite places." Leo finally met my gaze. "Hey, Jazmine." He gave me a half-wave followed by an attempt at a grin.

In the past, a half-smile from Leo was like sunshine for my soul. But not anymore. At that moment, it was like fire on my flesh.

"Hi, Leo." My blood started to boil.

Leo was the *last* person I wanted to see a week before my wedding. Or any other day, for that matter.

As I looked at him, some not-so-fond memories of our messy history came flooding in. Our ridiculous marriage pact. Him leaving me on our twenty-first birthday celebration to pick up Elizabeth. Me spotting him kissing her a week later. Us never talking again after fifteen years of friendship. The gaping hole that loss of friendship left in my chest. And the years I'd spent trying to repair it. The years of fond memories we had together were nowhere to be found.

All the anger I felt towards him started bubbling towards the surface. If I could've spit lava, I would have.

It must have shown on my face, because Hudson peered at me sideways. "Oh, right. You two know each other, don't you?" Hudson kept his tone innocent, but I knew he had to remember. It was only three months ago, after all, when my whole family started babbling about Leo at my birthday/surprise engagement dinner.

Memorable.

"You could say that," Leo replied, sliding his hands into his pockets.

"I didn't know you two knew each other." Kelly's eyebrows rose. I turned the full force of my glare on her. She squinted, assessing my worry. "Leo, why don't you take a seat? Jazmine, I need to use the ladies' room. Care to join me?"

"Yes. Absolutely." At least the adrenaline had given my legs back a modicum of strength. Enough for me to stand without falling over. I purposely turned my back to avoid Leo and Hudson's curious gazes, and strode after Kelly. Neither of us spoke as we wove through Gratalina's endless maze of modern tables.

The second the restroom door swung shut behind us, however, she didn't waste another second.

"What the *hell* is going on?" Kelly demanded. "Are you okay?"

I grabbed at a paper towel stacked on the restroom's counter and dabbed at my upper lip. "Leo Couture and I have a . . . *complicated* history."

She started tapping her foot. "How complicated?"

"Pretty fucking complicated, to be honest," I blurted, more curtly than I intended. I winced and crumpled up the paper towel, tossing it into the bin.

When I met Kelly's gaze in the mirror again, it had softened. "All right. Give me the short version."

I took a long breath and started pacing the suspiciously clean bathroom, appropriately decorated like the restaurant itself with pieces by local Mexican artists. "We were best friends since elementary school. Like real best friends. Our parents lived across the street and he and I did everything together. But we had a big falling-out when we were in college after things got a little more than friendly between us. He told me he loved me. I was young and wasn't ready for that kind of commitment and was superstitious about the timing of it all. I said some not so great things to him. I saw him kissing someone else . . ." I paused as the memory made my breath catch in my throat. "That's the short version."

The positive vibe that always seemed to illuminate Kelly's face dissipated. "Fuck, that *is* complicated." She sighed, running her fingers through her black, curly hair. "Look, Jazmine, I don't mean to sound cold. The last thing I want is to make you feel uncomfortable. But there's no way we could find another videographer of Leo's caliber and with his eye for detail and quick editing skills before Monday. And even if we could, Mercer would never approve a last-minute change like that. We are honestly lucky we snagged Leo in the first place. We never would have if I hadn't called in a favor from him. I mean, he makes *NatGeo* documentaries, this isn't typically his line of work. Plus, between the pace of the shoots we have planned, and how much is riding on this . . ."

Kelly was in an awkward position here, and I understood it. Mercer had spent a lot on this project. Her career depended on it.

So did mine.

I choked down the lump in my throat. There was no getting

out of this. There was nothing I could do. "I understand. And I'll be fine," I answered, trying to force some sort of pep into my voice.

Kelly peered at me more closely. "Are you sure? I'm truly so sorry you're in this horrible dilemma. I can't even imagine what you're feeling right now, and on the week before your wedding, for fuck's sake! I really want to make sure that you're okay."

"Yes. Totally okay." I straightened my shoulders. "This is a job, after all. I can be professional."

I had to be. I was doing this to save my career. I couldn't let Leo take that away from me. He'd already taken too much, anyway.

"Right. You are both professionals. We'll get through this." She flashed me her best forced grin. "Now, let's go back out there and face this fucked-up situation with some drinks."

Kelly pushed the bathroom door open, but stopped suddenly halfway out of it. "Oh. One more thing." She glanced over her shoulder. "Just so I have the full picture, did you guys ever . . . sleep together?"

My face flushed bright red.

Full picture, sure. What Kelly really wanted were juicy details. She was a magazine editor, after all. She couldn't help it.

"No." I pulled at the hem of my little black dress. "We came close but it never happened."

She raised a brow. "Huh."

I couldn't tell what she meant by that.

Walking back toward the table, I did my best to stifle the storm brewing inside me. *Deep breaths, Jazmine, deep breaths. You spent your entire youth around Leo, you can handle him now. Don't let him win.* But my attempt at mind-over-mattering the situation dissipated once I saw the empty seat waiting for me between Hudson and Leo.

Did they do that on purpose?

Hudson patted the chair, his eyes alight. Did he find this amusing? Or did he just not understand the gravity of Leo being there? It was my fault, really. I'd never given him the full scoop.

Despite the awkward seating arrangement, I slid into the chair. I wasn't about to ask Hudson to switch seats. I didn't want to draw any more attention to the god-awful situation.

"All good, love?" Hudson asked, eyeing me with his baby blues as I scooted closer to him. He reached over and ran his fingers over my shoulders.

"Everything's great," I replied, louder than I intended. "I'm great."

Hudson leaned in and kissed me on the cheek, which would usually be enough to calm my nerves. But that night, not so much. "Well, you look great. Doesn't my bride-to-be look beautiful?"

Everyone at the table chorused "*Yes*" practically in unison. Except for Leo. He sat beside me stiff as a board, like he'd suddenly forgotten how to move or speak.

"Let's order drinks, shall we?" I reached for the menu. "A lot of them," I added under my breath.

Right on cue, the waiter arrived, a middle-aged gentleman in a white buttoned shirt with a tiny mustache and dark hair slicked into a side part. He was carrying a basket of fresh chips with a side of salsa that he kindly placed on our table. "Hi. I'll have a shot of Patrón with lime, please," I spoke up before anyone else had the chance. "And you know what, I'll take one of your blue agave margaritas too."

Everyone at the table stared.

Kelly cleared her throat. It wasn't like me to order shots at a business dinner. But desperate times called for desperate measures.

"Wow. A shot of Patrón and a margarita. I'll have what she's having." Leo nodded toward me. "Let the party begin." And then he said something to the waiter in Spanish. I couldn't make out the words, but they caused the server to smile.

"A blue agave margarita sounds great. I'll take one of those too," Hudson added.

I glanced at him. "No shots?"

"Nah. You know I'm not a shots guy. I'm a beer and wine guy, but I do love a good margarita. When in Cancún, right?"

The table laughed, any tension from my drink over-order broken.

But I suddenly felt like a sinner sitting next to Saint Hudson. And then I felt even more devilish when Jack ordered a light Corona, Rosa ordered water, and Jennifer and Kelly each ordered one glass of wine.

Seemed like Leo and I would be the only ones drowning our sorrows in tequila.

After the waiter left, an awkward quietness fell once more. Luckily, Rosa spoke up before I started to sweat too badly. "So, Jazmine, Hudson, I just wanted to let you know that everyone at La Belladonna is so excited to be hosting your wedding. It's all anyone can talk about. It's such an honor!"

She smiled the most genuine of smiles, pure warmth and sunshine. You would have thought the red rose tucked behind her ear had sprouted there itself.

"And we're so honored you're hosting it," Hudson replied, flashing his trademark killer grin. "Thank you."

"Yes, thank you so much," I added. "The resort is *so* beautiful, even more so in person. I loved writing about it for last April's issue."

"Ah! Yes, we loved your write-up about us in the *Style&Travel* Cancún guide." Rosa giddily clutched her hands in front of her. "We have a framed copy hanging behind the front desk."

My eyebrows rose. "Oh wow. That's . . . very flattering. I'm so happy you liked it." My cheeks flushed.

"The way you talked about our resort, it seemed like you really understood our story. Our vision came through on the page. You're a wonderful writer, Miss Prado."

Her compliment felt like a wave crashing atop me and dragging me away from the shore. I was grateful to hear it, but it also cut real deep. Probably because, at that moment, I wasn't writing for *Style&Travel*—I was filming my wedding for them instead. *This better pay off like I think it will.*

"You really *are* a wonderful writer, Miss Prado," Hudson said, playfully nudging my shoulder. "Soon to be Mrs. Taylor," he added under his breath. Yet even speaking that quietly, the others around the table reacted, smiling at us like we were adorable.

As for me, I reeled, struggling not to visibly react.

Mrs. Taylor.

We hadn't discussed whether or not I would be taking his last name. We had barely time to talk about where we'd be living after the wedding (my place until we had time to go house hunting).

Not that I blamed him for assuming I would take it. That *is* tradition, and Hudson at his core is very traditional.

But was I ready to give up my Prado name? I wasn't sure. If I took Taylor, I'd want to hyphenate it, or at least keep both names like they do in my family's culture. But I couldn't exactly clarify that at dinner. This was not the kind of conversation to have in front of an audience.

"Mrs. Jazmine Taylor does have a nice ring to it," Jack from Mercer Media chimed in, holding up his water glass. My face only flamed even more. "To the future Mrs. Taylor."

"To the future Mrs. Taylor," the group chorused, lifting their glasses in the air.

Leo quietly snickered beside me.

For the first time that night, I turned in his direction. "What are you laughing at?" I muttered, just loud enough for him to hear.

His eyes widened like a kid who just got caught with his hand in the cookie jar. "Nothing." He smiled, looking from me around the rest of the table and back to me. "Just have a tickle in my throat."

Bullshit.

And that's the thing about having a history with someone. They can be out of your life for so many years, yet you can still read them like a damn book. I knew he was most likely snickering about the fact that "Mrs. Taylor" meant I wouldn't be keeping the Prado name. He knew my last name meant a lot to me. He probably thought I'd settled or something and it took all my effort in that moment to not correct it.

Seconds later, I saw the waiter heading toward our table, alcohol in tow. "Oh, thank God," I whispered. I practically pried the shot of Patrón out of his hands, threw it down my throat, and quickly chased it with my margarita.

After the tequila took hold, I stopped focusing on the details of dinner. Conversation went on—chatter about the wedding week. Yet all I could really hear was Leo. Breathing beside me, loud enough to pass for Darth fucking Vader. At least, that's how it sounded to me. It was infuriating. It kept drawing my attention and I fought to not let my gaze drift in his direction. Not to wonder what I'd missed in the last seven years.

Instead, I clenched my fists under the table and ignored him as best I could.

I started to sober up a bit as Hudson and I made our way back to our villa. He laid me down on the couch in his room, and I closed my eyes. When I opened them again he had emerged from the bathroom in a tight black shirt and gym shorts, and bent over to tie his shoes. It was not a bad view.

I moved from the couch and came up behind him, putting my hands around his waist and kissing the nape of his neck. He turned around and his mouth found my lips.

"You going somewhere?" I asked between pecks.

"Yeah, to the gym. They close in a few hours, and this doesn't happen by accident." He smirked, pulling up his shirt to reveal his perfectly toned six-pack.

My hands traveled over the muscles like magnets. I traced his abs like a sculpture in a museum. Pure perfection. "How long will you be gone?"

"Couple hours. Going to do some weights and then a quick run on the treadmill."

"A couple hours?" My eyebrows rose. "I was thinking we could do a workout of our own here." I tugged at the elastic on his shorts.

Hudson let out a quiet breath. His eyes caught mine, sparking. "We can when I get back. And . . ." He traced his fingers down my dress and over the curves of my body. "I promise to make up for the lost time." He leaned in and lightly brushed his lips against my neck, sending chills up and down my body.

Just mean, considering he was getting ready to leave.

"Oh." He stopped halfway to the door. "There wasn't a good moment to ask at dinner, but are you okay with Leonardo Couture being our videographer?"

I hesitated for a few seconds. "I mean, it's not my first choice. But what can you do?" I let out an awkward laugh that sounded like a cross between a hyena and a witch's cackle.

Hudson tilted his head. "Well, I'd love to know more about what happened between you guys, whenever you're ready to tell me."

Shit. I had been avoiding this conversation since the moment Hudson and I started dating. No one likes to talk about the first time they got their heart broken. Really broken. I'd rather just forget the whole thing ever happened. Forget Leo even existed. Forget that he was here to film my wedding.

"It's a bunch of boring bullshit, to be honest," I finally replied. "He means nothing to me now. It's all in the past."

Hudson leaned back, studying my posture. I couldn't read his expression. Did he believe me? "So you're okay?"

"I'm okay. Promise." I mustered up my best smile. "But also, do you *have* to go to the gym?" I pouted, more needy than usual.

"I'll be back before you know it," he replied, grabbing my chin and pulling me in for another quick kiss. "I love you."

"I love you too."

I sighed as the door closed behind him. Then I grabbed my phone to call Gal.

It went straight to voicemail, which meant she was most likely working late and had her phone on do not disturb. I decided to send her a text instead.

Guess who our videographer for the show is? Leo motherfucking Couture! Apparently, the devil is real and he's conspiring against me.

Gal was probably the only person who could understand the full gravity of the situation. Just thinking about it again made me clammy. But my phone remained silent. No helpful quips.

After staring at the wall for a few more minutes, I decided to go for a walk. Clear my head. I was at La Belladonna, after all, one of the most beautiful properties in Cancún. I owed it to myself to try to make the most of it, to salvage this strange evening.

I took Hudson's room key and stepped outside. The moment I exited our villa, the ocean breeze struck my cheeks like a wet slap. It was muggy tonight, the air heavy with impending rain that was supposed to start late that night and be gone by morning. From our front porch, I could see all the way down the gentle slope, across the dunes to the beachfront. Waves crashed white-tipped against the shore, the sound one long, steady drumroll.

I noticed a sliver of light above—a waxing crescent moon. It gleamed against the night sky. No full moon or eclipse to explain the chaos. Just nature showing off. Being beautiful.

I took a deep breath. Another. Despite the heaviness in the air, the familiar scents calmed me. Sea, salt, sand.

I kicked off my shoes and stepped off the porch, then off the stone walkway entirely. My feet sank into soft grass, as I strode toward the beach itself.

Behind me, the other villas dotted across the resort winked like jewels set in the face of the sand. I kept going until my feet hit beach, and then I sighed as I sank almost ankle-deep into the white sand. At least Cancún hadn't let me down.

I strode along the beach, parallel to the waves, careful to stay far enough from the surf to remain nice and dry. As I walked, I passed other villas. Couples lounged on the porch of one, drinks in hand. Another was filled with a group of girlfriends, laughing and dancing to the music they had playing from their phones.

Near the edge of the resort, I noticed a beachfront cantina. *Antonio's.* It had casual lounge chairs and a firepit out in the sand.

I had probably already had my fill of booze and food for the evening, but figured some more dessert couldn't hurt. Might as well treat myself.

Inside, the cantina looked too busy and loud. I could hear laughter and shouts spill out from the doors, and felt the sharp sting of air-conditioned air when the automatic doors breezed open.

Instead, I turned toward the beachfront firepit. Only a couple people were out here, braving the calm before the storm. One lounged in a chair next to the fire. There was a standing bar out here, sunk into the sand, with a single bartender cleaning glasses behind it.

One other customer leaned at the far end on one of the only two barstools, facing away from me.

I padded across the sand, still barefoot, to ask to see the dessert menu. But just before I reached the counter, the other customer turned my way, and I stopped.

Leo.

Of course.

I thought about leaving, but he was already staring at me, barely a table's length away, and I couldn't do it. I couldn't give him the pleasure of knowing he rattled me enough to split.

Instead, I decided to face this head-on. I took a deep breath and finished walking toward the bar, and leaned against it, right beside him. Head held high, strutting in my little black dress, heels in hand.

You got this.

"Okay if I join you?" I asked.

His gaze had already returned to the shelves of bottles lined up behind the bar. In the mirrored backing, though, I caught his eyes drifting in my direction, even while he pretended not to look.

"Of course." He waved toward the empty stool beside him. The air around us turned cold. Distant.

We were strangers now. Strangers with a complicated history. I slid onto the stool and rested my palms on the countertop. Behind it, the bartender was wiping down a series of glasses, taking his time coming over.

Maybe he sensed the tension between us too, and didn't want to interrupt.

"So, this is . . . weird." I tapped my fingers on the wooden surface.

"Yeah. This is weird," he agreed, taking a sip of his drink. Not sure exactly what it was. Some sort of amber-colored liquor on the rocks.

I leaned back in the high seat. "You really didn't know it was my wedding you were filming?"

I figured why not cut straight to the chase. We already hated each other, how much worse could it get?

"Nope." His shoulders rounded, defensive. "You really didn't know I was filming it?"

"No. Kelly never gave a name." But then, my wheels started to turn. How could he, "Mr. Attention to Details," not know anything about a project he signed on to? Things didn't quite add up.

"So you really didn't do any research beforehand on what you agreed to film? That doesn't really sound like . . . you."

He let out a light chuckle. "How would *you* even know what sounds like me?"

I could feel my heart pulse in my ears. My skin, prickly and hot. I wanted to shout, "Fuck you!" But I kept myself composed.

"Well, even if you didn't do any research, you would've had to hear about it, right?" I said. "*Style&Travel*'s been dropping big-bucks advertising all over social media. Photos. Videos. It's hard to miss."

"Believe whatever you like," Leo snapped, and I tensed, expecting a fight. Then his shoulders slumped a little. "Kelly needed a favor last-minute. I stepped up to the plate."

The air around us had gone from cold to fucking freezing. "I'm not a social media kind of guy. I promote my work on there, sure. But I never scroll through it. And I don't follow *Style&Travel*, or Hudson—"

"Or me." The words slipped out before I could think better of them.

Leo let out a huff. "But after our awkward—albeit entertaining—dinner, I got curious. You weren't on Hudson's account until the single post where he announced you're his fiancée, and told his fans to please download *Style&Travel*'s app to watch your wedding?"

I played with the ampersand around my neck. "Yeah. Well. That was by my request. I'm not into social media either." *I guess that's one thing we still had in common.* "I didn't want to be mentioned until I absolutely had to."

He replaced his glass on the table. "Funny how someone who isn't into social media is marrying a social media *star*."

"You really don't follow Hudson?" I squinted sideways at him.

"I'd never even heard of the guy before this. I told you—not a social media person." He cut a long, searching glance in my direction. "But Kelly loves him. She told me he was really sweet, and he has a loyal following." Leo paused, and ran a hand through his wavy hair that still fell around his ears. "To be honest, it never would have occurred to me to check if it was you doing this reality web show, Jazmine Prado. You barely even let me take your picture."

The sound of my full name on his lips, like *that*, made my whole body freeze up. Turn to ice.

Or fire. One of those two. Something that burned, at any rate.

I straightened in my chair. "I've changed a lot since we were kids, Leo *Couture*." A faint smirk at the corner of his mouth showed my retort landed. I sighed, relenting. "We are twenty-eight now."

"Come on, be honest, why are you *really* doing this show?" he asked, a hint of amiability in his voice. "It doesn't seem like something you'd enjoy doing."

"How would *you* even know what's something I'd enjoy doing?" I countered, using his own phrasing against him.

"Touché." His posture tightened. "I just . . . I just hope you're not doing something you don't want to be doing—"

"I am perfectly happy with my decisions, thank you." I held up my hand, interrupting him. We weren't friends. We hadn't spoken in seven years. I didn't believe he had a right to interject himself in my life like that. "This show is a great opportunity for me, that's why I *chose* to do it. It's a smart career move."

"Makes sense. I know your career is important to you." Something changed in his tone. Like he was remembering all the times I shut him down, waiting for the perfect timing for us to be together, waiting till I was settled in my career.

I looked down at his hand and my eyes went to his ring finger, which jogged my memory. Last I checked, he was engaged to Elizabeth. That was just a few months ago. I'd wondered when they'd be walking down the aisle.

"Is Elizabeth here with you?" I asked, tucking a strand of hair behind my ears.

"Elizabeth?" His eyebrows shot up his forehead, and he laughed. "No. No, we're not together."

I squinted. "You're not? Well, I'm sure you'll find your way back into each other's arms soon enough," I offered with a hint of sarcasm.

Leo lifted his drink and swirled the ice in it. The cubes clinked. "Probably not. She married someone else last week."

"What?!" I didn't mean to shout, but the news was shocking. "Elizabeth married someone else? Who?"

"Some guy she works with." Leo shrugged. "We were engaged for a month. But it didn't work out. And she got with someone pretty quickly after we broke up and apparently they eloped. So now it's officially over. I honestly think it's a good thing. Our relationship wasn't the healthiest."

Silence followed for what felt like minutes but I'm certain was just a few seconds.

"Wow." I finally regained my voice, and shook my head. "You and Elizabeth are officially done. It's the end of an era."

Leo grinned and took another sip of his drink. I caught the scent of it, something sharp and smoky. Whiskey. Last I remembered, Leo wasn't a whiskey drinker.

But then, I'm sure he's changed a lot over the years too.

"I imagine filming weddings isn't the type of thing you usually do?"

Leo suppressed a smile. "Not quite. But without that first opportunity Kelly gave me back at Discovery when I needed it, I probably wouldn't have gotten my first big photo series in *NatGeo*, which in turn wouldn't have led to my first documentary getting picked up by the Nature channel, etc., etc. It's important to pay it forward. Or back, I guess, in this case."

I traced a bead of humidity on the wooden tabletop before glancing at the mirror behind the bar again. In it, Leo stared at me. My cheeks felt a little warmer.

"So . . . you decided to get married in Cancún." He grinned. "Interesting. I feel like I'm discovering a lot of interesting things about you today."

I cleared my throat, and hoped the blush would die down. At least it was night, which helped obscure it a little. "The magazine picked the location, not me. It's just a strange coincidence."

"Huh. I'd say so." Leo drained the last of his whiskey, and went back to studying me.

"Hey, just as you said. Believe whatever you like."

"Fair enough." His eyes left the table and gazed out in the distance. "You know, the sky is really nice tonight." He squinted and pointed above. "The stormy clouds are casting a nice shadow on the sand. Looks almost luminescent, like it's glowing. And the way the moonlight reflects against the water makes the sky almost look like a sapphire. It's really stunning."

Leo and his damn details. I admired it. I just wasn't in the mood for it. I glanced in the other direction. That's when the bartender finally caught our eye, and set down the glass he'd been cleaning.

Next to me, Leo straightened. "Do you want me to order you some food? Or a drink? Some ridiculous Martini or something?"

My stomach flipped. Just like me, he must be thinking about our twenty-first birthdays. About thc drinks he bought me, before we went back to his parents' place, and lay out beside the pool, and . . .

And that's when I realized I had had enough of strolling

down memory lane for one night. I'd seen that production before, and I didn't like how it ended. I wasn't here to re-live it again.

I shot up from the stool. The anger over what happened that night rushed through my veins anew. Verbal vomit rose to the surface. "No. No. I have to get back. I've got a hot fiancé waiting for me back in our villa. We're going to have sex. Lots of hot, amazing sex. Probably a couple times actually. Hudson's a really good fuck."

Leo coughed, practically choking on air. He wasn't a blusher but his golden-brown cheeks had gone redder than I'd ever seen. "Lucky you?" he finally managed.

My own face could have started a bonfire. I spun to go, then turned back again, unable to stop myself from adding, "By the way, I'm not taking his last name. I mean, maybe if we hyphenate, or if I use both names, but I'm not *only* using Taylor."

What the hell was wrong with me? I was acting so immature. Why did I care if Leo knew this? And why was I telling him this before I'd even told Hudson as much?

Leo threw his hands in the air. "Hey, I'm not here to judge. You gotta do what's best for you." Then he sighed, searching my gaze. I wondered if he was cataloguing my eyeshadow color. But then his mouth turned down, and I realized I'd upset him, somehow.

Or maybe we'd upset each other, coming here. Talking like this.

"It's good to see you, Jazmine," he said softly. "Even if the circumstances are . . . unusual."

"Good to see you too," I managed through a tight throat. Then I turned away again, eager to escape the buzzing feeling at the back of my neck.

"Oh, Jazmine?" Leo called. I stopped dead, without turning around. He spoke to the back of me anyway.

"Congratulations. I'm really happy for you."

But for some reason, I didn't believe him.

Letting Go is Really Damn Hard

By Jazmine Prado

Getting over hurt is a process with no expiration date, and can take days, weeks, years and in some cases, maybe even a lifetime. The solution, according to professionals and friends alike, is to simply "let it go." Release the things that are no longer serving you. But if letting go was so easy, there wouldn't be countless self-help books dedicated to this very subject. On the contrary, letting go can be one of the most difficult journeys you'll ever have to make.

There's an old saying that goes like this: Holding on to resentment is letting someone live in your head rent-free. It basically means that when you harbor resentment, hate, and bitterness towards someone, you are giving them power over your thoughts, along with a cozy studio apartment in a distant corner of your mind. And the harsh reality is that many times, the person you're obsessing over, for whatever reason, moved on long ago. You're poring over every memory of them on a daily basis, but they haven't thought about you in ages. Ouch.

For some people, time is the greatest healer. And after reading a few books, reciting affirmations, and talking it over with friends around a pint of Ben & Jerry's, the obsession starts to fade, and the tenant begins to pack up their belongings. Others, however, just aren't as lucky. The reality is, certain people have a way of sticking around long after we've tried to kick them out. So, where do we go from there?

Maybe there's another path, one that doesn't require us to evict our pesky mental tenants, but still allows us to let go in another way. Acceptance can be a powerful coping mechanism, and despite what some may say, it doesn't equate to "giving up." In fact, I'd argue just the opposite.

For some, acceptance is the very key that empowers them to choose exactly how much time they spend lounging around with their mental tenant. This key can open the door to the hurtful memories, and it can also close it and lock it shut. Accepting that your mental tenant may be here for the long haul is one alternative to "letting go." And who knows, maybe through acceptance we can slowly reframe our perception of distant memories until they no longer bring us any pain at all.

Regardless, go easy on yourselves. Healing from hurt isn't a one-size-fits-all. Maybe for some, letting go is more about the journey than the destination or final result. In the meantime, I'll be reaching for another pint of Ben & Jerry's.

Chapter Eight

I lay in bed next to Hudson in his villa suite, staring at the clock, bewildered. 8:26 a.m. I couldn't remember the last time I was up at that hour.

I'm a writer. I liked to sleep till at least 10:30, noon being my ultimate preference.

Kelly asked us to meet her and Jack in the lobby at 10 a.m. that day, but I couldn't make my racing brain stay quiet until then.

I only got about three hours of sleep. There was too much on my mind. Too many unanswered questions.

I'd spent the last two days ignoring Leo, trying not to think about how he'd be filming our wedding, asking us personal questions in the lead-up to it, sharing this most intimate experience with us.

Now Monday had dawned, and I had to deal with the fact that Leo would be a part of my wedding. And I fucking hated it.

But most of all, I hated that I gave a shit.

I shifted closer to Hudson and leaned my head on his shoulder. His body was the perfect temperature, warm but not too warm, making an extra blanket unnecessary even when he blasted the resort's AC. I drew in a deep breath. He smelled of sun, and sweat, and a dash of old cologne that lingered from the day before. It was a sexy scent. A very Hudson scent.

I shivered as I sunk my cheek further into his skin, basking in all of his familiar, comforting goodness.

He didn't budge. Hudson was a heavy sleeper. But the heat of his skin comforted me. Like lying in the sand on the Cancún beach. The way we did just yesterday, side by side, ignoring the world for a quick minute before we went back up to his room and he tore off my clothes and went down on me before we had sex. I screamed louder than I ever had in my life. It was a good day. A day I wished I could go back to and stay in for ever.

I sighed, and Hudson twitched beneath me. I rolled away, not wanting to wake him. *One of us should at least get to sleep a little longer.*

After spending half an hour scrolling through a few of my favorite meme accounts, I opened the *Style&Travel* app, only to be taken aback by the thousands of comments on my profile. Besides me re-sharing some of my old articles, I only had two pictures up on my feed so far—both photos of Hudson and I on the beach. I had gotten a little better at posting to my Moments, but not enough to earn this level of traffic.

Then my stomach sank as I skimmed the first comment. *She's definitely pretty don't get me wrong, but he's Hudson Taylor. I would've expected . . . I don't know, more I guess.*

I let out a long breath. So much for waking myself up gently.

Underneath that comment was another. *She's like an exotic girl-next-door. Cute, attractive, nice body, but I would've expected Hudson to marry a goddess.*

I groaned. Not only because the commenter referred to me as "exotic," but also because being with someone like Hudson could sometimes be challenging. Having strangers question whether or not I was good enough for him was a hard pill I wasn't ready to swallow.

"Hey, don't read those." Hudson swatted at my phone, startling me. I glanced over to find him rubbing sleep from his eyes. "People will say all kinds of things when they can hide behind a screen. It's a waste of time to pay attention to it."

Easy to say that when everyone's drooling at your feet. I furrowed my brows. "But I thought we're supposed to interact with people who comment. Isn't that what Jack wanted?"

Hudson reached over and played with a strand of my hair. Slowly, he tucked it behind my ear, and his fingertips grazed my cheekbone. "You don't have to talk to everyone. Just a couple of people. When you do, only respond to positive comments."

"From the looks of it, there's not too much of that." I put my phone back on the night table, face down.

"There's more than you think." He booped my nose. "The bad ones tend to get more interaction, so they show up on top. People like to focus on negativity."

He moved closer and lightly kissed my lips, his mouth soft and supple. When I shifted closer to him in response, curling against him, I felt him dig into my hip, hard as usual in the mornings. It made my pulse skip, my face flushing as I traced my hands over his shoulders and down his back.

Hudson drew back just far enough to smirk at me. "Good morning, by the way."

"Well, good morning to you too." My fingertips trailed down his bare back. Hudson always slept naked. As for me, I slept in one of his T-shirts, large enough for me to swim in. With nothing underneath.

As if reading my mind, his hands trailed toward the hem of that T-shirt. Just the feeling of his strong, warm fingertips against my thighs made my heart jump, my chest tighten. Heat spread all over my body.

I knew everything was about to change. The cameras would be rolling. The mood would be different. I wasn't sure how I'd feel once the circus started, but I knew right then in that moment that I wanted him. Badly.

I looked up at Hudson and devilishly grinned before taking off my T-shirt and throwing it on the floor. His blue eyes widened as he inched closer to me.

"I think we have time for a morning quickie?" he smiled, before reaching his hand between my legs. I shivered at his touch, letting out a soft whimper.

He moved his mouth to mine, kissing me slowly before sucking at my bottom lip. He moved his lips down to my jaw, then to my neck, then to my nipples, sending more chills down my spine. Then in one swift motion, he rotated my body so my back was now towards him.

His hand trailed my lower stomach, clutching my hip bones and my ass before moving me closer. My body arched as he pushed inside me, sweat slicked between us.

"Oh, yes," I managed to utter. "Don't stop." I could feel his labored breaths against the back of my neck.

"I won't," he whispered, biting my ear.

His hand clutched my breast as he pulled me tighter to him and thrust harder. I moaned louder, my nails digging into the skin of his arms.

I loved this feeling. Our sticky bodies rolling against each other. Hudson deep inside of me. The way my toes curled more with every thrust.

Then, my phone dinged from the side table, and Hudson went still.

He released, turning me back towards him with a faint smirk. "Probably better check to see if that's Kelly," he said.

"Now?" I replied with a bite.

"You know I would never usually suggest something like that. But we are here for a job and there could be a schedule change or something. Just want to make sure everything is on track."

He was right, but I was not happy about it. Whoever this was, I was going to kill them . . .

I leaned over and grabbed my phone. It was Gal. *Can't wait to see you tomorrow!!* Our families and friends were arriving on Tuesday, and they would all be staying at the same resort. All flights and accommodation for our one hundred wedding guests (we were allowed fifty each) were paid for courtesy of Mercer Media.

Mercer was also paying for our honeymoon in Maui, which we wouldn't be filming, but Hudson negotiated for as part of the contract as long as we agreed to post photos from the trip to the app. We just had to survive the filmed wedding week first.

"It's just Gal." I set my phone back down and rolled onto my back, my earlier fire forgotten as reality had begun to sink in.

Hudson settled beside me. "What is it?" he asked, a playful smile on his mouth.

"Everyone will be here tomorrow. It's all really starting." I tried for a smile. I should be happy about this, right? *What was I looking forward to* . . . "I'm excited to see your parents again. And to meet your brother."

Hudson had one younger brother named Hunter, who lived in Toronto. We hadn't met yet. I'd only met his parents once, when they came to L.A. We spent the visit doing stereotypical Hollywood tourist stuff: the Walk of Fame, hiking to the

Hollywood sign. It had been fun, but I didn't feel like I really *knew* them after that.

Plus, I was nervous about his parents meeting mine. His had been so reserved and polite during that visit. Mine were . . . not.

"My parents can't wait to see you again too." Hudson traced a finger along my shoulder. "And Hunter is very excited to meet you. He's a little less outgoing than I am, so don't take it personal if he's quiet."

"Good to know." I wondered if Hunter had been cold to any of Hudson's past girlfriends. The warning sounded like it came from experience.

Then suddenly, a pit formed in my stomach. *What am I doing?* whispered a little voice in the back of my head. Was this too fast?

I shook my head. I was letting the nerves get the best of me. Before they could swallow me up, I levered myself out of the bed.

Hudson's face fell. "Where are you going?"

The expression on his face was almost enough to make me change my mind. To fall back into his arms and distract myself from my worries.

But the knot in my stomach wouldn't let me. "We've gotta go soon so I'm gonna take a quick shower," I said, before escaping into the privacy of our bathroom.

Once there, I leaned my forehead against the tiles, letting hot water wash over me, trying not to feel anxious about today. This week. The cameras, my career riding on my performance on thc show.

Hudson . . . Our families meeting. Our *wedding day*. Somehow, it still didn't quite feel real.

A little before 10 a.m., I still hadn't managed to do much

more than towel off and change into sweats. By then, Hudson was up and dressed too, so we headed to the resort café together.

The café was charming and quaint, filled with fresh pan dulce: orejas, conchas, bigotes (a cousin to the croissant) and churros—different from the ones in Spain, as the Mexican version was topped with cinnamon and sugar, not dipped in thick chocolate.

The smell of espresso beans and foaming milk filled the air, and I took a deep breath, savoring some of my favorite scents.

Kelly and Jack hadn't arrived yet, so we had our pick of tables. We planted ourselves at a seat near a set of wide bay windows overlooking the beach. I spotted a couple of intrepid people jogging along the white sand, and a handful more sprawled out, already at work on their tans.

Beyond them, the ocean frothed, deep gray speckled with white caps. It looked stormy today, despite the blue sky overhead. I wondered if it would rain later.

Maybe if it rains, they won't be able to film. Maybe we'll get a day delay before the theatrics all begin . . .

Then Hudson appeared with our drinks, startling me from my reverie. "I snagged some churros too," he commented, setting my usual Americano with cream and one pump of vanilla before me.

"Thank you," I said, taking a sip of my coffee. *So good.*

The churros weren't so bad either. In fact, I practically inhaled them, hardly leaving any for Hudson.

As I was wiping crumbs from my face, Hudson pulled out his phone. "Let's take some photos for our Moments."

"Right now?" I buried my head in my napkin. "I look like shit."

"Please. You look beautiful! And no one cares about how you look, anyway."

I do, I thought, biting the inside of my cheek. "Can you make it black-and-white at least? Everyone looks better in black-and-white."

"Black-and-white it is." Hudson winked and held up his phone in selfie mode, then snapped a quick photo. "Okay. Your turn."

"Um . . ." I squinted at myself on his screen, then tightened the bun on the top of my head. "I don't know."

"Jaz." He raised a brow. "You know we have to do this. It's part of the gig."

I glanced down at my coffee. "Why don't I just post a pic of my coffee? People love seeing food."

He smirked. "Not as much as they'd love seeing this gorgeous face." He reached over to tweak my cheek, which immediately flushed.

I usually live for Hudson's upbeat attitude. But right then, I wasn't quite in the headspace for it. "I think I'll stick to the food," I said, taking a photo of my coffee, with the empty churro container next to it.

I was in the middle of adding a caption—*How do you take your coffee? Americano with cream & one pump vanilla is my go-to drink*—when I heard someone clear their throat.

I looked up to find Kelly beside our table. I immediately admired her mustard-striped pantsuit—the perfect shade for Cancún in February.

She smiled. "How's the happy couple?"

"Never better." Hudson put his arm around me as Kelly took a seat. Then, almost immediately, he withdrew it to stand. "Let me get your coffee."

"Oh no, you don't have to do that—"

"I insist. What do you drink?"

Kelly shrugged her shoulders, defeated like most people in

the face of Hudson's relentless politeness. "I'll take a latte. With oat milk if they have it, please. Thank you."

After Hudson got back in line, Kelly scooted her chair closer. "How are you feeling about filming today?"

"Nervous. But good," I replied, with a half-hearted smile.

She hesitated, as though weighing whether her next words were a good idea. "Have you seen any more of Leo since Friday?" she asked softly.

"No." Which was surprising, considering he was staying in our villa along with the rest of the film crew—just as I feared. But so far, our paths hadn't crossed.

The rest of the crew had arrived last night so I hadn't met them yet, though I'd heard them chatting in the adjoining living-room suites.

I did, however, skim the brief Kelly wrote us with everyone's names and photos. I assumed she put that together after the awkward run-in between Leo and me, to make sure there weren't any other unresolved issues among our crew.

Meanwhile, Kelly kept staring at me, as if worried I was about to crack apart.

"There's no need to worry," I said, sounding a lot more confident about that than I actually felt. "I'm totally fine with Leo being our videographer."

Kelly tilted her head, assessing my face. I hoped she didn't pick up on the lie. "Glad to hear it," she finally replied. I couldn't read her, or tell if she bought it.

Right on cue, Hudson arrived to present Kelly with her latte.

"Thank you, Hudson." She glanced at me. "You really landed yourself a good one."

"I know." I linked hands with him as he sat back down.

Kelly took a long sip of her drink, then set it aside to fold her hands on the table. Just then, Jack from Mercer Media arrived and we all stood to greet him. He had the same "I mean business" look splashed across his face as he did when I met him the first night there.

There was something about Jack. A vibe I didn't quite like. Something I didn't quite trust. Lita always told me, when you feel a bad energy, listen to it. Don't ignore it. Pay attention to it.

After about ten minutes of small talk the conversation turned to what we came there for.

"We are very excited to start filming today," Jack said. "The number of app downloads are really impressive. We haven't seen anything quite like this before. People are excited and eagerly awaiting the first episode."

Hudson beamed. He was practically radiating sunlight from his fingertips. My palms, however, started to sweat. I gulped before squeezing Hudson's hand a little tighter, as if to remind myself I wasn't alone in this.

"So. The glam team will be up in your guys' suites in about . . ." Kelly glanced at a dainty gold watch on her wrist, "thirty minutes. As I mentioned in the brief, you each have your own separate team. And, I have to add this disclaimer again: we didn't get you guys glam teams because we think you need them; it's just about getting you camera-ready."

"I'm looking forward to it, actually." I grinned. I mean, who wouldn't want to get their hair and make-up professionally done daily, and have a stylist select outfits and accessories just for you?

"Wait till you see what the fashion designers sent for you guys. I mean, seriously stunning stuff! You can talk it all over with the stylist, but choose whatever you're comfortable with. Same goes for you, Hudson."

"Perfect. Thank you," he replied. I nodded my head in agreement.

"And Jazmine," Jack started. "I'm not sure if you've seen some of the comments, but people are calling you the girl-next-door with a little extra 'spice', That's a *good* response but we want to take that up a notch." Jack folded his hands. "We want you to be the *sexy* girl-next-door. The girl that everybody wants to be. So let the glam team go all out with you. Don't be shy."

I furrowed my brows. *Let the glam team go all out with me? Don't be shy?* I loved the power of make-up and good clothes, and I knew what it was capable of. But I had always been content without all that, too.

This was the second time since I'd met Jack that he'd commented on my appearance. I didn't like it.

I glanced at Kelly, whose jaw was tight and shoulders stiff, a posture that wasn't the norm for her.

"Jazmine," Kelly chimed in, "you just do whatever you're comfortable with—"

"Yes. Of course you need to be comfortable, I wasn't saying that." Jack held up his hand. "I'm just saying that this team of people we hired could make *me* look like a star, for fuck's sake, so just let them do their job."

I didn't even have to look at Kelly to know she was fuming. I could feel her frustration beside me like a blanket of fog.

I knew Jack was her superior with Mercer being *Style&Travel*'s parent company. But I still couldn't believe how he interrupted her. She was the Editor-in-Chief. A woman with years of experience under her belt. It was just . . . rude.

"Anyway." Kelly let out a long breath. "Just so you know, Leonardo and his film crew will be up in your suites to film you both getting ready."

I tugged at the neckline of my sweatshirt, which suddenly felt tight. "Leo will be in there while I'm getting ready?" My voice cracked a little on the word *ready*. Apparently I was going through puberty.

Kelly took another drink of her latte. "Not for all of it, of course. But we definitely want clips of you getting your hair and make-up styled."

"Exactly. People eat that shit up," Jack chimed in. "Is that a problem?"

"Nope. Not a problem. Totally fine. Absolutely fine." I had said the word *fine* so much over the last few days I should've gotten it tattooed on my fucking forehead.

"Great!" Jack smirked. "Then after you're both glammed up, Leo will take you to the first filming spot."

My stomach knotted, and my face clammed like it did whenever I had a fever. Except I wasn't sick. I was scared shitless for the show to begin. My skin burned, and I suddenly wished I had ordered an iced coffee instead of a hot one.

After going over a couple more minor details, we said goodbye to Kelly and Jack and headed back up toward our villa.

"I'll see you in a little bit, love." Hudson gave me a quick peck on the lips, before he went into his room and closed the door behind him. After a moment's hesitation, I stepped into mine.

Seconds later, I heard a knock. Expecting the glam team, I straightened my shoulders before opening it.

"Surprise! I'm here a day early." Gal swept past me, wearing a big beige hat and a long, tropical-patterned dress. Her usually slick straight hair had already gone wavy from the humidity.

At just the sight of her my lip quivered. I barely managed to slam the door shut after her before I put my face in my hands and burst into tears, all my stresses weeping out onto my skin.

Gal's face sank. She put her bag on the ground. "Oh my God, are you okay?"

"I'm fine. I swear, I am," I gulped between sobs. "Things have just been so . . . *stressful.* Seeing you made it all come out."

Gal wrapped me in a tight hug. "It's going to be okay. It's just one week of your life. Before you know it, it'll be over." She leaned back to wipe some tears off my cheeks.

"I know. And I just feel like such an ungrateful bitch even being stressed to be on the show like this, you know? I'm thankful for the opportunity, it's just . . . not something I'm used to."

"It's okay." She grabbed my hand. "You know what Lita always told us: You can have gratitude and still not love your situation. That doesn't make you ungrateful for what you have."

I shook my head as more tears started to stream down my face.

"And who gives a shit that Leo is here! It's kind of perfect, actually."

"How so?" I soaked up the rest of my tears with my sweater sleeve.

"Leo has to film you marrying the sweetest, hottest guy ever, for millions of people to watch. I mean . . . you won, Jaz." She squeezed my shoulders. "You fucking won."

Leo and I had spent our entire childhood competing. Since he had the more stable, visibly successful job, I thought he'd come out on top. But maybe Gal was right. The show. The publicity. The amazing fiancé . . .

Maybe I was the one on top now. *But why didn't that make me feel better?*

"Plus, you guys have been friends your whole life. Maybe working together will allow you two to let this all go. Put the past behind you. You never know?" She tried for a reassuring smile.

I chuckled. "I don't think I could be friends with him." I grabbed a tissue to blow my nose.

"I'm not saying *friends*, I'm just saying *not enemies*. Let bygones be bygones. Move forward in your life with Hudson." Gal handed me another tissue. "Don't give him so much power." She grinned. "So. How have you been otherwise? This resort is incredible."

Gal circled the room, eyes wide, lingering over the walk-in closet, the four-poster bed, the veranda with its sweeping curtains and floor-to-ceiling windows. "Plus this suite is massive!"

"I know. I feel really lucky to be here." I managed a real smile, then. "Also, my 'glam team' is supposed to be here any minute to do my hair and make-up. They're bringing a bunch of clothes designers they want us to wear on the show too."

"Sounds like a fucking dream." Gal picked up her small brown leather bag. I assumed the rest of her luggage must be in her room. Gal was not a light packer. "Well, I'll leave you to it. I've got to go check on Anik, and I have some work to do. PR never sleeps." She winked at me. "But seriously, call me if you need anything. Even just a shoulder to cry on again."

I smiled. "You're amazing, you know that? I don't know how you keep it so together all the time."

"I don't. I have my freak-outs. I'm just better at hiding them." Gal gave me another tight hug before sweeping back out the door.

After Gal left, I wondered how often she'd been hiding those "freak-outs" of hers. I hoped she wasn't hiding one right then.

Minutes later, another knock sounded. This time it actually *was* the glam team. Blue swept inside first—a famous make-up artist I actually recognized, who worked with brands like MAC, NARS, Smashbox, etc., and had a huge following on YouTube and Instagram. He was biracial with brown skin, and long curly hair that was pulled back in a ponytail exposing his shaved head underneath. He wore tight jeans, a Rolling Stones band tee, and lots of jewelry on his wrists and fingers.

Next came a celebrity hairstylist named Celine, decked out in a flowing gold dress that looked like it was straight out of the seventies and perfectly complemented her burgundy-red hair and broad, beautiful curves. Her hoop earrings tickled my cheek as she leaned in to give me an air kiss, careful not to smudge her deep-red lipstick.

"You have such beautiful dark hair," she announced, before even introducing herself.

A fashion stylist named Zoe followed her. According to Kelly's brief, Zoe was a Lebanese-American New Yorker who worked with some of the biggest designers in the world. Zoe wore a beige turban, a long-sleeved black sequin shirt, black leather pants and high heels, along with a silver nose stud. She was perfectly chic, with the softest hands I had ever shaken.

Last to join us was Jared, an assistant. He looked about nineteen and sported whitewashed jeans and a salmon T-shirt, his camel-colored hair cut high and tight. He looked like an escapee from a boy band.

After the introductions, Zoe and Jared left to fetch the clothes. Celine pulled more hair tools than I'd ever seen in one place out of her bag and started plugging them in.

"Why don't you take a seat right there." Blue pointed to the make-up chair he had just set up, with a large mirror in front of it. "I'm going to give you a copper smoky eye today and lots of bronzer and highlighter, to bring out the gold undertones in your skin."

"Sounds good to me." I let out a long breath and relaxed in the seat as Blue started to get to work.

Then, from the corner of my eye, I noticed Leo walk into the room. From the reflection, I could tell he'd donned his typical Leo attire: fitted black shirt, fitted jeans. Wavy hair. Camera in hand.

Air caught in my throat. I kept my gaze fixed on the mirror while he introduced himself to Blue and Celine. But eventually, his gaze found mine in the reflection.

"Hey, Jazmine."

"Hey."

"Wow, *Style&Travel* really pulled out all the stops." He looked around at the trays of eyeshadows, lipsticks, and other make-up items littering the counter.

"I know . . . This is all new territory for me, but I'm loving it."

"Those metallic shadows will look really nice on you," Leo added.

I swallowed, not really sure how to respond to his compliments. I still felt—well, not very fond of him.

"Right?" Blue chimed in. "They'll bring out the honey in her brown eyes."

I felt the heat rise in my body.

Then I thought about what Gal said. Maybe she was right. Maybe we should try and "not be enemies," especially since we'd be spending so much time together this week.

I cleared my throat. "Blue, Celine. Could you give me and Leo a minute, please?"

Leo raised his eyebrows at my request, but didn't comment.

"Of course." Blue hopped out the suite's door, and Celine followed. Now it was just Leo and I, alone in the room.

Suddenly, I became strangely nervous.

"Look." I crossed my arms. Uncrossed them again, fidgeting.

"I know when we first saw each other the other day, it was *weird*. But I just wanted to say, since we're going to be working together—there are no hard feelings on my end. And I was wondering if we could just . . . start over, maybe."

His shoulders softened. "I was actually going to suggest the same thing."

"You were?" I raised a brow.

He smiled. "This is your show, Jazmine. It's your big day." I winced internally at the show name reference. But he sounded sincere. "I just want everything to go smoothly."

My body relaxed a little bit and my arms loosened. "Okay. Well, thank you."

"And Hudson really does seem like a great guy."

"He is." I cleared my throat. "You know, you and I were both so young the last time we hung out. Young and stupid and just *so* dramatic . . ." I tried for a smile. He returned it.

Then Leo straightened, looking me dead in the eye. The air in the room grew cold, filling with tension so thick, not even the sharpest of knives could've cut through it. "You're right. We were young and stupid, Jazmine." His gaze intensified. "It meant nothing."

Chapter Nine

You're right. We were young and stupid, Jazmine. It meant nothing.

I flinched at Leo's words. Meant nothing? Was he referring to our years of friendship or the falling-out we had?

The logical side of my brain reasoned he was most likely referring to our fight (which, even so, would be a shitty thing to say). But the stressed-to-be-filming-a-show part of my brain took it to mean more. I was too on edge to be reasonable.

Maybe our past, our friendship, meant nothing to Leo, but it meant a lot to me. So much so, that I spent years forcing myself to get over it. To forget him. To try to let go of our unique history.

Why did he feel the need to say that?

My resentment started to creep up again. I found myself fighting to keep calm, to stop my blood from boiling over. Suddenly, this friend thing didn't seem like such a good idea after all.

I opened my mouth to say something, already knowing I'd regret it, when someone knocked on the door. "All good to come in?"

"Yes!" Leo answered, a little too quickly. Like he could tell I was ready to blow.

A woman in her mid-twenties entered holding some sort of accent light. She had long purple hair, glowing skin, and a crop top that revealed her tanned torso. Blue and Celine followed her.

"Jazmine, this is Esmeralda," Leo said. "She's one of my filming assistants. Mateo and Rex, my two other assistants, are in Hudson's room."

"Esmeralda. Nice," I said, way too loudly. *Nice?* I suddenly had the vocabulary of a frat boy.

"Good to meet you." Esmeralda smiled and shook my hand, then sauntered toward Leo. My eyes couldn't tear away from her. She was alluring. Sexy.

"Hey, I have to show you something," Esmeralda said to Leo and she pulled her phone out of her back pocket and played a video. They leaned against each other, laughing at whatever was on the screen.

I tried to ignore them, as Celine started curling my hair and Blue started to apply my blush.

But I couldn't help being curious. *What was going on between them?* I mean, the girl was gorgeous. I'm sure Leo was attracted to her. And based on her body language, she was clearly attracted to him. Were they work buddies? Work buddies who were fucking? Dating? I couldn't tell.

After Leo and Esmeralda wrapped up their mundane flirt session, they set up a light and camera on a stand in front of me, while the last of my hair and make-up was being applied. I glanced at the camera and noticed a red light.

Is it filming right now?

"Just ignore it," Leo said, practically reading my thoughts. "It will just be some B-roll."

"B-roll? What the hell is that?"

Esmeralda smiled, then bit her bottom lip. "Just some

behind-the-scenes-type footage with music added. No talking or anything like that. It's often used as filler, or for credit sequences."

I glanced at Leo.

"She's right. Just act like the camera's not there."

Wish I could act like *he* wasn't there. I bit my tongue on the retort, and tried my best to look natural.

How did I normally sit? Where did my hands go? Did I always grimace this much? I practically stared myself down in the mirror, willing myself to relax.

When Zoe and Jared returned with the clothes, I realized that Kelly had not exaggerated when she said there were tons of amazing pieces. There was everything from Prada, Dolce & Gabbana, Versace, Carolina Herrera, Oscar de la Renta . . . The list went on and on.

Zoe held up a short dress in classic blue, like a sapphire. It looked to be satin, with intricate buttons in the back. "What about this one?" she asked. "Feels very Cancún chic to me."

My eyes widened. The dress was stunning, but I wasn't sure if I could fit into it. "It's really pretty, but looks like it might be a little small for me? I don't usually wear things too tight."

Zoe pursed her lips. "You're about to be on camera, honey. The tighter the better. At least try it on." Zoe handed me the dress and motioned toward the bathroom.

Then, I thought about what Jack said: "Don't be shy" and "Take things up a notch." Jack was clearly a prick, but if I wanted this show to succeed to the point where I could be getting job offers left and right, did I need to start playing the game?

I accepted the hanger. "All right. I'll try it on," I said, before making my way to the bathroom.

I wasn't lying when I said the dress was small. I had to

wriggle just to get it over my hips, and hold my breath to button the thing.

It was short, and extremely fitted, practically painted on. Certainly not something I would pick for myself. I was hoping for casual, flowing dresses. Something you could slip in and out of between diving into the ocean.

This was . . . not that.

Still, I would admire anyone with the guts to wear this little number. I wasn't in love with it, but I had the sneaking suspicion that Zoe was going to push for it.

When I returned to the main room, I spotted Leo sitting on the couch with Esmeralda, laughing again. But he stopped the instant his gaze found mine.

His eyes sparked. Like he was examining the most intricate sky above and all of its shades, strokes, and colors.

His gaze stayed glued to me as I took slow, self-conscious steps into the room.

Everyone else stared too, even Esmeralda, who grinned in approval. At that moment, I started to think I might like her. But I couldn't stop stealing glances at Leo, watching him watch my every movement.

And suddenly, it was a no-brainer. If this dress could make Leo stop in his tracks, then maybe it *was* a good choice.

Yeah, keep looking. Keep looking at the woman you will never have a chance with again.

"Oh my God, Jazmine," Zoe breathed. "See? That dress is amazing on you. Hugs your body in all the right places."

"It really does look amazing." Blue clapped his hands.

Celine and Jared nodded. I looked over again at Leo, wondering if he was going to say something.

He didn't speak, but his inability to look away spoke for itself. Then Hudson walked in, and Leo ripped his gaze from mine.

"Hudson, great, you're here!" Leo practically shouted, hurrying in his direction.

Hudson looked even more handsome than usual, which I didn't think possible. His stylist had put him in a crisp white shirt tucked into black slacks. The sleeves were rolled up not far from his elbows, and accented with silver compass cufflinks. His hands were covered in unfamiliar rings, though among them I still spotted the coordinates ring I gave him. His hair was pulled back in a sleeker than usual bun, and his facial hair had been perfectly groomed to fit his face.

"Yep. I'm here." Hudson laughed. Then his eyes widened as he caught a glimpse of me. "Wow. Jaz. You look absolutely incredible." Hudson strode my way, gently cupping my chin before giving me a light kiss on the lips that sent a flurry of chills down my spine.

"Thank you," I replied quietly. "You don't look so bad yourself." I lingered there, our faces inches apart.

Until Leo spoke up. "That's perfect. Stay right there another second . . ."

My cheeks flared as I realized a camera was pointed at us. I ducked away from Hudson on instinct. Leo groaned, but I ignored him.

This was just B-roll, right? Warm-up.

"Wait," Zoe called, before I could duck very far away. "We have to add some jewelry."

I tugged at my Indalo bracelet and then at my ampersand necklace. I hadn't taken it off since Hudson gifted it to me, and I've had my bracelet since I was a teen. I wasn't ready to part with either of them, even for the show. "Any jewelry you want to add is fine, but I'd like to keep this bracelet and necklace on," I told her.

Hudson's grin doubled in size.

Zoe pursed her lips, then nodded. "Okay. I'll go for some white-gold earrings and bangles to match it."

After Zoe accessorized me with more jewelry, Leo introduced Hudson to Esmeralda and me to Mateo and Rex, his other two crew members. Mateo looked to be in his mid-twenties just like Esmeralda. I liked his bomber jacket and Converse. He seemed chill.

Rex then waved in my direction and I waved back. He looked to be in his late twenties like me, and he had a hipster side buzzcut and tattoos covering every inch of skin on his arms and neck.

They both seemed nice enough.

"So here's how it's going to go," Leo started. "Me and my crew will be following you guys around while Kelly and/or Jack puts you through your paces. I will be operating the main camera, A, and Mateo will be operating Camera B for different angles. Rex, my sound guy, will have a boom mic, and Esmeralda will be in charge of lights for indoor filming and reflectors for outdoor filming. In addition to action sequences, there will also be some 'talking head' portions, where I ask you questions on camera. None of this will be done in any particular order, to keep the most natural flow to your day possible."

Like any of this was natural. I stifled a worried frown.

"Once we have the footage, I will edit it according to the Mercer guidelines. Does that all make sense?"

Hudson and I nodded, although I had to resist the urge to ask about the phrase "talking head." Is it weird I pictured a disembodied floating head when he said that?

"Let's start with the talking-head sequence now." Leo glanced around the room. "Why don't you guys take a seat over there on that couch? Esmeralda, why don't you get some reflectors to capture the natural sunlight from the window, and a ring light on their faces. Rex, lapel mics?"

Everyone jumped into action.

I followed Hudson over to the couch. My palms started to sweat. I could feel my heart start to race. My chest tightened. Rex came up beside Hudson first and pinned a small mic to his shirt, with a chord that ran under his collar to a small pack that got clipped on the back of his pants.

Hudson seemed familiar with the process, but I couldn't help but think about where the hell that pack was going to fit on my tight dress.

"Okay if I attach this?" Rex held up the mic, and I nodded. Gently, he fixed it to the outer neckline of my dress, then passed me the wire attached. "Put this down the front of your dress, all right? We can hang the pack inside the skirts. I can talk you through it if you need help."

"I've got it, thanks," I replied, grateful I would be the one putting stuff down my own dress. I slid the wire down the bodice, ignoring the way it tickled my belly, and turned toward Hudson, who helped shield me for a moment while I fished the end of the wire out of my skirt to plug it in. I tucked the battery box under my thigh for the time being.

"Just so you're aware, whenever the light on the battery pack is on, we could be recording your audio," Rex explained. "We'll take the mics off at the end of each filming day, but there's a switch on the side to turn it off if you're ever somewhere where you need more . . . privacy."

I assumed he meant the restroom and such. Always recording our audio. Not creepy at all, Mercer Media. "Good to know," I said.

By the time we finished with the lapel mics, Esmeralda had finished lighting, and Leo turned the camera on.

Maybe it was the lights or maybe it was my nerves, but suddenly the room felt like a hot box. I could feel the beginnings of sweat forming on my skin.

"Hudson, why don't you introduce yourself to the camera. Tell us your name, where you're from, what you do, your favorite hobby, food . . . things like that. Ready?"

Hudson nodded and looked directly into the camera, megawatt smile turned up to a hundred. "Hi. I'm Hudson Taylor. You may recognize me from my outdoor adventures and travel expeditions, which I chronicle online. I'm from Toronto, Canada, and my all-time favorite hobby is snowboarding. My favorite food is Canadian pizza, which I know sounds cliché, but don't knock it until you try it. I have a cat named Garfield—"

"Wait," Leo interrupted, eyebrows shooting up. "You have a cat? How does that work?" He stared at me.

My face flushed. Of course Leo would remember my throat-closing-level cat allergy at the most awkward moment. Leo was allergic to cats too.

Hudson looped an arm around my shoulders in response. "Jazmine's actually never been to my place in Toronto, because of Garfield. After we get married, my parents will adopt him."

Leo tilted his head, frowning. "You've never been to his place? How long have you guys been together?"

I glared at him. "Is this relevant?" I grumbled, but Hudson elbowed me and nodded almost imperceptibly toward the cameras. Right. They're filming. I cleared my throat and pretended this was a normal interviewer. Not Leo, staring us down, judging me. Judging *us*. "We've been together for a year and almost nine months now." I gave the camera a huge smile. "That may not seem like a lot of time, but not everyone plays the on-again-off-again hot-and-cold-for-a-million-years game before they decide to get engaged."

Shit. I was verbal vomiting again. Aggressively, in fact. But Leo always did know how to push my buttons. And I knew how to hit his back.

Everyone in the room had gone dead silent. Filming was off to a great start.

After a moment's pause, Leo shook off his annoyance with visible effort. "Okay, Jazmine, it's your turn. Same as Hudson. Something like 'Hi, I'm Jazmine Prado, a journalist and aspiring social media star from Los Angeles, California. My family is Spanish-Moroccan from Marbella, Spain. I like cheap American nachos and way-too-sweet cocktails . . .' You know, stuff like that." He glared in my direction and followed it with a lopsided grin.

My stomach jumped. I hated that Leo knew so much about me. And also how to piss me off. And "aspiring social media star"? Really? I was inwardly screaming.

"Whenever you're ready," he prompted.

I looked at the lens. The clamminess came in full force. I opened my mouth, but no words would come out. Instead, I felt acid rising in my throat.

The lights suddenly felt brighter than peak Cancún sun. The couch beneath me felt like it was moving. Swaying back and forth like a cruise ship in the middle of the sea.

"Um." I blinked. I felt like I was moments away from a panic attack. Then I closed my eyes to ignore the camera. "Does everyone have to be in here? Could it just be the camera, or the camera and you, if you have to prime us with the questions? No offense, uh, everyone," I added. Luckily I couldn't see all of their facial expressions with the lights blinding me.

Leo scratched his chin. "Yeah, we could make that happen—"

"No." Hudson rubbed my shoulder. "That's all right, nobody needs to leave." He bent closer to me, and took my shaky hands in his. "Jazmine. It's going to be an entire week of this. You might as well face your fear head on. You can do this. Before you know it, you'll forget anyone is even here."

"People can leave. It's really not that big of a deal," Leo tried.

"Nah, man, it's fine." Hudson squeezed my hands. "Jazmine's got this. You do."

At this point, I wanted to crawl under the couch and hide. If it wasn't bad enough that I was on the verge of passing out, now my fiancé had to give me a pep talk in front of everybody.

I was completely out of my element.

"How about this," Leo chimed in. "Don't worry about saying anything specific. Just tell the camera whatever comes to mind. Like you did a few minutes ago responding to Hudson."

When I insulted you, you mean? I thought, but didn't say aloud.

"Okay." I took a deep breath and looked at Hudson. He flashed me two big thumbs up.

I forced my gaze back to the camera. *You can do this. You're totally fine.* "Hi, I'm Jazmine Prado. Some people call me Jaz, or Jazzy, in the case of my family." From the corner of my eye, I noticed Leo smirk.

I started to relax, just a little. "I'm a writer from L.A. I like to read, watch bad TV, and listen to cheesy pop music. My family is from Spain and Casablanca but are now mostly in Marbella. They're Spanish-Moroccan, yet I hardly speak any Spanish, so there's that. I'm pretty sure my grandparents secretly judge the hell out of me for it. I'm a Scorpio sun with a Taurus moon, born on a full moon. Oh. And I've also written a lot of articles over the years. I want to write a book one day, maybe even about vampires, who knows." I tapered off, my head starting to throb. "Is that good enough? Can I be done now?" I laughed nervously.

Although I was still somewhat blinded by the lights in front of me, I could make out Leo's eyes clearly. They were locked on the ceiling. When he finally looked back at me, his expression took me aback.

He almost looked . . . *sad*. Regretful. Not annoyed or upset anymore. There was just a vague sense of sorrow in the turn of his mouth.

He can't be sad over this . . . This must be all in my head.

"Yeah. That was great." His voice came out thick, too. "You can be done now."

I practically leapt off the couch. Hudson lingered to chat with the crew about the lights they were using, and the settings on the mics. As for me, I sprinted for the bathroom, my usual retreat whenever a bout of introversion hit.

In there, I turned off the lapel mic and gulped a few deep breaths of air, trying to calm my spinning mind. I wound up staying in the bathroom until Zoe knocked softly and told me the film crew were asking for me.

Outside, Hudson took my hand, and we followed Leo and the crew downstairs. In the lobby, Kelly waited with Jack.

"Jazmine, wow! You look wonderful!" Jack said as we approached. "That's exactly what I was talking about. Taking things up a notch." He gave me a thumbs up.

I clenched my fists. If my career wasn't in jeopardy, I would have flipped him off right there. I looked at Kelly whose lips were in a hard line. She let out a long breath, staying silent for most likely the same reason I did. I wondered in that moment how many other women under the Mercer Media umbrella had been forced to stay silent around Jack rather than risk losing their jobs or not being taken seriously.

Kelly explained how the rest of the day was going to go. Fittings. Wedding planning. All for the cameras, as we had already done most of the real fittings and planning beforehand.

As Kelly continued to go over our schedule, I noticed Esmeralda pulling at Leo's arm. She whispered something in his ear, and giggled. Leo cracked a small smile.

What's their story?

I stopped myself before the thought grew. *Doesn't matter. It's none of my business.* But I would love the most updated info. I was a journalist, after all.

"Why don't we start by heading down to the beach? We can get some shots of Jazmine and Hudson walking and holding hands," Kelly suggested.

As we all followed Kelly across the lawns, I pulled back a little to walk beside Leo, while he made adjustments to his camera.

"Thanks," I murmured. "For pissing me off just enough to get me to talk back there."

He managed a half-grin. "What are almost-friends-again for?"

I pressed my lips together, mostly to suppress the smile that threatened to rise up. *Remember your grudge, Jazmine.* Then my gaze drifted to Esmeralda, walking up ahead of us and chatting to Mateo.

"So," I said quietly. "What's with you two?"

Leo glanced at me. "We work together. We're friends."

"Just friends. Like you and I were?" I raised a brow.

"No. Not *those* kind of friends." He smirked.

My face burned hot. "So not the kind of friends who spend their young lives together, which apparently means nothing?"

Shit. I clapped a hand over my mouth. Something about being in Leo's presence in Cancún made my filter become obsolete. It seemed I hadn't gotten much better at that "think before you speak" thing. *Get your shit together.*

Leo's gaze found mine. "You know what I think, Jazmine?"

With an effort, I lowered my hand. "What's that?"

"I think you have a lot of bitterness toward me. Which is ironic. You know, considering."

"Considering what, exactly?"

Our eyes stayed locked. Mine narrowed as we both waited to see who was going to make the next move. It was like a really fucked-up game of chess.

"Hey, Jaz," Hudson called, knocking us out of our stare session. "Over here." Hudson was already barefoot near the shore. "Let's walk this way, against the sunlight."

"Great idea!" Leo yelled back. "Your husband's got a good eye for this stuff."

"Future husband," I clarified. "And yes, he's good with cameras. That's why he's got all those millions of followers," I said, proudly.

Leo chuckled. "Yeah, I'm sure all the shirtless shots of his six-pack have nothing to do with it. And I'm sure that's not what drew you to him either."

If I'd been glaring daggers at Leo before, now I glared swords. Was he really questioning my relationship? Was he really acting like I was that shallow?

But if he wanted to make this about Hudson's looks, we could make this about Hudson's looks.

"You know what, I have an idea." I grinned. "Hudson!" I jogged a few paces toward him. "I'm thinking for this shot, you should take your shirt off? Let's give the people what they want." I turned back to gauge Leo's expression. Sure enough, he was full-on glaring at me now. "This could be a nice touch, right? Since this is all anyone, including me, wants from Hudson, apparently," I added in a lower, dangerous voice. One Hudson couldn't hear.

Behind me, Hudson (who was never shy about displaying

his body) was more than happy to oblige. And I was more than happy to run my hands all over his perfectly chiseled abs and pecs in front of Leo.

I savored one last look of Leo's pure, unadulterated anger, before I took my fiancé's hand and strode off down the beach. Halfway to the water, Hudson picked me up and spun me around in the air, like I was light as a feather. I laughed, and my hair went wild, flying around both our faces.

The sun shone behind us, a bright yellow disk in an otherwise spotless blue sky. The waves crashed along the shore, the soundtrack to our romance movie. When he set me down again, it was slow, my body melting down his, until my bare feet touched sand. Then he tilted up my chin and went in for a kiss. But not just any kiss. The kind you'd see in a movie. Slow. Synchronized. Perfect.

He cupped my face between his palms, like I was delicate, breakable. He kissed me softly at first, our mouths moving in unison. You would've thought a symphony was playing somewhere in the background.

I kissed him back, harder, and for a moment was able to forget about the cameras and our audience. All I felt was the sand between my toes, all I tasted were Hudson's lips, his breath minty fresh. I smelled hot sand and salt water, and a breeze kicked up, blew my hair around his face once again.

I could have stayed there for ever.

Then we drew apart, and I remembered them all, staring at us. Silent, observant.

My whole body flushed this time.

Hudson certainly knew how to put on a show. Still, despite how weird it felt to have an audience, I couldn't help feeling a vicious kind of glee at Leo having to watch this.

I stared up at Hudson, wide-eyed and smiling, as the

cameras circled around. Then I glanced over, and caught something new in Leo's eyes. A look I hadn't seen in a long time.

A look of hurt. *Pain*. A pain I've felt before. A pain I was too familiar with.

It was the pain of a bruised soul. Of a broken heart. Of a shattered dream.

But I knew that look in particular on Leo. It was the same look on his face the last time we saw each other. When our fight broke us apart.

Suddenly, I felt a pang of guilt. Parading Hudson in front of Leo didn't feel so satisfying anymore. I was acting like the worst version of myself, and swimming in a sea of my own remorse.

And that was when I realized. Leo might have said our past meant nothing. But he was lying.

He was trying to hide the fact that it meant so much to him, too.

Chapter Ten

Gal and I sat next to each other on a couch in her suite in our plush white La Belladonna robes. Together we hovered over her tablet, watching the first episode of *Our Big Day*, which had just posted about an hour ago.

It felt surreal to watch myself on screen. That woman looked like someone else, her life a stranger's life. The dress. The make-up. The lighting. The brilliant angling of the camera. Not to mention my voice, which sounded like somebody else's to my ears.

Yet as I watched, I couldn't help picking up on how well the camera had done catching my good angles. Beside me, Gal must have noticed too. She nudged my elbow. "You look so *gorgeous*, Jaz."

My face flushed, and I sank lower in her plush, velvety couch. Her room at the villa a few rows farther back from the beach wasn't quite as large as mine or Hudson's, but it still had every amenity. Big floor-to-ceiling windows, a four-poster bed draped in gauzy white curtains. And most importantly, room service.

I plucked another churro from the tray we'd ordered to accompany our little viewing party. "This is so weird. I barely even remember saying all that."

On screen, I was talking about how Hudson and I met at a charity event in Malibu and how we went to get In-N-Out Burger afterwards and ate animal fries in the back of his rental truck. I was smiling, happy. But my eyes looked a little dead. Or maybe frightened.

I hoped no one else noticed.

Thankfully, the scene soon cut to us striding along the beach. The camera zoomed in as Hudson and I gazed into each other's eyes. There was something about the angle, the attention to detail, that told me—Leo filmed that part. There was no way it was Camera B.

We leaned in for a kiss, and I could practically feel Leo's emotions through the scene. Beside me, Gal had frozen with a flaky, perfectly baked oreja halfway to her mouth, staring. I sank into Hudson's arms as he picked me up, spun me in a circle, our lips connected.

When he set me back on my feet, Gal let out a breathless laugh. "Jesus. You two are so hot together. And damn, you know people everywhere are wishing they were you right now?"

But all I could focus on were the camera angles. The romantic way the sun hit the lens, and how the screen trailed us as we strode across the sand dunes toward the waves. It zoomed in on our clasped hands, lingered like a nostalgic lover, pining for the good old days.

It was my relationship, and watching it gave *me* butterflies.

As the episode ended I let out a long breath.

Millions of people just watched personal moments between me and my fiancé. They watched him kiss me, hold my hand, talk about where and how we met. How he felt about me.

As beautiful as the video was, I felt incredibly exposed. Naked.

"That was like watching a modern-day fucking fairy tale.

Well done." Gal finally bit into her oreja, then groaned. Whether it was at my romantic life or her pastry, I couldn't be sure. She washed the bite down with a sip of coffee, and flashed me a grin. "You guys really look like the perfect couple. Such natural chemistry. Everyone's going to love you two!"

"I wouldn't be so sure . . ." I said, still hung up on the comments section. I'd made the mistake of skimming it again when I was opening up the video.

It wasn't *entirely* bad. One viewer even said they'd named my coffee drink (an Americano with heavy whipping cream and one pump of vanilla) The Jazmine at the coffee shop they owned. That was flattering.

But there was a new favorite topic of conversation in the comments: my heritage.

I thought she was Mexican or Armenian or Italian or something. Any of those would be more interesting than Spanish-Moroccan or whatever she is, no offense.

If her family is from Spain, she should just say she is Spanish-American. No need to add the Moroccan. No one gives a shit.

And my personal favorite: *Go back to your own country.*

The U.S. *was* my country. I'm the proud daughter of immigrants. The internet was such a fun place.

People were still criticizing my looks too, of course, noting that my dress looked practically painted on, etc. But due to all that make-up and professional lighting, there weren't as many "Shouldn't Hudson be with a goddess?" comments. God bless the glam team. Goes to show you that with the right stuff, you can look otherworldly.

"You know," Gal continued with a wicked grin, "Leo really did a great job. He must've been bawling like a baby by the end of editing that footage."

I almost choked mid-churro. "You think?"

She raised her brows, perfectly shaped as always. "Are you kidding? People dream of revenge like this." Gal poured us another cup of coffee from the French press room service provided.

"I thought you said we should try to be friends." I took a careful sip, wishing for some vanilla flavoring. "Revenge doesn't seem very friendly."

"Being friendly doesn't mean you can't enjoy this turn of events. It's not like you *planned* this level of vengeance. It just happened. Plus, you're a Scorpio. Shouldn't you be living for revenge like this?"

"Leo's a Scorpio too."

"Exactly. Which makes it even better. Scorpios feel so fucking deeply, they can dish out revenge but they can't take it."

"True." I let out a quiet laugh. "Still. I don't think Leo cares enough to be bawling like a baby." I reached for one of the orejas. The crunchy cinnamon and sugar cookie paired perfectly with coffee, and was even better dipped in it.

"Maybe not." Gal shrugged. "But I'm sure editing footage of you and Hudson wasn't the happiest day of his life."

Suddenly, Leo's face at the beach came to haunt me once more. A look of sadness and pain that I'd seen at various points throughout our youth. A look that used to make me invite him over so we could spend the evening watching movies and eating cereal, talking about all the colors in the sky that day.

A look that made me realize that what happened with us meant a lot to him, regardless of what he claimed. A look that filled me with remorse.

My stomach soured. Suddenly the coffee and orejas didn't settle so well as the guilt of parading Hudson in front of Leo, coupled with memories of my verbal vomit, replayed in my mind. It was childish. And absurd. And unkind. If he wanted to be snarky to me, fine. But I needed to be better.

"Maybe we should go a little easier on Leo," I suggested, pulling at a loose string on my robe.

Gal froze mid-sip, then slowly lowered her coffee cup. "Wait a minute. You've spent years furious at Leo. And now, when you finally have the perfect revenge right at your fingertips, you want to go easy on him? Pray tell."

I shrugged. "Like you said, let bygones be bygones, right?"

Gal raised her brows. "Really." She took another sip. "Wow. So no more hating on Leo. Who are you and what have you done with my cousin?"

I rolled my eyes. "Have I really been that bad?"

"I mean, we've only been plotting his demise for seven years, that is, when I was even allowed to speak of him in your presence. So no, I guess you haven't been *that* bad."

I laughed, grabbing at one of the couch's pillows and putting it on my lap. "Hey. I have a question. Do you think I hurt him as badly as he hurt me?"

"What do you mean?"

I exhaled, shifting in my seat. "All this time I've been stuck on how much Leo hurt me. I mean, I knew we hurt each other, but I always thought what he did was worse, I was more betrayed . . . You know us, always competing." I laughed softly, unable to tear my gaze from the pillow in my lap. "But there was this look in his eye yesterday at the beach. It made me wonder if maybe he's been just as hurt. By me."

Gal sat her cup on the table. "Well, you did turn him down when he wanted to date you in high school. Then you made a marriage pact with him as a back-up plan."

"It wasn't a back-up plan! We were about to leave for college. I just wanted to focus on my career first and foremost." *And you thought he'd be there waiting when you finished doing that,* whispered a little voice at the back of my head.

I ignored it.

Gal ignored my protest, too. "*Then* after all of that, you turned him down again on your twenty-first birthdays."

"I didn't—" I started, but she cut across me.

"You gave him an ultimatum. Told him your relationship was over if he left. Which by the way, he shouldn't have left, but that's not the point. Then," she kept going, "after he left to pick up Elizabeth, you never reached out to fix it even though you guys had been best friends since first grade—"

I opened my mouth to speak but Gal got the jump on me again.

"Yeah, yeah. I know he didn't reach out to fix things either. I mean, fuck! You two are both so damn stubborn! But you told him it was over. And you never made an effort to seek him out or make things right . . . Shall I go on?"

A lump formed in my throat. I swallowed hard around it, blinking back the sting in my eyes. Gal didn't know that Leo actually did reach out to try to fix things.

She didn't know about the letter he put in my car. And how I didn't get it until a few days later. And how I saw him kissing Elizabeth in front of the coffee shop, his lips consuming hers with fire and passion and sensuality. And how watching that happen before my eyes bruised every inch of my soul.

I never told anyone about it. Even Gal, my closest confidant. Because it cuts too deep.

I looked over at my cousin, who was staring in my direction, waiting for my reply. "All right, I get it. I have to own my part in it. And I was shitty to him."

She let out a long breath. "Look, we've all done shitty things. You have, I have, Leo has. He isn't innocent in this either! He fucked up too! No one has *not* done shitty things at some point. We're all just human." Gal reached over to pat my hand. Reluctantly, I turned it palm up to squeeze hers back. She smiled at me. "All I'm saying is, you and Leo both hurt each other. But if push comes to shove, I'd still pick you in this fight, because you are my favorite person ever. That's also why I'm speaking truth right now," she added with a wink. "You can't speak lies to your favorite person."

I mustered up my best smile. It felt weak, but it was a start.

"And you know, oftentimes the people we love the most have a way of leaving the biggest scars." Gal let go of my hand to stretch and reach for her coffee once more.

My body stiffened. "I don't love Leo."

Gal sighed. "But you did. And he loved you. A lot. There's no need to keep acting like that didn't happen."

My breath caught in my throat. I was more comfortable in denial. I had built a home in it. I wasn't sure if I was ready to move out just yet.

"Just remember." Gal took another sip of her coffee. "We're down here in Cancún for your wedding, not some soul-searching retreat. Yes, there's some unfinished business in regard to Leo that you need to work through. But there's no need to get hung up on this stuff now."

She was right. But it seemed that "soul-searching" my past served as a nice distraction from my reality web show present.

At the moment, I had more change in my life than I did normalcy. And I've never done well with rapid change.

Still, I appreciated Gal's honesty. "Thank you for speaking truth." I grinned. "I couldn't handle life without you, honestly."

She leaned in for a quick hug, which made me relax, just a little. Gal had always had that calming effect on me.

"Even though you're a true pain in my ass, I couldn't handle life without you either." She grabbed the French press and topped off her cup with the last of it. "Fuck Leo. Fuck Hudson. Fuck Anik, for that matter. Our bond as family is for life."

I smiled, and this time it was effortless.

Gal grabbed at another churro. "You excited for the dinner tonight?"

"I am. A little nervous, too. You know, our fam and Hudson's have never met before. His parents seem very . . . well, nice, but reserved. Just promise me you'll keep an eye on my mom and Lita Durán because you know they like to start shit. It is one of your duties as maid of honor."

We kept the bridal party simple. Just a maid of honor and a best man—Hudson's younger brother, Hunter. A bunch of bridesmaids and groomsmen felt unnecessary.

"I'll do my best." Gal laughed. "But let's be real, those two are not easy to keep an eye on."

Never had one of Gal's truths ever been more accurate. I fired her an only half-apologetic grin. "Which is why you're the only one I can trust to do it."

She raised her churro like a toast, then hesitated, her gaze darting to the clock behind the wall. "Oh. You gotta go. Pretty sure the film crew will be hunting for you any minute now."

My stomach tensed once more, the coffee and churro swirling uncomfortably. She was right. We'd gotten a bit of a break this morning—no prep until the afternoon. But afternoon started in a few minutes, which meant it was time to face the music again.

Chapter Eleven

The long walk back to my own suite left my brain with more than enough time to run over everything Gal and I talked about. And in the midst of an over-thinking rabbit trail, I realized I hadn't heard from Hudson all morning. Not since I texted him after I woke up to his bedside note, saying he was going to a secret Cancún spot to get some videos and photos for his socials. That was hours ago.

I shot him another quick text, just a hello. Minutes went by. No reply. No sign he'd even received it.

I usually wasn't one to worry, but sometimes Hudson's daredevil-ish stunts he did for video content were a little too risky for my taste. I hoped he was okay. I hoped he was being safe.

It's fine, I told myself. *He's totally okay.*

I shook my head and let myself into my suite, expecting a barrage from the hair and make-up team. Instead, I found the rooms empty.

A little worried now, I strode across the hallway to knock at Hudson's door. No reply there either, and no noise from inside.

Maybe they went to shoot some B-roll elsewhere, I reassured myself.

Back in my own suite, I took a long shower, figuring someone would interrupt me if I was needed. But no one did. By the time I finished and threw on my robe, it was already 12:54 p.m.

Maybe I should check in with someone?

Just as I went to write Kelly a text, I heard a knock at the door. I perked up and hurried toward it, hoping for Hudson.

Instead, I opened the door to find Blue, Celine, Zoe, and Jared on the other side. To judge by the way their smiles dropped, I guessed my expression said it all. I was happy to see some familiar faces, but they weren't the one I wanted right now.

"How are you today, Miss Jazmine?" Blue asked, eyeing me a little too closely.

He had on a similar garb as the day before, but this time he'd swapped out his Rolling Stones tee for a vintage Bon Jovi one and he wore his curly, long hair down that day. He also had on black eyeliner, which looked pretty great framing his brown eyes.

"I'm good. How are you guys doing?" My voice cracked, but no one commented. They really were professionals.

"We're good," Blue answered as the rest of them started piling inside. Zoe rolled in new clothing racks and started shuffling through the garments. Celine started lining up her hair products on my vanity, and Jared lugged in a couple boxes full of accessories.

"Still not over the first episode," Celine gushed. "You looked absolutely fabulous. You and Hudson are just the perfect couple!"

I gulped as the sourness in my stomach returned. Just what I needed—a reminder of how many people watched me on screen. Of how many more would watch me again when the next episode dropped.

"Thanks," I managed, tugging at the hem of my robe. "But I can't take credit for the fabulousness. I swear, you people are magicians."

From her corner by the clothing rack, Zoe huffed. "Don't sell yourself short, babe."

"Although we *are* good at what we do, aren't we?" Blue interjected with a wink.

I laughed. "I'd say so."

"So, we talked about it and we came up with the best look for you tonight." Blue clapped his hands. To judge by the light in his eyes, I was either going to love or hate this next suggestion. He glanced past me at Celine. "We're going to go total retro."

Celine grinned. "I'll be giving you some big, loose curls . . ."

"And I've got a forties-style dress for you—super elegant, super chic . . . Pure perfection," Zoe added.

"Speaking of which . . . Jared?" Blue snapped a finger at their assistant. "We need that dress steamed ASAP."

While Jared leapt to do his bidding, Blue turned back and reached out to gently lift a stray strand of hair from my forehead and brush it back, studying me the way I imagined an artist would study a canvas.

"I'm going to give you the classic: winged eyeliner, red lip. Very glamorous. Golden era of Hollywood. It's going to be absolutely stunning."

"I even found these beautiful diamond earrings you can wear to match your necklace and bracelet," Zoe spoke up.

My eyes lit up. I really appreciated the way they were willing to work with my specifics. To let me hold on to some piece of myself throughout all this, at least.

"Sounds great," I replied, and I meant it. But as I toyed with the necklace in question, I couldn't help thinking about the one who gave it to me. Hudson. *Why hadn't I heard from him?* The seed of worry inching up my skin was starting to grow. I hoped everything was okay.

Almost at that instant, my phone buzzed, and a familiar name lit up the screen. Finally.

Sorry I'm just texting you now, love. Spent the morning on a scuba dive and then I had to edit the pics for my social. Phone died right after posting, it was a whole thing. Back at my suite getting ready now. Can't wait to see you soon!

I frowned, trying not to let my frustration show too prominently. He had time to edit video and post it to his social media channels, but didn't have a quick second to let me know he was okay?

I had come to find Hudson's constant social media posting endearing. But in that moment, I found it annoying as fuck.

I let out a slow breath, trying to calm my racing heart rate. *This is normal*, I told myself. *It's normal to get a little irked with someone when you're planning a big event with them . . .*

But a little voice inside my head kept telling me: this was how it would always be. Hudson putting his online image first. He needed to, it was his job, I understood that. I admired it. My career was my life too.

Still . . .

"Is Leo going to be up to film you getting ready?" Celine asked, distracting me from my irritation.

When I looked up, I caught her cheeks flushing almost as red as her crimson polka dot dress.

"I'm not sure . . ." I cleared my throat.

You and Leo both hurt each other, Gal's words played back in my ear. I wondered how he'd be when I saw him. How he'd be after a night of editing romantic footage of me and Hudson.

Sad? Distant? Over it? I wasn't sure.

How would I feel, if it were me in his shoes? My stomach reeled. I couldn't go down that thought path. The guilt would be too much.

"Oh, I hope he comes by," Zoe was saying. She smiled the biggest smile, her teeth so white they almost blinded me. "He's just so . . . *mysterious.*"

Mysterious? It took me a lot of effort not to snort. I pressed my lips together to suppress it.

I had never thought of Leo as mysterious. Perplexing, sure. Layered, yes. But mysterious? Not so much.

Maybe that was just because I knew him so well.

"He makes me so nervous," Celine added, her cheeks getting more rosy by the minute.

"Same. I saw him once at an art event in New York. He was staring at the art, all brooding . . . Jesus, is it hot in here?" Zoe waved a hand in front of her face, then shrugged off her cropped leather jacket and adjusted the emerald-colored turban on her head. "He's the kind of guy who could make me okay with disappointing my parents by dating someone who's not Lebanese. Though, I'm not sure what he is. And anyway, probably a moot point, I think he's with that film assistant."

"He's not. I asked him," I chimed in. "And he's half-Mexican, half-French."

Everybody stopped what they were doing. Even Jared, who had just returned from steaming the dress.

Zoe tilted her head. "You guys are friends?"

"Um, yeah." I shrugged. "We're friends." I was using the

word *friend* loosely. But I didn't think I needed to give them the whole history. Not then, anyway.

"Do you know what sign he is?" Celine asked. "My Virgo self is dying to know."

"Scorpio with a Pisces moon," I quickly replied. "He's got a lot of water in his birth chart." Completely opposite of Hudson's birth chart, which was all fire.

"Ooh . . ." Celine's eyes sparked. "No wonder he's so mysterious. So he's sensitive and artsy."

"Yes. And also athletic," I added. "He played soccer in college, at UCLA."

Zoe raised her brows. "Any idea what his type is?"

"Is he into redheads?" Celine butted in.

"Or dudes?" Blue said, followed by a snicker.

I laughed. "To be honest, I have no clue what he's into these days."

"How long have you two known each other?" Blue started to pull out the make-up brushes, and ushered me toward the chair. A reprieve I felt grateful for.

"A long-ass time," I replied as I settled into the chair and squeezed my eyes shut. After that, none of them pried, and I was happy for it.

A couple hours later I was all made-up and ready to go when I heard a knock at my suite's door.

"Come in!" I shouted.

My heart fluttered the instant I saw him. Hudson wore an all-black classic suit with his usual rings and low-bun hairstyle. He looked like a modern-day James Bond.

When our eyes met, he let out a long exhale and put his hand on his chest. "Wow. Jazmine. A man can only take so much." The way he looked me over from head to toe sent chills down my body.

My earlier annoyance with him quickly dissipated, replaced by the desire Hudson always knew how to conjure up in me.

He walked over and I tilted my head up to meet his. But he kissed my forehead instead of my lips. My mouth tingled, aching at being so close to his, yet still so far away.

I guessed he didn't want to mess up my bright red lipstick, or get any of it on his mouth. With an effort, I smiled and stepped back, without actually kissing him.

"You are truly beautiful." Hudson rested his palm on my cheeks. "And I'm sorry for not texting you sooner. I hope I didn't worry you." He ran his hand down my neck, across my shoulder, then trailed it down my arm.

My face felt warm. Especially when I noticed him take in the way this vintage dress hugged my body.

"It's fine. Just don't fucking do it again," I teased. I suddenly felt like putty in his hands. I had succumbed to The Hudson Effect—a state in which you can't help but be completely enamored by Hudson Taylor's natural charm. It was a force to be reckoned with.

Hudson turned towards Blue. "Excuse me. Would you mind taking a picture of us together?"

"Um. Of course!" Blue, for his part, only stammered a tiny bit when confronted with The Hudson Effect.

"Thank you." Hudson handed over his phone, then elbowed me. "You should get one too. For the app."

Oh. Right. He didn't just want a picture of us together or one of me in my amazing outfit. He wanted to share it with the world.

Then again, I should want to brag about being with him too. Shouldn't I? "Yes, right. Could you take one with my phone too?" I handed it to Blue.

Hudson flashed a grin of approval in my direction.

As we posed, I spotted Leo, along with Mateo, Rex, and Esmeralda, walking through the door. My vision narrowed. It felt like they moved in slow motion. Or maybe I did.

I swallowed hard. The moment of truth. How was Leo doing? And more importantly, was I going to try to smooth things over?

But when Leo met my gaze, the hurt in his eyes from yesterday was nowhere to be found. Instead, I caught a glimmer of something different. A spark of contentment. Almost as if he were happy to be there.

I wondered if he was hiding it better or if he just didn't care anymore. Maybe he hadn't cared in the first place. Maybe it was all in my head.

My hands clammed up. Suddenly, I regretted the conversation with Gal. Maybe our past meant nothing to him, after all. In which case, why was I so intent on dredging it back up?

"You guys look nice," Leo said, looking from Hudson to me. It was a very professional compliment. No emotion. Not so much as the bat of an eye. Casual and polite.

"I really like your dress, Jazmine," Esmeralda added, running her fingers through her long purple hair. She wore another short shirt, again revealing her tanned torso. This time I noticed a belly-button ring that I didn't see the day before. "I love the vintage vibes." She leaned her shoulder up against Leo's. He inched slightly away from her.

I glanced over at Zoe and Celine and shrugged. Leo claimed they weren't together, but who the hell knew. Apparently, I couldn't read him anymore.

"All right." Leo let out a long breath. "Ready to get down to business?"

Hudson and I nodded.

"We're going to start by having Rex attach your lapel mics.

Once you're ready to go, we're going to film you walking to the banquet hall. Just act relaxed and natural. Like the cameras aren't here."

Easier said than done. At least for me. But as we prepared and then tromped out of the villa onto the lawns surrounding it, I tried my best. I laughed at Hudson's jokes. I commented on how lovely the weather was that day.

When Hudson took my hand, I threaded my fingers through his and tried not to worry about how I looked, or if I was walking weird or holding my arms funnily.

We paused along the beach to watch the clouds for a minute. Well, also so the cameras could capture the perfect angle. It *was* beautiful, I had to admit. Clear sky, a couple of fluffy white clouds near the horizon, and the sun sinking orange and red behind them all.

I felt grateful for Hudson's steady presence beside me the whole time. At least I understood where we stood. He was upfront with me about himself, and what he wanted. A partner. A lover. Someone who met his criteria. We saw eye-to-eye on that. I appreciated that more than I could say.

As we walked, I tried a couple times for a kiss. But every time I leaned in, he turned his face away, or kissed my temple or cheek instead.

I knew the lipstick would take a million years to reapply perfectly and would probably leave a mark on his face. But still. Being here, in such a romantic setting, yet not able to fully embrace the moment felt like a missed opportunity.

Before long, it didn't matter, though. The cameras called a wrap, and we hurried to our next filming location—the banquet hall.

The moment we stepped inside it, I gasped. Kelly said it was reserved for high-end private events. Now I saw why.

The room sat on a higher part of the resort, on a low cliff overlooking the ocean. Broad windows along one wall gave us a stunning view of the cliffs below, the resort sprawled out to the right and the ocean waves breaking on the left, with the sun setting behind them.

Closer at hand, large dining tables lined the high-ceilinged room, each one with elaborate red rose centerpieces, delicate-looking china plates edged in gold foil, even gold silverware—goldware?

I stifled a smile at the thought. Beside me, Hudson leaned in. "Did they really get us a mariachi band?" he asked. "I love mariachi music!"

Sure enough, a mariachi band was setting up in the far corner. I also spotted a full bar, and servers with trays of what looked like uniquely colored Martinis, Margaritas, and highball drinks, ready to start passing around when the guests arrived.

Near the front windows, a sweetheart table had been adorned with candles, its chair backs festooned in silk ribbons. I guessed that was where Hudson and I would be sitting, so our guests could come mingle with us.

My heart skipped. This looked like a wedding, not just the dinner you have with your family *before* a wedding.

It made me wonder how much fancier the actual ceremony could get. Or how we were going to top tonight.

"You all right?" Hudson murmured at my elbow.

"Of course. It's beautiful."

"Not as beautiful as you." He reached down to cup under my chin with one fingertip, raising my face until I lifted my gaze to his. His eyes bored into me, red hot. But before I could reach for him, or lean in to close the gap between us and finally kiss him, the way I'd been dying to all night, he stepped back.

"Oh, look. There's Kelly."

Sure enough, Kelly and Jennifer stood at the far end of the room, near the bay windows. They both wore crisp pantsuits, Kelly's navy blue and Jennifer's dark brown. They each held a glass of white wine in their hands, too. Nearby, I spotted Jack from Mercer, perched on top of a table with his phone glued to his ear. His face looked tight and pensive.

I hoped he wouldn't come over when he was done with his call.

I also noticed Rosa chatting with a few resort staff as they added some last-minute decorations to the tables. Other than that, we were the only ones here so far.

"Well, you two look lovely." Kelly sauntered in our direction. Jennifer was beside her, the two practically walking in lock-step. "By the way, I got to sample some of the food for tonight. The paella is to die for!"

We'd opted for a mix of traditional Mexican cuisine and some dishes to honor my side of the family tonight. Just hearing the word *paella* made my stomach growl. I realized I hadn't eaten since the churros and orejas earlier.

Mamá Prado's paella was hard to beat, but I was looking forward to seeing what the chefs at La Belladonna had come up with. Everything I'd eaten at the resort so far had been exquisite.

Kelly showed Hudson and I to our table at the front of the room. The way the tables were angled, all eyes would be on us. My skin suddenly felt itchy. I reached for an iced water nearby and took a big gulp.

Esmeralda began setting up some lights, while Mateo propped up Camera B beside us. The added lights made me feel even warmer. At that point even my ass was sweating.

As I worked overtime to just breathe and steady my nerves,

I completely missed Hudson filming the banquet hall for his Moments. I only realized it when my phone beeped with the notification that he'd tagged me. Before I had a chance to look at what he'd posted, the mariachi band started to play "Hermoso Cariño."

I recognized the song. I'd heard it playing in the Couture house many times during my childhood. Whenever Leo's mother put it on, he'd beg her to change it to whatever rock band he was obsessed with at that moment. But Mrs. Couture never would. She was adamant about keeping pieces of her Mexican culture alive in their house.

I grinned and scanned the room for Leo. He stood a couple feet away with Camera A in his hands. Our eyes locked for a split second, before he quickly looked away. I flinched, wondering yet again what was really going on in his head.

Maybe he *was* mysterious.

"Ay, Dios mío!" I heard a woman yell from the front of the banquet hall. I recognized my mom immediately. The volume of Lucia Prado's voice was impossible to miss.

My breath caught in my throat. Suddenly, I wanted nothing more than to fling myself into her arms while she soothed away my worries by telling me stories about her life.

"Look at these flowers, these tables, oh my God!" Her voice rose with each exclamation in her dramatic Spanish accent. She wore a long, flamenco-style dress in a beautiful shade of sea green. Her hair was pulled up in a classic up-do, revealing shiny pearl earrings.

My dad strode up behind her, eyes practically sparkling as he examined the room. The fact that my penny pinching father didn't have to pay for my wedding made him happier than he'd been in his entire life.

He wore his typical ensemble: tucked-in, buttoned-up shirt,

and khakis, topped with a brown belt. At least that time he opted for a tropical-themed shirt.

"Omar, are you seeing all this?" Mom executed her trademark twirl. "You would have had to pay for all this, honey. Your salary would have been bye-bye. Thank Dios!"

"I'm thanking him right now." He reached over to a nearby table and grabbed a plate. "Lucia, there is gold on these plates. This fork is gold too!"

My mom snatched the fork out of my dad's hand and quickly dropped it into her purse.

I shook my head, suppressing a grin.

Mamá and Papá Prado trailed into the banquet hall next, both in black blazers and dress pants, just like they'd worn on the night of my birthday/engagement dinner. I hadn't seen them since then, so it had been a couple of months.

Lito and Lita Durán walked in next, also wearing blazers and dress pants. In their case, it surprised me even more. I couldn't remember the last time I'd seen them both so dressed up. It took an effort to suppress a smile.

It also made me realize: this was really happening. Web show and cameras and Leo drama aside, I was about to marry Hudson.

Emotion overwhelmed me. I couldn't even raise a hand to catch my relatives' attention. I just leaned against our table and watched my mother take charge.

"Mamá." Mom hurried toward Lita. "Look! The silverware is made of gold." Lita's eyes lit up. Seconds later, she was stuffing gold knives and spoons into *her* purse. At this rate, there would be no dinnerware left for the dinner. Yet all I could do was laugh, tears threatening the backs of my eyes.

Oliver and his husband Gabe arrived next, all smiles, hand-in-hand, each wearing a tailored gray suit and shiny shoes.

They didn't exactly match, but their outfits complemented each other perfectly.

My brother noticed us first. When our eyes met, mine started to water. I couldn't fight the emotion any longer. Even from a distance, I could tell Oliver struggled to hold back tears too.

I was so happy to see my family. I couldn't believe everyone had come down to Cancún for me. Touched didn't begin to describe it.

Finally, when I'd gotten the first rush of feelings under control, I started toward them.

"Holy shit." Lita's eyes widened the instant they found mine. "Jazmine."

The rest of my family turned at the sound of my name. They fell silent, their expressions stunned.

For a moment, I winced, worried. Did I have something on my face? Did I not look as stellar as I thought earlier in the glam team's room?

But then Lita added, "Dios, you look like a movie star."

And right on cue, my mom started crying. Like really crying. "My daughter *is* a movie star," she sobbed, grabbing a handkerchief from her purse, which rattled since she'd stuffed so many forks inside.

Lita started to cry too, then Mamá Prado. Behind them, Oli buried his face in his husband's shoulder. Even my dad looked a little misty.

"Come on, guys. Don't cry!" I said, my voice cracking and betraying me. "You're gonna make *me* cry, and I can't ruin this make-up."

Lita laughed and pulled me into a tight hug, thankfully only air-kissing my cheeks. "She's right. We must be strong for our Jazmine," she ordered everyone.

"I pulled some cards for you today," Lita said softly, referring to her Moroccan tarot deck. She never went anywhere without it. "I pulled The Sun card and The Star and The Lovers. Today is a good day for you. Fate is on your side." I smiled and she squeezed my hand. I hoped she was right.

Only after I'd made my way halfway across the room, hugging more and more relatives as my cousins and aunts and uncles piled in, did I notice Leo standing about ten feet away, camera raised. The moment I realized he was filming, I froze, staring.

That, of course, made the rest of my family take notice, and follow my gaze.

Shit.

"Is that . . . *Leo Couture*?" My mom squinted her eyes. We were all staring directly at the camera now. *Pretty sure Leo won't be able to use this footage.*

"Leo who lived across the street?" Lita asked, stepping up to my mother's side and raising a hand to shade her eyes, like some sailor peering out across the sea.

"Guys, wait," I tried. But no one paid any attention.

"It *looks* like Leo who lived across the street," Mamá Prado agreed.

"Maybe he just looks like him?" my dad interrupted. "Jazmine would have *definitely* mentioned if Leo were here."

"You need to get your eyes checked, Omar," Mom replied. Ironic, considering my dad's profession. "That is *definitely* Mrs. Couture's son. I never forget a face and he was at our house Jazmine's whole childhood, people don't change *that* much!"

"Why would Jazzy invite Leo to her wedding?" Papá Prado asked, turning in my direction.

"Maybe they're friends again." Lita didn't even bother to

glance in my direction, as I tried to wave for their attention. "You know young people these days. Yosef would never have let me stay friends with a man after we got married! He was too jealous."

"That's because you were in love with every man in Morocco when I met you," Lito chimed in.

"I was not, I was just *friendly*."

"Jazmine isn't friendly like that, Mamá," my mother spoke up, a wry smile on her face.

"You're right, she's too closed off," Lita agreed. Thanks for that one.

"*Hello*, I'm standing right here?" I strode up to my mother and waved a hand in front of her face. She ignored me in favor of squinting in Leo's direction.

"He certainly grew up nice, didn't he?" she murmured. "I haven't seen him in so long."

"He can *hear you*," I hissed under my breath, hoping he couldn't hear me, too. Then I remembered, belatedly, about the lapel mic hidden under the folds of my dress.

From bad to worse.

I chanced a glance in Leo's direction, and that only made my panic worse. He still had the camera raised, obscuring part of his face. But to judge by his wide grin—not to mention the way his shoulders shook with barely concealed mirth—he had heard every word my incredibly non-discreet family just shouted.

I looked at Oliver, who threw his hands in the air and shook his head. Finally, we both started to laugh too. There was nothing else I could do.

Where the hell is Gal? She was supposed to be moderating this.

"Jazmine, *is* that Leo Couture?" Lita finally turned back to me to demand. "Is he filming your wedding?"

They all stared at me, expressions ranging from curiosity to sympathy to outright vicious amusement. Lita and my mom loved anything that reeked of potential drama, I knew.

I glanced over my shoulder at Leo. He'd finally lowered the camera. He flashed me a grin, then shrugged, and set the camera down on a nearby table.

"Yes," I said, my gaze still on Leo. "Yes, he is."

The instant the words left my mouth, they all bombarded him with hugs and cheek kisses, as well as questions about his career, his life, his family.

I couldn't blame them. I mean, they hadn't seen the guy in years.

But when I glanced behind me, I noticed Hudson had approached. I couldn't be sure how long he'd been standing there on the outskirts of our huddle, arms crossed, an expression I couldn't read on his face.

Was he . . . mad?

How much did he hear? But he couldn't blame me for my family's over-excitedness over seeing an old friend, could he?

But there was no mistaking the downturn at the corners of his mouth, the frown lines across his forehead. I took a deep breath and pushed out of the crowd of my family to reach for his hand, then pulled him into our circle.

"Guys, look who else is here!" I prompted, a little too loudly. Mamá Prado was in the middle of giving Leo an enthusiastic, bone-crunching hug.

But then Lita wolf-whistled, eyeing Hudson's outfit from head to toe and back again, and the rest of the family finally turned away from Leo for a minute.

They rushed Hudson just as excitedly, with the same hugs and kisses. I watched as Hudson's annoyance reluctantly faded.

No one could stay annoyed for long with my family attack-hugging them.

"You two are such a guapo couple!" My mom batted her eyelashes, which appeared to be laced with eyelash extensions. "I watched your first episode on the flight here," she told Hudson with a proud smile. Then she turned to glance back over her shoulder. "You filmed that, Leo?"

Beside me, I felt Hudson tense, almost imperceptibly. *Shit.*

As for Leo, he was nodding. "I did."

"Well, you did a great job! It wasn't just us watching it on the plane either, lots of people were. My Jazzy, you're going to be a *star.*" To judge by the rapturous expression on my mother's face, she couldn't be more excited for it.

Even if I felt the exact opposite way.

My knees wobbled. I held on tight to Hudson's arm. I feared for a moment that I might fall over. *People on the plane watched us?*

Just then, I noticed Gal and Anik walk through the door. I gave Hudson's arm one last squeeze and disengaged to hurry towards her.

Gal looked chic in a knee-length lavender dress, and Anik looked equally elegant in a tailored pinstripe suit.

"Where have you been?" I murmured through gritted teeth as I wrapped my arms around her tightly.

"I'm sorry. We got caught up in . . . something." She and Anik traded grins. "How bad was it?" Her expression shifted into a grimace.

"Pretty damn awkward," I grumbled. Then I paused, considering. Despite everything, Leo had taken it well. And Hudson was only a *little* bothered. I sighed. "I guess it could've been worse."

Then I noticed another elegantly dressed couple enter behind Gal and Anik, and my whole body went numb. Hudson's parents. Along with a striking young man, who I assumed to be Hudson's brother.

"Shit, Hudson's family is here. Can you show the fam where their seats are, or distract them, or something? Just get them away from Leo. My mom especially."

"On it." Gal saluted, and Anik did too. He'd picked up on our family dynamics pretty quickly after being with my cousin for so long.

They departed just as Hudson came up and offered his arm. I gulped. As we walked towards his family, I noticed that Hunter's face looked completely expressionless. Not a smile in sight.

He did look a little like Hudson though. The more serious version. Tall, with dirty-blond hair and blue eyes, but Hunter cropped his hair short, and while Hudson was visibly muscular, Hunter had a leaner look.

"You look absolutely lovely, dear," Hudson's mother, Catherine, exclaimed as we approached. I gave her a hug, which felt a little like hugging a bird, she was so dainty. She wore a light gray blazer and matching skirt, her short blond hair loosely curled. "Congratulations, you two!"

"Thanks, Mom." Hudson hugged her next.

Hudson's father, Michael, crossed his arms and studied us like you might size up a prize horse at a competition. "You two make a lovely couple. We couldn't be more excited for you both." He sounded so formal.

Another rush of nerves hit me. How were Hudson's neat, polished parents going to deal with *my* family?

"Thank you so much," I replied, playing with my necklace. Another nervous habit I'd picked up, I realized.

"And Jazmine, this is my brother, Hunter," Hudson spoke up.

Hunter reached out to shake my hand.

"Nice to meet you," I said. Hudson wasn't kidding when he said his brother was quiet and stand-offish.

Hunter pumped my hand once and let it go without so much as a word. While Hunter and Hudson shared some resemblance, I didn't see much in common personality-wise. Maybe Hunter would warm up once I got to know him better. But no wonder Hudson became the social media star of the two.

"Jazmine, you must be so excited to have your wedding in the city your family is from." Hudson's mom smiled, glancing from me toward my loud, bustling family, still audible in the background as Gal corralled them toward their seats.

I blinked. "Actually, my family is originally from Spain. Marbella, to be exact. They're Spanish-Moroccan."

"I thought your family was from Mexico and that's why you were doing the wedding here in Cancún." Hudson's father frowned, as if I'd just answered a question wrong on a test.

I clasped my hands in front of me. "*Style&Travel* picked the resort. It's beautiful isn't it?"

"You guys didn't get to pick where you're getting married?" Hunter asked. It was the first time I had heard him speak. Even his voice sounded different from Hudson's, deeper and harsher.

"No, it's all part of the show," Hudson chimed in with a smile.

"You know, it must have been your last name that confused us, right, Michael?" Hudson's mother added. "I think that's why we thought you were Mexican." Beside her, his father nodded.

None of this was said maliciously, mind you. But it was clear they didn't know a lot about me. For some reason, that made my chest ache.

It doesn't matter, I told myself. *They have plenty of time to get to know you in the future.*

Besides, Hudson didn't live with his parents. With how much he traveled for work, and to visit me, he was hardly ever home in Toronto. And when he was, I doubted he used the precious little family time he had giving them all the lowdown on my life. When I met them in L.A. last year, they only had time for some dinners and sightseeing, which was hardly the moment to spill everything about myself.

"No worries. Common mistake." I forced a wide smile, hoping it would relax the Taylors.

None of them returned it. They were all openly staring behind me now, as someone started shouting at someone else. I recognized Lita's excited voice in there somewhere.

Standing there, I started to wish we'd had more time together before this. To them, I was a complete stranger. They knew nothing about me, and I knew next to nothing about them, either. If we hadn't rushed the wedding process thanks to the web series, we would have had more time together. Time to get well acquainted, to crack the ice. Time to make all this feel less rushed and awkward.

You're here now, Jazmine. You chose this, I reminded myself. *Make the best of what you have.*

As more and more guests began to shuffle in, Hudson and I showed his family to their seats—thankfully far enough from mine that they shouldn't cross over too much yet—and then Kelly came by to bring the two of us back to the front of the room.

As we walked that way, I leaned closer to him. "I know you said your brother is quiet, but you really weren't kidding, huh?"

Hudson smiled. "Don't take the flat effect personally. He's a painter, you know the whole tortured-artist thing. I promise, he's happy to be here."

I took Hudson's word for it. Then I wondered if I should introduce Hunter to Zoe, since she liked the mysterious types. Maybe she could liven him up.

From there, the dinner went on without a hitch. We ate, we drank, we listened to the mariachi band. Dancing started up, and we took advantage of the moment to introduce my parents to Hudson's. They all shook hands, smiled politely, talked about how handsome Hudson was, how pretty I looked. You know, small talk.

Then Gal smartly invited my parents to the dance floor, cutting the interaction short before they could say anything too untoward.

Besides the continual theft of the gold dinnerware, my mom and Lita seemed to be on their best behavior. I felt surprised everything was going so smoothly.

And then, the band announced the future bride and groom would dance next. The crowd on the floor parted, clapping, to make room for us.

Suddenly, my dinner didn't settle so well.

Hudson grabbed my hand. "Shall we put on a good show?"

I instinctively pulled my hand away. "I don't think I can."

"Come on, Jaz." Hudson actually pouted. "This is all to celebrate *our* wedding. We have to dance! Besides, you're such a great dancer. Show them your Prado moves."

That made me crack a smile. "I know, but . . ." I reached behind me and turned off the sound pack on my own mic. "It's going to be filmed," I whispered.

"Um. Obviously." He laughed. "That's the point."

"I just . . . I'm not big on dancing in front of people. Especially millions of them."

Hudson slumped. "Jazmine. We're doing a show, remember? You're going to have to get over the fact that people are watching."

I grimaced. "I know . . . But can we save the bride-and-groom dancing moment for the wedding?" I clasped my hands together. "Please?"

He sighed. "Okay. Well, at our reception, you owe me a dance."

I managed a weak smile. "Deal," I said, hoping by then I could muster up the strength.

He winked at me, though I could tell by his posture he was more disappointed than he wanted to let on for the cameras. "Let me know if you change your mind. I'll ask my mom to dance in the meantime."

"Great idea. She'll love that!" I bit my lower lip as I reached back to turn my audio back on. "And, I'm sorry."

But Hudson was already walking toward the dance floor, playfully swaying his hips to the beat. I wondered if I should have worked up the courage to join him. To try to squash my stage fright.

The people who had been staring us down turned toward Hudson now, whooping and cheering as he pulled his mother from the crowd. Across the room, I caught Gal's eye. She flashed me the *you okay?* smile we'd perfected over the years.

I nodded. No need to drag her away from the fun. She was already dancing with Anik.

But as I looked around the crowded room, I started to feel dizzy.

We were getting married in less than four days. Four days. And so many more people were going to witness it. On top of just the guests in this banquet hall.

And then I spotted my mom and dad salsa dancing in the middle of the floor and it hit me: the millions of people tuning in to the show were also going to get glimpses of my family. What if they started trashing my grandparents in the comments? Or my mom and dad? Or what if the homophobes went for Oli and Gabe?

They could say what they wanted about me, but my family?

I had written about my family in articles before. But I'd never said their names, never included photos, and I never posted any photos of them online. Having them on this show was exposure for them as well.

How could I put them in harm's way like this?

My throat tightened. I needed some fresh air.

Everyone was distracted on the dance floor, making it easy for me to sneak out. I grabbed a Margarita on the way out and the moment I stepped outside the bay windows onto a nearby balcony, my chest heaved. I literally gasped for air. The last time I struggled this much to breathe, I'd just petted a cat.

But after a few deep breaths, my chest finally stopped seizing.

I leaned against the railing and stared down the short cliff-side to the ocean below. The sun had set while we were eating, and the moon had yet to rise, so the sea looked dark, the only lights a distant glimmer from Cancún proper.

The resort itself had gone mostly quiet, except for little patches here and there. A restaurant, a few villas with the lights on. The outdoor bar where Leo and I sat a few days ago.

Was it really a few days ago already? It felt like just yesterday.

The sea breeze tickled my nose. It helped my head spins and the panic. Unable to face going back inside just yet, I found a patio table nearby, and took a seat on the wrought-iron chair beside it and placed my Margarita on the table.

I leaned back and stared up at the stars. A few minutes later, the sound of footsteps caught my ear. I tilted my head, only to see Leo walk through the doors and out onto the balcony, his camera swinging from one hand.

He froze when he saw me.

"Please tell me you don't have to film me right now," I called, with the most pathetic of pouts.

"No." He scratched his chin with his free hand. "Just getting some fresh air."

I sighed. "Me too."

"Do you mind if I sit?" Leo asked. My stomach jolted. I was surprised he wanted to.

"No, go ahead," I replied.

He took the chair opposite from me. I stiffened, not quite sure what to say. Luckily, Leo had less trouble finding his words.

"It's good to see your family again," Leo said, warmly. "They always make me laugh."

My shoulders softened. "Clearly they were very excited to see you too."

He cracked a small smile. "I can't believe Lito, Lita, and the Prados came all the way from Spain! I mean, I *can* believe it, because they would never miss your wedding. But still. To see them all in Cancún . . ." Leo trailed off.

I couldn't read his facial expression. Nostalgia? Pensiveness? Something else? "I know. I'm really grateful they made the trip."

"Was it my imagination, or were your mom and Lita stealing the gold dinnerware?"

I groaned. "Oh no, they totally did."

"As one does at a pre-wedding dinner."

We both started to laugh. It felt strange. Leo and I shooting the breeze so effortlessly. Like we used to. Talking like this, I almost forgot about our epic falling-out. Almost.

"By the way, I've read some of your articles."

"What?!" My eyebrows shot upward. "*You've* read some of *my* articles." It was one of the most shocking things I'd heard since coming to Cancún—and that was saying a lot.

"Well, yeah. I had to see if your work was up to par to mine," he said with a devious grin.

"And?" I tilted my head playfully.

"I mean . . . The bar is pretty high."

I rolled my eyes. Though, he wasn't lying about the bar being high. His work really was quite good.

"I'm kidding, Jazmine. Your work is amazing. You're a seriously talented writer." Leo ran his fingers through his wavy hair. It was a familiar gesture. A very Leo gesture. "I especially liked your piece from a few years ago, the one about why you shouldn't marry your best friend. That was a goodie."

"Yeah. It's one of my favorites," I teased, grinning.

He let out a stifled laugh before crossing his arms. "I noticed you've haven't written a story in a while. Is that 'cause of the show?"

My body jolted. Me not writing was not a topic I liked to discuss. I sat up straight in my seat. "No. It has nothing to do with that. I'm just . . ." I pulled at my Indalo bracelet. "I'm just doing *this* now."

Leo glanced at my wrist. His face scrunched. I forgot he knew all my tells. Then he leaned his chin onto his fist with a smirk. "You are such a bad liar, chica."

I glared at him. "I'm not lying." *Why not follow a lie with another lie?*

"Really?" He narrowed his vision, assessing my posture. I shifted uncomfortably in my seat. "Seriously, you should never play poker. Ever. You'd lose all your money in three minutes flat."

"Oh, come on, my poker face isn't *that* bad."

"Jazmine. I'm serious. Don't waste your money."

I took a sip of my drink. "Fine." I nervously tapped on the table. "The journalism industry has been a shit-show lately, thanks to pivot-to-videos and social media . . ." I cleared my throat. "It was basically this or not having a job. And I could never not have a job. Video is not my thing. But I'm hoping if I do just this *one* show, it will open up more opportunities to write for *Style&Travel*. Writing is still the long-term plan. It will always be." I let out a long exhale.

I felt like I was at confession. *Father forgive me for turning my back on writing and starring in a reality web show.*

"And you know, you could at least *act* like you believe my lies." I raised a brow. "You're the one with the thriving documentary/photography career. I'm just trying to save face here," I tried for a joke.

Leo flinched. He inched forward, leaning his elbows on the tabletop. He was staring at me harder than ever. As if he were memorizing every detail.

I understood. I wanted to do the same thing to him. Find all the ways he'd changed . . . and all the ways he'd stayed the same, too.

"Jazmine. We've known each other our entire lives. We skinny-dipped in eighth grade in my parents' pool; we've seen each other throw up, and fall down, and scrape our knees then cry about it. I mean, the list goes on and on." He folded his hands, every inch of his body focused on me, his muscles taut. "Things might be different with us now, but there's no need to save face with me," he said, his voice low and gentle. "Plus, you have a thriving career too. Being on a show is a big deal—even if you don't like it."

My skin burned hot. I looked away, tucking a strand of hair behind my ear. "Well, thank you," I said, looking up from the table and meeting Leo's gaze. Our eyes stayed locked until I couldn't hold the stare any longer and moved my focus forward, reaching for my Margarita.

"For the record," Leo started. "Video, like this, isn't my thing either. I love to make documentaries, but it would be really hard to have my wedding filmed. I would be miserable."

"So we still have one thing in common," I quipped, followed by a quiet chuckle.

"I think we still have more in common than you think."

The heat returned to my cheeks and started to spread across my body. I suddenly felt the need to fill the silence, and I did so in a way that was a bit . . . awkward. "This Margarita is really good, do you want a sip?"

"Do you want a sip?" Really? It was like I reverted to my twelve-year-old self, offering Leo a sip of my Slurpee.

"Um, sure." He shrugged. I slid the glass across the table. He hesitated for just a brief second, then slowly reached for it. As his lips gently pressed against the straw, right near my red lipstick stain, I found myself glancing away.

"Damn. That *is* good." He cleared his throat. "So it seems the mariachi band has the same taste in song choices as my mom." Leo took another sip before putting the glass down in the middle of the table.

"Oh my God, I thought the same thing! About how mad at you she used to get when you'd try to change her music?"

"I know, she would get so pissed. And then you, of course, would take her side. 'Leo, leave your mom alone,'" he said in a whinny voice.

I laughed. "Look. Elena Chavez Couture is a goddess. She can do whatever she wants and listen to whatever she wants."

"True." He leaned back in his seat.

"How is your mom, by the way? I miss her." I inwardly winced at my words. We'd lost more than just each other, when our friendship splintered.

"She's good. She misses you too."

I shrugged a little, suddenly uncomfortable with the force of his attention. I pressed my lips together and reached for the Margarita, sipping on the side of the glass instead of the straw were Leo's mouth just touched. As he watched me avoid the straw, his eyes slightly narrowed.

"How's the rest of your family?" I asked, attempting to move the attention elsewhere.

"Good. Dad's still at the restaurant. My sisters are in grad school up at UC Berkeley. They're all doing well."

"That's great to hear." I choked down another sip of the drink. "Hey, my family doesn't have to be in the episodes a lot, do they? Like, no talking heads or interviews or anything like that? I just don't want people to start trashing them online."

"No. They will only be in the episodes when they're with you. Like tonight, at the dinner, dancing, things like that." He ran a hand through his hair again. "But I promise, Jazmine, I won't put in anything too personal about them. I already told Kelly and Jack the same thing."

"Wow." A smile tugged at my lips. "Thank you." I couldn't believe Leo was looking out for my family like that.

He nodded. We stared at each other again until the sound of footsteps broke our focus. I looked back to spot Esmeralda.

"Hey, Leo. We need you inside for some shots," she said as she approached our table. She turned towards me "You okay, Jazmine?" Her eyes filled with genuine concern. I could feel the heat of Leo's gaze, yet I couldn't bring myself to look in his direction.

"Oh yeah. Just needed a little fresh air. I'll be in soon too."

"Well." Leo stood up and let out a long breath. "I'd better get back in there. Take your time though."

As I watched Leo walk away, I felt as though the fog was starting to lift. For the first time in years, I thought maybe, just maybe, despite the fact that we had both hurt each other so badly, we could put the past behind us.

Maybe we could actually be friends again.

Chapter Twelve

I hadn't dreamed about Leo Couture in years, but as I drifted off to sleep that night he somehow found his way back into my subconscious.

Like all my dreams, it started somewhere in the middle; the scene of our twenty-first birthday began to flicker into focus like an old movie projector whirring to life. We were at Taberna, just as before. Leo looked perfect. His chest and biceps strained against his long-sleeved, black shirt and his deep, hazel eyes sparkled under the dim bar light as they locked with mine. Leo slid his hand over mine, his thumb gently rubbing my palm, and a rush of heat swept up my arm and into my stomach.

The image cut to black, and with a blink of dreamlike magic we were in Leo's backyard once more. The stars twinkled against the night sky above us as we lay on our lawn chairs, promising to take each other to Marbella and Cancún.

"Let's do it. Let's have sex. Tonight," I said, propping myself up on my elbow as my eyes snacked on his body.

It was a perfect moment, just as it was so many years ago. Except this time, there was no phone call. No Elizabeth playing her games. Just Leo and me. Our gazes met and I could feel his desire boring into me. He leaned over and slowly caressed my face. My head swirled with the dizziness of anticipation and my hand found his body. I traced my fingers over his abs before tugging at the bottom of his top. I shot him a playful smile and he sat upright, tearing off his shirt in one swift motion.

He looked like a statue beneath the pale moonlight and my breath hitched in my chest. He was beautiful, and in that moment I saw him more clearly than I ever had. He grabbed my hand and took me upstairs to his bedroom. I could feel the heat rolling off his body as we lay on top of his bed. He looked at me with years of repressed longing in his eyes. Years of wanting our relationship to be more.

Leo gently pressed his lips to mine and a quiet moan escaped my mouth. I felt his firm arm wrap around my waist, pressing me into him. I breathed him in, every breath filling me with more and more excitement, until our gentle kisses turned into a passionate dance. I dug my fingernails into Leo's back and craned my head backwards. Leo dragged his lips across my exposed neck, leaving a trail of soft kisses that made me shudder.

The swell in Leo's jeans grew and I drove my hips forward. Another, more intimate moan, escaped my lips, telling the sweetest story. A story of repressed desire and love. A story that should have started a long time ago. I paused to drink in Leo's beauty and was met with a devious grin.

Leo shrugged off his jeans and I bit my lip. I stared with wide eyes at the bulge draping down his thigh. An electrifying pulse ached between my legs. My heart hammered in my chest as Leo tenderly removed my dress, leaving nothing but my bra and thong to conceal my body. His chest rose and fell as he searched my curves, his eyes beaming like a lighthouse in the night. Nothing in my life had ever felt so right.

Leo swallowed hard and shed his underwear. He stood

erect, his mouth curving upward. I felt wetness below and a satisfying shiver rippled through my body. In that moment I was ready to give myself to him. Fully. No need for marriage pacts. No waiting for the perfect timing. No superstitions holding me back. Nothing standing in my way.

I took off the remainder of my clothes and we both lay naked, mesmerized by one another. Finally, Leo climbed on top of me. He brushed a loose strand of hair behind my ear and whispered softly, "I love you, Jazmine Prado. I have always loved you."

His words tore into my soul, releasing a flood of emotions that had been walled off for so long.

Leo scooped a hand beneath my neck and pressed himself into me. I arched my back and wrapped my legs around him. Leo thrust again and our bodies instantly fell into tempo. He gently lay down flat on top of me, his chest firm against mine, and ground his hips with a rhythmic motion that left me breathless.

The world faded away until there was nothing left besides the two of us. I clung to the feelings of love and passion that swirled in my chest.

Leo grabbed the back of my thigh and raised my leg up higher as he pushed himself deeper inside me. My body quivered and I shut my eyes tight. A pressure began to build up within me, swelling with every thrust. I felt as if I were floating in a pool of ecstasy as my body drank up its waters with an unquenchable thirst.

The pressure inside me grew, threatening to erupt at any moment. I wrapped both hands around the back of Leo's neck. He quickened his tempo and my eyes flung open, meeting his. I gasped and moaned, pulling Leo into me again and again with each breath. Leo groaned and his back and stomach stiffened as he rocked his hips with a series of hard thrusts. My hands went numb and a flood of pleasure washed over me, spreading through my body like an untamable fire. My toes curled and I moaned myself awake with a start.

Shit. Fuck. What was that?!

I found myself back in my own bed, lying beside Hudson, who was thankfully still sound asleep. My body was wet with a thin sheen of sweat and my chest was still heaving from the dream. It took me a full minute to catch my breath, and even then I could still feel the warmth of Leo's touch between my legs. My throat tightened just thinking about it, and I was quickly consumed with guilt.

What just happened? What the hell did I dream?

I felt like the scum of the earth. Like I'd cheated on Hudson or something. I took a calming breath. *It was just a dream*, I assured myself. *It wasn't real, you didn't choose to dream this. You didn't do anything wrong.* But it felt real. Too real.

And as I drifted back off to sleep, I begged myself not to think about Leo again. Luckily, I got my wish.

Hours later I found myself in the make-up chair, getting ready for my bachelorette party that was taking place on that Thursday evening. We were in the final stretch of the series. Just like the last rehearsal before a Broadway show, adrenaline ran super high. Even though I'd only had two cups of coffee—not a lot for me—I felt like I'd drunk about a million.

In addition to my final-stretch jitters, I was bathing in guilt over my sex dream about Leo. I reasoned, though, that it was just my mind processing the fact that I had seen him again. It wasn't real. Not something to punish myself over. Not something to analyze and over-think.

I just wish I hadn't enjoyed it so much.

"I'm doing burgundy and plum today," Blue said as he lightly dusted my eyelids. "Going to make those eyes pop for your last official night out as a single lady."

"She's not a single lady, she's an engaged lady," Celine put in from where she stood behind me, curling my hair. "As a true single lady, I'm telling ya, there's a big difference."

"Come on, you know what I mean." Blue grinned at Celine over my head. "Okay, her last night out as a miss, how about that?"

Celine nodded in approval.

Meanwhile, I worked overtime to slow my racing pulse. I was getting married in two days with millions of people watching. The color drained from my face.

"You okay, hun?" Blue frowned at me in the mirror.

I forced a smile through gritted teeth. "Oh, yeah. Just a little nervous for the live ceremony on Saturday, that's all."

Partially true, but not the full truth. The full truth was, a lot of thoughts whirled inside my head that day.

One of them being that I dream-cheated on my fiancé. The other being how long it had been since I'd written a story. I hadn't published a single article since I agreed to do the show. That was three months ago.

Suddenly, it felt like the coffees I had earlier were eating away at my stomach lining.

I itched to write something. Anything. I was even game for a follow-up interview with Alan Yorkshire at that point. That's how desperate I was. And I knew myself. Jotting down my random thoughts in journal format wouldn't be enough. I needed an article, something to focus on. A topic to research. A deadline to hit.

Yet my mind remained blank when it came to article ideas. I was counting down the days until our wedding was over. Not just because the show would be over too, but also because I planned to start pitching pieces to *Style&Travel* ASAP. I couldn't imagine they'd say no to my pitches after the success of the show. And I assumed the millions of people who had been tuning in already meant it was well on its way to success.

"I don't blame you for being nervous. A live ceremony would freak me out too!" Zoe's chipper voice knocked me out of my thoughts. She rummaged through the beautiful rack of clothes beside me like a lion hunting prey. Except this lioness was on the hunt for my camera-ready bachelorette attire. "I couldn't even give a speech in front of my class in high school," she continued. "Getting married in front of millions would probably kill me."

Shit. My palms went clammy. *Thanks for the reminder, Zoe.*

"You might want to look for some funeral clothes for me while you're at it," I replied with a nervous laugh. "Because I'm pretty sure I'm going to die too."

No edits. No fuck-ups allowed. The whole wedding would appear in real-time.

Not ideal for someone like me.

"Oh, you'll be fine." Celine sprayed some dry shampoo on my roots. "Plus, you'll have Hudson right there next to you."

"And if you need something a little stronger, I've got you covered," Gal interrupted as she strode through the door.

She was like a one-woman pharmacy. Gal had everything from Tylenol to cannabis oil to Xanax to antibiotics stuffed in her purse.

"What would Dr. Gal prescribe me for nerves?" I joked.

"Well, hopefully having a day off tomorrow will help cool them down naturally." Gal grinned at me. "But a hit of a joint might not hurt either." She laughed.

Friday was a no-filming day, in preparation for the live

ceremony on Saturday—as well as for recovery from our bachelor nights. I don't remember the last time I had looked forward to something so much. Maybe when I was six and my parents bought tickets to Disneyland?

Tomorrow, I planned to do absolutely nothing camera or social-media related. Including posting to the app. All the posting and responding to comments was a lot of work. Mercer could get pissed off if they wanted to, I needed a break.

"Jazmine, I forgot to tell you." Zoe finally turned from looking through the clothes. "I had some time to kill this morning, so I read your *Style&Travel* article about the resort. They have it featured at the front. It was so good! I think we need a follow-up article now that you're here in person."

A follow-up article?

And then, I had a story idea.

Coming to Cancún for my wedding, to the resort I wrote about in last April's issue, except all through the perspective of a bride. I could talk about the resort, highlight the owners again, show their wedding process, talk about the dining and activity options nearby. Plus, it would make for the perfect piece to publish after the wedding.

Suddenly, color flooded back into my cheeks. I felt more alive than I had in months. I couldn't hide the smile tugging at my lips. "You know what? That's a great idea! I think I'm gonna talk to Kelly about a follow-up article!" I grinned at Zoe. "It would be perfect to run after the show!"

"Plus, you could get quotes from your glam team . . . Just saying." Zoe winked. "I'm always up for some press."

"Um, me too," Blue added.

"Me three." Celine grinned at my reflection.

"Me four," Jared shouted from the hallway as he backed in, balancing a tray of fresh coffees. His assistant duties knew no bounds. "Americano with one pump of vanilla and heavy cream. Aka, The Jazmine." He set the cup on the counter beside me.

"Thank you." I smiled. I was already brimming with adrenaline. Why not add more caffeine to the mix?

After going through practically every outfit on the rack, Zoe put me in a stylish black pantsuit with a matching black tie. The suit was fitted very tightly to my body, the perfect mix of classic and sexy. She paired it with black spiked stilettos—the highest heel I'd ever worn in my entire life. Completely worth tripping over. As I checked myself out in the mirror, my phone buzzed with a text from Hudson.

I hope you have fun tonight, my love. I promise I won't be out too late. I'll come over to your suite when I get back. I will probably be full of booze. Feel free to take advantage of me. ;)

My legs weakened. I wish I could blame it on the stilettos, but I knew what it really was. Thinking about Hudson coming to my room. Probably smelling of cigars and cheap liquor, looking for a good fuck.

My body tingled. And yet . . .

The guilt over my dream came to haunt me again. *It wasn't real.* I pushed the thought away.

Right as I set my phone down, I looked up and noticed Mateo and Esmeralda walk into the room.

"Wow. Love the outfit, Jazmine." Esmeralda eyed my get-up. "And those shoes!"

Esmeralda had been super-friendly toward me ever since she walked up on me and Leo's conversation the night of the pre-wedding dinner. I was beginning to really like her. She had such a positive presence and energy. I wasn't surprised she and Leo were friends.

"Doesn't she look amazing?" Gal prompted. She shut her laptop—my cousin had stayed in my room as I was getting ready, while also catching up on emails and phoning clients the whole time. Talk about multitasking—and being a badass boss. Right then, however, she rose from her seat. "Guess I've gotta get myself ready now." She air-kissed my cheek. "See you in a bit."

"I hope you're not planning anything too crazy," I called after her.

She flashed me an over-the-shoulder grin at the door. "I make no such promises."

After Gal left, I stared at the door, waiting for the rest of the film crew. *Huh.* I glanced at the clock and then at Esmeralda. After a moment's silence, I cleared my throat. "When will Leo get here?"

"Leo isn't coming," Esmeralda said as she set up the lights. "Mateo and I are going to film your bachelorette. Rex and Leo are going to be filming Hudson's. We had to split up today, since there are two parties."

"Oh. Of course." I hoped the disappointment splashed across my face wasn't too obvious. But hearing that I wouldn't see Leo at all that night made me a little bummed. I was looking forward to seeing all the colors and details he'd notice throughout the evening. Things I wouldn't catch otherwise.

But maybe it was for the best. Maybe it was good I wasn't going to see him that day after the dream I had. It would give me some more time to forget about it.

And then I wondered: why did he choose to film Hudson's party instead of mine, especially after the friendly exchange we had at the family dinner? I highly doubted a bachelorette with mostly women made him uncomfortable. Leo had never had a problem hanging out with the girls. Case in point, yours truly.

Maybe he thought he'd get better footage at Hudson's? Or maybe he wasn't interested in experiencing my party with me. *Damn it, Leo.* He had a way of making my wheels turn, even when he wasn't present.

After filming some segments of me walking around in my outfit, Esmeralda and Mateo escorted me outside, to where a limo idled. The door opened and out popped Gal in a shiny gold jumper. Her long, black hair was stick straight. That, along with the jumper, made me think of 1970s Cher. She looked ready to party.

"There's the bride-to-be!" she shouted, placing a crown on my head and tossing a white sash over my shoulder. It read *BRIDE* in purple glitter.

"Do we have to do the sash?" I grimaced. "Doesn't really go with the look."

Gal pursed her lips. "You *have* to do the sash."

When I stepped inside the limo, I found Kelly and Jennifer, a couple of my old journalism colleagues and a few cousins, as well as Oliver and Gabe. I was thrilled that Oli was here for my bachelorette party instead of tagging along with Hudson's.

Leo, take note.

I held my arms open for all the obligatory cheek kisses, coos and compliments. All while Gabe raided the mini-bar that ran along one wall of the limo.

It took a minute for it to sink in, just how big this car was. The bar had a whole ice-bucket section, champagne glasses, the works. I grinned as Gabe passed me my drink, only for Oli to immediately tap my glass with his.

"Congratulations, Jazzy. I'm so happy you found the perfect

partner for you, like Gabe is for me." His eyes sparkled as he said it.

Yet somehow, the words only made my stomach churn faster. I loved Gabe to death. He and Oli were my favorite couple around.

But was Hudson really my Gabe?

We were a great match, that I was certain of. But not every love story is soulmate level—if you even believe in that sort of thing.

Before I could get too in my head about it, the door crashed open, and Zoe, Celine, Blue, and Jared all hopped in the limo. "Surprise!" Celine crowed, and I laughed, glad they'd taken up my offer to join us.

I reached over to pour them some drinks—at least, until Gabe swatted me away, and Gal informed me that serving the drinks was not the bride-to-be's job.

I settled into the back of the limo, squashed between Gal and one of our cousins from Spain, listening to them chatter away. My heart felt so full it could burst. These were my people. My family. My friends. I felt at home among them.

And yet . . .

I couldn't help feeling one friend—someone who had once been my *best* friend—was still missing.

And then I felt guilty all over again, because why was I thinking about Leo on the way to my bachelorette party?

I shook my head. *Why am I so fucked up?*

Gal noticed and frowned. "Out already?" She tapped my glass.

I hadn't even noticed the champagne on its way down. But sure enough, the flute was empty now. "Oh . . ."

"Let me refill it." Gal waved at Gabe, while the limo started winding its way through Cancún's narrow streets.

But I caught her arm, stopping her. "It's fine." I cleared my throat, when it looked like Gal might scold me. "I just want to pace myself, you know?"

"All right." She leaned back in her seat. But she didn't resume her chat with our cousin. She kept her eyes fixed on me, watching. Studying.

I just hoped she didn't notice too much. The last thing I needed was an on-camera confrontation with my cousin about why I looked freaked out on what should have been one of the happiest nights of my life.

The limo rolled up to the first stop of my bachelorette, an upscale restaurant called Gratcia Del Oro. And I couldn't hide my laughter once we walked into our private room in the back.

Splashed across the large table were dildos, glasses filled with margaritas and garnished with penis straws, and at the other end of the room, a larger-than-life penis cake.

Gal really went for it. My whole face flushed bright red, especially as the cameras zoomed in on the décor.

"Oh, my God."

"You didn't think I'd miss an opportunity to send you off in style, did you?" Gal grinned, far too pleased with herself.

As I moved toward the large table, I noticed Jack from Mercer by the door. It appeared he stopped by to talk to Kelly. I pulled at the bottom of my blazer. I hoped he wasn't planning to stay long. I didn't want to spend my bachelorette with Jack.

But then my eyes lit up. I had a thought.

Though I knew it probably wasn't the right time, I was anxious to talk to them about my article idea. Kelly would need to get the final approval from Jack anyway, why not pitch them the idea right then?

Now or never, right?

"Hey, could I talk to you guys over here for a sec?" I motioned toward the corner of the room—the only section not covered in penis-themed décor.

Jack stiffened before nodding his head. Kelly's brows furrowed as she trailed me toward that area. "Absolutely. What's up?"

"Well. I was just wondering . . ." My hands started to tremble. I was never usually nervous pitching a story. I was confident in my ability to write. I cleared my throat, hard. "I wanted to talk to you both about a possible article idea to run right after the wedding. A story about coming to this resort in Cancún and getting married here. I thought it could be like a follow-up article from the first I wrote in last year's April issue. I could talk about being at the resort in real life, re-interviewing the family who owns it, showing their wedding process, and all of this could be through the lens of a bride . . . Thoughts?"

Kelly glanced away and put her hand on her chin. Right then, I noticed her nails, painted a pretty shade of pale pink. It looked beautiful against her dark-brown skin.

Jack stayed completely still. Pensive.

I held my breath until one of them finally spoke.

"I think that's a great idea," Kelly broke the silence, a smile stretched across her face.

I perked up. "Really?" My soul swelled with excitement. Hope pulsed through my veins.

"Well, if I may be honest . . ." Jack chimed in, raising his hand like he did in the coffee shop. "Mercer is still being pretty tight with the print editions—"

"I'm okay with an online-only piece," I interrupted, aware I was coming across as desperate.

"Okay . . ." Still, Jack seemed unconvinced. "Well, that's something I can definitely discuss with the team at Mercer later. But would you be open to doing a podcast to *talk* about your experience? Or maybe even a separate video series, we could do an after-the-wedding shoot."

My face flushed. Just what I'd hoped to avoid. "Honestly?" I bit my lower lip. "I'm not looking to do this just to share my point of view. I'm looking for something to write." My forehead scrunched. "I just thought, after the show, Mercer might be more open to running a few stories from me?"

My gaze turned to Kelly. Her full lips turned downward. She moved to face Jack. "I think it could be a great story to run! Having a Jazmine Prado print byline will be great for us after the show." My chest rose a little.

"All I'm saying is, I can't guarantee it," he said, sternly. "But why don't you shoot me an email with the full pitch when we're done. Sound good?"

I was completely deflated. Like a balloon popped mid-air. For a moment, I couldn't move; I could hardly even breathe. Kelly's face dropped along with me. It appeared she guessed wrong when she said Mercer would be begging me to write for them after the show.

I forced my lungs to intake oxygen. "Okay. That works." I tried not to sound like I'd just had my hopes pulverized.

Then I wondered, would they ever take a story from me again? Was all this just a way for Mercer to get a show with Hudson? My stomach surged.

I slapped on my best fake smile for Kelly and Jack. I was getting frighteningly good at those.

"Jaz! Kelly! Have a seat." Gal waved us over. And that was Jack's cue. He hopped on a call before walking out the door.

Kelly gave my hand a quick squeeze before we moved back to the table and I took my seat at the head.

I glanced at Mateo, holding his camera nearby. At Esmeralda, standing behind a soft box light on the other side of the room. I swallowed hard. I had been filming for the last few days but for some reason I was hyper-aware of being filmed in that very moment.

Some food and more drinks appeared, as Gal announced a very dirty game of bingo. We went three rounds before she rose from her chair, pretty buzzed at that point, and stood at the front of the room, clapping a hand onto my shoulder.

"Okay, let's go around the table and say why we all think Jazmine and Hudson make the perfect couple." She clapped her hands.

"Come on. Do we have to—"

"I'll start." Gal completely ignored me. "Three words. His fucking abs." I would blame her comment on the liquor but she'd say that sober too.

I rolled my eyes. "How the hell do his abs make us the perfect couple?" Gal could convince people of almost anything, but this seemed like a hard sell.

"They don't. But they make me extremely jealous." She laughed. "But in all honesty, I think you guys are great together because you respect each other, and both care very much about one another. Plus, his ass ain't bad either."

"I thought you said abs."

"His ass is great too." She shrugged, like it couldn't be helped.

I groaned. "Oh, sweet Jesus."

"I like how sweet he is with her," Oliver chimed in, thankfully. "He's always getting her thoughtful gifts and doing little things to show he cares. I like that."

"Another thing I have to add," Gal started again and I hoped this time it wasn't about Hudson's ass. "No drama. None of this back-and-forth, will-they-won't-they? bullshit. You two are straightforward and consistent."

I nodded pointedly at the camera, reminding Gal that we were being filmed at this very moment. Leo would be editing this.

She shrugged and mouthed, "What? It's true."

I shook my head and quietly chuckled, but when I looked up, I spotted a familiar face walking through the door.

Leo.

I felt my lips break into a smile, larger than I would have expected. His eyes met mine and he smiled too. Us gazing at each other from afar like this felt familiar. Like that time we spotted each other from across the gym at the homecoming basketball game, sophomore year.

And then I wondered why he was there. Why did he leave Hudson's party to stop by mine? Regardless, I was happy to see him.

"I really like how supportive Hudson is," Kelly spoke up, knocking me back to the present. "And she supports him too. They're a great match."

As the servers walked in with another round of drinks for the table, I started to feel lightheaded. Then, my eyes began to throb and my head started to pound like someone was doing construction inside of it.

Migraine.

I blinked a few times as the room violently spun. The filming lights pointed in my direction suddenly seemed brighter. I squinted, unable to look at them. My forehead went damp and my body warmed. I rubbed my head but the pain grew worse until it became insurmountable. My heart raced faster than the music playing in the background. A wave of nausea followed.

Suddenly, I was working overtime to not lose my lunch. Or more accurately, my dinner.

I rose, stumbling over the chair. I think I said something, but I wasn't sure what. Then, I ran to the single-person restroom in the back of the restaurant. The moment I got inside, I started to puke. My head pounded harder. I was seeing spots.

After a couple seconds of reprieve, the room spun more quickly, which caused more vomit to come flying out. A few minutes later, I heard a knock at the door.

"Jazmine, it's Leo. Can I come in?" I pulled myself up off the floor with difficulty and unlatched the door.

"Hey, I saw you leave and I just wanted to make sure—" His eyes widened the moment he saw me sitting on the floor, knees to my chest, shaking. "Oh my God. Are you okay?"

"It's a migraine," I said, between labored breaths. "I haven't had one this bad in years." I got migraines from time to time, Leo knew this. And when I did get them they would often come on suddenly, out of nowhere, and hit me pretty hard. These days they were usually triggered by too much screen time. But since I wasn't writing at the moment, and therefore on my computer a lot less, I wasn't exactly sure what brought *this* level of a migraine on.

"Oh no, I'm so sorry." He frowned. "Do you want me to get your brother? He's the nurse, I'm sure he'll know what to do."

"Yes, please." I nodded. Just moving my head ever so slightly made the pain worse. The room went blurry again but I still could make out Leo's silhouette as he inched towards the door. "Leo, wait!" I called after him.

He crouched down beside me on the floor, meeting me at eye level. Even with his face so close to mine he was still fuzzy. It was as if I was looking at him through an antique glass window.

"They're never gonna take another one of my stories," I said, eyes closed and rubbing my temples.

"What are you talking about?" he replied softly. Almost a whisper.

"You know how I told you I was doing this show to help my writing career? Well, I just pitched a story idea to Jack and he rejected it. He said I could email him about it later, but I could tell it won't make a difference. At this rate, I'll probably never be writing again."

Maybe it was the pain from the migraine. Or maybe it was the disappointment from Jack shutting me down. Or maybe I just wanted to vent to my friend like I used to. But I was spilling my feelings to Leo, right there on the bathroom floor.

And seconds later, I was spilling in a completely different way. I turned towards the toilet and threw up again. Once it stopped, I sat back against the wall and took a deep breath, trying to suppress the acid climbing up my throat.

Leo reached over and handed me a towel and a bottle of water from the complementary cart in the restroom. He put his hand on my shoulder. It felt warm. Comforting.

"You know Jack's a dick, right?" he said. "And a dumbass if he doesn't see the value in your work."

I grinned, even though it physically hurt me to do so. "He really is a dick, isn't he?"

"Truly. He's the worst." Leo nodded. "And you're not done writing, Jazmine. You're just getting started."

I looked at him and blinked a few times, trying to clear the spots that were obstructing my vision. I opened my mouth to say something but instead I grabbed my face as the pain become more intense. "Oh shit."

"I'm gonna go get Oli." Leo jumped to his feet and stepped outside the door.

A few minutes later, Leo did not return but Oliver walked inside and assessed me as he would one of his patients, hand to the back of my forehead.

"What do you think triggered it?" my brother asked.

"Not sure. Maybe I had too much to drink or something?" I said, as I wiped the towel against my mouth.

"You only had one glass of champagne," he pointed out, which was true. Though I'd tried to disguise it by pouring myself a margarita and swirling it around at dinner every now and then, I hadn't had a sip since that champagne in the limo.

"And alcohol has never triggered one before, right?" Oliver asked.

"No," I replied, closing my eyes. The throbbing had spread across my entire head, to the back of my neck, and my ears were even pounding at that point. I put my head between my knees, desperately trying to take deep breaths.

Oliver's eyes widened. "All right. I'll grab Gabe. We need to get some meds in you and get you back to your suite. I'll monitor you and call the resort's physician."

"What? We can't leave the bachelorette party, they need to film it! Don't you or Gal have something I can take so I can get back to this?"

"Jazzy, I'm sorry. But do you want them filming you in a ball grabbing your head and vomiting all night? Because it looks like that's all they're going to get."

I let out a long huff. "Fine." It didn't seem like I had any other option, anyway.

Between the three of them, Oliver, Gabe, and Gal managed to get me back to my room with minimal camera interaction. My head was so foggy by then that I didn't even remember how it happened. One minute I was at the restaurant in my suit, and the next I was lying on the couch in sweats, Gal and Oliver sitting beside me.

"No fever. Blood pressure good. Heart rate slowing down a bit." Oliver continued to monitor my vitals. "Anything else you think could have triggered it? Did Gal give you one of her pills?"

"Hey! I resent that," Gal grumbled. "I wouldn't give Jaz anything that would make her feel bad. Only stuff that would make her feel good."

"Did you try any food you haven't tried before?" Oliver asked. He was Sherlock fucking Holmes that night. "I'm wondering if it could be a migraine triggered by a food allergy. Sometimes those crop up later in life, too, like you can eat shellfish one day just fine, and the next . . ."

"No . . ." I interrupted him, not wanting to think about seafood right now. I gulped hard, suppressing the bile rising up my throat. "Not that I can think of."

Oliver handed me a water bottle. "Here. Don't want you to get dehydrated. Sip slowly."

I grabbed the water and took the smallest sip possible, hoping it would settle well. I waited a minute, then two. So far so good. Whatever meds Oliver gave me were finally starting to take the edge off the pain and were helping me feel more relaxed. But I was still fighting the lingering nausea from the migraine-triggered dizziness. Good times.

"Well, I'm gonna go let Kelly know that you can't film for the rest of the evening." Gal grabbed her phone. "You need to rest."

"Shit." I started rubbing my temples again. "Shit, shit, shit. You think they got enough footage? They only got me at my first stop."

Gal shrugged. "They'll just have to deal with the fact that

this is going to be a Hudson-heavy episode. Leo already said he could edit it like that, so it shouldn't be a problem."

"You talked to Leo?" The last few hours were a blur but I remembered him stopping by the party and coming into the bathroom peak-migraine. Thanks to the pain I was in at the time, and the pills that were presently in my system, I couldn't remember exactly what we talked about.

"Yeah. He came by a little bit ago and asked how you were doing. That was nice of him to get Oliver. I feel awful that I was mid-shots and missed you stepping away. Glad Leo noticed."

"Well, he doesn't miss anything." My brow furrowed. "Did he say why he came by the party? I thought he was supposed to be at Hudson's all night."

Gal shrugged. "I guess he decided to switch places with Mateo and was going to spend some time at your party, but obviously that didn't work out so well, migraine and all."

"Huh." A grin pulled at my lips.

"Hey, do you want me to let Hudson know you're back at your suite for the night and not feeling well?"

"No. Then he'd just try to leave his own bachelor party. Just let him have his fun. And get enough filming in for the both of us."

"Good call." She nodded and stepped out the door to call Kelly. Right as she did, my mom stepped in, wearing a silky pink robe with intricate floral stitching. Her robes were always over-the-top.

"Honey!" She held out her hands. "I heard you had a migraine! How are you feeling?" She knelt down near the couch.

"I mean, I've been better."

"I know just what you need." She shot back up. "My olive-oil lemon drink. One tablespoon of olive oil with some lemon juice. It helps with headaches. Nausea. You will feel good as new."

My mom truly believed olive oil was a gift from the gods, a cure-all for anything. She put it on everything. Literally. Not only on paella and couscous, but also on her skin, her hair, and even our cuts and scratches. I'm convinced if she could have married a bottle of olive oil instead of my father, she would have.

"And the olive oil they have in the kitchen here is amazing! Nothing like that cheap shit you always keep in your house. No offense, honey, but it's true. I'll be right back."

She scooted out the door towards the villa's kitchen. I glanced at Oliver, my vision still a bit blurry. "Did you tell her about the migraine?"

"No. But I'm guessing Gabe did when he went back to our suite. Our room is right across from mom and dad's."

"That must be painful."

"It is." He rolled his eyes. "Seriously. I don't know if it's because they're on a high since they don't have to pay for your wedding, but the sex is nonstop. It's torturous. I've been sleeping with earplugs in so I can at least muffle the sound of mom yelling, 'Oh, Omar.'"

I laughed, practically choking on my water.

Oliver's eyes narrowed. "How are you holding up, though? Be honest. I'm sure all of this is very overwhelming."

"I'm okay. Well, not at the moment, since I had the migraine from hell. But otherwise . . . I'm okay." My stomach ached again.

The wedding in two days. Jack waffling over my story. Reuniting with my ghost from the past. Dealing with harsh comments online from complete strangers. My relationship being watched by millions.

Oliver was right, this was all very overwhelming.

"Hudson really is such a great guy," Oli continued. "I think it's sweet of you to do this for him."

I squinted. "Do what for him?"

"The show." When I didn't react, Oli laughed. "I mean, come on, it had to be his idea. Clearly filming this wasn't your suggestion. You hate being in front of the camera."

My chest went tight. I hated that my brother didn't know the real reason I decided to do the show. How my career was on the brink of failure, and I agreed to do something that was completely not me to try to salvage it.

"Jazzy, I was just talking to Lita and the moon is in Gemini tonight, so we think maybe you're just overthinking things and maybe that caused your headache?" my mom announced as she charged back through the door. "But you're going to love how you feel after drinking this."

I let out a quiet groan as I sat up on the couch, looking at her and then back at Oliver.

"What's wrong?" he asked, concern consuming his gaze.

It was time to come clean. I sighed, loudly. "It wasn't Hudson's idea to do the show. It was *mine*." My eyes stuck to the floor. "I was about to get fired, and it was the only way I was able to save my job."

Oliver tilted his head. "What?"

"You were going to get fired?" My mom's mouth hung wide open. "Jesucristo!"

"Yes. I was about to get fired." I cleared my throat. "Not because of anything I did wrong. The magazine has been moving toward video and podcast content, and they aren't running many written stories anymore. So it was either do the show and keep my job or start over with no job at all. And to be honest, I have gotten fired before. Twice, actually. I didn't leave those other magazines because I 'wanted a change.' They did lay-offs, and I was let go."

"Honey, why didn't you tell me?" Mom came up beside me on the couch.

Oliver moved closer too.

"I didn't want to let you down," I said, my voice scratchy from impending tears I fought to stifle. "You always told me how important it was to have a career and follow your dreams and how lucky I was to be born in the U.S. so I could work to achieve those dreams. And how you weren't able to achieve yours after you got pregnant with me. And you even took me to your psychic friend who told me to stay focused on my career goals and not relationships, and I just . . ." My bottom lip started to tremble. "I didn't want you to be disappointed with me."

Oliver reached over and took my hand.

Mom's eyes started to water. "Oh, honey." She sniffled. "I think I might have . . . How you say, *pro-heck-ed*?"

"Projected." I smiled, in spite of myself.

"*Projected* . . . my own feelings about not becoming an actress onto you. I didn't want you to be like me, to give up your dream, to not have your own career. To have to depend on a man. I don't think the message was wrong, but I went about it the wrong way by putting so much pressure on you." She put her hand on my shoulder. "And I may have paid my psychic friend to tell you that."

I laughed. "I know, Mom. But you doing that just showed how much you wanted that for me, you know?"

And it was also really manipulative, but that was a conversation for another time.

She slumped. "I'm so sorry, Jazzy. I really am. I went about this all wrong. But I do want you to know, I'm very proud of you." She smiled. "And you know what? I never got to become an actress but I have a great life. I have you. And I have you." She reached over to take Oliver's free hand. "And I love your father very, very much." Mom let go of my hand only to wipe a tear from her cheek. "Dios! This is why you have a migraine. You're stressed. You're too stressed about all this work stuff! When you were a kid, even as young as kindergarten, you would get so stressed at school, that you'd come home with bad headaches. The teachers thought it was loco!"

"Huh. That's right." *Maybe it was Jack's rejection of my pitch that did me in? Me internalizing it all?*

Then, I vaguely remembered telling Leo about Jack in the bathroom. *You're not done writing, Jazmine. You're just getting started*, I recalled Leo saying. I appreciated his words.

"It's too bad I can't switch places with you," Mom continued. "I would be great on camera!"

"We know, Mom." I laughed. So did Oli. "We know."

"Just promise me you won't do anything you don't want to do again. Especially not because you think you might disappoint me. Because you could never disappoint any of us. We love you."

Oliver nodded fervently in agreement.

A lump formed in my throat. My eyes glassed over. "Thanks, guys. I love you, too."

"Now," Mom grabbed her olive oil concoction from a nearby table. "Drink your drink. It will help, I promise."

I looked over at Oliver and shook my head slowly, disgust written all over my face. I'd tasted this concoction, or something like it, far too often. It knew it would not help right now.

"I'm just gonna take this," Oli said, plucking the drink from my mom's hands. "Jaz should stick to water for now. Nurse's orders."

"*Thank you*," I mouthed.

And as I lay there on the couch, the pain, dizziness, and nausea starting to subside a little bit, I thought about dreams. About how I wasn't even sure what mine were anymore.

As much as I wanted to deny it, my career as a journalist at *Style&Travel* was coming to an end. I hoped I was wrong. But my gut told me otherwise.

I woke up an uncertain amount of time later, confused. Mom and Oliver must have left, because I didn't see them anywhere. But sitting in front of me, where my mom had been sitting, was Hudson. My heart skipped a beat at the sight of his beautiful blue eyes.

"How are you doing, love?" He put his hand on top of mine.

"Better, now. I had a bad migraine earlier, but I'm okay." I grimaced, and wished I'd had a chance to brush my teeth to get rid of the lingering vomit taste before he showed up. I shifted now, and reached for my water bottle.

Hudson stared. "What?! I'm so sorry. You should've told me. I would've come to take care of you."

I took a long drink of water before I narrowed my eyes at him. "That's exactly why I didn't. It wasn't a big deal, and you deserved to have a good night, even if I couldn't."

I couldn't tell him the entire truth. I couldn't get into how stressed I was; it would only worry him more.

And then, he gently put his hands on my face and moved in for a kiss. I closed my eyes and leaned in, but only until his warm, familiar lips brushed mine. Then I remembered how I'd spent part of the night throwing up.

I jerked away from him as though stung.

Hudson blinked at me. For a split second, I could have

sworn I saw hurt in his eyes. But a moment later, it smoothed easily into worry. "Is something wrong?"

My heart raced in my chest. My palms went clammy, the same way they'd done at dinner, right before the migraine hit. I grimaced and bit the inside of my cheek. I probably didn't have anything left in me to hurl, but I'd be damned if I was going to do it in front of Hudson. Days before our wedding, no less.

"I'm fine," I replied, my voice constricted, and completely unconvincing. "Just, um . . . still feeling a little off, so . . ."

"Oh." Understanding dawned in his eyes, followed quickly by relief. That set of emotions made my stomach churn even worse. "Oh, of course, Jaz. I'm sorry." He stretched out alongside me on the couch and offered an arm. "Come here."

I blinked at him, confused, until I realized that he just wanted to cuddle. Only then did I turn my face away from his, and sank against him, my back curled against his body.

We'd never really done this. At least, not without having sex first. Because, let's face it, the number of times I've turned Hudson Taylor down for sex before . . . well, I could count them on zero fingers.

I squeezed my eyes shut. What was wrong with me? And why did my dizziness only seem to get worse as Hudson lazily traced a hand up and down my arm, raising goosebumps along the way?

I tried to calm my breathing. Tried to remind myself: this was Hudson. The most beautiful and sweetest guy I'd ever seen. The best one I'd ever officially dated. The love of my life.

. . . Wasn't he?

"Hey." Hudson ran his fingers through my hair. I tensed like a deer in headlights, afraid he could sense my train of thought. "Relax, Jaz. Get some sleep."

I turned, shooting him a weak half-smile over my shoulder. He kissed the back of my neck, softly. Sweetly. The kiss lingered on my body, left my skin warm with his heat. It made me rethink my instincts for a split second. Maybe it didn't matter that I wasn't feeling well, maybe I should just enjoy one of our last "single" nights together.

But instead, I turned away to face the empty room again, staring at the doorframe, wide awake, while Hudson's breathing slowed into sleep behind me.

Follow Those Dreams, You Won't Regret It

By Jazmine Prado

If you dare to dream, anything can be possible.

Have you ever come across someone and felt incredibly inspired? Almost as if they spoke to you on a deeper level and made you feel like you could take on the world? Well, that exact thing happened to me when I was in fourth grade. I remember it like it was yesterday . . .

It was a Tuesday afternoon and I'd finished my homework early and had the rest of the day free. After eating a bowl of cereal with chocolate milk (don't judge, it's a great snack!), I hopped on the couch to find something to watch. As I scrolled through the channels I stopped when I came across a show about women in music. I've always been super into biographies, and all things music, so this immediately caught my interest.

About halfway through the show, a song started playing that was familiar to me. And then, I saw her: Selena Quintanilla-Pérez a.k.a. Selena. (Yes, she is iconic enough to be known by one name.)

Known as the Queen of Tejano Music, Selena was a Mexican-American entertainer, fashion designer, and more. And the moment I saw her, I was mesmerized. *Her voice. Her smile. Her style.* She was so magnetic, so talented, so well spoken. In that moment, I felt inspired and I was so upset to discover that she had been taken from this earth so soon (sobs!).

But I wanted to learn everything I could about this amazing artist, so I listened to her music, read as much as I could about her, and watched the movie *Selena* based on Selena's life.

I enjoyed the movie for many reasons, but for a child of immigrants, it touched me on another level and motivated my young mind to dream in a way I hadn't dreamed before.

I always knew that I wanted to be a writer. All it took was my grandma gifting me a pen and a journal to open my mind to the possibilities of what one could do with words on paper. As a kid, I envisioned myself as an adult traveling the world to visit magical locations, Mai Tais in hand, writing stories while gazing at beautiful sunsets.

Sure, my job as a journalist has equaled a lot more time with my laptop on my couch, than Mai Tais and sunsets. But truth is, I couldn't imagine myself doing anything else.

Following your passion takes guts. Following your dreams takes grit (and it's never too late to chase a dream!). Doors will slam in your face. People will reject you. People won't believe in you. But as cheesy as it sounds, if you can believe in yourself, if you can believe in your dream, then that will be the fuel that will carry you along the way.

Life will always be full of ups and downs, but those dreams of ours, those seeds of desire that we planted long ago, are there for a reason. Water them. Feed them. Give them ample room to grow. Because when it comes time to reap the harvest, you'll be so glad that you did.

Chapter Thirteen

I woke up migraine-free with my head on Hudson's chest. It was 11:34 a.m. We'd slept in a little, not setting an alarm since for once we had no filming to prepare for. Nowhere to be but here.

Thank the gods.

"Good morning," he said, kissing my lips and wrapping his arms around me. I sunk into him even further as he held me in those chiseled arms.

I kissed him again. "Thanks for coming by last night, and for cuddling with me. It was nice."

"It really was." He brushed back a strand of my hair that had fallen into my eyes. "And just think, starting tomorrow we get to *cuddle* for ever."

My body stiffened as adrenaline came coursing through my veins. I couldn't think about the wedding or the live show without feeling like I was about to fall off a cliff. My armpits went damp and I pulled away, fanning my face.

"Are you okay?" he asked, tilting his head with concern.

"I'm totally fine," I lied. "You're just making me too hot. Metaphorically and physically speaking."

He grinned, and ran his finger gently along my collarbone, sending heat all the way down to my toes. It wasn't helping the situation at all. “I don’t have to be anywhere for a couple hours . . . Should I order us some room service?”

Hudson had planned to spend the day before our wedding with his family, taking them to some popular Cancún spots to spend some quality time together. Seemed like a great plan at the time, since Hudson had been so busy. Now I greedily wished we’d planned to spend the whole day together. I needed some time alone, just the two of us.

“What about some waffles? And ‘The Jazmine’ for you, of course,” he added with a wink.

I let out a laugh, forcing my worries to the back of my mind. “Yeah. That sounds perfect.”

While Hudson ordered, I went to take a shower to try to calm the storm brewing inside me. This was the first morning I didn’t immediately jump to watch the next episode of *Our Big Day* on the *Style&Travel* app. Or read any of the comments.

Instead my mind buzzed, glad to be preoccupied with other things. Like how I would get through the live ceremony the next day. I grimaced. Okay.

When I finally finished toweling off post-shower, I walked back into the main room to find that room service had already arrived. *Guess I took a longer shower than I thought.*

“Breakfast is served.” Hudson gestured at the table, already set with waffles and my coffee drink.

“Wow. This all looks amazing.” My stomach grumbled. I was pretty hungry, despite my jitters. I topped my waffle with lots of butter and syrup and took my first bite.

A long groan followed. “Oh my God, these are so good,” I exclaimed in between bites.

“They really are.” Hudson shoveled a forkful into his mouth. “I can’t remember the last time I ate waffles.”

"Are they not approved on your sculpted Greek god fitness plan?" I teased.

"All things in moderation, right?" He grinned and took another huge bite, wiping his face with a nearby silk napkin. "So, Jack from Mercer Media stopped by my bachelor party last night."

"Oh?" I took a sip of my coffee, wondering if Jack crushed his dreams at his party too.

"He had a very interesting proposition for me. For us, actually." Hudson sat up straight.

"Really?" I raised a brow. What proposition could Jack have for us?

"He said the show is doing extremely well. Meeting all of their expectations and then some. Apparently fans really like seeing us together, and getting access to our lives."

I blinked a few times. "That's . . . good to hear." If a little weird. But hey. Maybe I was wrong. Maybe I just caught Jack at a weird moment. Maybe they *will* start publishing my stories again.

Hudson took a long sip of his black coffee, then set the cup back down, tapping his fingers on the table. He looked nervous. But Hudson was never nervous.

I leaned forward in my seat. "Is something wrong?"

Hudson's gaze jerked back to mine. "Not at all. Just, basically, Jack was wondering . . ." He cleared his throat. "He was wondering if we'd be interested in filming our honeymoon, too."

I almost spat out my bite of waffle. It took all my remaining self-control to wash the bite down with a gulp of The Jazmine before I responded. "Our honeymoon in Maui?" My voice came out louder than I expected it to. "Isn't it a little late for that?"

"It wouldn't be anything over-the-top. No film crew. Just footage from my phone and camera. Vlog-style. He told me I could submit the footage after our honeymoon ends. Then they'd have someone edit it and put it up on the app. Sort of an after-show special. And since I'd be filming it, we could control exactly what we want to show. It would be easy-peezey." He grinned at me.

I felt like Hudson was trying to haggle with me. To convince me this would be a lot more low-key than it actually sounded.

Now I know why he was so nervous.

"I don't know . . ." I bounced my foot under the table. "I'm not sure how comfortable I am filming our honeymoon. I was hoping after *Our Big Day* I wouldn't have to appear onscreen ever again."

"Jaz." Hudson leaned forward. "They're already writing up proposals for us to do new spin-off shows with them. You know, things like . . . *Our first year of marriage. House-hunting. Travels.* The possibilities are endless. Whatever we choose, though, they definitely want more."

A lump formed in my throat. More shows with *Style&Travel*? Would this be my life now? I suddenly found it difficult to swallow. "They want to follow our lives for, like . . . ever? Who do they think we are, the fucking Kardashians?"

"We could be. Or even bigger." Hudson's eyes glistened, brighter than I'd ever seen before. Like a child walking downstairs on Christmas morning to a heap of presents. "That's what Jack thinks, anyway."

My feet started to twist into the carpet. "Well, couldn't *you* just do shows with them? Fun, adventure-type stuff like you do online?"

"Maybe here and there, sure. But people want to see more of *us*." Hudson reached across the table for my hand. I stared down at his palm, leaving him hanging, unable to move. Unwilling to. It felt like if I took his hand now, I'd be agreeing to . . . all of this. Everything. I didn't know.

Hudson's smile tightened around the edges. "Jaz. You and I together have become our own brand."

"Our own *brand*?" I couldn't help it, I huffed aloud. I didn't like being thought of as a product.

"Yes. And it could be a profitable brand, too. To have the backing of a company like Mercer . . . It's an amazing opportunity."

I knew how he felt. Because I used to have that comfort. The backing of a big company behind the work I loved. But I didn't any longer.

Right then and there, I knew for certain I wouldn't have a future writing at *Style&Travel*. From here on out, they'd only want me for shows. With Hudson. About our lives. No more writing about my own topics, my own ideas. My own stories.

My nausea suddenly returned, worse than ever.

I peered at Hudson on the other side of the table. His nerves had vanished. Instead, he looked excited, eyes filled with hope, his smile wide. He wanted this. It would help his career, expand it. Make him more popular and well-loved than ever.

And it killed me, because I wanted him to have that. He deserved that kind of publicity and recognition. I just didn't want to sacrifice my own dreams for him to get it.

The realization made my head swim. Could I really ask Hudson to do the same; to give up on his dream because of me? Would he resent me, if I couldn't be a part of these shows? If I said no?

I gulped. It seemed we were no longer on the same page with life.

It took me a few moments to find my voice. "And this is

something you'd really want to do," I said slowly, already knowing the answer. *Please say no. Please say no.*

"I think this could be a natural evolution for my personal brand. It would take me to the next level. I wouldn't be limited to just videos on YouTube or TikTok or Instagram. And I think, because our show is so successful, it puts us in a strong position to negotiate. Jack said we could do whatever shows we're comfortable with, even brainstorm pitches ourselves. It could become a long-term partnership."

"Hudson, I'm a *writer*." I leaned back in my seat. "I'm not made to be on camera. I'm words. I'm paper. I'm old-school. This show was supposed to be a one-off for me. I only did it in the hope that they'd run some more of my stories, which I doubt they're even going to do at this point—"

"Maybe that could be part of the deal," Hudson interrupted. "If they want shows from us, they also have to run your stories."

"Yeah, but . . . Then I still have to do the shows. I just . . ." My head pounded. The thought of more of this, the filming, the anxiety, those commenters online dissecting every part of my life . . . My stomach knotted and my hands started to shake.

Hudson reached across the table and grabbed them. "Hey, Jaz. Look at me."

But I couldn't look up right away. He put one hand on my cheek, waiting.

"You know what? This is something we can talk about later. Today is our day off, right? We'll talk about the honeymoon after the wedding."

Slowly, I raised my head to meet his blue eyes. They looked sad. Heartbroken. I knew this was not the answer he was hoping for.

"Okay." I let out a slow breath.

"And if you really don't want to do the honeymoon filming, we won't, okay?"

I nodded, my breath coming a little easier. "Thank you." I kept my eyes locked on his, even when they started to water.

Hudson searched my gaze. "But would you be willing to at least talk with me about the possibility of another show later on? Maybe an idea that would make you more comfortable?" He scooted closer. "Because this *is* something I would like to explore with Mercer." His hand fell from my cheek, only to wrap around my palm once more. "I want us to have a bright future together. To be able to retire down the road without any worries. To have a good life." Hudson continued gently, "This could put us both in a position of long-term financial security. You know?"

As I looked up at him, my stomach sank all the way down through the floorboards. He wanted this so bad. And that worried me. I forced myself to speak through the lump in my throat. "Yeah. Definitely. We can talk about it."

A relieved smile tugged at his lips. His shoulders softened. "Thank you." He clasped my hands and raised them between us. "But look, all that matters right now is that we love each other and we're getting married tomorrow. The rest of this we can figure out later, all right?"

I nodded. But I knew it wasn't that simple. Nothing ever was.

Then he tugged me closer for a slow kiss. But I couldn't sink into it the way I normally would. I couldn't lose myself in his touch, the feel of his palm against my cheek.

All I could think about was how disappointed he was going to be when I told him no. Because I couldn't do it. I couldn't become a show personality. I couldn't be a star, no matter how much Hudson wanted me to.

It just wasn't me.

* * *

After Hudson left to meet his family, I lay on the couch and stared at the ceiling. So many thoughts chased through my head, almost too fast to focus on. I couldn't shake the look on Hudson's face. How he lit up at the prospect of more shows. He wanted this more than he could express in words.

It broke my heart to know that something he loved so much could bring me so much sorrow.

But then I started to think about timing. About how much stock I've put in timing throughout my life—at times to the point of fault.

The reality was, the timing of our wedding had been so rushed. Because of the show, we were getting married only three months after our engagement. Which was completely my doing, I knew. But by trying to save my career, had I hurt my future marriage?

I practically jumped off the couch at the sound of my phone beeping. A text from Gal. Grateful for the distraction, I clicked it open.

Not sure what you are doing but Anik and I are going to chill by the pool. You in?

I assumed I'd spend my day off with Gal and my family, but after my conversation with Hudson, I needed some time alone.

Just gonna lay low and rest today, I replied.

Seconds later: *K. Text me if you need me. Love you!*

I put my phone down on the couch and lay motionless again. I needed to go for a walk. Distract myself. I remembered Rosa told me about an adorable bakery and café in downtown Cancún called Pan Amor. I had a couple books I brought along for the flights, so I grabbed one of those.

An afternoon full of coffee, pastries, and reading sounded like exactly what I needed.

I put on jean shorts, a T-shirt, and flip-flops, threw my hair in a messy bun and headed down to the hotel lobby, trying to keep my breath steady as my nervousness continued to creep towards the surface.

In through your nose, out through your mouth, I quietly chanted to myself. Luckily, there were a couple cabs waiting outside the resort, so I was able to hop in one quickly.

The whole ride, I kept my window down, the warm sea breeze dusting my cheeks. It cleared my head a little bit. Enough for me to appreciate the blue sky overhead, the sunny, brilliant day. By the time the driver pulled up outside the café, my heart rate had almost returned to normal. I paid him with a smile and headed inside.

Pan Amor looked exactly how Rosa described it: red-brick walls, cozy puffy chairs, and the scent of great coffee drifting through it all. Warming the space. Making me smile just to inhale. I wove between the wooden driftwood tables dotted with little cute accent plants, until I spotted a free one.

The seat was near the window, perfect for people-watching as resort-goers and locals alike wandered past on the street, dressed in bright colors, everyone smiling, happy.

It lightened my heart. At least *some* people were appropriately enjoying Cancún.

When the waiter passed by, I ordered my coffee and some fresh bigotes. As I sank my teeth into the buttery, flaky, delicious pastry, I felt free for a moment from my stresses.

I wished I could just hide in that café for ever. Away from the cameras. Away from my responsibilities. Away from these new expectations being piled onto me.

Away from everything.

I felt like I no longer had a grip on my life. That it was slipping like sand through my fingers, impossible to catch.

I inhaled another bigote before I felt centered enough to glance around the café. The moment I did, however, my jaw practically dropped to the floor. I spotted a familiar face on the far side of the room, bent over a laptop.

Is that . . . Elena Couture?

Leo's mother had an extra-large coffee cup beside her, and she was alternating between typing and jotting down notes longhand in a notebook. She wore a lilac dress, her brown skin practically glistening against it. She had pearl earrings in her ears and a thick, gold bracelet on her wrist. She looked as glamorous as I'd remembered her to be.

Right then, as if she could sense my gaze on her, she looked up. Her eyebrows shot up, and her smile flew wide. The next thing I knew, she was leaping from her seat, leaving both her notebook and computer behind to hurry across the café toward me.

"Jazmine! Oh goodness, mija, I can't believe it!"

I barely had time to stand before she barreled into me, her arms going tight around me in one of her trademark crushing hugs.

I worked hard to swallow tears.

Mrs. Couture was someone I always looked up to. She had it all. The thriving romance novelist career. The ideal relationship. The smart advice. The flawless style. And, she made the best tamales around. I couldn't believe I had run into her here—especially after the day I was having.

I cleared my throat of any dangerous lumps and pulled back just far enough to grin at her. "What are you doing down in Cancún?" I blinked a couple times too, just to make sure she wasn't a mirage.

"I still come down to Mexico about once a month. My sister is the manager at a hotel nearby and doesn't live very far from here. This is one of my favorite cafés to work out of when I come to visit." She gestured over her shoulder toward her corner. "I have a book deadline I'm trying to hit."

"Oh. I should get out of your hair then." I slowly backed out of the hug, not wanting to impose on her time.

"Are you kidding?" She waved an impatient hand. "The book can wait. I'm so happy to see you! Leo told me you're down here for your wedding. You're filming a show for it?"

I furrowed my brows, surprised Leo would have mentioned me and my wedding at all. I always assumed I was far from his mind. "Yeah. I wish Leo would've told me you were here. I would've invited you."

"No need." She shook her head. "I wouldn't want to intrude."

"You could never intrude. You're practically family!" The minute I spewed out the word *family*, I had to suck in a sharp breath again to hold back a sob fest. I knew if I let one single tear fall, it could open the floodgates. Safer to hold them in, *stay strong.*

She grinned. "How has it been going with Leo filming? He said you were just as surprised as he was to see you, but that's all he said."

Huh. Leo shared more than I would have guessed. *Interesting.*

"Yeah, I was definitely very surprised." I laughed a little nervously. "But it's been going well. It's . . . nice to see him again." That was the truth.

"I'm so glad." She clasped her hands in front of her heart. "Would you like to join me at my table for a little bit? It's not every day you run into Jazmine Prado in a café in Cancún. I need to take advantage of this."

She sounded so much like Leo in that moment, it did strange things to my head.

I picked up my coffee and we walked over to her table. As soon as I took a seat, my anxiety lessoned a little bit. It was so comforting to see a familiar face, especially a familiar face I enjoyed so much.

"So, you have another book deadline?" I eyed her notebook and rose-gold laptop. "I know you already know this, but my family reads all of your books. I'm kicking myself for not being fluent in Spanish, because I'd love to read them. They're always singing your praises and talking about all the juicy drama . . ."

Her grin stretched across her face. "That's very kind of them. Actually, English rights just sold for one of my books. I'm in the process of translating it. I'll send you a copy once it's done."

"That would be amazing! Thank you."

"You've turned out to be a great writer yourself, Jazmine. I always enjoy your pieces. One of my favorite essays of yours was *Caught Between Two Worlds.* I could very much relate."

I felt the heat rush to my face. I couldn't remember the last time I'd been so flattered.

"Wow. Thank you so much!"

"I visit your website from time to time for story updates. Haven't seen one from you in a while, though." She tilted her head. "Are you still writing?"

Her question felt like a punch to the gut. It was also ironic since Leo noticed the same thing a few days before. "Not at the moment, no." I slumped in my seat. "The magazine isn't running many pieces right now. That's why I agreed to do the show. I wanted to keep my job afloat."

"Ah. I see." She flashed me the type of understanding grimace that only a fellow writer could muster. "Writing is a very hard career. All these apps and social media platforms and videos aren't making it any easier."

I rolled my eyes. "Tell me about it."

"But if you love to write, you should keep writing. I'm sure there are other publications you could write for, if not for *Style&Travel*. You have a great body of work as a resumé."

More heat rushed to my face. She was very generous with her compliments. "Thank you. I would love to write anywhere at this point, honestly. It's just . . ." I tapped my fingers along the table.

Elena frowned, peering at me closely. "What, mija?"

"My career is very important to me. You know how my mom is—she raised me to support myself and follow my dreams hard."

Elena nodded. She'd heard my mother's story enough times herself, all about the movie-star dreams she never grasped after she got pregnant with me.

"But I think somewhere along the way, I started to confuse my career with my whole identity. So when the industry started to change, I couldn't . . ." I paused and let out a huff. "Gal told me to adapt to the changes. Like start a blog or build a social media platform, that kind of thing. I never really took it to heart because I'm good at my job and I stubbornly assumed it would always be there."

I stopped for a brief moment to gather my thoughts. Across from me, Elena waited patiently for me to pick up the thread once more. I shook my head. "But when faced with the prospect of losing my job, I tried to adapt in a really big way by agreeing to this show. But now it seems I might have lost my job anyway, so it was all for nothing." My eyes found the floor, stinging. I blinked a few times. "And let me tell you, I *hate* being on camera. I hate all these people knowing my personal life. I hate that viewers can love me one minute and plot my death the next. I hate that I have to think about if I look good enough. All of this is just . . . Not me."

I glanced up from my monologue and noticed Elena staring at me intensely, her dark-brown eyes processing my every word.

My cheeks flushed with embarrassment. "Shit, I'm so sorry. I haven't seen you in for ever and here I am dumping all this on you." I laughed weakly. "Bet you're glad you came to this café today."

Elena folded her hands on top of the table, her shoulders stiff. "Have you ever wondered why I don't write my books in English, even though I'm fluent in the language and live in the U.S.?"

"I have, actually." It would be a bigger market, I knew. Plus, selfishly, I'd always wanted to read one of her books.

"It's because it's very important to me to stay authentic to who I am. And a big part of that is representing my heritage. This might sound foolish and stubborn, especially considering that in the English market I could make more money and reach more people." She smiled at me, then, almost as if she'd been able to guess what I was thinking. "But I don't care about that. My romance novels always take place in Mexico. I was born in Mexico. My stories have to be true to the people, to the culture. To *my* culture. And that means writing them in my native tongue. I'm happy to translate if the English rights are ever bought—and one of them just was, which made me very happy. But it will always be Spanish first. Believe me, a lot of people, even people I very much respect, like my agent and some of my editors, have told me I should change this. Write in English first, because it is easier to sell Spanish rights than vice versa. But this is something I will never change."

She reached over and put her hand on top of mine. "Mija. When it comes to your career—and your life in general—it's good to take advice. But it's also good to know where you draw the line. To maintain your authenticity. You're a creator—only *you* can create what you have to offer the world." She leaned back in her seat then and waved a dismissive hand. "Sure, maybe you could have blogged or started a Pinterest or whatever the kids do these days. And Gal gave you good advice: finding out all the possibilities, and considering if you want to or can adapt is a good idea. But you should never *adapt* to the point where you lose yourself or wind up doing something you hate. Life's too short to be unhappy, Jazmine."

I smiled. *Life's too short to be unhappy.* Such a simple statement, yet so difficult to follow.

I couldn't remember the last time I made a choice just because it made me happy. All of my choices had revolved around saving my career. Except saying yes to Hudson's proposal, of course. But even then, I turned our wedding day into a career move.

My stomach sank.

"I understand that your career is important to you. My career is very important to me too. And we do have to pay our bills, after all. But I can't imagine not writing anymore, or being on a TV show. For others, that would be a dream, but for me?" She shook her head and clicked her tongue. "What makes a person happy is unique to each individual. That's why you can't run your whole life based on others' advice. We all have to follow what we're pulled to."

So true. *But what if you and your fiancé are now pulled to different things?* I worried my lower lip with my teeth, sinking back into the thoughts I'd been trying to ignore since this morning.

"So, tell me about your man!" Mrs. Couture asked, shifting to a smile.

I struggled to return it. Poor woman. I'd already dumped on her about my career. The last thing she needed was another doubt-filled rant from me. "Oh. Well. He's . . ." I looked down at my shiny, four-carat diamond ring. It was massive, and perfect. Just like Hudson. Ironically, this ring didn't really feel like *me* either. Just like the show. This wedding, all of it.

"Jazmine?"

"Oh. Sorry." I picked at my fingernails. "He's wonderful. Kind. Handsome. Smart. Amazing, actually. He's good for me on paper. And I'm perfect for him on paper too." I paused. "I'm just a *little* worried that . . . we're not on the same page anymore." I sniffled as my eyes started to water.

Keep it together, Jazmine. Don't open those floodgates.

"If I'm being honest, everything just feels off. I feel as though I've lost myself—in this madness of the show, in my relationship with Hudson." My bottom lip started to quiver. "I don't know who I am anymore."

I couldn't fight it. A few tears trickled down my face. Not so bad, all things considered. But still.

Elena handed me a napkin. The words *I don't know who I am anymore* played over and over in my head. I didn't even know I felt that way until I said it out loud.

"Do you love him?" Elena asked gently.

"I do. And I know that he loves me too." I grabbed another napkin. "But being on this show has opened my eyes to the fact that what we want in life might be very different now. And what brought us together in the first place, was that we wanted the same things."

For a minute, I felt a little guilty sharing all this with Mrs. Couture. But I knew she was a safe person. A trustworthy person. Someone who I'd always been so comfortable with. Someone who would take secrets to her grave.

Plus, she was removed enough from the situation that I could speak to her freely. She didn't know Hudson the way Gal, my family, friends—hell, even my boss—did. Her opinion would be unbiased.

Elena leaned back in her seat. "All I know, mija, is that love is a very powerful thing. The *most* powerful thing. Love is the reason why we keep going. How we survive. And that's true of all types of love. Romantic love, family love, friend love, self-love, love of our art. I'm talking about the real deal, not manipulators or abusers who misuse the term." She pointed a finger. "Real love is the most beautiful thing about being human. If your fiancé loves you and you love him, you'll be able to work through anything. Even his disappointment. Because your love for each other will overcome it all." She smiled softly. "But I'm very sorry you're feeling this stress right now. Is there anything I can do to help?"

"No. Honestly, you've done enough just by listening." I wiped a couple more tears off my face, then wadded the napkin in my lap. "So thank you, very much."

"One other thing." Elena looked away for moment. "Just remember, it's okay to change your mind. About anything, really. Nothing is permanent. It's never too late. Like I said before, you only get one life." She squeezed my hand. "Do what makes you happy." Then she smiled. "So, when is the big day?"

"Tomorrow."

Elena nodded. "I know you'll do what's right for you."

I swallowed thickly around a lump in my throat. "By the way . . . I know it's last minute, but you're more than welcome to come if you're free." I smiled. "It's at La Belladonna. Four o'clock. No pressure though."

Mrs. Couture opened her notebook to write down the information. "Of course I'll be there. Wouldn't dream of missing it." She flashed me one more lingering look. "Congratulations, sweetheart."

"Thank you." I drew in another deep breath. Mrs. Couture was so easy to spill your guts to. "Well, I better let you get back to writing. I appreciate you talking with me."

"Of course. And Jazmine," she added, as I rose from the table. "Don't stop writing. You're too good at it."

Leaving the café after seeing Mrs. Couture, I felt a lot different than when I had arrived. Just talking to her made me feel so much lighter.

But at the same time, I was even more confused about my relationship. I did love Hudson—I knew that without a shadow of a doubt. And I knew he loved me. But was it the kind of love that could overcome all our impending issues?

My head pounded. And under it all, I kept thinking, *You should have thought about all of this sooner. It's too late now.*

But I reminded myself of what Mrs. Couture had said: *It's never too late.* I could still change my mind.

Did I *want* to change my mind?

One thing I was pretty certain of: I wasn't doing any more shows. I couldn't spend another minute doing something I hated so much. And I would need to be stubborn about that fact.

I also wanted to pull back from social media. Hudson had gotten used to us tagging each other and posting about our relationship. I knew he loved me being a part of his world. But I couldn't do it anymore. It wasn't good for my mind. It wasn't good for my health.

I was dreading the thought of telling him that social media would be off the table too. *Fuck me.*

After wandering Cancún mindlessly for a few more hours, I retreated to my suite to order room service. But I'd barely hung up the phone when I heard a knock at the door. *That was fast.* I swung it open.

But it wasn't room service.

I opened it to find Leo on the other side.

Chapter Fourteen

I hadn't seen Leo in twenty-four hours and my chest tightened at just the sight of him. I couldn't tell why. Was it stress? Anxiety? Missing Leo after just one day apart like I did when we were young?

I wasn't sure. But the ache was different in my chest.

He was in his typical Leo garb: dark jeans, black long-sleeved T-shirt hugging his toned arms and body. As always, his brown hair was wild and wavy falling just below his ears and highlighting his sharp cheekbones. A five o'clock shadow fell across his face, and his hazel eyes glistened when they met mine.

"Hey, how's the migraine? Long gone, I hope?" Leo grinned.

I nodded. I didn't trust myself to speak around the heaviness in my throat.

"Sorry to bug you. Esmeralda left a plug for one of the lights in your room. Okay if I come in and grab it real fast?"

"Of course."

He stepped inside and assessed my stiff body language, scrunching his brows. "You okay?"

"Yeah." I shrugged. "I'm fine." I knew my answer was less than convincing. After the conversation I had with Hudson that morning, and the talk with Mrs. Couture that afternoon, my mind was on overdrive.

His eyes softened as he studied me. The air in the room grew heavy.

"Hey." He paused for a few seconds, squinting as if he were trying to solve the complexities of the universe. "I don't know what you have going on tonight, but I gotta grab this plug and run back to my room to do a few things. But after that, would you wanna grab some coffee to catch up? Maybe seven? There's a café right down the street, Amora Java. They're open till at least nine."

I flinched, taken aback by the fact that he'd want to have coffee, just the two of us. It felt like a lifetime since we'd hung out at a coffee shop—one of our favorite pastimes.

I wondered if I should mention that I'd just run into his mom, ironically, at a coffee shop. But I figured I'd wait. I hadn't had time with Leo like that in seven years; I didn't want to scare him off. Plus, it was just coffee. No alcohol involved. There'd be people around. It seemed innocent enough.

"Sure. That sounds good," I said, a hint of reluctance lingering in my voice. "Should I give you my number in case anything changes or if you're running late or something?"

Leo scratched his head. "Oh. Right." He pulled out his phone but didn't unlock it. Then, he went still. "Is it the same number as before?" He raised a brow.

I tugged at the ends of my sweater. "Yeah. It's the same."

He put his phone back in his pocket. "Mine's the same too." Leo cleared his throat. "All right then. I'll see you soon," he said, before leaving my suite with the light plug in hand.

After about an hour of lounging on the couch and snacking on a quesadilla courtesy of room service, I threw on my shoes and headed toward the coffee shop.

The walk was short, about ten minutes. But I loved the way the night breeze delicately stroked my face the entire time, and how I could taste the salt from the ocean air lingering on my lips.

As I approached the shop, it felt like fate had brought Leo and I together after all these years. And maybe it was for this. To finally clear the air and close the hurtful chapter that'd been a part of my story for far too long.

I ran my fingers over my Indalo bracelet. I was counting on its good luck and protection right then.

When I stepped inside, I inhaled deeply, cracking a faint smile as the scent of espresso tickled at my nose. This coffee shop had a completely different vibe than the one I went to earlier that day. It was modern, with clean, minimal décor. Wooden tables and chairs scattered throughout, some accent lighting, and a barista bar. Jazz music hummed softly in the background.

I spotted Leo right away. He saw me, too, and murmured something to the barista as he waved me over to a corner table.

I found myself wobbling a little as I walked toward him. When I got closer, he rose to give me a hug. Friendly. Little more than a pat on the back, really. Not like how we used to hug.

"I ordered for us both already," he said. "I was just waiting for you so they didn't get cold. I got you your Americano with cream and a pump of vanilla. When I saw you drinking it on the show, I couldn't believe it was still your drink!"

"Yeah." I let out a huff of laughter. I've had the same coffee order since high school. "You still do the same but with hazelnut instead?" I countered.

"Of course. Hazelnut is so much better than vanilla."

I rolled my eyes. Our drinks arrived and Leo passed me mine, his fingers briefly brushing over the top of my hand.

"Thank you so much for getting this." I took a sip and savored the delicious blend. It was perfect. Leo had gotten the order just right.

"I ran into your mom today," I said, clutching my hands around the warm cup. He smiled and gazed straight into my eyes. It was an inviting, cordial gaze.

"She literally just texted me and told me. I can't believe that happened! She was *so* happy to see you."

"She's the best," I grinned.

"She is. I kinda like her." He took a drink of his coffee, gaze still fixed on me. "So what else did you do today besides hanging with my mom?"

"Oh, you know," my back went stiff, "just freaking out about the live ceremony tomorrow." *And about Hudson wanting us to do more shows*, I thought to myself. "Any tips to ease the nerves, Mr. Cameraman?"

Leo shifted his weight in his chair, eyeing me with an inspective look. "What about being live makes you so nervous?"

"Um, the *live* in front of millions part," I griped. "What if I fall on my face, or vomit, or shit my pants or something?! Everyone will see! You can't edit that shit out, literally."

Leo choked on his coffee, his laughs sputtering in between coughs. "Now *that* would be an entertaining show."

"Don't say that!" I reached across the table and playfully smacked his shoulder. It was an old reflex that used to come about whenever Leo would tease me. Funny, how quickly one could fall back into old patterns.

But for a split second, I wondered if it was inappropriate, considering the present state of our friendship, or lack thereof. But Leo's hysterics proved me otherwise.

A moment later, his laughter quieted. Leo cleared his throat. "You know you're overthinking this, right?"

"Oh, I know." I chuckled. "But that doesn't make me any less freaked out."

He folded his arms over his chest, wrapping one hand over his bicep. His muscle bulged in response, testing the tensile strength of his fitted shirt. "Just try and pretend the cameras aren't there," he offered. "You know, zone them out."

"Pretend the cameras aren't there." I tapped my finger on my chin, like I was actually considering it. "How did I not think of that," I countered sarcastically.

"I know, it was a shitty suggestion. Hmm." He pursed his lips together. "What about having Lita pull some tarot cards for you, or make you one of her special teas?"

I shook my head. "I thought of that. But then I run the risk of the cards being bad and her making me some gross drink to counteract it. I don't need any bad luck tomorrow."

"Ah. Good point." Leo drummed his fingers on the table. "Clearly, I'm not very good at the live-ceremony tips. But what about Gal? I'm sure she has something that can calm your nerves. Does she still carry around her bag of goodies?"

"Yes." I snickered. "And it's grown substantially."

"Why am I not surprised?" A grin tugged at his lips. "Did you know that the first weed gummie I ever tried was one Gal gave me from her bag, junior year in high school? I made the mistake of having two, not knowing that you're supposed to start slow. Let's just say soccer practice that day was a bust. I couldn't stop laughing. I kept falling over. I think my coach knew but didn't say anything. I went home after practice and pretty much ate my whole kitchen."

I burst into laughter. "How do I not remember that?"

"You were going out with Brian Doyle at the time so you were doing your own thing." He rolled his eyes.

"Ah, the Brian Doyle phase," I reminisced. "Why did you hate him so much?"

Leo sat up a little straighter. His posture went tight; his face pensive. Like he was inwardly rehearsing his words before saying them. "He just . . . wasn't good enough for you." He shrugged. "You were pretty selective of the few people you dated, and Brian, I just never understood."

My stomach fluttered. Heat found my cheeks. "Well, he did end up being kind of an asshole, so you were on to something." I paused to take a sip of my coffee. The warm drink made my face flush even more. I wished in that moment it was iced. "And let's be real, you were clearly the opposite when it came to selectiveness," I teased.

"What can I say? I find beauty in everyone." Leo smiled as his eyebrows danced upward. Just then, a barista came beside our table, offering us a complementary plate of conchas. I could never say no to conchas. Leo couldn't either. It was one of his favorite pastries that his mom made—at least, it was growing up. We both said thank you and the moment the barista stepped away we dug into the Mexican sweet bread.

"So what do you have going on after this gig?" I asked between bites.

"That's actually what I'm in the process of deciding." He let out a long breath. "I got an offer yesterday to do a documentary about the Amazon rainforest, to bring awareness to why we should be preserving it and protecting it, and all that. It's with a reputable production company and currently in a bidding war with all the streaming networks. They want me to film and produce it and they said I could have the freedom to pick my film crew. It was a pleasant surprise."

My breath caught in my throat. A documentary about the rainforest? All the big networks want it? This was a huge deal. "Oh my God, Leo, that's amazing! What's there to decide?"

"Well, it will be at least six months of filming in South America. And I don't mind being away for that long, but I do like to see my family when I can, and six months is kind of long. My mom thinks I should do it though."

"So do I. Who cares if it's six months!" I raised my hands in the air. "It sounds like a great opportunity. And the time will fly by. Plus, it's not like you have a wife and kids waiting for you at home or anything."

Leo lightly flinched. His shoulders stiffened. It completely slipped my mind that he and Elizabeth broke off their engagement not that long ago. And she just married someone else.

"Sorry." I shook my head. "I didn't mean it that way—"

"I know you didn't. And you're right." He nodded. "Now is a good time to do something like this since I'm *very* single."

Very single. I wondered what exactly he meant by that. No girlfriend in addition to no casual relationships and no random hook-ups? As far as I remembered, Leo was rarely *very* single. He always had someone in his life. He was a magnet. It was part of his charm.

"And I'll probably do the doc," he continued. "I just wanted to think about it before committing, at least until I get back to L.A."

"Well, that's amazing that they even offered this to you." I took the last bite of the concha in my hand, wiping my mouth with a napkin. "It's really cool that you've stuck with your dreams, Leo." I beamed. "That you've accomplished so much."

My voice cracked at my words. My eyes started to burn. Leo was keeping with his dreams. Finding success. Staying true to himself. I admired it. It made me ache to do the same.

His face softened. "You okay?"

"Yeah, I'm good," I lied, sucking in a long breath and stuffing down any impending tears. "It's just very impressive is all. You should be proud."

"Well, impressing Jazmine Prado is no easy feat, so I'll take it." He smirked.

"I'd say impressing *you* isn't easy either."

"It's not. Which is why you should be so honored that I'm impressed by you."

I pressed my lips together, my hands clutching around my cup a little tighter. "Ha. Probably not now though, huh? Doing this show?"

Leo's face grew stiff; his jaw tight. "Always, Jazmine." He inched forward. "Now. Then. I've been impressed by you since first grade."

I swallowed hard. "Well, thank you for saying that."

"Did you ever follow up with Jack via email about that pitch?" Leo asked, before taking another sip of his coffee.

"Oh, right." I shifted in my seat. "I mentioned that in the bathroom during my migraine from hell. To be honest, that's all very fuzzy. I was in a lot of pain and also vomiting my life away so only remember bits and pieces. Hopefully I didn't say anything too weird?"

"No, not at all." Leo grinned warmly. "And I'll repeat what I said in case you don't remember. Whether or not Jack takes your pitch doesn't matter. You're not done writing, Jazmine. You're just getting started."

My chest slowly rose.

"I'm serious!" he continued. "What you've accomplished, your career, it doesn't define you but I know it means a lot to you. So you should know that you've already accomplished a lifetime worth of things—winning awards, writing for huge publications, having viral stories. But even still, the world's only seen just a sliver of what Jazmine Prado can do. I truly believe that."

The energy that Leo had in that moment, the belief he had in me and my writing, was moving. And I knew I needed to find that energy for myself again.

"You know, you saying that, about me just getting started with writing, is the only thing I remember clearly from the conversation. And I appreciate it." My lips turned upwards. "You've always been really supportive, Leo. And it's always meant a lot."

Just then, I reminded myself what I came to the coffee shop for: to get some closure. I wasn't sure when I'd have an opportunity to talk with him like this again. I wanted to make the most of it.

"And not to completely change the subject, but . . ." I cleared my throat, "do you think we should talk about, you know, the elephant in the room? What happened between us?" I crossed my ankles and rapidly bobbed my knees up and down.

"You know, I was just about to suggest the same thing." Leo put his half-eaten concha back down on the plate, wiping his hands in a deliberate manner. "As nice as it's been to sort of shoot the shit, I know we have some air to clear."

I was relieved my request wasn't too left-field for him. We'd always been simpatico. It seemed we still were.

"So where do you think we went wrong?" Leo asked, leaning back in his seat. "I mean, we were young, we made mistakes. I made mistakes. Big ones. But the biggest mistake we made, in my opinion, was letting it break us. Letting fifteen years of solid friendship just pour down the drain."

My entire body flooded with heat. "You're right." I almost reached for him, then thought better of it and curled my hand back around my coffee cup. "Leo, I need you to know that I'm really sorry about how things went down between us all those years ago. I shouldn't have given you an ultimatum like that. I was shitty to you. I was jealous. Immature. Stupid." I bit my bottom lip. "I'm just . . . I'm really sorry."

He reached over and squeezed my hand, just once. The touch was all too brief but his heat lingered on my skin long after he withdrew it.

"I was shitty to you too. I should have never left that night. I shouldn't have answered my phone. *I* was so immature and stupid. And I should've reached out to you more to make it right." His eyes found the table and he brushed away a few crumbs. "I thought you made it clear that you didn't want to hear from me anymore and I didn't want to crowd on your space. To push you. But I do wish I'd tried a little harder."

When his gaze moved up, the flecks of gold in his hazel eyes shone brighter than before. It reminded me of staring into his eyes in my youth. And then, I thought about why I never reached out to him. *The kiss.* "Well, it wasn't just you who didn't reach out. I know I never tried to make things right either, but I did have my reasons."

"You knew I wanted to hear from you, right? Did you think I didn't want you to reach out? Because I checked my phone so much it was embarrassing."

I let out a little laugh. "No. It wasn't that." I took a deep breath. "It was because I saw you kiss Elizabeth in front of The Coffee Shop." As soon as the words left my mouth, my eyes started to sting. I hated coming back to that feeling. It was like removing a scab on a wound and restarting the healing process all over again.

"Oh." Leo's face dropped. "*That.*"

"Yeah, *that*. I'm fine now." I waved a dismissive hand. "But seeing you kiss Elizabeth right after our fight . . ." my voice squeaked, "was hard for me. You leaving, and then seeing that, I felt betrayed. And it hurt me so much that I just couldn't talk to you again."

Leo slumped. "I'm so sorry, Jazmine. I really am."

"Thank you." I nodded. The air between us felt super-heated, like baking in the middle of a desert in the dead of summer. Or maybe it was just me. But I was starting to sweat. I rolled up the sleeves on my sweater. "Did you know I was in my car that day?"

Leo's face scrunched. He let out a long sigh. "I did."

I looked away. "Wow," I muttered. I always assumed that he saw me. Leo didn't miss anything. But confirming that he actually did see me was harder to hear than I thought.

"The truth is, I was just being petty as fuck." He shrugged. "I saw you in your car and I was upset that you gave me the ultimatum of not being friends anymore, and that you ignored my letter, and that every time I called you it went to voicemail. I was hurt. And I wanted to do something hurtful." He picked at a sugar sachet on the table. "Honestly, it's something I regret every day. I know how you are. I knew I ended it right then with what I did."

His mouth turned downward. He was just as remorseful as I was.

"Just so you know," I cleared my throat, "I wasn't ignoring your letter or your phone calls. My phone was off for most of the week and I didn't get your letter until that very moment in the car. I was about to call you and apologize too, and then I saw you."

"Hmm. Great." He smiled thinly but it wavered at the edges. "Boy, would I do things differently if I could go back."

"Me too." I absently twirled a loose strand of hair around my finger. "Do you think we were maybe too attached to each other? I mean, we spent practically all our time together as kids."

"Maybe. I didn't care though." He grinned, for real this time. It was his typical lopsided Leo grin. A grin that always brightened up a room. "I just loved being around you, Jazmine. You're like the flavoring of life. You make things that are usually bland suddenly interesting."

"Flavoring of life?" I raised a brow. "Maybe *you* should be the writer?"

"Ha," he chuckled. "I'll leave the writing to you."

We sat in momentary silence as the gravity of our conversation sank in. "When I published my first article I thought of you," I said. "You were the first person I wanted to tell."

"I thought the same thing when I got my first photography gig." He smiled sadly. "It was weird not sharing that with you after talking about it for so many years."

I nodded in agreement. "Do you think things would be different now if we'd stayed friends all these years?"

His eyes locked with mine and I struggled to read the emotion in them. "You wouldn't be walking down the aisle tomorrow, that I am pretty certain of."

My stomach flipped and my palms began to feel clammy. I wiped them on the bottom of my sweater. Leo searched my eyes before vigorously shaking his head.

"Sorry." He put his face in his hands. "I probably shouldn't have said that."

"It's okay," I said, putting on my best happy face. "I know what you mean."

He scooted forward. "Look, all of this is in the past now. And you *are* getting married tomorrow. This is *your* time. Your moment. You shouldn't have any unfinished business lingering in the way. So I'm glad we were able to talk about this. And I hope you know that I'm really sorry for hurting you."

"I'm really sorry too." And right after I uttered the words, I felt a little lighter.

"Come on," he said, his voice gentler than ever. "I'll walk you back to your suite."

The ten-minute walk back went by in a flash. We spent the whole time laughing again over Lita and my mom stealing the gold dinnerware. And before I knew it, we were back at the villa and in front of my suite.

I opened the door with my key card and we both stepped inside. "Thanks so much for the coffee," I said. "And for inviting me in the first place. You're the bigger person." I drew a deep breath, hoping he couldn't see all the emotions raging through me. "You win."

"I always do." He winked. "But seriously, I'm glad too. It was really nice to talk. And it was *long* overdue."

"That's for sure."

We stared at each other. Silent. Part of me wanted to ask if we could do this again. Catch up, get coffee when we were both back in L.A. Or even just start texting each other again. But would that be appropriate? I wasn't sure.

"We should do this again sometime," Leo offered, practically reading my mind. "Maybe when we're back in Cali. You can bring Hudson if you want?"

Bring Hudson? I felt my eyes widen. "Really?"

"Yeah. I mean, that's what friends do, right?" he said casually. "They get coffee with their friend and their spouse?"

I nodded. "Yeah. Um. That could be fun."

Coffee with Hudson *and* Leo. That would be . . . interesting.

"Well," he said as he moved towards the door, "at least

you've only got one more day of filming and then you'll be done being on camera for ever."

"Ha," I said with a huff, thinking about Hudson's earlier proposition. "Not exactly."

He stopped cold. "What do you mean?"

"Oh. Hudson wants us to do more shows together, but I'm telling him 'no.' I can't put myself through this torture again." The second the words left my mouth, I regretted them. I knew I shouldn't be telling Leo this, not before I told Hudson, at least. But I had spent my whole, young life telling Leo everything, so it just sort of slipped out.

"Wait a minute. Hudson wants you to do more shows? Did he just meet you?" Leo turned his hands up, his face contorting into a look of disgust.

"What are you talking about?" I spouted back.

"You clearly hate this. You're miserable!" His voice was louder this time. "As you said, you were only doing this *one* show for the hope of more writing opportunities. That writing was the long-term plan."

"Yes," I said, matching the volume of his tone. "Which is why I'm telling him I'm not going to do it—"

"But the fact that he would even suggest that to you is just . . ." He scowled, but he looked more angry at himself than me.

"What? Is just what?"

His pupils flared as his eyes locked on mine. "Look. I know I'm probably over-stepping here by asking you this. But I still care about you, so I have to." He paused and took a deep breath. "Are you happy?"

My throat locked up, trapping my words inside my chest, and I forced myself to swallow. "What the fuck does that mean?" I finally got out.

"Are you happy, Jazmine? Because when I came up here earlier to get the light plug, you looked really sad. And I wondered why you would look so sad the night before your wedding. Is this why? Is it because you might be doing more shows?"

I flinched, angry that he was able to read me still. "Yeah. I'm happy," I snapped.

"Well, you seem *thrilled*."

My cheeks burned red. I could feel the anger pulsing through my veins. "Are you really going to start a fight with me after we just cleared the air? After we just put the past behind us? After we were starting to become friends again?"

He took another step closer. "I'm not trying to pick a fight with you. I just . . . I think you're not being honest with yourself. And I can't not say anything about it. I'm sorry."

"Leo." I crossed my arms. "I'm super grateful we were able to talk things out tonight and get some closure, but the reality is, what I do with my life is none of your business."

He retracted sharply like he'd just been stung. "You're right, it's none of my business." He raised a hand. "But tell me this. What happened to the girl who never did anything she didn't want to do? Who wouldn't take any shit from anyone? Who wouldn't do desperate things to keep her job with a company because she knew how talented she was and knew that she could reach any goal that she wanted? What happened to that stone-cold drive, that fiery ambition?"

"What are you saying?"

"I'm saying you're better than this." His voice grew even louder. "You're better than thinking all you're worthy of doing is starring in someone else's show, especially when you don't even want to do it in the first place."

His words burned like venom, even though I knew they were true. I'd lost some of my confidence after my first editorial lay-off. And I buried the rest of it after weathering another. My past awards and viral articles and respect among my peers couldn't shine through the dark cloud of being let go. Of feeling like I failed.

From then on out, it became about staying afloat instead of rising above. I'd lost the wind in my sails. And it hadn't returned since.

Regardless, though, Leo didn't know what it was like to be in my shoes. He wasn't with me when I experienced those losses. "You know, it's just not that simple," I countered. "Sometimes, you just have to take what you can get."

"No," he said, sternly. "No. That's not the Jazmine Prado way. You don't settle. That's not the girl I knew. That's not the girl I'm in love with."

My mouth dropped. Suddenly, I felt like I was breathing through a straw. Not enough oxygen getting to my brain. Because surely he didn't just say what I think he said.

"*Was* in love with, when we were young or whatever," he clarified, fumbling his words.

Leo swallowed hard, his hazel eyes glassed over. He exhaled loudly. And then I saw it again: the pain. The pain I glimpsed on the beach our first day of filming.

The pain I caused him. The pain we caused each other. Years of unnecessary heartbreak. Years we will never get back.

His hands spread at his sides. Defeated. "Okay. I've said too much. I gotta go."

"Leo, wait."

He spun back around, his gaze hot on mine, wilder than before. More desperate. I took a step toward him. When he didn't flinch away this time, I took another. Until we stood face to face, inches apart. So close I could catch the familiar scent of his cologne, a warm, spicy smell that reminded me of our college years.

"*Was* in love with, or *am* in love with? What did you mean?" My jaw went tight.

Leo sucked in a deep breath. Then he calmly clasped his hands together. "I can't get into this."

"You can't just say all this to me without an explanation! We literally both *just* apologized for everything, we can't start this weird cycle between us again—"

"Okay, fine. Yes." He threw his hands in the air. "I still have feelings for you. I didn't plan to tell you, obviously. It just slipped out."

The world went quiet. The room narrowed around us, until all I could see was Leo. Leo, taking another step toward me. Leo, breathless, staring, filled with emotions he'd never let me see before.

He somehow still looked just like his eighteen-year-old self, his dark eyes alight with hope and desire. The night we first really kissed.

"I've loved you since the first grade, Jazmine." His voice was low and soft, and my heart hammered against my ribcage. "I'll always have feelings for you." He lifted one shoulder, let it fall again. "That's just how it is. I've tried for years to get over you. Tried to fill that hole with other people. I've come to accept that I just never will. No matter how hard I try. I can't." He stepped back and went still. "And now that you know this, I'm not sure if us being friends is such a good idea. I don't see that working out so well." He ran a hand through his hair, the same hair I used to love watching fall across his forehead. "And I'm sorry that this slipped out right now, and for telling you all this. I shouldn't have." He grimaced, wrenching that hand from his hair to press it over his mouth instead, as if he could push those words back inside and take them back.

"But more than anything, I just want you to be happy. And

that's the God's honest truth." He shook his head again, harder this time. "And now, I really think I'd better go."

I blocked his path to the door.

We stood inches apart, our chests rising and falling fast, almost in sync. He took a step forward, and I mirrored him, until I was pinned against the door.

His warm breath caressed my cheeks. He smelled sweet as candy. Like sugar that would melt on your tongue.

His gaze shifted to my lips. I couldn't help it. I did the same. This close, I remembered how soft his lips had been against mine. Supple and smooth, with the perfect amount of plumpness. A pleasant wave of heat rippled through my body, starting at my toes and racing its way up until it swirled around in my head, leaving me a little dizzy.

There was a part of me that wanted to kiss him. To press my lips into his. To feel his tongue against my teeth. To run my hands through that messy hair of his while he cupped the small of my back and drew me closer.

But I didn't kiss him.

Because I loved Hudson. And I was marrying him in under twenty-four hours. No matter what past feelings still lingered for Leo, I could never do that to Hudson. I could never cheat on him.

It seemed that timing or fate wasn't on Leo's and my side. That maybe all the time we would ever have together was frozen in our past. Where our love for each other would live, and possibly die one day, too.

Maybe he'd always be just a ghost from my past, haunting me until the end of my days. A ghost who understood me better than anyone.

As I stared into Leo's glassy eyes, a frown on his lips, I could tell he was fighting to resist kissing me too. But he wouldn't.

Because even if he'd hated Hudson, he would have never let me cheat. He'd know how the guilt would eat me up inside, how I'd hate myself for it.

We wrenched our gazes apart and our chests hitched.

Slowly, so slowly I could have stopped him if I'd wanted to, and oh, a part of me *wanted to* . . . Leo reached his hand behind me. His arm grazed my lower back. Then he grasped the door handle, and pulled it open.

I swallowed hard as he brushed past me, near enough to touch. But he might as well have been a million miles away, for all that mattered.

He cleared his throat. "See you tomorrow," he whispered. And then, he was gone.

Chapter Fifteen

I woke up alone in my suite.

It was the first time I'd slept without Hudson since we arrived in Cancún. We'd decided to sleep separately the night before our wedding to keep with tradition, build up anticipation . . . and so we wouldn't risk him seeing my wedding dress (because who needs the bad luck?).

I got about one hour of sleep that night. One.

After Leo left, I couldn't stop thinking about him. I spent some time attempting to meditate with black tourmaline, burning the last of the palo santo, and pulling a few tarot cards. But nothing could clear him from my mind.

The way his voice sounded. *I've loved you since the first grade.*

The pain in his eyes as he said it. The heartbreak. How it broke my heart, to watch his crack. Thinking about it made my chest go tight, my breath catch.

I knew *something* would always exist between Leo and me. But to hear that? Regret over my past mistakes taunted me.

But more than that, I couldn't stop thinking about Hudson. How I truly loved him and committed to him, but how we clearly wanted different things. How we were no longer on the same page. And how it didn't take much to get us on different wavelengths.

But the circus couldn't be stopped. And I wondered how it would all shake out after we said "I do." I wasn't sure. But one thing was for certain, I needed to reacquaint myself with the girl I once was, and the woman who I wanted to be. And who I wasn't, was a reality star.

I wouldn't do any more shows. And I would be stern with Hudson about that fact.

How much would he resent me for crushing his newfound dream with Mercer Media? I pondered.

Guilt and fear swirled in my stomach, a dangerous mix.

I lay in bed and stared at the ceiling, thinking about how Mercury had just gone into retrograde and hoping that because of that, something would go wrong with the live stream. Maybe the cameras would fail. Maybe the app would crash. Maybe astrology would save my ass. A girl could dream, right?

Somewhere in between staring into space and being lost in thought, the glam team arrived.

Just like me, they seemed off. Stiff postures, tight lips. Bloodshot eyes from lack of sleep. They appeared to be just as stressed as I was about the big day.

Even the air felt different. Still. Focused.

Maybe it was because we were about to go live. Or maybe my crew worried about the show coming to a close? I tried to ask Blue, but he just patted my shoulder. "Don't worry about me. You're getting married in a few hours!"

That set off a fresh storm of panic in my gut, and made me fall silent once more.

After that, Blue remained relatively quiet as he finished my make-up (which was unusual for him). "I can't believe it's only hours away," he tried again a few minutes later, as he dusted on some eyeshadow.

"Me neither," I replied. The shakiness in my voice frightened me.

"You better keep in touch with me when this is over, girlie." Blue moved on to my cheeks, adding the blush. "We're friends on social media now. Plus I've worked on your bare face. We're practically family at this point." He pursed his lips as he worked.

"I promise I'll keep in touch," I replied with a laugh. "You live in New York, right?"

"Yeah. But I'm in L.A. a lot too. We have to meet up."

"Oh, me too! I want to join the meet-up," Celine added in a cute, whiny tone, curling iron in hand. She was giving me loose, flowing curls, adding in random extensions to make my long dark hair look even more lush, full and fairy tale-like.

"Me three!" Zoe chimed in from where she was working on opening a massive box.

My wedding dress.

"Don't forget about me. I know I'm just the assistant, but I have feelings too." Jared made an exaggerated pout, and we all laughed.

Poor Jared got stuck with all the worst duties during the show, including multiple coffee runs for me. He was a good sport about it, though.

It's amazing how quickly you can feel bonded to people. In less than a week, the glam team really had started to feel like family, the way Blue said. I was grateful for their steady, calming presence, especially when I'd found myself knee-deep in the comments section. They had become a fun reprieve from all the chaos surrounding the show.

"So, where are you and Hudson going to live in L.A?" Blue

peered at me in the mirror before he went back to filling in my brows.

"We're going to start house-hunting when we get back. Until we find a place, we'll just stay at my apartment, and—" I stopped mid-sentence. My heart started to race. My vision blurred and I blinked a few times. I could hardly see myself in the mirror.

"You good?"

I blinked again. Blue and his mustard-colored Nirvana shirt grew a little clearer.

Though my vision was coming back, I still felt like I was on the verge of hyperventilating. "I'm okay," I gasped. "I think . . . I just need . . . some water, is all."

"Jared, can you get Jaz a water bottle?" Blue snapped his fingers, motioning toward the kitchen.

"Right away."

As Jared practically sprinted out of the room, Kelly walked in, all smiles, wearing a lovely pale-blue pantsuit. Her black, curly hair sat up in a sleek topknot.

I inhaled deeply, held it, then exhaled slowly through my mouth, working my hardest to compose myself.

I didn't want Kelly to think anything was wrong. I mean, I had made it that far.

"How's the bride-to-be?" She tilted her head while assessing my face.

I must have done a good job at faking calm, because her posture relaxed and her mouth curved upwards.

"A little nervous about going live, but good."

Jared returned with the water bottle. I opened it and took a huge gulp. The cool, refreshing taste of the water helped a little bit. At least it soothed some of the burn in my chest.

Behind Jared, I noticed Gal. She was all glammed up:

smokey gray eyeshadow, shiny nude lips. Contour that brought out her high cheekbones. Her dark hair was straightened and shiny, and the maid-of-honor dress (one of many sent by top-tier brands), which I let her pick out for herself, was a classic little black dress, complete with a low neckline and a cinched waist. It fit her like a glove. She was drenched in jewelry too, silver bangles and diamonds.

The moment I saw her, my posture relaxed. She looked flawless. More than that, she looked like Gal. My cousin. My confidant. My rock.

"Gal." I whistled, grateful for the change of subject. Glad I could pay attention to someone else for a change. "You are gorgeous!"

She waved a dismissive hand. "Oh my gosh, *you* are gorgeous. And you don't even have the dress on yet!" She took in my appearance from head to toe, nodding all the while.

I tugged at my white robe, the one with the word *BRIDE* emblazoned across the back. "Thanks," I managed, trying not to let my nerves show.

Blue took over for me, practically gushing. "Right?! Jaz is going to look like a straight-up princess." He swiped a final coat of lipstick across my already-lined lips. "She's major bride goals."

I chuckled and glanced over my shoulder. My smile quickly faded.

There, standing in the doorway, was Leo. His eyes looked wide and sparkling. His grin lopsided, coy. As if nothing had happened yesterday. As if he was fine with all this.

But as I kept looking, under that serene veneer, I could see a hint of his anguish.

My hands went numb.

"Hey, Jazmine." He gave me a sheepish wave.

"Hey, Leo." The room around us fell silent. He held a camera in one hand and a coffee drink in the other.

I turned towards Kelly, curious as to why Leo was here with a camera. "I thought we weren't filming anything besides the live stream today?"

Everyone stared at me now, including Leo. He was probably wondering why I would question his presence.

"He's here to get some behind-the-scenes footage for the bonus content that we'll be releasing in a couple days," Kelly explained. "You know how it goes."

"Oh. Okay. Cool." I rubbed my hands to try to get some warmth back into them. They felt cold as ice.

Moments later, multiple phones in the room started to ring. Both Gal and Kelly stepped out to take calls. Everyone else got back to work. Which left me alone with Leo, while the beauty team began to clean up their supplies.

"Hey, I got this for you." Leo handed me the coffee drink. "You know they put 'The Jazmine' on the official resort menu today?"

I managed a smile. This must have been a peace offering, after our intense chat last night. "Thank you." I took a sip and grinned. Just right. "How are you doing?"

"Good." He put the camera down and stuffed his hands in his pockets. "I'm good."

He didn't seem good. I knew him too well to be fooled.

Plus, I've learned if someone keeps repeating that they're good, chances are they're probably not very "good."

"Hey, guys?" He glanced at the glam team. "Could you give me and Jazmine a minute?"

As everyone shuffled out, it suddenly felt like déjà vu. On their way past, Blue eyed me curiously, Zoe grimaced with confusion, and Celine flashed me a little thumbs up of encouragement.

Once the last person had shut the door behind them, Leo inched a little closer. "Your hair and make-up look beautiful, Jazmine." He studied me as an art student might study a painting. "Absolutely beautiful. Really stunning."

My skin went hot. "Thanks." I looked away, blushing hard. "So . . ." I started as I fiddled with my lucky charm on my wrist. "How are you doing, really? I wasn't sure. After last night."

"I'm fine. Promise." A weak grin pulled at his lips. His gaze shifted away, though. "How are you doing?" He watched as I pulled at my bracelet. "I know I said some . . . *things* I shouldn't have." He cleared his throat. "And I'm really sorry about that. I truly am. I should have kept my mouth shut. I'm usually so good at that, but not around you, apparently."

We both grinned.

"Leo. I, uh . . ." I gulped. My eyes started to water. I blinked them hard. *Keep it together.* "I wanted you to know, I've really liked working with you. Just, seeing you again, really. I've missed you." My throat went tight. "A lot, actually. And as hard as it was to hear, you were right about me not really being myself lately, losing sight of who I am—" That did it. A couple tears snuck down my cheeks.

Leo reached for a nearby tissue and dabbed at them. "Jazmine. It's your special day. You can't cry now. You've got to save that for the altar." He smiled warmly. "Plus, you can't ruin that perfect make-up."

I let out a weak laugh and peered up at his hazel eyes. "Look. I know in the past I made a lot of mistakes. But I don't want to do that anymore." I grabbed another tissue and carefully dabbed under my eyes, trying my best not to ruin Blue's creation. "I want to have you in my life, as a friend, in any way you're comfortable with. If it's too hard, I completely understand. I know it's selfish of me to even ask. But I needed to let you know, the door is always open on my end." I sniffled. Finally got my tight throat under control.

As for Leo, he knelt down in front of the make-up chair, his knee brushing mine. He was close enough now for me to see the struggle behind his eyes. But the hope, too. "I would argue that Leo Couture and Jazmine Prado *have* to be friends." He smirked. "Fate keeps bringing us together."

Right then, he sounded like the Leo I once knew. And loved.

"It sure seems that way." I chuckled as I wiped my nose.

Leo reached over, hesitated, and then slowly placed his hand on top of mine. "I want to be in your life, too."

"You do?" A rush of relief spread through me. I didn't know what I expected. But I guessed I'd been afraid that maybe, after all this time, it might be too late for us.

"I do," he said, and smiled that familiar smile of his. My skin went warm all over again. "I want to be in your life in whatever way you'll let me. I know what I said yesterday, that it maybe wasn't a good idea. But I thought about it and I realized through all this that I'd rather have you in my life on your terms, as a friend, than not in my life at all. And I promise, moving forward, I'll keep my mouth shut when it comes to your life, at least I'll try anyway." He winked. "And as strange as it is, I'm happy to have been a part of your wedding." He paused. "By the way, did you invite my mom?" He raised a brow.

I let out a little laugh. "Yes, I did. After running into her yesterday, I couldn't not. You know I love that woman." He grinned, and I shook my head, smiling back. "You two are so much alike," I added.

"I learned from the best." With a shrug, hc rosc to stand, and squeezed my shoulder. "Only happy tears from now on, okay?" He leaned in, and I stiffened, until he gently wiped away a smudge of mascara with his thumb.

I thought this was supposed to be waterproof. I swallowed hard in the back of my throat, as his thumb lingered on my cheekbone for a heartbeat.

Then he pulled back. "I'll go get the make-up guy."

"Thanks."

Leo paused on his way out. "You really do look beautiful, Jazmine. I'm really happy for you."

I smiled and nodded. And as Leo stepped outside, for the first time in seven years, I felt like I could finally put this behind me. That I would no longer need to stuff it, or hide from it, or not speak of it, but actually let it go. Forgive him for his mistakes and forgive myself for mine. I finally got what I had been waiting for: closure. No more unfinished business. We could move on at last and be friends again. It was one of the greatest gifts I could have received on my wedding day.

But my joy over Leo didn't last long as visions of the live ceremony flashed through my mind. My stomach soured. I felt like acid was eating me from the inside out.

I clamped my hand over my mouth, dry heaving just as Blue walked back in.

"Jesus, Jazmine!" He flinched and waved his hands at me. "What happened?!"

"I'm sorry," I groaned. "Fucking live show jitters." I pointed at my face. "Already wrecked the mascara."

He tutted, but grabbed his brushes at the same time. "Don't worry, sweetie. I got you."

After Blue touched up my make-up, Zoe ordered everyone except for her and Celine out. It was time for the dress.

And what a dress it was. A frothy white confection, with a simple bodice and sweetheart neckline, that flowed into a crinkled, lace-effect train that billowed out from my waist to trail a full three feet behind me when I moved in it. When I'd tried it on a month ago with my mother and Gal in attendance, they had gushed over it.

But now, staring at it, it felt more real than ever. Imminent.

I was about to walk down the aisle in this. In front of millions of people.

I felt like I was having an out-of-body experience. I watched the other two fluff the gown, readying it for me. I took Celine's hand when she offered, and carefully stepped into the bodice Zoe held open for me. I sucked in a breath as they zipped it up the back, then carefully hid the zip in the layers of crushed silk.

All the while, I stared at the girl in the mirror. She looked like a complete stranger. Like a princess, a little girl's fantasy dream of a bride.

But not like me. Not at all.

I felt like an imposter. Like I didn't belong there. *This isn't me*, something screamed, deep in the recesses of my mind.

What am I doing?

My whole body tensed when I heard a knock. Kelly peeked inside. "Jazmine, your *familia* just got here—" She stopped dead, eyes going wide. "Oh. My. God. You look *stunning*. They're going to freak out when they see you!" She clapped. "I'll tell them you'll be out soon. And Leo will be filming your reveal, too, for the bonus content."

I nodded, silent.

A few seconds later, Rex arrived to attach my lapel mic. I hoped my dry-heaving episodes from my stage fright had finished. That would not be pleasant audio.

"Thanks, Rex," I murmured as he attached the final cord.

"You ready?" Zoe reached over and grabbed my hand. Celine took the other. Blue put a hand on my arm. "You got this, Jaz," Zoe said. Blue and Celine nodded.

"All right." I let out a long breath. "Let's do this."

I stepped out into the living area where my family waited. All at once, there they were: my mom and dad; Oliver and Gabe; Mamá and Papá Prado; Lito and Lita; Gal and Anik.

They went dead silent when they saw me, which was rare for them. You could have heard a pin drop.

I noticed Leo near the window. The natural sunlight lit the side of his face. But the camera he held had sagged to his hip, half forgotten. He was beaming. The same smile he gave me when we went to our junior prom together and he first saw me walking down the stairs of my parents' house.

We locked gazes as he shook his head and mouthed, *Wow.*

I smiled, my eyes going a little misty again. I let out a long breath, then forced the impending tears back inside. Leo was right. Save those for the altar.

Beside Leo stood Esmeralda, Mateo, and Jared. Rex followed me out of the bedroom and joined them. Kelly stood not too far away, smiling wide and wiping a tear from her eye. Next to her was Rosa, the La Belladonna event planner, who must have snuck in while I was getting dressed. She sniffled pointedly, too.

Apparently brides made people cry.

"My bebé. My beautiful bebé!" My mother rushed toward me, arms wide. "You look like a princess, Jazzy." Her eyes welled with tears. "An actual princess." She paused. "Where the hell are the tissues around here?"

Without a word, Zoe handed her the box she'd been clutching. I could tell that was going to get a workout.

Even my dad grabbed one, as he smiled at me. "You look so beautiful, honey."

"Thanks, Dad."

I looked to Gabe and Oliver next. Gabe was already low-key crying. Oliver struggled to resist. "I've never worked so hard not to cry in my life," my brother groaned, his voice cracking.

"Me too," I croaked back. "But you'd better stop, before you fuck up my make-up." I laughed as I pointed to my face.

He rolled his eyes. "Oh, what the hell, bring on the tears." He threw his arms around me and squeezed tight. "I am so happy for you, Jazzy."

"Thanks, Oli." I swallowed hard. *Keep it together, Jazmine. Blue can only touch up so much.*

After I released Oliver from my clutches, Mamá and Papá Prado each gave me a kiss on the cheek. "I am so happy for you, mi amor," Mamá Prado cooed.

Papá Prado smiled over her shoulder and gave me a reassuring wink.

"Gracias," I replied. My grandparents' faces lit up. Figured I could bust out my little Spanish for them. I mean, they did come all this way.

Then Anik walked over in his crisp, pinstriped suit to give me a side hug. "You look beautiful, Jaz. Congratulations."

Gal followed hot on his heels, only to grab my face in her hands. "I can't believe it!" Her eyes were glassy. "Saying I'm happy for you wouldn't be enough." She let her hands fall from my cheeks, only to catch my hands. "I love you so much, Jaz."

I squeezed back, nodding and pressing my lips together hard. I knew if I tried to speak, the waterworks would start to flow.

Lito Durán walked up next. "He better be good to you." He pointed a finger.

"He is, Lito," I laughed. "I promise."

Lito rolled his eyes. He often showed his love by acting grouchy. I couldn't help grinning at his antics, my chest tightening. Then Lita shoved my grandpa aside and threw her arms around my neck, sobbing. "Jazmine. I so happy."

Right on cue, she started to wail. Like, *loudly.* I usually wouldn't have cared. If anyone deserved to cry on me, it was her.

But she was sobbing on the dress. And I imagined the glam team was silently panicking.

I shot Gal a "please help me" look, and she quickly sprang into action.

"Come on, Lita." Gal grabbed Lita's hand. "Let's go find your seat before the cameras start rolling."

"Jazmine," Lita added before Gal led her out the door. "This is a big year for you, I can feel it."

Then I recalled what Lita said on my birthday back in November. That she looked at my birth chart and that my theme for the year was love. *That must mean I'm doing the right thing . . . right?*

I took in a long breath and just when I thought I might earn a reprieve, Hudson's family appeared in the doorway just as Gal and Lita exited.

My stomach knotted.

My future mother-in-law, father-in-law, and brother-in-law filed inside, all beaming. After that day, they would become my family. Yet I hardly knew them. They were practically strangers.

Maybe *I* should have spent the day with them yesterday instead of Hudson. Maybe he should have done the same with my family. Although, at least Hudson had had more than a few family dinners with mine. I'd only barely met his.

What am I doing?

"Jazmine, you look absolutely lovely!" Catherine exclaimed, opening her arms wide. No one could deny that this woman was kind. From what I knew about her, I really liked her. And she looked lovely as well, her short blond hair curled and a dark purple dress highlighting her eyes.

But it didn't change the fact that I didn't really *know* her.

"My son is one lucky guy," she was saying.

I forced a smile. "Thank you. That means a lot."

"You really are a sight," Michael added, offering me a polite hug. "Welcome to the family."

I gulped, and my face burned hot. Somehow, I made my voice work. "Thank you so much." I could feel the back of my neck growing damp.

"Congratulations." Hunter shook my hand. His lips turned upwards at the corners. This time, he seemed a little less standoffish. Maybe he just needed a little time to warm up to a new person?

He resembled Hudson more than ever in his best-man tuxedo and groomed facial hair.

"We are just so excited for you two." Catherine clapped her hands together. "And thank you for letting us have Hudson yesterday. It was so great to spend some time with him."

I waved a hand. "Oh, please! I'm glad you guys got to spend the day together."

"We're planning to come out to L.A. when you guys get back from your honeymoon." Catherine nudged her son. "I'm even going to try and convince Hunter to come along."

He smirked. "I got a gig painting a mural on a building in Toronto. I told my Mom, as long as I get that done, I can come along."

"That would be great," I replied, inwardly scheming about how to get Zoe in town at the same time so I could set them up.

Catherine fluffed her hair. "Hudson said you guys have a couple days of meetings with that Jack fella when you get back from Hawaii, but maybe after—"

"Wait. What?" I furrowed my brows.

"The meetings with Jack? About the prospect of you two doing another show? It's so exciting, it was all he could talk about yesterday!" Her expression brightened at that. "But Hudson said we could visit after that. Just let us know what works best for you."

Meetings with Jack? Did Hudson schedule meetings and not tell me? Did he hope he could talk me into it on our honeymoon?

I'd told him I'd think about it. I definitely didn't agree to anything like this, though.

But maybe his mother had misunderstood. Maybe Hudson didn't set up any meetings. Even so, if she were wrong, the fact that he even *brought up* the possibility of us doing a new show, and that it was all he could talk about even after our discussion, spoke volumes.

He wanted this. Badly.

My chest went tight. "Yeah . . ." I mustered up my best smile. "We'll let you know, for sure."

"All right, well, we'd probably better get downstairs." Catherine leaned in and gave me a butterfly kiss on the cheek, so as not to smudge my make-up. "See you in a bit, sweetheart."

Michael and Hunter each waved, and all three backed from the room.

As I watched them leave, it hit me. Because of my decision to do this show, Hudson had gotten a taste of a life beyond his social media channels.

Now he wanted more.

More shows, more fame, more of us together as a brand. Our *relationship* as a branding tool. The very thought made me sick. Yet I knew from here on, there would be no going backward for him. Once he'd tasted this level of notoriety, he wanted to keep going. The social media success he had was one thing, but a web show watched by millions on top of that just made him want more.

It all made perfect sense, but still, I'd awakened the fame beast. I had changed his course, and ours, for ever.

We couldn't begin our marriage like this. Wanting two completely different things. We were setting ourselves up for failure. I had been trying to ignore it all morning, but everything felt wrong.

We can't do this. Can we?

"Almost time!" Kelly walked toward the front of the room. "Everybody ready to head down to the ceremony room?"

"Now?" I was having trouble catching my breath.

"Yes, *now*, silly. The live show starts in half an hour." She did a little happy dance. Only when she got a better look at my face did she pause. "Are you feeling okay, Jazmine?"

I could practically feel myself paling. Thank God for all these layers of blush.

What do I do, what do I do . . .?

What I did was dry heave again. I gagged right there in the middle of the room.

Kelly stepped back, her eyes wide with concern.

"I'm fine," I blurted, in my least convincing tone ever. "Live-show jitters, that's all. It's been happening all day."

And that's when I realized. It wasn't just the live show that was making me nauseous.

It was the getting married part, too.

Fuck. My conflict was so obvious, yet I hadn't even seen it until that very moment. Denial could be a real bitch.

Of course, Leo chose that moment to catch my eye. He lowered his camera, and as he stepped closer to me, I noticed him tap something that turned off the little blinking red recording light. "You good?" he whispered.

I couldn't speak. I couldn't move. Finally, I forced out the words, "Has anyone seen Gal?"

Gal was my sounding board. I knew she would give me an honest opinion. Let me know if I was doing the wrong or right thing.

"She's already down there," Kelly answered.

That's right. She took care of Lita. Shit.

"Come on. We'll meet her in the atrium before you have to walk down the aisle," Kelly murmured, hooking an arm through my elbow.

Still dazed, I let her lead me from the room. But as we stepped out of the suite, my body started to tremble.

What the hell do I do?

Do we just go through with the wedding while the whole world is watching, and work things out later?

Do we call it off and explain what happened in the app?

No. We couldn't call it off. Too many people were watching. This was *live*, for fuck's sake.

Plus, we were contractually obligated to finish *Our Big Day*. It's not like we could just walk away.

. . . Could we?

If I could just talk to Gal for a few minutes, brainstorm the best way to do this . . . I hoped we'd have enough time.

But I could barely make my legs work. On the threshold of the villa, I tripped over the hem of the gown. For some reason, my ankles decided to betray me.

Luckily, Leo stood beside me, and he moved fast enough to catch me. But when he leapt forward, he dropped his camera, and I heard something crack, followed by muttered curses from the other tech people.

I grimaced at him. "Shit. Sorry."

"No worries. The lens is fine, that's all that matters." He smiled. His eyes searched mine, and a frown line appeared on his brow. "You sure you're okay?"

"Yes." With an effort, I straightened. I shook my ankle out and gingerly put my weight on that foot again. It held. It'd be fine. "I have to be," I added, because Leo still didn't look convinced.

But the words didn't seem to placate him. In fact, his frown only deepened.

Luckily, Kelly intervened, gesturing at us from the walkway that led up through the resort's grassy green lawns to the banquet hall built into the cliffside nearby, overlooking the ocean, where the ceremony itself would be taking place. "Let's go," Kelly called, tapping an invisible watch on her wrist.

"Here, let me help with the dress." Esmeralda sprang to my side from where she'd been handling Leo's camera. She hoisted the skirts up in both hands, high enough that I could walk without accidentally tripping on the train again.

"Leo, can you . . .?" Kelly gestured at him.

With that, Leo offered me his arm.

My whole face turned beet red. Or, it would have, if I'd been able to blush through all of this foundation. "I'm fine," I insisted again. But Leo just held his arm there, intractable, until finally I caved in and looped my hand through his. We all made our slow way across the resort and up the steps to the banquet area.

It was a beautiful day. Perfect, cobalt-blue sky, a brilliant, blinding yellow sun in the middle of it, and not a single cloud in sight. The ocean whispered against the beach as we strode near it, a constant, low rumble that should have soothed my nerves. But today, it worsened them. The ocean sounded like my mind right now. Turbulent. Crashing on a hard shoreline.

By the time we reached the main resort building, I could already hear a roar of noise coming from inside. We ascended a few short steps, and then there we stood in the main atrium, closed double doors the only thing separating us from the banquet hall. The live cameras.

My heart leapt into my throat. Through there, our wedding guests waited.

Through there, I'd find Hudson at the altar. And millions of viewers on live TV ready to devour every word we said to one another.

"Just in time," Kelly gasped, as she practically bolted from my side to dart through the main doors. As they opened and closed around her, a swell of sound emerged.

The sound of a band. Playing the intro songs Hudson and I had picked out weeks ago.

Wait . . . "What time is it?" I said. Or I thought I did. But it didn't feel like my mouth was working properly anymore. I pressed my lips together, licked them, and tried again, glancing at Leo.

But he just swore and glanced at his wristwatch. "Live cameras rolling in one minute," he said. "Jazmine, I'm sorry." He touched my shoulder briefly, his palm hot on my skin. "I have to get in there."

"*What?*" I practically yelled. We were going live already? We couldn't be! I hadn't even seen Gal yet, hadn't gotten a chance to get her advice on how to handle this . . .

Leo yanked the doors open. Another burst of sound escaped as he dodged inside.

And Gal emerged on his heels. My heart skipped a beat.

Finally.

In her hands, she held two bouquets. One smaller, for her. The other huge and elaborate, spilling over with white roses.

"Here you go, bride-to-be," Gal exclaimed as she handed me the bridal bouquet. "Let me just adjust the veil." She bit her lip and leaned in to do it. "Your dad's just inside the doors—"

Then she stopped dead, catching a glimpse of my expression. With a confused frown, Gal tilted her head. "Jazmine. What's wrong?"

"I . . ."

And right then, the music changed from within the hall. We were live.

Chapter Sixteen

The moment the doors swung inward stole my breath away. Red roses on white silk ribbons dripped from the ceiling, looking like inverse flowery icicles or chandeliers. Matching delicate white scrollwork benches lined an aisle of gauzy white fabric, so delicate it reminded me of sea foam. Every inch of the surrounding hall, aside from the enormous floor-to-ceiling windows overlooking the sea, had been swathed in silk.

I couldn't imagine how much it all cost. It looked like a ballroom fit for a princess.

Nothing at all like the hall had looked the last time I was in here, introducing Hudson's family to mine at the first dinner of this wild week.

Had it really only been a week? Somehow it felt like so much more time had passed.

More time, and yet really, none at all. Because I still had so much I needed to do. So much I should have said and done before now.

That's when I noticed the cameras.

Not just the two from Leo and Mateo, but at least five more on various cameramen's shoulders, people I didn't know, people I'd never even met before. There were even a few standing cameras along the balconies and hovering near the main arch of pure white roses and green climbing vines. A spill of flowers underneath which Hudson and I would pledge ourselves to one another for the rest of our lives.

I couldn't even fathom how many people were watching at that very moment. Or what they'd think the moment I stepped onto this aisle, and they could all see me.

The thought made me lightheaded. For a moment, the room swam before my eyes, and I feared I might faint. *Deep breaths. Deep breaths.*

"Jazmine, what the hell is wrong?" Gal hissed.

I opened my mouth to speak, but Rosa got there first. "That's your cue." She nudged Gal toward the archway at the front of the aisle.

Gal looked at me, searching. She knew something was wrong.

But there was no time to talk. No time to get her sound advice. We were too late. The music was playing. The guests had been seated. The world was already watching.

The wedding had begun.

Gal masked the concern on her face as she stepped forward, under another archway that mirrored the one on the main stage, and onto the aisle.

I watched the back of Gal as she glided along in her maid-of-honor dress. She looked flawless. The whole venue looked flawless. Like something out of a movie.

I guess it sort of was.

Even so, a little voice in my head kept whispering, *This isn't right.*

"Mr. Prado." Rosa waved him over.

The moment my father and I locked eyes, he started beaming like he'd just won the damn lottery. "Jazzy, you are so beautiful."

It made me tear up. But he probably assumed they were happy tears, because he just offered me the handkerchief from his vest pocket, ever the gentleman.

"Thanks," I managed, my throat thick, and dabbed at my eyes. I thought about talking to him. Asking if he really thought this was the right move for me.

But at this point, only I could make that decision. And it felt like it had already been made for me. By these cameras, by our families, by all the people gathered here to celebrate *Our Big Day.*

"Get ready," Rosa interrupted. "You two walk next." She was smiling too. Everyone was.

Everyone but me.

My knees went weak and I reached out to steady myself on the doorframe.

As for my dad, he seemed too enamored with the décor to notice my emotional turmoil. Probably for the best. His eyes sparkled as he stared around.

"Wow, look at all this, Jazzy," he murmured. "You have the perfect wedding. The perfect man. Your own show. You are living the dream."

My entire body tightened at his words.

I don't think this is my dream.

Then, as we stood there in the archway, just out of sight of the rest of the room, the Wedding March began to play.

Everyone in the room rose. Goosebumps pricked my arms, and I shivered.

When Rosa nodded for us to move forward, I tensed from the crown of my head all the way down to my toes.

"Okay, mi amor. It's time." Dad held out his arm.

I shook my head. *Here we go.*

As I started down the aisle, my arm interlocked with my

father's, everything shifted into slow motion. It felt as if we walked through quicksand. Or against a windstorm. Resistance pushed against us.

With effort, I looked up, and spotted Hudson at the far end of the aisle. I couldn't make out his face yet, but I could see him standing ramrod straight in a classic tux that fit his tall body perfectly. His hair had been pulled back nice and sleek.

Even from a distance he looked like a classic movie star. A guy most people would give a kidney to marry. An all-around lovely person, inside and out.

Yet suddenly, I felt like the air had been sucked out of my lungs. Like I was falling into the deep, dark ocean, weighed down with sorrow like blocks of cement on my feet.

Just like how I felt before I agreed to do the show. When my career was sinking along with me.

I took the life vest Kelly threw me then. I hitched a ride on the S.S. *Hudson Taylor*, hoping for smoother seas ahead. I'd tied my career to Hudson's, and in doing so, set us both on this course.

I'd had help along the way—Gal as my intrepid navigator. But no one else could help me now. I had to decide for myself. Pull myself out of the waters. Build my own ship.

Navigate life my way. Like I used to.

I'd lost my confidence. I'd lost my enthusiasm. I'd lost my belief that I could kick down any wall that I wanted.

But I couldn't rewind life. I could only move forward. I needed to embrace my strength and claim the power that I knew I had.

I had to decide what was best for me. For my dreams. For the life I wanted, the career I wanted, even the type of love I wanted.

After all, this was my future. The rest of my life.

My mom may have been wrong to pressure me so much

early on over my career. But regardless of her mistakes, it shaped me. All of me.

I truly loved being a writer. I loved that the Google search for me said "award-winning journalist." I loved the feeling of putting fresh words on paper.

My career status didn't define me, it didn't determine my worth. But writing set my soul on fire. And some fires shouldn't be put out.

I felt alive for the first time in months when I pitched a new story, and felt ill at the idea of spending the rest of my life filming shows.

At the worst possible instant, it all crystalized. I was walking down the aisle toward my future.

But Hudson Taylor was not my future.

I was my future.

I loved him and I wanted to keep my commitment. To him, to finishing the show. But I knew I couldn't. It wasn't fair. Not to Hudson. Not to me.

We neared the altar. Hudson raised his gaze to mine, finally, and his mouth dropped.

His eyes raked over me as he drank in every detail, like he was dying of thirst in a desert, and I was the water, appearing just in time to save him. He looked at me the way you look at your dreams. He wanted this, wanted me.

And it broke my heart in half, knowing what I needed to do.

I *did* love Hudson. So fucking much. Hurting him, especially in this way, was the last thing I wanted to do.

But the truth was, I loved myself *more*.

And I couldn't go through with this.

I locked eyes with Hudson, meeting those baby blues as he smiled—the kind of smile that lit up his entire face. *He will never look at me like that again.* A gaping hole opened up in my chest.

And then we were there. Standing at the foot of the altar.

My father took his time lifting my veil and draping it back over my hair. He leaned in to kiss my cheek softly.

"Congratulations, Jazzy." His voice came out gruff, like he was fighting back tears.

It made me tear up, too.

I watched until my father had taken his seat beside my mother in the front row. She had a tissue in her hand and was already bawling into it. Oliver, beside her, also misty-eyed, beamed at me.

I remembered my mom's words from the other night. "*Just promise me you won't do anything you don't want to do again . . . Because you could never disappoint any of us, Jazzy. We love you.*"

Would they still feel the same after this? I wondered.

But deep down I knew they would. They were my family, before anything else. They, at least, would always have my back. And I would always have theirs. I knew that much, and it gave me the confidence to lift my chin a little.

As I did, I spotted Leo's mother in a dusty-blue dress and matching hat. Elena smiled and gave me a little wave. When I didn't smile back, her smile dropped away. Even half a banquet hall away, I felt her scrutinize my expression. When she mouthed, *It's okay*, I had a feeling she knew what was about to happen. And I remembered her words: "*It's okay to change your mind . . . it's never too late.*"

I faced the altar. Gal met my gaze first. One look was all it took. A faint rise and fall of my shoulders, barely detectable to anyone else. But she saw it. She knew. Her eyes shot wide and her lips formed words, almost without her seeming to decide. *Shit*, she mouthed.

I stepped up to the altar. Hudson reached out for my hands,

but I kept them wrapped firmly around my bouquet, down at my waist.

He froze. "Jaz?" He kept his voice quiet, soft enough that I hoped the cameras couldn't hear. But we were mic'd. Everyone in the ceremony was mic'd, and this was fucking live, of course they would hear it. "Is everything okay?"

Suddenly, I couldn't even look at him. I couldn't gaze into his kind eyes. It hurt too much.

So I turned to Leo instead. I'd only glimpsed him from the corner of my eye, yet some sixth sense, some part of me, always tracked him, even when I didn't want to. He stood with a camera raised, at the foot of the altar. Just a stone's throw away.

"Um . . . Could we turn the cameras off?" I asked as quietly as I could.

Leo raised a brow, and lifted his face away from the lens to meet my gaze. "You mean . . . right now?"

"Yeah." I let out a long breath. "Right now."

Suddenly, Jack from Mercer jumped up from his front-row seat beside Kelly. "Absolutely not," he barked. I grimaced. Either I didn't speak as quietly as I thought, or Jack was wearing an audio link to our mics. I didn't know which option felt weirder.

Jack fired Leo a stern glare. "The cameras stay rolling. Our sponsors paid good money for this; whatever is about to happen, we're all going to see it. That's the name of the game."

A game I should've never played in the first place.

Still, after a long hesitation, I nodded, angrily, just once. I might have hated it, but I understood. I was the dumbass who signed up for this.

A Grand Canyon-sized pit formed in my stomach.

But then, as I watched, Leo shut his camera off anyway. "She asked for privacy, she gets privacy," Leo said. He motioned at Mateo, who a moment later did the same.

"You wanna lose the rest of your payment for this gig, fine." Jack turned to glare around the rest of the room. "The rest of the cameras in here are staying on."

The other cameramen, ones I'd never met, continued to point their lenses my way. I couldn't blame them. They didn't know me. They didn't know what I was about to do, either.

There was no getting out of it. This horrible moment was going to be broadcast live. To millions of people. As the thought of that reality sunk in, I knew there was a chance that me doing this could possibly hurt Hudson's career, his livelihood, his brand, too. But as awful as that possibility was, I had to put myself, my health, and my emotional well-being, first.

The least I could do, though, was try to minimize damage. I reached behind me and turned off the battery pack for my lapel mic. But then I noticed a microphone above us, and remembered Hudson had a mic too, as well as Gal.

Fuck it. I made my bed, now I had to lie in it.

I stepped forward, finally gathering the strength to meet Hudson's eyes. I let my bouquet drop—though I noticed Gal snatch it up before it landed on the floor—and reached for his hands.

Mine shook when they clutched his.

"Don't do this, Jaz," he whispered. "Please."

"I'm so sorry." My eyes started to water. The heartbreak that washed over his face hit me like a punch to the gut.

"I have to," I breathed.

"You don't." He was shaking his head, his forehead scrunched. "You don't, we can just . . ." But whatever he'd started to say drained away when he noticed the resolution on my face. He fell silent. Waited for me to speak instead.

I swallowed the world's largest lump, lodged dead center in my throat. How could I even breathe right now, let alone speak? Yet somehow, I managed.

"I can't live in your world." My voice cracked. "I tried to, and I just . . . I can't." He parted his lips to say something, but I shook my head a little, and he let me continue. "You and I both know what you want for us. More of this. More of us on screen, more and more shows." Before he could protest, I pulled one hand from his and raised it. "I don't blame you. Fuck, your dreams, your ambitions are one of the things that drew me to you in the first place. And you should keep chasing those, Hudson." I put my hand back on his and tightened my grip once more.

He squeezed back, tightly, like he was holding on for dear life. Sorrow sprang up behind those deep-blue eyes of his, and I nearly caved in. I nearly said *forget it, let's do this*.

But I couldn't. For myself and for him.

"This is my fault," I whispered. Tears leaked from my eyes now, and it killed me that before I could make a move, Hudson was the one to wipe them away with his finger. Gently. Sweetly. The same way he'd always taken care of me. "I pushed you to do this show, I rushed us into this, it's my fault. And I know you said we could figure the rest out later, but the thing is, we can't."

"Jaz . . ."

I shook my head fiercely, and wiped my eyes with the heel of one hand, sniffing long and hard, smudging my mascara in the process.

It took me another second to compose myself. "Hudson, you love this life more than you know. And I *hate it* more than you know. But *you* should be able to have it. You deserve to pursue your dreams, and the lifestyle you want. But to do that . . . you need to find someone who's a better fit for you than I could ever be."

This time, he didn't try to interrupt. His gaze softened. Turned almost . . . wistful.

I closed my eyes. "Hudson, you should have everything, because you *deserve* everything." I caught my labored breath and opened my eyes once more, hoping, praying, that he could see the sincerity there. "You're an amazing person. And I really do love you. So damn much. That is why I have to walk away. I'm so sorry."

For a moment, he was silent, biting the inside of his lip. He glanced up at the ceiling, and I noticed tears sparkling in his eyes. Fuck. That sight nearly undid me.

He blinked a few times, before he was able to glance at me once more. He tried on a rueful smile, but it only made him look more torn apart. "I knew I should've waited till our honeymoon to mention the new shows to you." He shook his head, still wearing that terrible smile. "I knew it would scare you away."

"I'm glad you told me now." I squeezed his hands hard. "It's better that we know now. It would've been even harder to come to this conclusion later."

With a deep breath, Hudson bent to kiss the back of my hand. Then he let go, and took a step back. Away from me.

The air rushed in between us, the flood of oxygen so sudden that I felt dizzy. The room had faded into the background as we spoke. For a moment it had been just the two of us standing there, alone in the world.

Now I remembered everyone watching.

Hudson ran a hand through his hair. "You might be right." He pressed his lips together. Composed himself. "I guess we'll never know."

With another hard swallow, I reached down and gently

pulled the large diamond off my finger. I extended a hand, cupped Hudson's to turn it palm-up, and placed the ring on it. Then I folded his fingers around it, closing his fist tight.

"Thank you. For everything." Tears were streaming down my face now. I let them. "You've been such an important part of my life. I will always cherish the time we had together. I'll always be grateful for you."

His eyes glassed over. "Me too, Jaz. Me too." He leaned in and folded his arms around me. I buried my face in his chest and held on to him as tightly as I could, for one last time.

When I finally pulled away, I left half my make-up all over his handsome shirt. I grimaced in apology, but Hudson just shook his head, trying his best to smile, though I could tell he was minutes from a breakdown himself.

That's when my navigator swooped in. Gal wrapped her hand around my wrist and gently tugged me backward. "Come on," she murmured. "Let's get you home." She led me off the altar, toward a side door.

For the first couple steps, the room around us remained silent. And then, all at once, *noise*. Shouts, whispers, cries. Calls between the cameramen. Jack from Mercer had whipped out a phone and started barking into it. Kelly rose and tried to wave at me, her expression a mask of concern.

But Gal had a tight grip on my arm, and she wasn't about to let me go.

I was more indebted to her in that second than I could ever express.

We raced from the banquet hall, and I tore my gaze from the hubbub, my mind reeling.

A million memories flashed before my eyes. So many things Hudson and I had shared, that we never would again. So many choices I could never take back.

When we finally burst free from the labyrinth of corridors around the banquet hall, into the fresh sunny air, the sea crashing in the distance and the salt breeze tickling my nose, I let out a loud sigh and fell to the sand. I dropped my head between my knees and wept. In my wedding dress, on the beach, in broad daylight where anyone could see. All the tears I'd fought so hard to hold back at the ceremony, over this past week even, came pouring out.

That had been one of the hardest decisions of my life. But as painful as it was, I knew I'd made the right choice.

Even so, there would be consequences. And I would have to face them sooner or later.

But, as if reading my mind, Gal knelt beside me, rubbing my back in small circles, reminding me. "Just breathe, Jaz. Just breathe."

For now, that was all I needed to do.

Posted by Jazmine Prado on the *Style&Travel* app at 10:15 p.m.

Look. I know a lot of you are mad at me right now and I completely understand. What I did was shocking, and unexpected, and everyone has a right to feel how they want to feel and process however they deem fit.

Although I don't owe a public explanation, I do promise I will speak on it soon.

But I will say this: what we see on social media or a web series, etc., is never anyone's full story. It's just fragments. Highlight reels. A drop in the bucket of who we really are as people. As human beings.

I don't have all the answers, but I do know that we are all on (or should be on, at least) a path of ever-evolving self-discovery, and that sometimes that path wavers and mutates in unexpected ways at inconvenient times. And when it does, we should follow it.

Because if we're not living a life that makes our hearts sing, then we are doing ourselves a disservice. Life's too short to be unhappy.

xx, Jazmine

Chapter Seventeen

Post-wedding: about three months later

The sun in Marbella was different than the sun at home, I swear. Or maybe it's just the sky, bluer somehow.

I perched on one of Mamá and Papá Prado's striped deck-chairs, gazing off the balcony at the gently sloped hillside around their house. Multicolored houses with red-tile roofs dotted the hill, in between bursts of lush green trees.

It took a herculean effort to tear my gaze from the sunny view, and focus instead on my laptop. Poised beside it sat a glass of horchata de chufa, which I paused to sip before I continued writing.

It's been three months since my almost-wedding-day, three months since I chose the path that was best for me with the world watching, I wrote, and then I stared down at the words, stunned that so much time had passed.

Then again, since I'd spent those months alternating between writing, sprawling on this very balcony, or being fed a truly impressive amount of food here at Mamá and Papá Prado's and at Lito and Lita Durán's house, so maybe it wasn't surprising that the time seemed to have flown past.

After the news broke of our split—which was pretty much

instant thanks to all of those live cameras—I knew I had to get away. Marbella seemed like the perfect place. Just the right amount of familiar. Plus enough distance to stay under the radar.

On social media, I was the bitch who left Hudson Taylor at the altar. During a live ceremony. With millions of people watching. What did I really expect?

But it was eye-opening to me how quickly online love can change. How "fans" are fleeting. How fame is fleeting. Those already mean-sounding comments sections turning into a war zone. With all weapons aimed at me.

It all got so much worse than I expected. Once I got back to L.A, on a same-day flight Gal booked for us, I had a few scary encounters with fans from the show. One of them confronted me in the airport to throw her (thankfully not too hot) coffee in my face. Another one followed me, threatening to kick my ass.

Hence, my extended Spanish escape.

Once I got to Spain, I deactivated all of my social media accounts. Every last one.

My profile on the *Style&Travel* app was the first to go. Between all the "cunt" and "whore" comments and racial and xenophobic slurs, not to mention people telling me to kill myself . . .

I didn't need that shit in my life.

Even just remembering it sent my stomach sinking to my knees. I took a long, slow breath, closing my eyes, and concentrating on the sun against my face, the feel of the balcony tiles beneath my bare feet.

The online ugliness couldn't touch me right now, I reminded myself.

There was some support mixed in, but it was few and far

between. Commenters even went after my family, including Gal. Hudson had to practically beg his fans to stop.

They didn't, not completely, at least not where I was concerned. But they let up on my family a bit, at the very least. Thank goodness.

It broke my heart that my family had to deal with the harassment because of me. Just thinking about it started my heart racing, my anxiety spiking once more.

I grabbed a piece of selenite that I had sitting beside my laptop and looked up at the cobalt Marbella sky and took another deep breath. It was crystal clear. Beautiful.

I'd been forcing myself to stop and smell the roses. Be in the moment. Practice gratitude. Recite affirmations. All the things one does after they've gone through something really shitty. It helped a little.

So did the video therapy sessions I'd been doing with Dr. Rivers, a therapist a former colleague recommended.

I needed to work through being disliked by so many people online, anxiety, and many other things. Some can brush the haters off, for others it becomes soul-shattering. Apparently, I was one of the latter.

I was still working on it all. But as Dr. Rivers said, "One day at a time."

One day at a time. My heartbeat started to steady. I'd gotten better at taming my racing heart these last few months.

The higher-ups at Mercer Media were furious that I didn't go through with the wedding. At first I thought they might sue me for breach of contract, but they ended up giving me some grace in that regard.

Why?

Well. If Hudson and I were a good "brand" as a happy couple, we made even more sensational news breaking up the way we did. The controversy led to more views and coverage than Mercer could've ever anticipated. It was *all* the gossip blogs talked about. Even some entertainment news channels covered it.

And Hudson came out on top. People loved him even more after I left him. He was the hero and I was the villain.

I had come to terms with that. Mostly.

Hudson got a new show out of the mess, at least. Mercer Media offered him a *Bachelor*-like web series called *Finding Mrs. Taylor.* It would premiere in a couple months.

I smiled thinking about it. He deserved this. I knew the show would take off. How could it not with such a winning, perfect lead? And maybe, that way, he would find the perfect woman for him, too. The kind of woman who was happy being in his world. A world that had ballooned since that live show—he now had over twenty million followers and counting. Looks like in breaking his heart, I helped him become even *more* internet famous.

At least, that's what I've told myself.

Hudson called me the day after I left. He was more than gracious. More gracious than I would've been if the situation had been reversed, to be honest.

He said that he understood where I was coming from. He agreed that once our rose-colored glasses faded, it would have been clear that we were on completely different wavelengths. He promised he didn't hate my guts.

I tried my best to believe him.

Our relationship had shifted from romance to a friendship. I wouldn't call it a close friendship, but we texted here and there to catch up. Mostly about his new show.

He was about to become an even bigger star. And I couldn't be happier for him.

Or more relieved to be out of the limelight myself.

Though Kelly was more understanding than I expected, I obviously lost any chance of a journalist position at *Style&Travel.*

Kelly, however, didn't stay there much longer either. She was not pleased with how Mercer handled things and she took a job with a huge fashion publication where *she* got to call the shots, not the higher-ups. She said I could pitch her anytime.

She and I also launched an investigation with Mercer Media against Jack Paulson. We didn't like some of his creepy comments towards Kelly, and myself, and found others who complained of a hostile and inappropriate work environment under him. Exposing Jack was one of the best things that came out of the show.

As for my current work life, a handful of publishers were clamoring to know what happened. What was going on inside my head. They wanted my side of the story. They wanted to hear my truth.

All it took was a proposal write-up, a few chapters as a sample, and before I knew it, I had a literary agent, and multiple book offers on the table.

I was a bit surprised at first. A memoir from Jazmine Prado, "the most hated woman on the web," didn't seem like much of a hook to me.

Publishers disagreed.

Though the circumstances weren't ideal—this isn't exactly how I'd pictured launching into the next phase of my writing career—I was still thrilled. Becoming a published author was a huge accomplishment. Something I had always dreamed about. I was writing. I was in my element. I was happy.

The book wouldn't be just a tell-all about why I left Hudson at the altar. It was also about following your dreams, finding your passion, and doing the things that make you happy, sharing the lessons that I learned the hard way. I was approaching it like one really long journalism piece, so I didn't feel too overwhelmed.

I got Hudson's blessing about the book. I knew I didn't need to get his blessing, but I wanted to let him know about it. I didn't want any bad blood between us. But considering he'd always lived his life in front of the camera, he didn't mind me writing like this about mine.

Even so, I had expected my first book to be . . . lighter. Or maybe just less personal. But at least this way, I controlled the narrative. Not someone at Mercer Media. Me.

In keeping with that, I'd decided I would reactivate my social media accounts once the book launched—comments off, no DMs, just posts I'd put up about the book. I'd set hard boundaries. Rules I could live with.

My way of adapting, as Gal always told me I must.

I stretched and shook out a crick in my neck. My concentration was shit at the moment. Maybe it was the warm sun, or maybe it was the fact that I'd already written a couple thousand words that morning, and my brain was feeling done for the time being.

I leaned back in my chair to take another sip of my horchata de chufa, when a book on the patio table caught my eye.

Amor en Cancún by Elena Chavez Couture. I grinned. Her newest one.

Mamá Prado was probably reading it. Though there was a strong chance she'd already finished it and Papá was reading it in secret.

Hopefully I could read it myself soon. I'd been working on my Spanish since I'd gotten here. I wanted to take advantage of my surroundings.

I reached over and delicately lifted the novel, careful to keep the leather bookmark in place. It smelled like newly cut paper and freshly printed ink. I ran my finger over the word *Couture* on the cover.

Leo.

After the wedding devolved into chaos, Leo reached out via text and email. I was glad. We had mostly emailed back and forth since. It felt nice to be friendly with him again.

I did miss him. A lot. He was currently in the Amazon filming his documentary.

Maybe there would be a time for Leo and I in the future. Maybe there wouldn't be. I wasn't sure. But he would always play a role in my life. My first love, who I'd always love. Always have a connection to. Who I'd always save a piece of my heart for.

I sighed, placing the book back on the table and returning to my laptop.

Besides my immediate family, Gal, and my grandparents, I hadn't told anyone I was in Spain. Not Hudson. Not even Leo.

After being on the map in such a big way, I needed to be off-grid for a while. Especially while I was writing my book.

Or, spaced out in memories while writing, as the case may be.

I sighed and glanced down at my phone. *Good, another distraction.* In this case, a text from Gal.

I tapped it open.

Care package coming your way, should be there tomorrow. In the meantime, I just paid upfront for you to get your coffee and pastry at Costella's on me today.

I smiled. Costella's was one of our favorite cafés in Marbella. We loved getting pastries there when we'd visit with our families as teens. My phone dinged with another message.

Give them my name and they'll know what to do. Go soon please. And send a pic so I can live vicariously through you!!

I let out a laugh. Gal had been sending me care packages every few weeks filled with things I loved from home (like my favorite face cream and lip balm). Plus little notes from my family, who had been very supportive of my decision.

I gazed up at the sky for a few seconds before replying.

You're the best. Thank you for always being so thoughtful and making me feel loved.

A lump formed in my throat. I felt really lucky to have Gal in my life. And I had been trying to be more expressive about that.

She sent back a bunch of heart emojis. I grinned, and set my phone face down on the table.

After finishing up on writing for the day, I closed my laptop and walked back inside, where Mamá Prado was chopping tomatoes in the kitchen. The whole place already smelled amazing from something simmering on the stove. Like tomatoes, olive oil, maybe some garlic?

Even though I fully planned to take advantage of the coffee and treat Gal sent, I already couldn't wait to come back after and devour whatever she was cooking.

I drew the sliding glass door behind me, shutting it quietly, and picked my way around the colorful, mismatched table and chair set to give my grandma a side hug. "I'm gonna go to the coffee shop, but I'll be back soon."

Mamá Prado leaned back from the gas stove to hug me back, careful to twist sideways so her somewhat smudged apron wouldn't touch my clean clothes. "Okay, mi amor." A smile tugged at her lips. "But don't fill up too much. You have to save room for my salmorejo with diced jamón ibérico and couscous. Plus the leche frita I'm making later."

Yum. Mamá Prado made the best leche frita. My mouth salivated just thinking about the sweet, milk pudding with a fried crunchy shell.

"I won't. I promise. Love you." I blew her a kiss. Then I wove through the rest of the house, past the antique bookshelves and the colorful paintings on the walls, through the funny little passage between the living room and the dining area, and out onto the street outside.

Here, even the streets themselves served as decorations, paved with marble tiles and inlaid with pebbles in swirling patterns that changed every few blocks.

I marched along them, past houses and little shops in every color—bright oranges, hot pinks, deep blues. Even the white buildings, with their terracotta rooftops, looked picturesque.

A little part of me couldn't help imagining what Leo would say about all these colors. I beamed thinking about it, and made a mental note to email him a photo later.

The grocer on the corner shouted my name and waved. I grinned and waved back. Around the corner, I passed a couple with an adorable little dog who lived next door, and paused for a moment to chat about how their days had been.

I loved this town. The way it felt big and small at once. Like somewhere I could hide out, but still be completely myself.

Plus, it had really good coffee, which I appreciated.

As I walked, I thought about all the decisions that had brought me here. My life had taken such a dramatic turn. And a lot of my choices this last decade hadn't been great. Some I regretted.

But whatever else, they were still *my* choices. Making choices—good ones and bad—is part of being human.

That's all I am. A messy, ambiguous, sometimes confused, often fucked-up human. A work-in-progress.

As hard as this season of my life had been, it had given me some good perspective. Whatever else, I was grateful for that much. And I realized that when Lita said my theme for the year according to the stars was "love," she wasn't wrong.

But it wasn't the type of love I expected.

It was learning to love myself again. The greatest love of all. Something I'm still working on. But every day I fall a little more in love with myself. And I think we're going to be very happy together.

Finally, I rounded the corner and spied the telltale green awning of Costella's. I could already smell the pastries, the scent of butter and fresh bread and spices drifting from the open doorway.

I waved cheerily to the shop owner through the window, then ducked through the shop door, which had been painted canary yellow, all the better to stand out against the pale blue of the building itself.

Inside, a faint hum of chatter arose from the other patrons, scattered around the handful of narrow tables and iron chairs. For a second I just closed my eyes and took a big breath.

The espresso machine behind the counter hummed as if in welcome, and I stepped toward the glass countertop, ready to order.

That's when I froze.

I blinked, sure I must have been hallucinating. *What the fuck?*

But no. The scene before me remained the same, no matter how hard I squeezed my eyes shut and reopened them. There, right in the corner of Costella's, wearing his same black T-shirt and dark jeans combo, sat a familiar man. Grinning at me. Waving.

Leo Couture.

I could feel my pulse beat in my eardrums.

How did he know I was here? I furrowed my brow.

Then it clicked. *Fucking Gal and her "coffee and pastry on me."* This was a set-up. I shook my head. But I smiled, too.

Across the room, Leo stood. But the shop wasn't that big. A few steps, and he was close enough to hear me.

"Leo. What are you doing in Marbella?" I was surprised I managed to speak at all. "I thought you were supposed to be in South America for another three months?"

With each step he took, my heart beat faster and faster. The techniques I'd learned over the last few months to tame my racing heart were useless in that moment.

When he reached me, a smile stretched across his face. His eyes sparkled as they caught mine.

I could feel my cheeks grow warm. My knees buckled a little. I'd never seen him look at me like that before. Hot and cold warred in my veins, and it took all my energy to keep upright. To wrangle my thoughts into an order that made sense.

"So, I have a proposition for you," he started, still with that sly grin I'd always loved. "And I think you *might* like it."

"And you came all the way to Marbella to tell me about it?" I dared a weak smile, because his serious face could've killed me. "I'm sure an email would've cost you less."

He didn't smile back. He reached out instead and, ever so gently, curled his fingers around mine.

It felt like my heart stopped beating for a second.

"The thing is . . ." Leo squeezed my fingers lightly, sending a flurry of heat all the way down to my toes. "I think we should give this dating thing another try. Start over. Clean slate. See how we work together, now, at this point in our lives. I think we deserve a real shot, at least." He shrugged. "Plus, we're still twenty-eight. And I'm thinking if our marriage pact is still valid, we should at least *try* dating first," he joked, before reaching over and tucking a strand of my hair behind my ear. When his fingertip grazed the delicate shell of my ear, it sent shivers down my spine.

"Leo . . ." My throat tightened as I stared at him, admiring the way his wavy hair fell perfectly around his ears, framing the face that I gazed at for most of my youth. A face that had changed and grown, but also, stayed so familiar. My eyes started to water. *Dammit.*

Leo reached up and brushed his fingertip along my cheekbone. Wiping a single renegade tear away. I let out a soft, huffy laugh. He did, too.

"What if it doesn't work out? What if we end up hating each other again?" I said, sniffling.

"That could happen. And it crossed my mind too. But I'd rather take the risk." He inched a little closer. "That's what life is, isn't it? Just a series of risks? Some risks work out, some don't. But if you never take them, you'll never know the outcome."

Now his smile returned, spreading, slow but steady. "I'd like to date you, Jazmine Prado. Fall off the grid with you. Figure out the next phase of life with you. I want to give it a real try as more than friends . . . if you want to, that is." His voice went low, full of emotion.

"What about your documentary on the Amazon?" I furrowed my brow. "Aren't you still in the process of filming it?"

Leo nodded. "I have a break for a month, and then I do have

to go back for another three." He let out a slow breath. "But, you know, if things work out, we can just do the long-distance thing. You've done that before, right?" He smirked.

As I peered into Leo's hazel eyes, which looked more gold than green that day, I thought about how he was still in the process of filming his documentary, and I was still in the process of finishing my book. I had no idea where the next year would take us.

Is the timing right? worried a little voice at the back of my head, like it so often did.

But the thing I've realized? If you wait for the perfect time to do . . . well, anything, actually—you'll be waiting for the rest of your life.

The timing was right when you wanted it to be right. So right then, it was just perfect.

Plus, I'd be damned if I didn't give dating Leo Couture a real chance. My past self was screaming with glee. It seemed that fate for the first time was finally on our side.

"Okay," I breathed, only very slightly choked up. "Let's do it. Let's give this a try." I took a step closer, and his hand brushed my shoulder. Slid down my arm, until he cupped my elbow. Drew me forward another step, our faces a mere breath apart now. We stood so close I could feel his every inhale. Watch my exhales tickle his cheeks. I bit my lip. My eyes locked on his. Those familiar, ever-changing eyes. The ones I'd missed so badly over the years we didn't speak.

The pain I'd glimpsed hiding behind them in Cancún? It was gone. All I saw now was happiness. The brightest, most painfully clear happiness I'd ever seen in my life.

I knew my eyes mirrored it right back.

"So . . ." He lifted one hand. Hesitated. Then brought it to rest against my cheek. His palm felt warm. Reassuring. At the same time, his breath caressed my face. He smelled familiar, like coffee and cedar and *Leo.*

My body tingled.

"Can I take you out tonight?" he asked. "A real, official date?"

I blushed hard. A first real date for Jazmine Prado and Leo Couture. What would that be like?

I peered up at him from beneath my lashes, coy. "Hmm. I dunno. I mean, I *did* tell my grandma I'd be back soon . . . She's cooking tonight."

Leo rolled his eyes. He knew I was making him work for it.

"We could go over there?" He arched an eyebrow, casual. "You know I love Mamá and Papá Prado. Although Papá Prado still won't let go of that time I beat him at golf our junior year. Clearly I should have let him win."

"Clearly. He's very bitter about it." We both laughed. Then the laughter faltered. Faded. Before I knew it, we were gazing into each other's eyes as if for the first time. "What if we go over there tonight and you can take me out on a real, official date tomorrow? It can be your big chance to smooth things over with Papá Prado," I teased.

Leo chuckled. "That sounds perfect."

Then I reached up and slowly wound my hands through Leo's mess of wavy hair. He grinned and titled forward. I raised my chin, and finally, *finally*, our lips collided.

Nothing between us anymore but heat and desire. I wrapped both my arms around his neck, and his slid around my waist to pull me flush against him, hoist me up.

I gasped, lips still tight against his, when my feet left the floor, but he just grinned and ducked his head to keep kissing me, as he spun us in a slow circle, right there in the middle of the café.

He tasted the same. A little sweet, just like always. I parted my lips, let his tongue slip through to curl against mine, like he wanted to savor me just as much as I did him.

When he finally set me back on my feet again, and we broke apart, just far enough to suck in fresh air, our arms still tight around one another, bodies still pressed tightly together, the whole café burst into applause.

I laughed, and buried my face in Leo's shirt.

He raised his hand to cup the back of my head, holding me there. I could feel his chest vibrate as he laughed, then lifted his other arm from my waist to wave. "Lo siento por el show, amigos," Leo said with a big smile.

"No te preocupes," someone shouted, and more people laughed.

Somehow, the attention didn't bother me this time.

I tipped my head back, chin resting on his chest, and grinned. He beamed right back, and leaned down to kiss me again, softer this time. Just a light peck. Yet the brush of his lips on mine was enough to send chills all through my body.

Kissing Leo again after all these years felt good. *Really good.* And I was excited to see how things would evolve between us as we started our new journey as more than friends.

But one thing was for certain, no matter what happened with Leo and I—I would never announce our relationship status publicly. You won't see pictures of us on my social media.

And if things went well, and down the road we got married, it would *not* be in front of a live audience. Because some things are too fucking special to share with the world. And to me, this was onc of those things.

Epilogue

Jazmine Prado is Writing Her Own Rules *(Draft Copy)*

By Lorenzo deCampa

The world watched as award-winning journalist Jazmine Prado made headlines choosing herself, her dreams, and her personal happiness, over a fairy-tale-esque life with social media star, Hudson Taylor. Just this week, Jazmine released her debut novel *Write Your Own Rules*—a book about following one's passions and staying true to ourselves, and it also gives more insight into what happened leading up to that infamous day when Jazmine left Hudson at the altar during the live and final episode of *Our Big Day*. Pre-order sales alone have already put the book in bestseller territory. I was lucky enough to get an early copy, and let me just say, you're in for a treat. The book is a beautiful page-turner that will leave you feeling inspired and encourage you to pursue more of the things that bring you joy.

For the interview, Jazmine and I decide to meet in a private room inside a coffee house in West Los Angeles that's not too far from where she's been spending the earlier part of the day in meetings. When Ms. Prado arrives at the coffee house the air immediately changes. Her presence is calm, cool, collected—a completely different vibe from what millions witnessed on that final episode of *Our Big Day.* And also completely different from the day I first met her at her cousin's PR firm, where I confessed my dreams about wanting to become a writer. Side note: getting to interview Jazmine, who has been an inspiration of mine, is a dream come true.

She looks stylish in a casual black pantsuit and snakeskin patterned pumps with her lucky Indalo charm bracelet on her wrist. Her hair is pulled back in a low, sleek ponytail bringing attention to her silver hoops and striking features. We exchange some friendly small talk as we walk into one of the private rooms and take a seat across from each other.

Jazmine: This is weird, you know, being interviewed for a story when I used to be the one doing the interviewing.

Lorenzo: I can only imagine! I promise to make this as painless as possible.

Jazmine: Ha! Thank you.

Lorenzo: How does it feel having a book out in the world?

Jazmine: Surreal. It's always been a goal of mine, publishing a book. And I always thought if I did it would be fiction, something light. But I am really proud of *Write Your Own Rules* and I just hope that it inspires people to not only follow their dreams, but to do so in a way that works for them.

Lorenzo: What was the book-writing process like for you?

Jazmine: At times, it was a fun, creative process . . . I would pull tarot cards and eat pastries while writing under the moonlight. But most days, it consisted of pretty much lots of coffee and no sleep and overthinking every word. A very healthy thing to do, and not at all stress-inducing.

We both laugh. I have always enjoyed Jazmine's sarcastic humor and wit, which shone in her articles and shines even more so in the book.

Lorenzo: Do you miss writing articles, doing the journalist thing? I'm sure you don't miss the busy pace.

Jazmine: The pace never bothered me, to be honest. But I definitely don't miss wondering what publications are going to be pivoting-to-video next and making cuts. No offense.

Lorenzo: None taken. It *is* a reality.

Jazmine: It is. But there are options to adapt in a way that works best for you. That's what I learned . . . the hard way. But I learned it, nonetheless.

Lorenzo: If there was one thing you would want readers to take away from *Write Your Own Rules*, what would that be?

Jazmine: That you're never stuck. Someone once told me that it's never too late to change your mind, and I think it's one of the best pieces of advice I've ever gotten. We can change our minds and start over whenever we want to. Life's too short to be unhappy.

Lorenzo: Very true. Thank you for that. Seems so simple yet so hard at the same time.

Jazmine: That's what I thought too. But then I came to realize that nothing is more important than your own happiness. So I try my best to stay focused on that, even on my not-so-happy days.

Lorenzo: The world is very aware of Hudson's love life at the moment with his show *Finding Mrs. Taylor.* But what about you? Are you seeing anyone?

Jazmine sits up straight and crosses her arms, a smile pulling at her lips. She looks the other direction briefly before turning back towards me and meeting my gaze warmly.

Jazmine: I appreciate the interest, I really do. But that's just something I'm going to keep to myself. However, I will say this: I'm happy. I'm very happy.

After Ms. Prado leaves, I go to my car and I spot her standing just a few feet away. She's facing the other direction and as I begin to walk towards her to thank her again for the interview, a car pulls into the parking lot.

"Leo!" Jazmine shouts. "I saved you a spot." She motions to the parking space she's standing in front of. After the car pulls into the spot, a man steps out of it with a coffee in his hand. He is easy on the eyes, with wavy brown hair, sharp cheekbones, aviator sunglasses, and an air of mystery and intrigue about him.

"'The Jazmine,' for you, of course." He holds up the coffee, a smirk plastered across his face. "Figured you'd be too focused to order one during your interview."

"You were right," she says. "Thank you. You're the best." She grabs the drink out of his hand, pulls him close, and kisses him. The chemistry between them is undeniable. Like magnets. A force I haven't seen between two people in a long time. It's alluring—something that's hard to turn away from.

"How'd the interview go?" Leo asks.

"Good!" she replies. "It was short and sweet, which was nice after a day full of meetings. And the interviewer was really kind!"

"That's great!" Leo beams. "Well, you know what we have to do now, don't you?"

"Oh, come on, is it really necessary?" Jazmine says before taking a sip of coffee.

"Oh, it is." He inches closer to her. "We're going to walk to the bookstore I passed on the way here and go see your book on the shelves."

She lets out a long huff. "Are you literally going to drag me to every bookstore in the area this week?"

"I am." He playfully raises his brows. A smile follows. "Mainly the ones you don't have signings at since we'll already be going to those. And every time we go to these stores I will be buying a copy of Jazmine Prado's debut novel masterpiece."

She laughs, and playfully nudges his shoulder. "I think you have enough copies."

"I think I'll never have enough copies." They go in for another kiss.

"Shit," Jazmine sighs. "Okay, fine. But I get to pick the restaurant we go to after."

"Deal." Leo reaches for her hand. "But it better be somewhere good."

As I watch Jazmine and Leo walk hand-in-hand down the street, smiling and laughing and so obviously in love, Jazmine's words, "Life's too short to be unhappy," echo in my mind. And then it gets me thinking . . . As I continue to go through life and try to write *my* own rules, "Life's too short to be unhappy" is the main rule that I want to live by. And I have Jazmine to thank for that.

The author of this article revised this story before submitting for publication, and redacted the part about Jazmine and Leo to respect her privacy.

Acknowledgements

Good on Paper was a project I started working on a couple years ago and it was seed of an idea about two people (Jazmine and Leo) who were a little messy, who made mistakes, who were figuring life out and themselves out and somehow found their way back to each other after all those years.

However, the book ended up evolving to become Jazmine's story, her own personal journey, and I loved the idea of Jazmine choosing herself and re-evaluating what she wanted for her life and making decisions based on what made her happy—not what anyone else wanted or expected from her. The direction I decided to take the story made it a little outside of the "rom-com" box so I always assumed it would be challenging to get it published. So the fact that it *did* get picked up by a publisher has been such a dream come true!

To my editor Kate Byrne, thank you so much for acquiring *Good on Paper* and for all of your amazing encouragement and optimism about this book! You really understood this story from the get-go and I am forever grateful to you for taking a chance on me and this project!

To my agent Louise Fury at The Bent Agency, thank you so much for believing in me and this book and for always cheering me on and being in my corner! You're one fierce Cancer and I appreciate your tenacity and constant support!

To all the entire editorial team at Headline—copy editors, designers, assistants, marketing folks, etc., thank you so much for all the love, support, and care that you put into this book!

To my family and to my friends in the writing community, creator community, astrology community, thank you for sharing in my wins, encouraging me during my losses, and for showing me and my work so much love!

To my amazing friend, Jessica Alvarez Palmer, you are the friend everyone deserves (enter Oprah meme). But in all seriousness, thank you for all the countless hours you allowed me to verbally process this project and for reading it at its early stage and offering me so much great insight and encouragement. You are my chosen family, my Scorpio sister, and I feel lucky that our paths crossed all those years ago!

And to my husband, Brent McCluskey, thank you for your unconditional love and unwavering support. For encouraging me to pursue the things that make my heart sing. For being my biggest fan and the love of my life. For being so much than just "good on paper." Every moment with you is a gift. You are human sunshine. Thank you for making my life brighter.

HEADLINE
ETERNAL